Madeleine and the Mists

Mary Catelli

Published by Wizard's Wood Press, 2015.

MADELEINE AND THE MISTS

First edition. March 4, 2015.

Written by Mary Catelli.

Chapter 1—News and Decisions

In her solar, Queen Katherine sewed. An innocent amusement, it kept her harmlessly, even usefully, occupied.

When King Walter had appointed her regent while he judged the dispute between Lord Peter and Lord Magnus, he had astounded her. The law permitted it, she knew, but in her native land, a new and foreign queen would not receive such a post.

Her ladies-in-waiting chattered. One laughed. The sound only trapped her further into her thoughts. King Walter had explained that it would be a gross breach of custom, for the queen not to serve as regent. He had not explained how she could safely receive the position, because it meant nothing. She stabbed the cloth with her needle.

Her ladies-in-waiting fell silent. She looked up to see to the cause.

In the doorway, the gray-haired Lord Osgar bowed. He looked over the ladies, in all their brilliant gowns, and his gaze tracked across the room to her, wearing dark green.

Katherine lowered her sewing. She had hoped once, that wearing more sober colors would make her seem more fit for the regency. Now, she would not surrender them, because the ministers would know why and jeer at her. At least, they reminded *her* of what dignity the post should hold.

Lord Osgar gestured at the women.

As if his words would mean something, she told them to leave the room.

The ladies-in-waiting left. In the hallway, out of his presence, they giggled over young men among the courtiers. She wished she could follow them.

Lord Osgar gave her a letter. She marked the seal: King Walter's. Before, he had sent news to his councilors, who might or might not tell her of it. He had never sent her a letter.

"Is this about the matter of Lord Peter and Lord Magnus?"

Lord Osgar bowed again.

Hoping, she broke the seal and opened the letter. Words leapt out at her: Lord Magnus, treason, arrest. She shook her head and tried again, from the start. She could not manage it, the words would not stay in place, but she mastered the gist. King Walter had ordered Lord Magnus of Owlscourt to take the disputed land, Lord Magnus had raised men from his vassals to do so, and King Walter had arrested all of them for treason.

Katherine stared at the paper. The messenger must have been fast. Once this news reached the court, it would buzz like a bee hive—and a bee hive struck by sticks.

It held something about preparing for trial, and the men's imprisonment. She could not read that part.

Lord Osgar cleared his throat. From his expression, he already knew the news.

Katherine stiffened. "The King's Grace put forth this—insanity?"

Lord Osgar bowed once again. "Madame, the orders have been given. If you have reason to countermand them—" He paused an insolent moment. "—I will convey your new orders."

If she had no reason, he would destroy the orders. That she knew.

As an unimportant princess, she had dreamed of becoming a queen, and no longer negligible. Her fingers tightened on the letter. She wished King Walter had declared her too young, too inexperienced—too womanly!—to serve as regent rather exert this web of control over her.

"You may leave, sir."

His fourth bow was insolent. "The King's Grace sent more. When you collect yourself, I will bring the proclamations for your signature." He left.

She walked to the window. The garden spread in the sunlight, in incongruous good cheer. Flowers in bloom sported butterflies and bees.

She closed her eyes. The air was warm and flowery. She wondered what had inspired King Walter to *this*. He had not acted so capriciously before. Ambassadors might hide such faults from the mere bride, but her father had chosen him for politic reasons.

She looked at her sewing. She could finish her gown—the only thing she could be certain of doing today, besides pray that someone would give her a means to act. She sat again, and hauled the cloth into her lap.

In the solar, Madeleine embroidered a tunic for her husband— golden trumpet flowers on blue—and tried not to think on why she had chosen the pattern. Lords had summoned their men for generations, and John was as bound to obey as any of them.

Outside, Gilliane's voice rose in complaints about how Donald had abandoned her for the circuit. Madeleine's mouth twitched. Settling peasants' disputes about chickens was no reason to leave Summerfield, but it was more important than Lord Magnus's summons. She followed the reasoning entirely.

She took another stitch. John would obey the summons for no more reason than his oath, but there were other reasons for obedience. It still baffled her: Donald and Andrew thought they could defy Lord Magnus. Refusing the summons gave him the right to throw them from their lands. Once, not realizing that she was in earshot, Nichola had spoken of a lord who told Andrew—but no lord could order Magnus to desist. The king himself had ordered the summons.

Gilliane flounced into the room. Like a little mouse, Nichola skittered after her, snatched her sewing, and sat to work. Three sisters in the hall, thought Madeleine merrily— well, sisters by marriage.

She picked up some thread. Gilliane, her mouth set, stared at her rather than sewing. Nichola bent over her work, so intent that she must be deliberately ignoring her. Madeleine threaded her needle. With the study Gilliane was giving her face, she wondered if Gilliane would complain about her looks again, as if she had deliberately had broad cheekbones and a pointed chin to make her face unusual, in order to spite Gilliane—when John had never complained.

"Donald sent a messenger," said Gilliane. "He won't return tonight."

Your husband was here two nights ago, thought Madeleine. *Mine* has left over a fortnight ago. She started another flower.

"There's plenty of work about the estates," said Gilliane. "Bad enough when three do it. With only two...."

There ought to be *none*, thought Madeleine.

"What are you making?" said Nichola. "You hadn't started to embroider it last time." She looked imploringly at Madeleine. Madeleine glanced at her, wondering what was so dreadful that Nichola was willing to intervene—but she spread out the tunic, showing the yellow trumpet flowers on the blue.

"Lord Magnus's badge," said Gilliane with a sneer. "A tribute to John's—loyalty."

Her eyes wide, Nichola glanced at Gilliane. When she looked back at Madeleine, her face took on a contemptuous look. Madeleine glared at them. Gilliane had complained of the convolutions of the estate so often, but Lord Magnus now had reason to settle them, by giving all the lands to John.

Childish laughter rose from the garden. Madeleine smiled. Then, Summerfield held more pleasant things than her sisters by marriage. She rose to her feet.

"You could still hire Bethia," said Gilliane. "She's raised children—you would not need to hover over her."

"I find Rosie suitable," said Madeleine.

"Andrew's mother didn't hover over him," said Nichola.

Or John or Donald, thought Madeleine—and so, though she and their father had died less than a month before she had met John, John had worn black and shown no other signs of grief. She left.

Nichola's voice came after her. "Half a witch—did you know she told me that she knows a way through the Misty Hills in *one day*? It must take weeks."

Only by some routes, thought Madeleine, and you asked how John and I had reached Summerfield so quickly.

She hurried down the stairs and tried to calm herself. She wondered if Gilliane ever grew weary of her grievances.

She emerged into the sunlight, which smelled of John's grandmother's roses. Flowers of pink and pale red brushed against her. She drew a deep breath. Her son played in the grass, and his nursemaid knelt by him.

Rosie scrambled to her feet to curtsey. Sandy looked from his wooden knight only long enough to smile. Madeleine gestured Rosie back to her charge and sat on a bench, where she and John had spent hours. She sewed another yellow flower. Sandy's knight clattered against stone.

Hoof beats sounded in the courtyard. She looked up. Gilliane's complaints held that much truth: Andrew and Donald were unlikely to return this day. John was unlikely to return without news arriving first, of how Lord Magnus's private war had fared. She lowered her sewing.

"Something wrong, my lady?" said Rosie.

"I'll see," said Madeleine. She walked through the roses. In the courtyard, a messenger dismounted.

Gilliane and Nichola left the house. As a groom took his horse, the messenger bowed. Madeleine, still half hidden by the roses, walked toward the gate. He mentioned Lord Magnus of Owlscourt. Gilliane disclaimed any need to summon Madeleine for the message, he could tell them without delay.

"Lady Elspeth sent me."

Madeleine scowled. Why would Lord Magnus's *wife* send a message? What could have—she listened as the messenger said that the king had proclaimed Lord Magnus a traitor for the men he had gathered—that that large a force could only have one purpose. She slowed with every word; she reached the gate but had not the strength to open it.

Her breath came fast and shallow, and she could not master it. King Walter had ordered Lord Magnus to gather men. John had fulminated about it, how the king should have enforced justice himself.

She forced herself to listen. "Taking the men captive—many of them didn't survive."

Madeleine's hand went to her face.

"I believe Lord John to be alive, but injured. . . ."

Madeleine could not hear him anymore. Taken alive, but for how long? Injured or not, traitors faced only execution. She walked forward.

The click of the gate's latch drew their attention. Gilliane smiled at her. Madeleine was glad she had not faced her when she heard the news.

"My lady?" said the messenger. Madeleine nodded. He repeated the message: Lord Magnus of Owlscourt and many of his men had been taken as traitors, for assembling as an armed force in excess of the law and for resisting the king. "Lord John was alive afterwards, and among the prisoners taken with Lord Magnus to the Lindon Tower."

Cold as she felt, she could remember it: half way across the kingdom, on the other side of the Misty Hills. The king wanted neither an escape nor a rescue.

"A trial?" Her voice was a croak.

His sure tone slipped. "Not—at once, my lady. The King's Grace is summoning the nobles to attend court. For the trial, and executions."

Madeleine saw only John, wounded and imprisoned, awaiting certain execution. She felt helpless. Then she remembered an execution she had once seen, and envisioned John on the block.

Gilliane said not a word, certainly none of sympathy. After a glance at her, neither did Nichola. Madeleine thanked the messenger, not knowing how she found the words, and wandered back into the garden. Behind her, Gilliane dismissed the messenger to the kitchens. He thanked her but said that within an hour, he would leave. He had other messages.

Madeleine shivered. For other wives—widows—"So Lord Peter got what he was after," she whispered. She wrapped her arms about herself against the chill.

A voice floated in, saying that someone had been right, but Madeleine could not even make out who had spoken. She walked on. A bee bumbled by her, from one rose to the next.

Sandy crowed over his knight, and then stopped, looking at her. Madeleine crouched and held out her arms. Sandy threw himself across the garden, and she snuggled him close. He almost warmed her. Her free hand stroked his blond curls—the hair he had inherited from his father.

Sandy was easier to comfort than she was. He did not know of his father's danger. She felt cold again. Or, for that of matter, of his own and his mother's.

She swallowed. Her dowry had been small and might be all she could claim. The king could seize John's lands as well as execute him, and Andrew and Donald would give her nothing that they did not have to. She stared at the garden wall. If the king acted as unjustly to her as to Lord Magnus, he might even deny her dowry. Indeed, considering how King Walter had treated Lord Magnus, Donald and Andrew might lose their lands, as well.

A breeze stirred the branches, sending petals flying from roses past their prime.

She already thought of John as dead. Her stomach felt like a cold weight. John whom she had held warm and living in her bed, not a fortnight ago—who had laughed and kissed her the next morning and tossed a laughing Sandy into the air. . . .

Sandy wriggled, and she forced her breath out. John would want Sandy safe, she told herself.

"Mama?" said Sandy. Madeleine looked back at the garden. Rosie, her face pale, curtseyed.

Sandy would be all she had left of John. "Go with Rosie," she said. "Mama has to plan."

"Oh." Sandy considered that. "Papa come soon?"

In the courtyard, Fergus scowled at the crowds. He had to manage; with Annette arriving soon, he needed to arrange the chambers—but what inspired this? The day was sunny and pleasant, but court had not held such throngs since King Walter had left. But here they stood, brilliantly clad, glittering with jewelry, and every one of them talking.

"Have you heard the news, Lord Fergus?" said Lord Gavin of Hawkehill. His face was grim.

Fergus bowed. Lord Gavin was no petty gossip—and even if he had been, he could not offend a great noble. Annette would be furious about the danger to her prospects. His mouth twitched. "I have not, my lord."

"About the king and Lord Magnus?" said another man.

Fergus could not think what to say to that: the stable boys—the beggars on the streets—knew the king had gone to judge between Lord Magnus and Lord Peter.

He must have looked blank. The story poured from many mouths.

"Whatever business we have on our lands," said Lord Gavin, "however urgently that business requires us, we must abide the king, and this trial."

He sounded poisonous. Justly, thought Fergus, but neither Lord Gavin nor any other lord would defy the king. His mouth tightened. Besides their duty, King Walter could punish them.

"How many lords must suffer because of this!"

Summerfield lay in Lord Magnus's domains. He forgot Lady Madeleine's match for weeks at a time, but not after such news. He hoped his voice sounded idle. "Is it known which nobles are held?"

"The clerks can tell you," said a lady, carelessly. "They are preparing for the trial."

Fergus thanked her and left, inching his way through the gossip.

He had thought of Madeleine only as showing how court could bring poor matches as well as good. Now, he could caution Annette the more about choosing wisely—if Madeleine's poor match did not utterly foul Annette's chances.

He barely managed to return a greeting; he did not stop.

Though, if Madeleine had married with her father's blessing, she might still face this. He would never have warned her that marrying John of Summerfield brought her into danger with the king, because he would never have dreamed that it would. He shook his head, still surprised by the decision.

He stepped inside, to darker corridors. Clerks and servants bustled.

"Sir," said a young clerk, pale, but speaking firmly, "what business do you have—"

"I heard that you have the names of the nobles captured with Lord Magnus," said Fergus.

The clerk hesitated. Another, grizzled clerk said, "See him," and pointed.

Fergus thanked him. Minutes later, he studied the list where it read, "John of Summerfield."

He thought John had brothers. The list did not show them; perhaps Madeleine's plight might be better that it seemed. He handed back the list. Still, her plight was evil enough.

He heard horses outside. More people came to court. He handed back the list. Even with his goddaughter's husband in prison, he had to receive Annette.

The servants flitted about like ghosts; they scurried by the garden gates and talked among themselves. Then, Madeleine conceded, she only picked at her sewing herself.

It seemed a long time had passed when horses thundered into the courtyard. She rose and found herself moving stiffly; perhaps a long time had passed. The shadows had shifted.

She walked toward the gate. If the king had not reached Harthill, the trial, and executions, could not have happened. Stray branches caught at her clothing, and she freed her veil from a bold rose bush. John might have died of his injuries, or the rider could have come some other business. She swallowed.

"Where is Lady Gilliane?" Donald called. He handed his horse to a surprised stable boy as Andrew dismounted. Nichola and Gilliane hurried outside. "We heard the news."

In her bewilderment, Nichola received Andrew's kiss without much attention. "But, what could any of us do?"

Donald looked across the courtyard at Madeleine. "There are the marriage articles. Very confused, those articles were."

Madeleine's eyes narrowed.

"You're Lord Fergus's goddaughter, aren't you?" said Donald.

"Yes." Drearily, Madeleine thought that she could appeal to Lord Fergus for help. His high birth meant he could protect her, but then, marrying John might have alienated him. Her father, having gotten such a nobleman for her godfather, had expected her to marry as well, and John had met her under Lord Fergus's care, at court, in search of a husband. Lord Fergus might never have forgiven her that.

"Pity," said Andrew. "Seeing Lord Fergus at court might remind the king of you."

Madeleine felt chilled. She had been right about a want of generosity.

Andrew innocently met her gaze. "The last thing we want to do is remind the king of Summerfield."

"But this news has greatly distressed you, dear sister," said Donald. "You will not wish to trouble yourself about money after such news."

Madeleine's voice was soft. "John would wish me to know the affairs concerning Sandy."

"Why then," purred Gilliane, "we shall tell you. I know that John complained of them. Hopelessly convoluted, he said, even when they ordered that some of the rents be paid to him."

"Aping their betters," said Madeleine. Great nobles had land enough to order rents paid to the younger children; a couple with an estate as small as Summerfield should have let their younger sons seek service. "He also complained of the impossibility of change."

Gilliane smiled. "We shall see."

Despising herself for weakness, Madeleine still could not look at Gilliane. Nichola could not meet her gaze, and Andrew almost looked abashed, but neither one would stand up to Donald and Gilliane. She could not stalk them and prevent them from meeting without her. She inclined her head. They might even be protecting themselves from the king's rage—which the king had shown, was to be feared.

She watched as they went into the house, and walked into the garden, looking for a suitable window. Knowing what her foes intended might give her some way to plan. Someone had to provide for John's widow and fatherless son—if it had to be the widow herself. In a shadowed corner of the garden, Madeleine sat and waited.

"A dowry-less woman from the Misty Hills." Gilliane's voice rang as if everyone else in the house were deaf.

Madeleine grimaced. Gilliane had wanted John's bride to be as meek as Nichola, leaving her mistress of the household, down to her nephew's nursemaid—but her dowry had been small.

"Plain, brown-haired—she will not marry again and take herself off her hands—as if we would miss her dowry. . . ."

Madeleine's eyes closed. At court, a sharp-tongued Lady Lettice had said that no one could find anything pleasing in her face. Gallantly, John had said that her pointed chin and broad cheekbones made her face heart-shaped. He had inveigled an introduction out of Lord Fergus soon after and found half a dozen ways to praise her nut-brown hair.

She remembered the execution, the way the blood had spouted, and put a hand to her mouth.

"Nice figure, though," said Andrew, slyly.

Madeleine glanced at the rose bushes around, to confirm that they hid her. Andrew would have been too afraid of John to say that even in his absence, without being sure of his death. Sickened, she wondered what the noble had told them—the noble that Nichola had spoken of before the news. They had known of John's danger, and they had let him go.

"It will draw the king's attention," said Donald. "Having a traitor's wife at Summerfield."

"Then there is Sandy," said Gilliane. "Without another heir, Sandy will hold the lands."

A reasonable, a truthful statement—but why did it remind Madeleine that many children died young? That if she took Sandy to her father's house, John's brothers might demand his return, so that their heir would be raised in their house.

Madeleine fled the garden. This was a fine terror to build up out of nothing. John's brothers had never been fond of her. Now, they worried that the king's caprices could harm them— a prudent fear—and noted that Sandy was their heir. What reason had she act as if they plotted her death and Sandy's as well? That would be as unreasonable as the king's acts.

But the king had given her no reason to believe him unreasonable, before the arrests. Indeed, less than Donald's bland refusal to let her hear his plans.

She pressed her hands together. Whatever the marriage articles said, Donald held the lands, and Gilliane was mistress in the hall. And—he had evaded Lord Magnus's summons. He could deal with her more easily than with his overlord.

After some minutes, she climbed the stairs. The breeze carried the scent of roses, and Nichola's voice, asking the gardener whether they could be rid of the roses.

Madeleine stopped in her tracks. The bushes were their grandmother's roses, and John loved them. . . . Madeleine's hand went to the wall. That certainty, of John's death, had been obvious, but to destroy the roses—

She looked out the window. The bush there blossomed pale pink, the flowers so profuse that she could barely see any leaves. John had carried an armload of them to their chamber, one night when she was far gone with Sandy. Madeleine swallowed. The night they had first arrived at Summerfield, John had crowned her with blood-red roses, and visions of John, laughing, warm, alive, gave way to a flood of red.

She turned from the window, gagging. What cause had she to complain of Nichola? This was no fairy tale where the good king would set aside injustice. The only thing that could save John was a pardon, which the king would not grant.

She climbed toward her chambers. Her godfather—Lord Fergus's rank had impressed her father but would not win a traitor's life from the king. He did not even attend the king; he stayed at Harthill, where the court awaited the king, where the queen remained.

As she lifted the latch, that thought stayed put. Where Queen Katherine was. In the king's absence, the queen—even a new and foreign queen—was regent.

A regent could do much. She could grant pardons, for John, for Lord Magnus, for all his men.

For a moment, she seized the door, not to open it, but to keep from falling. She thought of John's arms, warm about her, and leaned against the doorframe. Not even envisioning his death had weakened her like this burst of hope—and that thought did not calm her, either.

She took a deep breath. It did not steady her. She tried to think sternly. First, she had to reach court. Then she had to get an audience. Then she had to persuade the queen.

Nothing of this kept her hands from shaking.

Inside, she went to the nursery and kissed the sleeping Sandy.

Chapter 2—Plans and Disappointments

The next day, the morning light was gray and chilly. Lying in bed, Madeleine looked out the window and contemplated the mists. The night had held perfervid dreams of John, enough to make her blush, but now was time for waking thought. John's family would not aid her. She shifted her head on the pillows. If they, in fear of the king, imprisoned her, they would be safe; she could appeal to neither Lord Magnus nor King Walter for help, and not only because she had no way to send a message.

She had to leave without their knowledge. She thought of the mare in the stable, but the servants were theirs and not hers. To ride off like a great lady without servants would invite robbery—or an accusation of theft.

Madeleine rolled onto her side. The blankets caught, and she pulled them free.

She and John had made their way from the Misty Hills to here without much money, and afoot. A widow might do that, rather less merrily than she and John had fared, but she could say that she had quarreled with her husband's family.

She pushed back the blanket and went to the window to say her prayers.

Sandy's voice rose next door. Madeleine remembered Andrew's words and shivered. She did not want to leave Sandy here.

She contemplated the road to the palace with a two-year-old. Her teeth worried her lower lip. Still, it was not impossible. To pass themselves off as a widow and child of lower rank, they needed clothing. She looked in her wardrobe. Courtiers might sneer at it, but the wearer of such fine wool was a lady, however lacking in grandness. She picked a dress for today, where they knew she was a lady, and dressed, and thought. There was the clothing to be given to the poor, if nothing else. Perhaps she could get to the strongbox for money.

Sandy laughed as Rosie brought him downstairs.

Madeleine shook out her veil. And Rosie. It would be indecent for a knight's daughter to unattended, but Gilliane had inspired little loyalty in the nursemaid.

Voices rose from the kitchen. One was Rosie's. The air smelled of baking bread. Sandy sat on the hearth, eating bread and half the honey on it, the other half being smeared over his face; it almost matched his curls in color. The cook Rhona shifted bread in the oven, flooding the room with heat. Rosie leaned over a table and talked the laundry maid's young man.

Madeleine stopped in the doorway. Once she had told Rosie about the Twelfth Night gift she made for John. Every servant in Summerfield knew it before the day was out.

Rhona laughed and put aside the wooden peel. "You're a fine one to talk, with Finlay in your past."

Rosie turned pink.

"My lady!" called Rhona. Rosie blinked. Madeleine came forward before the servants could wonder why she eavesdropped.

"Honey!" said Sandy, through a mouthful. Madeleine kissed his forehead, where the honey had not reached. Rhona sliced the loaf with the great bread knife and reached for the honey pot.

Madeleine looked at Rosie. Finlay had sneaked into Rosie's bedchamber in the night. Her shrieks and blows had roused the house. Madeleine fought to keep her face impassive. She could not wake Rosie in the night and hustle her off on a journey.

Rhona held the bread out and shook her head. "Sad thing, about Lord John."

Madeleine bowed her head as she murmured her thanks for the bread and the condolence. She could barely taste the honey.

Clothing and money first.

"Shall I tell them that you are not ready to receive them?" said Lady Beatrix. The lady-in-waiting stood by the door, her hand on the doorframe, awaiting the order.

"Tell that I am ready," said Queen Katherine, deciding even as she spoke. "Within the great chamber."

Lady Beatrix curtseyed and looked baffled—as if she thought that waiting would sweeten the drink. Katherine knew better. Even when she sat in the great chamber, with the servant announcing, "The Queen's Grace will see you," and the nobles being ushered in, that knowledge was not shaken.

"Your Grace." The nobles' clothes were travel-stained; they had not paused to change. They bowed to her, but stiffly. She inclined her head and braced herself.

"Your Grace," said a lord. "We received a summons to court, from your lord husband."

"Your prompt response," said Katherine, "honors the king."

His nostrils flared. She wondered if she should learn his name, or whether the number of nobles that she must placate meant that she should not even try.

"We could not believe its contents."

"What did it say that you wish to have denied—or confirmed?" she said.

Faces hardened before her.

"It can not be true," said a white-haired lord, "that the king ordered Lord Magnus's arrest." His lined face was set in such despair that she wished she could wipe it away.

"The king," she said, "has given his orders."

"This is folly!" said the first lord.

For once, Katherine longed for the sewing in her inner chamber. Some things she could do as regent, if she evaded the ministers, but not this.

The sole window let in only dim light. By it, Madeleine looked over the clothing. She pulled out a rusty brown dress and threw it over the blue shawl. She could wear her own chemise. Even for a knight's daughter, the clothing was none too fine.

Father Parlan hovered, his disappointment on his face.

"We must not be profligate," said Madeleine. "I do not think Lady Gilliane realized I needed the cloth."

"You should trust in Divine Providence more, my lady." His voice was thin. "Consider the lilies of the field, they toil not, neither do they spin—yet Solomon in all his glory was not arrayed like one of these."

John might have died of his wounds already, Madeleine thought bleakly; I am trusting that this will not be in vain. "Providence has provided that you have not given the clothing away already." Providence, she prayed, would bring her safely to court.

The chaplain muttered about miserliness.

"Why, did not Lady Gilliane give you the money for the poor?" said Madeleine. Her heart beat faster. Gilliane had left for the village and could not gainsay her about the strongbox, but she could hear rumors.

"No, my lady," said Father Parlan.

"I will have to see to that."

And now she had a reason to open the strongbox. She resolved to get him the alms before she left.

"You should trust in God more," said Father Parlan.

Madeleine considered a moment. "Perhaps I should go on a pilgrimage. Implore divine aid for John."

Father Parlan blanched. "Robbers, my lady, and bandits—and insolent nobles—the way holds too many perils, in these troubled times."

"I would bring a guard." Her heart pattered faster. "Surely you could convince my brothers to support my holy purpose."

Father Parlan drew himself up. "Your good brothers by marriage could not spare the men. They must protect the good folk of this estate from evildoers."

By candlelight, coins glittered. The yellow of the candlelight tinted their colors, but Madeleine could name them, still. Coppery pennies. Silver regals. And golden angels. Far more than a few, or even a dozen; they had a hoard with several scores of them.

"With this much gold," she whispered, "why is Gilliane complaining so much of money?" Her words echoed strangely, and she bent over the money again. The pennies and regals she gathered by the handful. Her hand hesitated over the angels. A woman with gold could afford servants. She bit her lip. On the way, she could buy little with it, for fear of questions, but at court, she might need to bribe.

The coins glittered in the candlelight.

Andrew and Donald owed Lord Magnus scutage, for not obeying his summons.

Before she could lose her nerve, Madeleine snatched up a third of the angels. She would have to hide the coins well, so that Father Parlan did not guess—she locked the strongbox before she could frighten herself and put the coins back.

Madeleine climbed to her room. Sandy napped; she could speak with Rosie in secret, and then keep her too busy to gossip, until sundown.

In the nursery, Sandy lay on his stomach, his face turned to one side. Rosie stood next to the bed.

"Been a lot of rumors about you, my lady," Rosie said. "Said you would go back to the Misty Hills." She shook her head. "I could not stand such—glad I never have to."

Madeleine wondered—she had had no time to eavesdrop, and Father Parlan disapproved of gossip—but she still had no time for anything but what lay before her. "You could not leave Summerfield for good?"

"Never leave Summerfield at all. Never will." Rosie looked at the door. "All the dangers of bandits."

"You can avoid them," said Madeleine, walking closer, eyeing the nursemaid.

Rosie's eyes were wide. "Oh, they won't let you! They find travelers *anywhere* they go."

"If it were that dangerous," said Madeleine, "I wouldn't be here. I went from Candlewood to court half a dozen times, and Lord John and I traveled from Candlewood to here."

Rosie hesitated. "I couldn't—" Suddenly, her voice strengthened. "Besides, I could not leave my mother."

"Leaving?" Gilliane stood in the doorway.

"Oh no, my lady." Rosie looked horror-struck. "I assured my lady that I *couldn't*."

"True enough," said Gilliane. "Rosie is bound to the estate. She could not leave to look after a child."

"Oh no, never," said Rosie. "Besides—the Misty Hills." She shuddered.

"And there is no need. Sandy being heir to Summerfield, he will not leave for his father's—misfortune."

Madeleine felt very alone. With Rosie or without her, she had to leave before Gilliane guessed the truth. But no knight's daughter would travel alone, and for a lone woman—were not the dangers as great as Rosie feared?

She gave Gilliane a sidelong glance. Her sister by marriage had guessed *something*, to come here.

"Come, Rosie," said Madeleine. "We don't want to wake Sandy."

Gilliane knew she had her.

The chapel was dark, the sanctuary candle a red glow behind the glass. The crucifix was only dimly illuminated, with shadows cast across its face. Madeleine knelt and tried to pray.

The clothing she had chosen was not good. A baseborn servant might receive her mistress's leavings, and no one would wonder at such a servant traveling alone.

Her hand trembled as she lit a candle. The tiny glow shook and took long to blossom into a yellow flame. Madeleine stared at it. She could pass herself off as a peasant woman, whom no one had to heed. Her mouth trembled. It would increase the dangers. If she were assaulted, robbed, and murdered, it would help no one, least of all John.

The head on the crucifix hung, weary, burdened, in pain. Words came to her: God has chosen the weak of the world to confound the strong. . . . She turned her face away. Was she too good to dress like a peasant, even to save her husband's life—and perhaps her own, and her son's?

She rose heavily to her feet.

The crescent moon hung over the sunset. It gave little light, but the sunset was enough. In the garden, Sandy chased a butterfly while Madeleine spoke with Rosie. "Go see your mother tonight, see that all is well with her." She was pleased at how steady her voice remained. "Stay the night to ensure it."

Rosie's mouth opened and shut like a fish's.

"Your mother should have someone to watch over her. Within an hour, I will take charge of Sandy."

Looking uneasy, Rosie nodded.

With a sad smile, Madeleine walked through the garden in the gloom, and through the courtyard, to the chapel. She thought of lighting a candle as well as praying, but it would take a miracle to hide one before the St. Christopher statue. She had need enough for miracles without adding to it.

Chapter 3—Travels and Encounters

The moon set not long after the sun, but she had walked by starlight before.

In her chamber, Madeleine lit the candle. She dropped her sewing beside it. If anyone saw her, she could claim that a bad dream had woken her, and being unable to get back to sleep, she sewed.

She wondered if there was a patron saint of people who sneaked about in the night.

She dressed. The shawl felt odd; heavier than the veil she was used to, it swathed her hair instead of letting the loose ends hang below.

When she had married, she had grown used to the veil. She would grow used to the shawl, too.

The money pouch she fastened to the belt. She took up the satchel with its blankets and food, slung it over her shoulder, and carried the candle to Sandy's nursery. Rosie had not been so bewildered that she had returned from her mother's. Candlelight glinted from Sandy's blond hair.

She could leave him asleep, return to her bed, smuggle the clothes back to Father Parlan, sneak the money back into the chest—and all more easily than she could win her way to court. No one would blame her. No one would even know that she dreamed of saving John, and Lord Magnus, and all the captives.

Madeleine closed her eyes. O God, Who led the children of Israel through the Red Sea and guided the wise men by a star to the Savior, grant us, we beseech You, safe journey and favorable weather, so that, under the guidance of Your holy angels, we may reach our destination and, in due time, the gate of eternal salvation. She opened her eyes. Sandy had not moved. Through Christ our Lord.

"St. Christopher, patron of travelers," she whispered, "pray for us, and protect us from evil."

She put the candle down and bent over her son. Sandy stirred. She wrapped him in a blanket and took him in her arms. He slept on, his head tucked against her shoulder. Madeleine ducked to blow out the candle. The air filled with the brief scent of smoke. For a minute, she let her eyes adjust. It would be brighter outside, where the walls did not block out the starlight.

Nothing sounded except the crickets. Feeling foolish, Madeleine put her hand on the wall to guide the way. She walked out and down the stairs. Sandy seemed to weigh more heavily by the minute, but she could not wake him.

In the starlight, the village slept. She could not go through it. Sheep might stir in their pens, a dog might bark, a baby might wail—someone might rouse in the night. She shifted Sandy's weight, to rest more securely across her body.

A woodcutter's hut stood an hour from the village. She could rest there. At dawn, she could dress Sandy and be off before anyone noted that neither she nor Sandy had risen from their beds to eat.

But they would, in due course.

She walked through the fields. The road inched into the woods, where leaves hid stars from her. She walked on.

Branches sheltered the road. In the gray morning light, Sandy rubbed his eyes and stared. Madeleine, feeling stiff in every limb, hefted him against her shoulder. She had been so tired that, in the hut, she slept without dreams, and though she had not had any difficulty waking early, in the morning cold, she was still yawning.

And the morning air was still chilly.

"I'm *tired*, Mama," said Sandy. "I don't *wanna*."

"Shush," said Madeleine, without much hope. She was too tired to care. A cranky child would draw no more attention than an easygoing one.

A little more, she conceded. She stroked Sandy's hair with her free hand, pressing his hand to her shoulder. He rested there and drowsed off; he had slept no better in the hut's cold, hard bed than she had.

She flinched at the thought of carrying him to Harthill, but she had nowhere to leave him.

She came around the last trees. Ahead, the village at the crossroad stood among the fields and pasture. Her shoulders slumped in relief. The sun warmed the air some, outside the woods, and the village stirred. She needed fellow travelers, because there might indeed be bandits along the way: west through Lord Magnus's lands, then west through Lord Patrick's, around the Misty Hills; then south, still in Lord Patrick's lands. She did not know who was overlord in the next lands. It did not matter. She need only look for travelers heading to Harthill.

The inn, which the village had grown up around, sat central to it—a better position than even the church's. It had more people about it, too. Then, perhaps mass had already been said for the early travelers. Grooms saddled horses; the mounts were not good enough for a noblemen's, or even a knight's, but respectable nags such as a merchant or a priest might ride. Madeleine kept her ears cocked. The grooms complained that a troupe of players was leaving, with a few leers about a woman in the troupe.

"Goodmen! Whose horses are these?"

All three grooms looked at her.

"I wondered who else travels these roads, after I got lost last night."

"Lost," muttered one, glancing over her clothing. She looked back. He would find no grass stains.

Another groom said, "Merchants, heading toward Vinton."

Madeleine's teeth closed on her lower lip. Vinton was south, toward Harthill, but a traveler needed to go west—or east—to get about the Misty Hills. No one knew better than she that the hills' perils were not all outsiders' imagination.

"Players heading west," said the first groom.

Madeleine considered how things vanished in the players' presence, how the women whored, and how, in their company, she would be taken for a player. Bad enough that she traveled without a maid.

A groom led out mules. Other men, roughly clad for travel, came out with bales to load onto them. Several of the men sported beards. Sandy stirred. "What's that, Mama?"

The drovers carried the bales easily. Colors showed through the gaps in their wrapping. The West Dales were known for their woolens and dyes, though their dyes were not quite as famed as the Misty Hills'. In their northern reaches, men commonly went bearded. "Cloth, dearling," she said. She pulled closer to the wall, where she would not get in the way. People, dressed as merchants, emerged from the inn. Better still, two were women. She approached.

Dame, she reminded herself. Passing herself off as a peasant meant she could not call the merchants Goodwoman. She twitched. But it was too late to claim to be a knight's daughter, or even a merchant's.

"Who are you?" said the younger woman—though her hair was laced with white, it was not the pure white of her companion's. The older woman appraised Madeleine and Sandy. Neither looked taken with her.

She remembered to bob her head respectfully. "Dame, I am seeking companions for the road. I am a widow, returning to my father's house."

"A likely story," muttered the older woman.

"We are headed only to Vinton," said the younger woman.

"But the road there has more travelers, and I would have more choice. . . ." She sounded plaintive, and she fought down her resentment. She needed them to have pity on her.

Someone stumbled from the inn, in motley; though grimy, the outfit held hints of its original red, blue, and green. The man leaned against the wall. Madeleine flinched away, hoping he was not drunk already. He staggered round the wall. Sounds of nausea emerged. She winced.

The younger woman said, "You may come."

Madeleine thanked her, earnestly.

Going south—she went toward the Misty Hills and her father's house, but Vinton did have more travelers, and the route might distract Donald and Andrew, to think she returned to her father's house.

Sandy twisted. "Down, Mama."

Madeleine lowered him. With all the hooves about, she would have to watch him, but better that Sandy should walk than she carry him all the way. He sprinted after a marmalade cat. Madeleine ran after him. The two women gave her disapproving glances. She did not doubt that if Sandy distracted her, they would leave her behind.

She snatched her son up. Sandy squirmed.

"If you chase after everything," Madeleine said, "Mama will carry you everywhere."

Sandy pouted. She wondered how long the rebuke would last. But minutes later, the mules trudged off, with both of them walking alongside.

"Madame." The messenger dropped to one knee. His head bent in blatant relief.

Queen Katherine inclined her head, trying not to show how much his appearance alarmed her. He shook from weariness.

"Treachery and treason, Madame! In Eastwyck—I alone escaped. My companion perished at rebellious hands."

Katherine drew a deep breath. How could this have happened so suddenly? Without tales of gathering weapons, or armed bands, preceding it? She would have thought her ministers had kept the news from her, but they looked as baffled as she.

The messenger swayed.

"Do you know—" He looked as if he had not stopped for anything once he fled the murderers. "Did you learn who led the traitors?"

"They spoke of Lord Ivo, but I do not know who he—I thought this news more—"

"Even so." She hesitated. He looked on the verge of collapse.

"They spoke of lords who claimed the king had wronged them, that their lands, like Lord Peter's, are unjustly held, and the king will not—"

The ministers shifted.

"Others said that lords took advantage of the king's—preoccupation." He stumbled over the word.

Queen Katherine inclined her head. "The news is more important than the names of the culprits. You did well,—"

"Somerled, Madame," he said.

"My lord—" Katherine glanced about the great chamber. "Tavish. Deliver this good man to a servant, and give orders for food and a bed. I will see to his reward once he has eaten and slept."

Somerled looked ready to weep in gratitude. Lord Tavish looked as if he had bitten on something sour—as if he had ever done as much service for the crown as the messenger.

With Somerled gone, Katherine spoke again. "It is a thousand pities that the King's Grace could not have put this treachery down as swiftly as he did Lord Magnus's. We must act in haste. The conflagration is not large. Yet."

The ministers rumbled with agreement, one saying, "So we must."

"The men must be raised."

After a frozen moment, Lord Osgar said, "The lords do not wish to raise armies without the King's leave."

"Nevertheless," said Katherine, "the forces must be raised."

Lord Osgar brightened. "A messenger shall go to the king! On our swiftest horses, news can come and go quickly."

While Katherine still stared at him, Lord Osgar gave orders. A clerk hurried toward the door.

"Since when has that authority been denied the regent?"

The frost in her voice stopped the clerk, but Lord Osgar did not twitch. "If the King's Grace hears that we proposed sending a messenger and then forbore. . . ." He shook his head.

The clerk darted out. She knew that she could not keep a watch on Lord Osgar, to prevent his sending a messenger, and then the messenger would tell the king not only of the rebellion.

"Stop," she said. In the hallway, the clerk looked banefully at her. "Ensure that the slander the rebels spread of the king is in the letter."

She was not certain that it was slander, but it might stir King Walter.

As the door closed behind the clerk, she looked at the minister with narrowed eyes. If they had known what message Somerled bore, they would have kept him from her. "What other matters must be dealt with?"

One said, "Your Grace, that order about the Stoneriver bridge—"

Katherine suppressed a smile. Sometimes, evading her ministers meant that she could act. "Was there something wrong with it?"

After a moment, none of them had the courage to say that the bridge, on the king's land, should not be repaired from the tolls. Some travelers would be glad of that.

The mules plodded along the dusty road. Winifred, the older merchant woman, muttered about tolls and imposts. Pasture gave way to fields as she spoke of how the king wasted his time playing favorites among the nobles when he should protect the merchants from them. She seemed oblivious to the sun's heat.

Then, thought Madeleine, Winifred must be used to this travel. Sandy clung to her hand, too tired to cry out about sheep, or chase butterflies, or even to whine. Though she had heard all Winifred's complaints before she was certain of the woman's name, Madeleine could not bring herself to draw away. Fiona, the other merchant woman, argued with a mule driver, and they were the only women with the caravan.

"They didn't dare these fees in the old days, under the king's father," said Winifred. "King Michael would not permit it."

"But aren't the lords about here prisoner?" said Madeleine. She wondered what had happened to her sense, but not enough to stop speaking. "They're Lord Magnus's men."

Winifred's mouth twisted. "Some didn't bother."

Madeleine felt cold. How many of Lord Magnus's men had proven to be as much rascals as Donald and Andrew?

Fiona returned. She nodded at a hill ahead, where a castle stood. "There's a place where they can complain about the king." Winifred gave her a sour glance. "Lady Nora's husband was Lord Magnus's man."

Madeleine's heart seemed to pause. Fiona could not have guessed—"Captured with him?"

"Where there's life, there's hope," said Fiona, "and there's none."

Madeleine opened her mouth and shut it again. Many men must have died. Nothing she did would do anything for those widows, fatherless children, and mothers.

"No protection there," said Winifred. "The heir can raise the toll. Or the guardian, all pious about his duty to the fatherless—"

"I want to go *home*, Mama," shrieked Sandy.

Winifred and Fiona looked at Sandy with distaste.

"We are going home. A new home. . . ." Sandy wailed. Madeleine picked him up. In two more days, they would be at Vinton, and she would not need to fear revealing anything more to these travelers.

Sandy subsided. Madeleine glanced at the castle. Widows and children needed their rights upheld, and for that, they needed their overlord. A pardon for the prisoners would free Lord Magnus to do that. But for now. . . .

She closed her eyes. "Oh God," she whispered, "Creator and Redeemer of us all, grant your servants departed this life full remission of all their offenses, that they may obtain your pardon and so enter into the fullness of eternal joy. We ask this through Christ our Lord."

Her foot kicked a stone, and she opened her eyes again.

The sky was rosy with evening, but the air still steamed. Madeleine looked with longing at the ford before them. The water had to cool the air.

"At least," said Winifred with relish, "at a ford, there is not a noble standing with outstretched hand for a fee."

The first mules splashed into the expanse. The water rose only to their fetlocks. Madeleine stopped by the bank, where a cool breeze touched her. She pulled off her shoes and stockings, and Sandy pressed closer to her. Madeleine tucked the clothing away and picked him up.

Abruptly, someone loomed behind her and lifted her off her feet. She gave a startled shriek. Sandy threw his arms about her neck.

A great, red-bearded man, a roughly clad drover, laughed. After a second, Sandy grinned. The man tromped into the waters. "You and the tadpole shouldn't have to wade in the mud."

Her heart slowing toward normality, Madeleine cast her eyes down. It *would* keep not only her shoes but her feet dry. She thanked him demurely.

Another drover called over the waters: "Pretty lass like you won't be a widow long!"

Madeleine froze. That, she had not thought upon, and here, she had no help to call if a drover took insult at refusal.

Then, she had implied that she had not been widowed long.

She blinked, as if holding tears back, and felt tears actually welling. She blinked again. One trickled on her cheek.

"Don't cry, Mama!" said Sandy.

"I'm sorry," said Madeleine, sniffing. "But it was—it was—" Unable to think of what to say next, she sniffed again. "My John would not have let me cross on my own."

The drover looked aghast, and then resigned. He trudged out of the water and lowered her—even if as abruptly as he had taken her up.

Madeleine put her shoes back on. The sun gleamed red, shining on the road and fields; the waters glittered red. They still had time to travel, and these merchants would travel, getting her closer to the end of her journey.

Beneath the fierce noon sun, Winifred and Fiona wished Madeleine well and walked away with their wares and the mules. Madeleine stood at the crossroads.

Sandy shifted in her arms, which ached with weariness, but she did not dare put him down. She looked about the heat, noise, and dust and tried not to look ignorant. Her clothing had seemed rough at Summerfield, but now she wished it were rougher, and her feet bare. No one would pick her out as a noblewoman, but someone might remember her.

Her feet ached as it was. She would keep her shoes.

Merchants lined up their pack donkeys with oaths and blows. A handful rode by wagons. Outside the town, drovers packed a lowing herd of cows into a fenced enclosure. A troupe of entertainers separated the travelers from their coins—with a juggler keeping a rainbow of balls in the air, but Madeleine put her free hand on her purse.

Sandy's gaze went to the juggler. He wriggled. "Down, Mama, down!"

"Shush," said Madeleine.

A wagon trundled off the street. A company of travelers clustered before the central cross. They did not dress like merchants, and carried no merchandise. She looked more closely. Every one of them wore a scallop shell: pilgrims.

Madeleine let free a sigh of relief. The pilgrims shifted, and she scolded herself for its prematurity. She still had to ask. And a lone woman—she approached. The chatter she overheard was about the shrine of St. Adelaide. The company was mixed: elderly who, though spry, did not look accustomed to overpowering strangers, and many women. Rich peasants, poor peasants, townsfolk—certainly no one as high as a knight. Madeleine slowed. In her clothing, she could pass herself off as a pilgrim, but they would wonder at her sudden appearance.

A dark young woman looked sharply at her.

"Goodwoman," said Madeleine, "is this the road to Harthill that you are on?"

The woman nodded. Other pilgrims glanced at Madeleine.

"I need—my husband died, and his family. . . ." The words did not flow. "My family has gone to Harthill, in service."

The pilgrims still looked unwelcoming. Madeleine felt as if the lies would choke her.

Sandy looked at them with wide eyes. "Papa?" he said. Madeleine stroked his hair and dared to hope that the faces were less inhospitable.

"Recently?" said a man, his dark hair heavily laced with silver.

"We got the news just three days ago," Madeleine said. She wondered how long she would have to lie.

"We go to St. Adelaide's shrine," said the man. "You are going the way we are, and then some." He lowered his voice. "And St. Adelaide is the patroness of widows."

"Adding to our pilgrimage the good deed of aiding the widow and the fatherless," said the dark young woman. She smiled.

"I would be glad of her intercession," said Madeleine. The first pilgrims walked down the road, and she fell in with their company. Down the road, surrounded by plowed fields, she remembered that St. Adelaide was also the patroness of prisoners. That did not take the bitter taste from her mouth.

A bright-eyed old woman came up to admire Sandy. "Little chick, with yellow fluff." Sandy buried his face in Madeleine's shoulder. Still smiling, she glanced at Madeleine. "The king get to the estate yet?"

Madeleine, not sure what she meant, shook her head.

The woman laughed. "They'll regret that. Bad enough when the lord descended for his share. Now the king as well?" She rolled her eyes. "His family will have to deal with *him*, you may be sure."

Her dead husband's family. Madeleine blinked. Not yet, not yet—but if the king executed John. . . .

"Don't cry, Mama," said Sandy.

"Fond of him, were you?" said the woman.

Madeleine nodded and swallowed. Wailing over a husband not even dead yet—she would never get to the queen if she crumbled on the third day of travel.

The dark young woman appeared by her shoulder, holding out a scallop shell.

"I'm not—I may not stop at the shrine—"

"It's on the way, and we are making a circuit, so you will visit - *some* shrines." She smiled. "And you do not want to repeat your sad tale to every curious soul."

And lie every time. Madeleine thanked her and attached the shell to her shawl, juggling Sandy to manage it. He ran a finger over it.

"My name's Katrine."

"Madeleine. And this is Sandy."

"Edna," said the old woman.

"There's a monastery ahead," said Katrine. "We'll stay the night there—under a roof."

A honking gaggle of geese came down the road toward them. Two goose-girls, sticks in hand, looked ready to dispute the way.

Katrine rolled her eyes. "You will find a pilgrimage instructive in patience."

She had no choice, Madeleine reminded herself. If she went on her own, she might never arrive.

Ahead of her, a tiny old man began a hymn, his voice deep, and the other pilgrims picked it up. "Revive us again, God of our salvation." It could only help to pass the miles, thought Madeleine, and joined in. "His salvation is near for those who fear him, that glory may dwell in our land." She choked on the words. "Mercy and truth will meet; justice and peace will kiss one another." She plodded on, thinking bitterly as they sang, "Truth will spring out of the earth; justice will look down from the heavens." That, she reminded herself, was what she sought.

Thin clouds covered the sky, without darkening the day much, or lessening the heat. Fergus looked about the courtyard. Lady Annette had to come this way—and after all the work he had put into readying the chambers, she had best come soon.

"Uncle Fergus!"

Annette ran across the cobblestones. She stopped for a band of nobles—she knew that much of court—but leapt on the instant she could. Her brown curls flew behind her. More like a child than a maid ready for marriage, thought Fergus.

Her arms looped about his neck.

"I am glad you arrived safely," said Fergus.

For all the heat, Annette shivered. "It was so crowded on the way." She lowered her voice. "Is it true, about those arrests? About this—Lord Magnus?"

Fergus nodded.

"I heard that the king didn't expected so many to obey the summons." Her mouth pursed. "It will bring nobles to court—but a nobleman who could think of marriage now—"

His mouth twisted wryly. "Come inside." He watched her mercurial expressions a moment longer. If he told her of *his* connection to the matter, she would spread the story of his goddaughter's husband over the court within an hour.

He hoped that he would have spoken, if he could have aided John of Summerfield, but he could not.

A village clumped below the hill where the monastery stood. Against the clouds of red and orange, the buildings were black. The sleeping Sandy heavy in her arms, Madeleine wondered how long it would take to get to their beds—if it was where Katrine meant.

"That's the monastery," said Katrine. "A service at the church, and then to bed."

Madeleine nodded. The road felt longer than it must have been; they reached the village before the sky was dark.

Lit by only a few candles, inside the church was darker than the outside. The priest with the pilgrims—Father Kennard—appeared from the gloom. "Your husband's name?"

"John," said Madeleine, too surprised to answer otherwise.

Father Kennard vanished again. She joined the others in the pews and laid Sandy aside. He was too soundly asleep to be woken by the hard bench.

In the midst of the prayers, Father Kennard intoned, "Have mercy on your servant John, departed this life, and on his widow and child—"

Madeleine stared at her hands. Even reminding herself that Donald and Andrew might find her if she told the truth, and that the pilgrims might suffer if the king discovered they had helped her, did not diminish her dismay at the pretense.

"Eternal rest grant unto him, o Lord—"

The prayers might be premature, Madeleine found herself thinking, but perhaps not much. With John's wounds— perhaps, not at all. She bent her head over her hands and prayed, passionately, for success.

Katrine lifted her head from being bent over her hands. Prayer had brought her no light on their companion. She rose with the rest, but as they filed from the church, she eased toward Father Kennard.

"She's hiding something."

"Perhaps she's just grief-stricken," said the priest.

Katrine's mouth twisted. Outside the road wound on. They would travel on it. She would discover if her prayers for knowledge would be answered.

Sandy shifted against Madeleine's shoulder. Katrine looked away. On pilgrimage for a husband—and to escape one whom she did not pray for. She wondered if Madeleine knew how lucky she was.

She let out her breath slowly, and left the priest to go toward her. "I could help you carry your boy, if you liked—"

Madeleine looked over. "When he's more awake, I will be grateful."

The sun was setting, the road went up a hill, and Drostan's horse trudged on. A good steed, even for a royal messenger, but if he did not find the king soon, he would need another.

At the height, the valley was clear. Drostan surveyed the banners. In the still air, it was impossible to make out their devices, but he could pick out the colors. He did not want to foolishly hope, but those were the royal banners, finally.

His gaze flicked over the valley again. A gallows—he had not noticed it before, but a score of men hung there. His mouth tightened.

The horse went down the slope. Considering the number of messengers the king kept, he made it difficult enough for any to find him. He would hear about how long this had taken. Had he know that King Walter was here, he could have made in journey in half the time—but that was past. Now he had only to ride down to the castle, answer the guards' hail, and reach the king's chamber.

There, on bent knee, he presented the letter. He breathed a sigh of relief as the king broke the seal. Not only was the reputation of the king's couriers at stake, so too was the matter of the message. He had seen Somerled only briefly, but rumor had run rife in the messengers' quarters.

The king read in silence. Then his gaze went to the top again, and he read it again.

"Sire?" said an attendant. Drostan glanced over. No, a minister, with a chain of office. He wondered how tired he was to make such a mistake.

King Walter handed the letter over. After reading it, the minister said, "An urgent matter."

"We must still deal with the West Dales," said the king.

Drostan blinked.

"They are not in open rebellion," said the minister.

"Yet," said King Walter. "The spark may yet be crushed, as it can not be in Eastwyck."

Drostan glanced between them. Somerled, he thought, and then, Benneit.

"You can hardly wish," said King Walter, "to expose me, undefended, to the malice of my foes!"

Drostan shifted his weight. The king waved a hand at him. Drostan, taking it as dismissal, bowed deeply and sidled from the room.

A gray-haired servant touched his arm. "Be wary. He's quick to—justice."

"He's not quick in Eastwyck," said Drostan. "His men were murdered there."

"You must have seen the gallows."

Clouds lowered—not great, sooty thunderheads, but while lightning might send them running for cover, rain would slow them, and so would mud. And those gray billows promised rain.

Sandy ran about the monastery's courtyard, laughing. The pilgrims talked and glanced at the clouds, but Father Kennard had not returned from speaking with the abbot. Madeleine wondered how far they could travel before the rain struck.

Then the priest, his face grim, moved slowly through the doorway. "Abbot Ellar told me of another way, by down the road to the pastures—"

"How much farther is it?" said old William.

"We can reach the next town by nightfall. . . if all goes well," said Father Kennard. They could not escape the wet, Madeleine thought, but the priest did not glance at her. "Robbers in the woods would make the shorter route a delay."

"Robbers?" said a young man. "We will show them wiser ways! A good stout staff—"

Tormod, Madeleine realized. He had not seemed so ferocious on the way. Other young men, and not so young men, among the pilgrims looked as fierce.

"A holy pilgrim leap into such an affray?" said Father Kennard.

"It's a pious act, preventing their plundering—"

"When the aged, the young, the women, surround you?"

"An act of charity," said Tormod, holding his staff loosely, "and you can go around—"

"And," said Madeleine, "wait while they nurse you back to health?"

The pilgrims laughed. Madeleine did not smile. If these fools were injured, she—she would go on alone, robbers or no.

"The road to the pastures," said Father Kennard.

They tramped through the pastures beneath clouds. In the forest, rain began. Madeleine pulled her shawl forward—but nothing would keep them dry if they journeyed in this weather.

"Don't *like* rain," said Sandy.

The showers had stopped, the sunset even broke through the clouds, but mud clung to her feet, and she and Sandy, like the pilgrims, were wet, their clothing stiff and chaffing. And this from showers—she hoped they suffered no worse along the way.

The town stood ahead, across the river; it lay dark between the sunset and the sunset's reflection in the river. They would spend that night there, but they had yet to reach the bridge.

"Is he too heavy for you?" said Tormod.

A better act of charity, Madeleine thought, but. . . . "He's half-asleep. I don't think it's worth waking him." Sandy stirred and sighed. She closed her mouth before she woke him without shifting him to another pair of arms.

"Halt!" came from bridge. Guards there spoke to the first pilgrims, and the news spread: a toll. It came with angry murmurs, and declarations, "They didn't have that *last* time."

Old William said, "All very well for the merchants—greedy folk, ought to pay. But poor *pilgrims*? An offense against God and man. The lord'll suffer God's curse for interfering with pious duties."

While they rummaged for coins, hoof beats sounded from the bridge ahead. Madeleine stood, paralyzed with the thought that she had been found. The pilgrims shuffled aside. Madeleine went, grimacing with her own folly and the muck underfoot. Commoners gave way to nobles. She hoped no one had ever scrambled into such grime for her.

A thin, pale nobleman rode by after a minute. He cast a disdainful glance over the company. Madeleine was certain he would not remember her if Donald or Andrew asked.

The pilgrims filed over the bridge, their coins clinking.

A guard jeered. "Did you think the men that caught the robbers feed on air?" He flipped one coin in the air. "Or that the lord doesn't have to buy their provisions?"

Madeleine dropped hers, and a guard said, "And him." He pointed at Sandy.

Madeleine did not stir. She could afford it, but to reveal that she was not concerned about money—she did not want to expose even pious pilgrims to that temptation. Sandy shifted in her arms, to stare, wide-eyed.

"You said," said Katrine, fiercely, "a coin for everyone who *walks* across."

"How hard-hearted you are," said Father Kennard. "To have no mercy on the widow and fatherless—to increase your toll beyond its appointed bounds—"

The captain called, across the bridge: "Let her go."

Madeleine scurried.

Father Kennard led them down dark, narrow streets, not hesitating when townsfolk glanced at them and whispered, or when dogs barked. Madeleine did not realize, until they were under it, that they passed a gallows. She glanced up. Men—bodies—hung from it. Not yet rotten, their clothing not yet ragged, but they had been dead some time. Sickened, she looked away. Sandy stirred and raised his head. Madeleine hurried on, interposing her shawl.

"Rogues, all of them," said an old woman, Helwise. "We're safer for their deaths—they had no shame, they would have robbed even pilgrims."

"The guards robbed us," said Tormod, surly.

"Not of everything," said Katrine. "Those knaves—"

"Are dead," said Madeleine, her voice small. Katrine looked at her. "With my husband so lately dead—"

Helwise snorted. "Then give thanks to God that he did not die shamefully."

He might yet. Beheading was not that much more honorable than hanging. She swallowed her horror. In the journeying, in all her deceit, she had almost forgotten why she journeyed.

Sandy, she realized, stared at the gallows, despite her efforts. Perhaps because of them.

In an alley, William spoke with a townsman; he returned, indignant. "The lord *didn't go*. Lord Magnus summoned him, he got a messenger from—someone else—and he didn't go!"

"That we knew already," said Edna. "No lord who went could be here to lay a toll on pilgrims."

Madeleine glanced among them. The toll was more to them than the treason. She swallowed.

She woke with a gasp, in gloom. Like the last of sunset, red glowed to one side—but it was too late, even for that.

It took Madeleine flustered seconds to sort out the room: the rough blankets, the harsh logs beneath the straw, the warm lump that was Sandy, sleeping beside her. Other pilgrims snored, or slept in peace. She had woken no one with her dream. She lay back against the blankets. The fire, banked down, glowed dully red.

Sandy snuggled closer. Scraps of moonlight colorlessly illuminated the room. Unlike her dream. She shuddered and did not close her eyes again, for fear of that flood of red.

After a week of travel, the pilgrims chattered around their campfires. Sunset gleamed golden, but the trees shadowed them. Sandy slept in the crook of Madeleine's arm, wrapped in her shawl. Madeleine, almost as weary, did not move for fear of waking him. She had learned their stories: one in thanksgiving for her daughter's recovery after a difficult labor, another in petition for a good harvest, a third more to travel than in piety (though those pilgrims did not admit it aloud). Sad-eyed Colina had told her how the lord—another one who had failed to obey—had imposed a new fee and, their last hope was pilgrimage and prayer for a miraculous softening of heart. A handful had come in penance and ate only bread and water. They chattered as freely as the rest about weather and how it would affect the crops, and if they would find more lord making new exactions, and whether the roads had really gotten as bad as old William claimed.

Her feet agreed with old William. Running away with John had not been so hard.

Katrine leaned back from the fire. "Take care with Sandy. We aren't that far." She pointed at the hills ahead. Mists rose up from the valleys there—as mists did in other valleys, but in these ones, it never faded. Madeleine's tongue touched her lips. She had not realized that they would come this close to the Misty Hills. She eyed them. They were enchanted, Katrine was right in that, the king had less power in them than even in the unruly West Dales, which had owned him as king much later, but their company was safe enough, being outside them.

To say *that* would make the pilgrims wonder.

"It. . . it would be too far for him to reach."

Katrine lowered her voice. "The mists aren't bound in place. They—reach out. He shouldn't tempt them."

What nonsense, Madeleine thought—but she had to keep her voice calm. "How can you tell? There are mists elsewhere."

"Why, monsters!" William looked indignant. "Dragons and—wicked things—come out."

Dragons she could not deny, and she could not know too much. To divert the talk, she said, "We must reach Lord Patrick's lands soon. Leaving Lord Magnus's."

Katrine shrugged. "One overlord's like another."

Her overlord was the king; Lord Magus held directly from him, and Katrine came from his demesne lands. She thought Katrine could tell the difference between King Walter and King Michael his father.

"Watch your tongue!" Across the fire, a pilgrim leapt to his feet. Silence fell about. "You know what happened to Lord Magnus—do you think you think *you're* more powerful than him?"

Everyone tried to look away. Almost everyone—Father Kennard hurried over. Madeleine straightened the blanket about Sandy in her own effort to ignore it.

"Don't tell me that king won't find out! He went hunting in the Misty Hills itself!" The man sat on the ground. He gave the priest, whose mouth was opening, a baleful glance. Father Kennard looked flustered, and did not speak.

"In King Adair's day," whispered Katrine mischievously, "a block of wood was disguised as Prince Leod, and a lord's men died about it, so the prince could escape. Bet you that no man would die for King Walter like that."

Old William snorted. "Bet you that no man died for Prince Leod like that."

Men died for Lord Magnus, thought Madeleine.

Old William said the food was ready. Madeleine eased Sandy to the ground. She could leave when the pilgrims reached the Misty Hills, which could be traversed in a day, whatever Nichola thought.

She took the porridge, but her thoughts flitted back as she ate. Leaving the pilgrims would be folly. Wiser for a woman to have company than to travel alone, and this company would last to well past the other side of the hills.

Sunset gilded the mists. In those mists—a day's travel by an enchanted path, weeks by an unenchanted one—lay Candlewood. There a widowed Lord Thomas, and his son Lord Jasper, lived. There the body of his wife, Lady Sorcha, was buried.

There John had won his way from Candlebrook, to woo and win her.

Madeleine's spoon scrapped the bowl's bottom.

The road wound its way through a mire. Sandy shrieked at a bird flying over the road, from one patch of rushes to another. Its body was black, but red flashed on its wings. "Red!"

Pilgrims smiled at him.

In the front of the company where Sandy had run, Madeleine looked ahead. The road wound into a pinewood; pools and mud still lay to the left, but on the hills beside it, mists lay. They went near the Misty Hills indeed. In fact, near the path that she and John had taken.

Sandy scurried back to Madeleine. "My *legs* hurt, Mama. Carry me!"

Madeleine picked him up and walked. Pines closed around, shading the road and scenting the air. The hill doves' call sounded, too loud to be called cooing, more like the tolling of a bell.

Madeleine smiled sadly. When she was a child, the doves had nested outside her window, but she had not heard them since she had wed John.

Hoof beats sounded on the road. Madeleine winced. Those were not merchants' horses. The pilgrims moved into the trees without visible resentment, but she had not quite mastered being a peasant. Her foot slipped on the black mud beneath the golden pine needles, and she steadied herself on the nearest tree. The hoof beats slowed on the road.

For a moment, she tried to convince herself that the horsemen slowed for a patch of mud or some such, but so far from picking up pace again, they slowed still further. Her heart pounded. What would a nobleman want with pilgrims?

The horsemen pulled up by the company. They wore the green of Summerfield's livery.

One rider spoke with a pilgrim. She could not make out the words, but she felt coldly certain of her danger. Other nobles dressed their servants in green, but these riders wanted something with these pilgrims.

Madeleine stepped behind the tree.

The man's voice rose, and some words were clear. "She's mad. . . passing herself off as a widow! Her husband lives. . . Madeleine."

She felt wintry cold and drew a steadying breath. It was little help, but she could think.

Running would make noise and draw attention. Despite her hammering heart, Madeleine wrapped her shawl about Sandy, prayed that he would keep quiet, and inched into the woods. The slope rose steeply, with gray rocks cropping from it. She picked her way through wet leaves and damp earth, and thanked God that they would quiet her step. Trees grew gnarled as she reached the height, and tangled roots lay like rope over stones.

Mists rose above the hilltop. Madeleine faltered, for a moment, among the twisted pines.

But her flight told both the pilgrims and Donald's men that she was the Madeleine they sought. With the mire behind, and Donald's men on the road, she had no other path.

A rock jutted from the ground ahead of her. Madeleine climbed it and looked over her shoulder. The pilgrims and Donald's men searched through the trees. They knew.

She took off the scallop shell and laid it on the rock. Katrine or another might find it. She hoped they could forgive her the deceit. She hoped they would still pray for her.

St. Adelaide, she prayed, pray for me, and for the prisoners.

"Mama?" Sandy's voice was hesitant.

"Shush," she breathed. Lord, have mercy. Christ, have mercy. Lord, have mercy. Blessed Mary, pray for us. St. Joseph, pray for us. St. Peter, pray for us. St. Valentine, pray for us. St. Nicholas, pray for us.

The voice was cold. "She must be up the hill."

Standing against the mists would reveal her, if anyone glanced this way, but the men climbed the slope. Madeleine scrambled up. Seeing the mists filling the valley like porridge filling a bowl reminded her that she had not lived in the Misty Hills for three years.

Sandy wriggled around. "Oooo."

Her mouth twitched. It was just as well she had come afoot. Horses from outside the Misty Hills did not fare well inside them.

"There she is!"

Even against the wet earth, even from far down the hillside, the footsteps were loud enough for her to hear. Madeleine looked at the trees about her, twisted over the rock, and picked one half-bent one, odd even among these. She climbed down, picking her way through rock, mud, and pine needles so profuse as to be slippery, with Sandy a weight in her arms. When he wriggled, she tightened her arms, and thanked God that he was still too bewildered to chatter. Every now and again, she glanced back. Shouts followed her, muffled by the mass of the hill, but the men climbed after her. The tree turned into a shadowy shape quickly, but she was down in the valley, the ground flat ahead of her, before it vanished in the mists.

If she could not see it, Donald's men could not see her from the hilltop. She let out her breath. Her heart calmed. Hunting her would mean venturing into the mists.

From the way the shouts echoed, the men had reached the summit. Her assurance vanished. Madeleine darted behind the nearest tree. Sandy ooed and reached for a gnarled branch. Madeleine lay fingers to his mouth and whispered, "Shush."

"If we go after her, who's going to tell Lord Donald that Lady Madeleine vanished into the Misty Hills?"

Madeleine's breath whooshed out.

Minutes later, footsteps descended the hill's other side.

Sandy wriggled. Madeleine lowered him to the ground. "Don't go up the hill," she said.

The nearest tree had a gash in the bark, and he went to poke at the amber ooze. Probably only the fascination of that kept him obedient, but the sap was not poisonous.

She touched her belt pouch. The gold might prove more useful here than for bribes. She sat on the nearest rock and poured the coins into her lap, where she sorted them into the pouch again, despite their variegated sizes: silver in the bottom, copper over them, gold on the top.

"Gold is solar," she said.

"Mama?" said Sandy.

Madeleine fastened the pouch. "Come, Sandy, we're off to see your papa."

"Papa come soon?"

"We have to go to him." Madeleine's mouth felt stiff. She wondered if she could see John, if her petition failed.

Sandy scrambled over. She would not think about her petition failing.

Only a handful of trees were visible ahead of them. Most were vague, mist-veiled. She took Sandy's hand and walked.

The noises of the pilgrims and Donald's men, already faint, vanished. The pine roots were thick and knobby, and many places were slippery with mud. Sandy's attention was soon bent on his footing, his concentration so complete that even when climbing, he did not remember to complain of being tired. A flock of hill doves tolled about them.

Not a flock, or only loosely, because they were birds, but a flock of doves was a truelove of doves. John, in a merry mood, had waxed lyrical on the trueloves of the Misty Hills.

Her face felt stiffer than ever. She must ensure that Sandy did not watch his father's execution. She forced herself to remember the way through the Hills. If she did not pick up the path's proper end, at the stream, it took as long to go through the Misty Hills as it did to pass through the land outside them. Some enchanted paths took longer than the distance should, and some never ended—when the king would not delay that long.

Sandy's grip on her hand tightened as he stepped on an enormous root. Madeleine slowed, to allow him to keep up.

Chapter 4—Mists and Monsters

Katrine turned the scallop over. Neatly placed on the rock. Madeleine—Lady Madeleine—had not dropped but discarded it. Apology? Or delight in escaping base-born companions?

"At least Lord Donald did not blame us for fetching her so far from her family and home." Tormod sounded dazed—as dazed as most of them felt. No one had taken another step on the road since Lord Donald's men had left. They would be hard put to reach shelter that night.

She was as dazed as any, Katrine admitted, straightening. One man had said that her brother by marriage, not her husband, had sent them. She did not want to consider that too long, or too deeply. Lady Madeleine's husband had to be one of Lord Magnus's men.

"The liar." Ysabel thumped her staff on the ground. "St. Adelina is the patroness of *widows*."

"Also," said Father Kennard, without inflection, "of prisoners." He looked down the slope. "Let us go."

They walked down, on the knotted roots and slick leaves. Katrine's hand tightened on the scallop. Whispers spread even before they could have heard them speak.

Colina pulled toward Katrine. "How could she have told *us* such lies?"

"When she did not know us?" said Katrine. "When her own brother by marriage meant her ill?"

Colina sniffed and muttered that Lord Donald was distressed by Lady Madeleine's plight, but Katrine did not listen. Clever, clever, *clever* Katrine, to have guessed that

Madeleine hid something. If she had *thought*—she pocketed the scallop. "Let us pray for her."

"When she *lied* so?" said Colina.

"Our Lord came not for the righteous but for sinners," said Father Kennard, in reproof.

"And," said Katrine, "if Lord John was taken in battle—how *could* Lord Donald *know* that Lady Madeleine is not a widow?"

She looked down the road. Through the trees, the sunlight slanted and made the pine forest glow until it seemed carpeted in amber. Her mouth tightened. "Let's go. We need to sleep tonight."

For the fourth time, Madeleine thought that she heard water running, and then they reached a hilltop, and she found she had mistaken the rushing of the wind. Bushes clustered in the valley. In the woods, it was always difficult to make out whether you traveled in a straight line, but those red flowers were new.

Sandy scampered toward them. The right direction, for once. Madeleine followed. Something crashed in the bushes. Sandy pulled back, and Madeleine reached him in three strides.

After a moment, she made out the gray deer. Its flanks gleamed with a dull metallic sheen, like lead, as it fled through the brush. A fawn ran alongside. Madeleine breathed a sigh of relief. Those deer never did worse than lure travelers from the path. They might not do that on purpose.

Perhaps they meant the path was near. When she and John had reached its end, they had seen a stag and doe in the brush.

She walked as if she could out-walk the memory. Sandy looked on the verge of wailing, and Madeleine said, "Race you to that tree." She pointed at a forked one. Laughing, Sandy ran. Madeleine hurried after, as if running as hard as she

could. Before they reached the tree, Sandy had forgotten the
end, and ran and ran, up the slope to the hilltop.

In the valley below, a stream ran over rocks. White and
crimson flowers sprouted here and there, the blossoms and
leaves low among the stones. The path lay beyond.

Onward, to the queen, Madeleine thought. She smiled as
broadly as Sandy, even as she pulled off shoes and socks.

They had to splash through it, but the stream was cold.
Sandy's first enthusiasm vanished. When they got out, Sandy
complained as she pulled back on stockings and shoes, on still
wet feet. She had to rub off grime before it rubbed their feet
raw.

But they had reached the path. Though it was little more
than a trodden line in the plants and dead leaves, marked more
by mud than any other sign, she knew its secrets.

They walked through birches. The white bark and even the
pale green leaves faded into the mists. A thicket of ferns grew
to each side, so thickly that they narrowed the path. Though
Madeleine sent Sandy ahead of her, ferns still pricked and
poked, and Sandy grumbled.

When it felt as if the birches would last forever, firs
appeared ahead. Despite the dimness, Madeleine could see the
dead needles that formed the forest floor, not broken even by
moss. The path was dirt among the golden needles. Madeleine
and Sandy walked into the gloom. The fir bark, dark with
moisture, bore not even lichen.

"Witches?" said Sandy.

The dark was enough to make Madeleine think of fairy tales
as well. Tendrils of mist reached through the trees.

"No witches," she said. "See, no houses for them."

Sandy nodded sagely. Madeleine glanced back. The mists outside the firs—were they as bright as they had been? She had ventured into the Misty Hills at midday. Even without Sandy, she could not have crossed the hills before sundown.

"Stay here," she said. Sandy stared at her, but she would be able to see him. His face was a white gleam in the firs' shade as she walked back to the birches.

The mists lay in wisps among the trees; only in layer upon layer, did they obscure the hills behind, and the sky overhead. Madeleine drew a deep breath, racked her memory, and recited a charm. It worked better than the charms she had learned outside, against rain: the mists thinned, and she could see the sun through their veil, silvery over a hill.

She hurried back to Sandy. They would stop as soon as she found some shelter for the night.

Firs spread out ahead. Mists kept her from seeing anything beyond them. Madeleine walked. Sandy yawned and pulled close to her. She hoped he did not insist on being carried soon.

The firs grew larger, like cathedral pillars, and then larger than any pillar she had ever seen, even at Harthill. She walked past one, and behind it, a gap in the trees let in misty light. It shimmered on the pool that caused the gap. No stream flowed in or out of it: a perfectly still, perfectly round pool of black water. It reflected like a dark mirror and showed no hints of its depths.

A pair of brilliantly blue water lilies blossomed in the center of it. Madeleine's heart hammered in terror.

"Pretty!" said Sandy.

Without thinking of rebuking first, Madeleine snatched him up. The black tarns held madness. Enough of the water would reduce Sandy to a simpleton.

"Witch's?" said Sandy, leaning over. It made it hard for her to carry him, with his weight so uneven, but she could not threaten to put him down.

"You must not go there," she said. "It's bad."

Sandy looked unconvinced. Madeleine nearly groaned. She would have to go much further before camping—far enough that Sandy could not wander back. "Papa wouldn't like."

Sandy leaned back, to her arms' relief. "Bad pool—keeps Papa away." His head rested against her shoulder. "Witch keeps Papa away."

Madeleine did not argue with that.

The mists showed, faintly, the colors of sunset. Madeleine crouched by a cliff face, holding her son. Ferns grew on the cliff overhead. Sandy already slept, having invoked blessings on his family and cuddled in her shawl, with a blanket under them and over them.

She ought to sleep. Sandy would wake early in the morning, and the sooner they started, the sooner they would reach the other side. She had laid the golden coins about them, to avert what the metal could avert. She had nothing more to do but sleep.

Her gaze went to the colored mists.

She knew where this path went. If she left it, she could reach her father's house by noon.

She shivered.

Her marriage had not pleased her father, but her arrival, with Sandy in arms, seeking shelter, would be taken as penitence. She was less sure of a welcome at court. Lord Fergus might have been as offended by the elopement as her father. She could only hope that he would help her reach the queen. At that, she could only hope that the queen would grant the pardon.

She told herself, sternly, that she had yet to fail. She dropped her head down on the ground beside Sandy. If she could not sleep like Sandy, she could pray—more good than the fretting had done her.

She remembered the words: But he must pray with a firm heart, never wavering. . . .

"Lord have mercy," she whispered. "Christ have mercy—"

"I'm *cold*, Mama!" Sandy wailed in her ear.

Of course, you're cold, Madeleine thought furiously, if not coherently. It's cold. Then her son tugged on her shawl, letting in air. She woke to the gray, bone-chilling morning. The ground was like a grave, and she had never felt so stiff before. She hugged Sandy under her shawl, as she inched up, to sitting. She had thought they had slept meanly before, but they had usually had hay, and always had more blankets.

Cold still leached into her legs. With a groan, Madeleine rose. Gray mist enveloped the hills with its usual morning thickness. She could barely make out the coins; in this gloom, they did not glint. Not daring to forfeit their protection with her thoughts muddled, she paced inside the circle. She and Sandy had far to go, but this night had passed in peace, and they had escaped Donald's men. She stopped and closed her eyes. I will praise You, Lord, You have rescued me, and have not let my enemies rejoice over me.

"I'm *hungry*, Mama!"

Madeleine opened her eyes, shifted Sandy to her hip, and reached for the satchel. He took the bread without more talk, letting her eat, but when done, he said, "My *legs* hurt, Mama!"

He had walked more yesterday than on the days before, Madeleine thought. Her arms ached, and she lowered him; she would have to carry him enough today.

Sandy pouted. Then his hand went to his mouth. "What's that, Mama?"

Lilies rose from the ground about the path; the flowers were pure white, the stems and leaves, silver touched with green.

"Morning lilies," Madeleine said.

Sandy leapt to touch one. It dissolved beneath his fingers, and he gawked.

"They're magic," she said. "You can gather them, sometimes, if you just touch the stalk." The stem would dissolve then, leaving the flower intact for the hour or so before it melted into mist.

His face contorted with thought. She could not remember at what age she had mastered the art of gathering them, but she had been older than Sandy. He reached out. A stem dissolved, sending a lily to the ground, but his snatching fingers dissolved the bloom.

With him distracted, Madeleine gathered blankets and coins.

"What's that, Mama?" No longer concerned about the lilies, Sandy leaned forward.

Madeleine stopped. "Lean back, or you'll have to walk. Mama can't carry you."

Sandy pouted and leaned against her. "What's that?"

On their left, Madeleine realized, leaves twitched. Twittering came from the brush. A flock of tiny birds burst out and flitted over the path, their wings iridescent in the misty light. "Rainbow birds, Sandy."

"Oh." Sandy laid his head to her shoulder. "Pretty."

Madeleine shifted his weight. She had not realized how much the pilgrims had helped her with carrying Sandy. She silently prayed for their well-being.

The trees here were smaller than most, rising barely over her head, and the brush underfoot grew thickly. The mist lay heavily about—more than it had the day before, more even than she remembered from her childhood.

"Down, Mama!" said Sandy, squirming. Madeleine followed his gaze. Silvery rabbits nibbled at grass. As good a time as any to rest, thought Madeleine and let him down. He scampered after them. Madeleine kept her gaze on him, but the rabbits never seemed to draw him away.

Not like the deer then, she thought. She swung her arms. Not like misty rabbits, either; they did not dissolve into mist to avoid Sandy.

A shadow fell: a bird, flying through them, with a hooked beak—a raptor. The shadow grew larger, and closer to Sandy.

Madeleine jumped forward. One hand threw her shawl about her son, and the other tossed the other side of her shawl into the air, almost before she thought of baffling the hawk about how big Sandy was.

A white hawk swept through the air. The rabbits vanished as if they had melted.

Sandy wailed. Madeleine's heart hammered. She had not needed to protect him, the hawk was far too small to have carried him off, but that thought did not calm her heart.

She gathered Sandy into her arms to comfort him.

"Rabbits got 'way?" Tearful, Sandy looked at her.

"Yes, the rabbits got away."

Sandy sniffed. Madeleine's heart slowed. Unlike her tales of being a widow, she thought bitterly, it was even the truth.

Too unnerved to sit again, she walked on, carrying Sandy. Walking with a child, or carrying him, was not the best way to travel. Even on this path, she would have to spend another night in the Misty Hills.

Flowers, white and pink stars, appeared along the path. Madeleine walked more quickly. A vale appeared ahead of her. All the trees growing there were saplings, and the forest floor between was filled with moss and small blue flowers, bent over, like silent bells. She groaned. "Dead Men's Bells."

"Who's dead?" said Sandy.

"Just a story," Madeleine said. She muttered the mist-parting charm again. The sun appeared. It was sinking, but had not gotten far.

Sandy wriggled. She did not even dare hint at putting him down again as she walked on. It was a bad sign when Dead Men's Bells grew where they had not grown before, but she heard no sound like bells ringing.

Nevertheless, she took care not to step on any of them.

When the trees thickened to shadow the forest floor and the flowers ended, she sighed in relief and walked briskly. The farther from the flowers, the better.

As she climbed the opposite slope, she thought she saw folk ahead of her, two or three people by the path. She hesitated. News would fly; it might even reach out of the Misty Hills.

Standing here, dithering, only gave it more time to spread.

She walked quickly, but when she reached that place, she saw not so much as a trodden-on leaf.

Hours later, gray mists turned charcoal. Madeleine climbed a rocky slope. Sandy lay like lead in her arms; he had slept for the last hour. No Dead Man's Bells grew in the rocks. She sat with a thud. Sandy stirred. She fumbled for bread and cheese. She would not have any difficulty sleeping tonight.

Lord, mercifully hear me. Christ, make haste to aid me. . . . Her eyelids drooped as she prayed. She barely laid the gold coins out before curling up on the ground.

The hiss was low, but Madeleine could not mistake it for anything else—especially when the air had grown warmer, and smelled like heated metal. She eased her eyelids open. Moonlight touched the mists and glinted from an eye like a well, liquid and dark.

The shadow dragon turned its scaly nose toward her. Its forked tongue licked the air, an even darker shadow against the faint gleam of its scales. Madeleine's arms tightened. Sandy shifted but did not wake.

The dragon's tongue came no further than the coins; the gold did keep it back, then. Its head shifted from side to side, and its shoulders bunched as if to pounce. Madeleine glanced down the sinuous body. Moonlight glinted from scales as large as her hand.

She met the dragon's gaze and whispered, to avoid waking Sandy, "The Lord is my Shepherd, I shall not want."

The dragon was unblinking. Madeleine admitted to herself that she had hoped that prayer would drive it off. No matter. "He makes me to lie down in green pastures; He leads me beside the still waters."

Tired as she was, she finished the psalm without falling asleep. The dragon showed no signs of melting into the mists. Madeleine forced herself to close her eyes. Watching would not scare the dragon off, and she had far to go.

The next morning, Sandy complained of the chill again. That could not keep Madeleine's attention from the hillside. The stone had not shifted, but where grass and brush had grown, they had been trampled. Mud showed claw marks so deep that she could plunge her hand into one to the wrist.

She gave Sandy breakfast and urged him to eat quickly. A yellow butterfly flew by as they finished. With a squeal, Sandy chased it down the path. Madeleine, glad of the respite, followed.

She was very glad, when, near noon, she walked into daylight unveiled by mist, and onto a road. Though barely wide enough for a cart, the way was a road, the air about it laden with dust. She stood still a moment.

Carts trundled toward her. Madeleine stepped back into the trees, drawing Sandy with her. She thought of changing her story. Coming through the Misty Hills meant she was ahead of her pursuers—if they still chased her. But if she still claimed widowhood, Sandy might yet betray her. Even if she were so wicked as to instruct him in lying, would he remember?

She swallowed and realized the truth. Her husband was in service. She had stayed with his family, but they had quarreled with her. She traveled to her family at Harthill. Being the truth, it might even put off pursuers looking for a lie.

She reminded herself: if she did not travel quickly enough, it would not matter whether Donald's men found her.

Sandy peered at the carts. Madeleine looked at the horses drawing them and kept him on her hip as she walked. The carts trundled by, their drivers giving her a few glances. Madeleine lowered Sandy to the ground. "Let's go."

Sandy skipped along. "What's that, Mama?"

"A chapel," she said. A chapel to St. Christopher. They were not near enough the town for anything else. "Let's go in."

A bank of candles stood before the crucifix. Beside it, a statue showed that she had guessed correctly: St. Christopher stood to one side. A wooden giant almost swamped by carved waves, and the Christ child on his shoulder, one hand upraised, his face serene, confident.

Sandy put his fingers in his mouth.

Madeleine pulled out a golden coin. She would have to rearrange before the town—but not here, where any passerby could see her. She dived deeper in the pouch for a small silver mark and slid it into the box, before taking a taper and lighting one candle. The yellow flame burned steadily, in thanksgiving. She pulled out another coin, considered it a moment: for a second candle, for their continued journey, and the petition at the end.

Her hand shook as she put the coin in. It rattled against the box. No matter how earnestly she pleaded, she might not succeed.

Chapter 5—Rumors and Appeals

Less than an hour from the chapel, trees yielded to fields and a village with an inn. The inn sign bore an elegant golden stag, and the inn's condition was such that merchants and nobles would find it serviceable. Madeleine resolved to pick her traveling companions here. Sandy clung to her skirt. Then, no players distracted him here.

As she joined the crowds, other women stood or walked about, but they were from the nearby village and not pilgrims. These travelers were merchants and drovers, grumbling about the levies the king had imposed on ship-borne goods and tolls on the land. Some complained about what the king had done to Lord Magnus—if he dared that with high and mighty lords, who knew who would be next?

"Ah, who cares about lordlings?" said one drover. "Lord Magnus and his men will hang no deader than they would have died at Lord Peter's swords."

Madeleine's free hand tightened on her skirt. If the king had enforced his own decision, no man would have had to die.

A cow lowed. Madeleine forced herself to look about. She wondered if she would be the only woman on the road. Then two shepherdesses drove a bleating flock of sheep. She wondered whether they would let her join them.

One merchant argued with a woman about whether to leave at once. Madeleine looked over. The woman wore clothing as fine as the man's. Madeleine took up Sandy and walked over.

The fire glowed orange in the camp. Madeleine settled Sandy against her and stared into the depths, where the base of the flames glowed blue, and the coals red.

A drover, white-haired but still spry, came back from the village, cackling. "See that castle up here?" He pointed to where it was side-lit, by the sunset.

"Did you buy the eggs?" said Ysenda, the merchant's wife.

Still cackling, he handed them over. As Ysenda knelt to bury them in the coals, the drover said, "Full of nobles. Lord got the word early, 'bout the treason, but figured he got no need to hurry. Now he's 'offering hospitality'—to every noble looking for a night."

Madeleine looked at the fire again. He was troubled by his guests while John—she let out her breath. He had not disobeyed his lord, as Donald and Andrew had; he had hardly brought his problems on himself.

She remembered John, feeding a log to the fire in their chamber, one winter night. Her mouth tightened. She did not *want* to be just.

Smoke rose.

Malcolm pulled up his horse and scowled. He had heard enough tales of unrest that he had returned without having concluded his betrothal, and had pressed his men-at-arms on the muddy journey, but he had seen nothing. Though everyone had heard of the troubles, and some had even said the king's messengers had died.

Dark smoke billowed. The fire was large.

Kristine, he thought. He had looked for a husband for his sister, but not seriously. He intended to marry himself first, and so his sister waited at home.

He spurred his horse. He only vaguely heard his men's shouts as he rode through ravaged fields, where little would be harvested. Nothing moved about the castle, neither besiegers nor defenders. The gate stood open, and he thundered within. No one moved inside, either, and buildings burned.

Kristine, Malcolm thought again, but no bodies lay about the courtyard.

Other horses charged into the courtyard. Arche pulled up beside, and shouted orders about the fires.

Malcolm's mouth worked. Nothing Arche did would make the castle habitable again. And the first question was whether anyone would inhabit it. He yanked on the reins and spurred his horse back outside.

"My lord!" shouted Arche. "Take guards!"

Malcolm did not stop. This time, he saw the bodies sprawled about the village. Only a handful—many peasants must have escaped—but his mouth set as he rode for the woods. In the trees' shadow, he cast about for tracks. He startled a rabbit and, later, a small flock of birds, heard his own men coming behind him, and began to wonder. If they were dead, where were the bodies? If they lived—were they prisoner?

"Malcolm!" Kristine ran through the woods toward him. Her eyes were red, and she still cried. He looked about the trees, but he saw only the servants and men-at-arms. His own men rode up. He dismounted.

Kristine threw her arms about him in a manner that would make it impossible for him to fight to protect her. She sobbed.

"Hush, hush," he said, stroking her hair.

"If I had—if we hadn't—" Kristine looked up at him. "I wanted to go maying. Ide told me not to be a foolish child, but I *ordered* her to go maying—"

She put her hand to her face. None of them carried flowers, they must have discarded any that they had picked, but if she had not insisted, everyone in the tower would have died.

"Come, Kristine," he said, "let's go back."

"Why?" Ide stalked down the hillside, though bent over her staff. "We aren't going to live there."

Malcolm closed his eyes and forced a commanding note into his voice. "Come back to the tower."

Trudging back only drew the eye to how right Ide was. The peasants wept at the fields, or looked with dry eyes, past weeping.

"You should have concluded your betrothal, my lord," said Ide.

He looked indignantly at her—a poor relation, fit to chaperon his sister, but not to advise him.

"Who's going to marry his daughter to a lord whose lands are like this?" She gestured at the smoke. "Or take his sister?"

Arche scowled at such bold language to the lord, but, thought Malcolm, he could hardly contradict it.

Malcolm turned to him. "We will take my sister and the servants to the convent—the Order of the Holy Name."

Arche did not meet his gaze. "My lord—will the convent be safe?"

Malcolm opened his mouth and shut it again. And then his voice hardened. "You and various others of my men will escort Lady Kristine to court—to our Aunt Triona. If she is not safe there, it is past my power to protect her."

He looked about. "At least—while these knaves are free. My other men and I will recover the bodies, from the village, the castle, the woods, for burial. Then, we will hunt down the knaves like any rampaging beast."

Arche shifted. "Lord Magnus."

"If I can not wed, what matters if my lands can not pass to my son?"

"Couldn't believe it," the driver said.

The cart jolted over a rut. Madeleine rested her weary feet against the board. Soon the ride would be enough to have her walking again, even on this hot day, but for now, her feet hurt too much.

"You'd have thought that the king had a right to the pond." The drover snorted. "No, he doesn't even *say* he does, but he says he has a right to the golden ducks. Since when does a king own the golden ducks?"

The king owns all the swans in the land, thought Madeleine, but she was not certain about that. The golden ducks—if she could only win John and the others, she would not care if the king claimed every waterfowl in the land.

Ysenda rode up. "Traveling well, young Sandy?"

Sandy bobbed his head. Madeleine suppressed a smile.

Ysenda chuckled. "Well, there's your end." She pointed out a dot along the river: Harthill. It looked different when she came by this route. Madeleine's heart beat not faster but harder; each pulse drummed in her ears. The press about the gates was greater than she remembered.

"You'll need help there?" said Ysenda.

Madeleine shook her head.

The drover gave her a sidelong glance. "You're sure of your family."

"Oh, yes," said Madeleine. At least as far as her welcome went—her godfather had always done his duty. Many lords would not have brought a goddaughter so low in rank to court.

Ysenda looked discontented. Madeleine considered a moment. "I think my mother would be happier I went alone." So she would, if Lady Sorcha were still alive, and she went to meet her. "So that nothing could go further—"

The deceit choked her words.

"An evil thing, things said that can not be retracted. Why, Effie—she lives back in Farrington—she. . ." Ysenda rambled with a tale about Effie and her daughter.

Madeleine pressed toward the castle, through streets filled with vendors and their customers. People of all stations hastened through the streets, as much as the press allowed. Servants of the nobility squabbled loudly in front of merchants who sold everything from perfumes to sweets—but seemed not to have enough for all the nobles now. Madeleine smiled sadly. She had been right about the crowds. The nobles answering the king's summons were more than ever came to court on their own. It was harder to get through the crowds—but then, she remembered, always before she had had an escort to make her way.

Sandy gleefully pointed out each shop sign and exclaimed at the liveries.

Madeleine heard more grumbles about King Walter than she had ever before at court. New taxes, new confiscations for unknown cause, new fines, and darker mutters about Eastwyck—and no one dared appeal to the king.

No one spoke of appealing to the queen. Madeleine wondered. No one in all the court, where the queen received petitions every day. Perhaps they knew something she did not.

Sandy gawked at a sign over an inn. It showed a green lion. "What's that, Mama?"

"A lion," said Madeleine. Such innocence.

"*Lions* are *yellow*."

"It's—the lion's from far away," said Madeleine. Sandy leaned against her shoulder. Her thoughts returned to the queen. Tales of the queen had not spoken of whether she was feather-headed, interested only in clothing and gossip. King

Walter might leave authority in her hands because he knew she would merely sign what wise councilors put before her.

Madeleine squared her shoulders and plowed on toward the castle.

A tavern door opened ahead of her, so swift and hard that it slammed against the wall. Madeleine stopped; so did the crowd about her. A popinjay staggered out. His clothing was brilliant in scarlet and gold, but he carried a sword by his side, and she thought he knew how to use it.

A circle opened up about the man, larger than any juggler would get for his act. The nobleman swirled around, his hand on his sword hilt. The crowd retreated farther.

"We don't take this! We don't *have* to take this! The king thinks. . . ."

Another nobleman emerged. His finery was as gaudy, but his walk was steadier. "The king thinks a great deal. We shall persuade him otherwise." He laid a hand on the drunk's arm. "Once he returns from his progress—so we must make plans."

After a minute where Madeleine scarcely dared to breathe, the drunk lurched back into the shadowed tavern. Before he could take it into his mind to argue again, she hurried past and turned a corner. The royal castle loomed overhead—an old fortress. Its towers and walls held few windows, so as to make attack more difficult. Madeleine shivered. He must have been drunk to talk like that in public, but many other proud young noblemen must have said the same in private. The less proud, or less young, must have thought it. She wondered if conflict would break out at the trial—if the men would live to be executed.

She walked. The air grew warmer with the afternoon.

Shop signs slowly disappeared. Though the buildings stood as close together, they were larger, and so fewer. Here and there, a flowery scent escaped from a garden not wholly given over to vegetables. Madeleine slowed.

Laughter rang from one window. Two young ladies stood, dressed and bejeweled, by the window before a grave chaperon ushered them away.

Madeleine's tongue touched her lips. Lord Fergus had never taken the same quarters twice while she was at court. He had said that influence could depend too much on the place to not follow it. This time, she had no letter from him, directing her escort to his quarters.

A vendor hawked sweets from a coppery tray. Madeleine glanced at his tray: those foreign fruits, orange in color and heavily sugared, that were Lord Fergus's favorite.

"Could you direct me to Lord Fergus's quarters?"

The vendor looked quizzically at her. Sandy put his fingers into his mouth.

"He's in the castle, goodwife, in the lion's lodgings."

Madeleine's stomach felt cold as she thanked him. The castle was large, and the nobles would be crammed in. Even so, residing in the castle was a mark of favor, useful in obtaining an audience.

She managed not to slow, as the castle walls loomed higher and higher, and their shadows fell on her, but her stomach curdled.

The castle stood before her. Even in summer and this close to noon, shadows fell on her, and the air was cooler. She stopped. She wondered if she were afraid to face the queen.

The panic that thought brought confirmed it. Remember John, she told herself fiercely.

At the castle gate, servants darted about, like shoals of fish. The guards looked bored. Madeleine walked past them. In the courtyard's clamor, she tried not to look confused. Lord Fergus was not so great that he had a grand apartment, deep within the castle. She picked out the door and darted over. When no one challenged her, she hurried down the dim corridor—past maidens giggling about jewelry and three gentlemen indignant over a game of cards—toward his lodgings. Some servants glanced at her but said nothing.

The door had lions carved on the lintels. She rapped on it. Her mouth felt dry. Sandy stared at the lions. When he tried to reach for them, Madeleine wondered. Lord Fergus might not be there, but there should be servants. She rapped again.

The door flew open. "His lordship gave orders that the servants weren't to disturb him."

"I am no servant. I must see Lord Fergus—"

"A likely story. The child looks not the least like him."

It took Madeleine a moment to interpret that. "The child," she said frigidly, "is my husband's. Were I coming to lay a child to Lord Fergus, I would have done so when he was a babe."

Sandy, his fingers in his mouth, stared.

"And Lord Fergus. . . ."

The servant slammed the door. Madeleine stared at it a moment. Then she sat on the floor, her skirts spreading about her, and put Sandy in her lap.

Servants hurried by. Many gave her strange glances. Rumors, she thought wearily, but rumor would not matter if she could not reach the queen.

Sandy fretted. She rose and knocked again.

"Be off with you, you wretch!"

"I must see Lord Fergus. . . ."

Sandy wailed. Madeleine tried to hush him. The door behind the manservant opened with a surge.

"In God's name, is there not enough trouble in the realm?"

"Lord Fergus!"

He stared at her face. She tried to quiet Sandy. Lord Fergus had once admitted, with a harrumph, that her features were distinctive. His tone had implied that was dubious compliment, but she needed it more than beauty, now.

"Lady Madeleine—what. . . ." Lord Fergus glanced over her clothing.

The manservant glanced uneasily between them and stepped out of the doorway.

The low fire lit the room badly. Orange touched here and there, leaving shadows all about—but Madeleine did not need to see Lord Fergus.

"Nothing can be done for Lord Magnus of Owlscourt," said Lord Fergus, "or for any man taken with him. The king will not countenance it. What every wise councilor has advised against, he will not give up for some country lass."

Lord Fergus leaned forward. "For you and the boy, perhaps." He glanced at the hearthrug, where Sandy, curled up, slept. "In my household, you will be safe. If the king's temper cools, he can be persuaded to mercy for the widow and fatherless."

"It would please me," said Madeleine, "if he could be persuaded to justice for a husband and father—but the king is not here, Lord Fergus. Had I wished to appeal to the king, I would have gone to him."

Lord Fergus scowled. Firelight and shadow painted his face in orange and black.

"The queen is here. Also, she is regent."

Lord Fergus paled.

Madeleine sat quietly. She had things to say—and had said them.

"Queen Katherine knows the king's orders."

"And will obey them?"

Lord Fergus raised an eyebrow, making Madeleine feel young and foolish. "His ministers will see to it. She's young, flighty, thoughtless—at her age, they do not blame her, but they keep a good eye on her." He snorted. "A better eye, yet, with Lord Magnus's example before them. There is trouble—

armed rebellion—in Eastwyck. The ministers do not wish to join Lord Magnus. They sent for leave to raise a force, lest they be taken as rebels."

Madeleine felt cold—Lord Magnus had had the king's leave—but said, "I wish to speak with her."

Lord Fergus sighed. "This is futile, Lady Madeleine, and you know it. Even if the queen granted a pardon, she could not give you a troop to escort you in safety."

"I came here."

"Even for your husband, you should not have. Especially not—" He glanced at Sandy. "You might not even need the king's protection. Your father has regretted the ill will."

That jolted her. She had not heard—and then her back stiffened. Her father had sent word to Lord Fergus, then, but not to her. "Whatever possessed my father to make you my godfather?"

His eyes narrowed.

"You neglect my spiritual upbringing. You should urge me to 'forget my father and my father's house' rather than my husband."

His mouth tightened.

"And it is *anyone's* duty before God to rescue the innocent from destruction."

"Child, you could bring down more of his wrath!"

Madeleine's mouth twitched.

"You think he can not? He has not harmed the families of the—traitors. Neither their wives nor their children. Even Lord Magnus's have gone unmolested. The lords who are fostering his sons have heard nothing. Neither have his daughter and her husband. You yourself suffered nothing before this mad flight of yours."

"They will hear enough when the king declares their estates forfeit," said Madeleine.

"The queen," said Lord Fergus, "has her orders."

"And is so *fond* of the king that she will obey without question?"

The fire sighed. A log sank into the coals. Lord Fergus sat back. "For you and the child to have reached here so quickly, you must have traveled quickly."

Madeleine opened her mouth and shut it again.

He looked over her clothing. "You can not dress like that at court."

"*You* must be Lady Madeleine."

A young woman bounced into the tiny room. Her brown hair sprung about her face in a profusion of curls. Madeleine, still half awake, pulled up the covers and blinked. Not a servant—plain though that green dress was, the fabric was good.

A maid in a drab dress followed her, more quietly.

"I am Annette, Lord Fergus's niece. He told me of your situation." Her gaze went to the clothing lying at the bed's foot. Her mouth pursed.

Madeleine wondered whether Lord Fergus had mentioned John at all, or merely her clothing.

"My uncle had to be about the queen's business this morning." She touched Madeleine's shawl. "This, I suppose, gets given to the poor."

"Not now," said Madeleine, "I wore it here. And one does not know. . . ."

Lady Annette lifted an eyebrow but took the bundle from the maid. She shook out a dress in dove gray, and then another in blue. "He said we were much of a size. . . ." She laid out chemises to go with them, and a plain cap. "And I brought some clothing for your son." She looked about.

Madeleine looked at the trundle bed, where Sandy curled in the blankets. "If our talk did not wake him, he is still tired."

Lady Annette pouted. "I sent for a bath. . . ."

Madeleine rose. "Let us see if Lord Fergus still has an eye for the ladies."

"The gown won't quite do for court—but we can manage."

Madeleine wondered if Lord Fergus had decided to keep her here by force, if need be. "If all goes well, I will not need that." After a moment, she added, "And if all goes ill, my only need will be for mourning."

Clean, in the gray gown, Madeleine emerged from the room, holding a likewise clean Sandy. The cap felt odd after her shawl. It covered even less of her hair than the veil she had worn at Summerfield.

As a maiden, she had gone bareheaded at court. She had been at court before. She should not act like a country chit.

Lady Annette sat by the breakfast. She smiled with particular warmth on Sandy. Madeleine took some porridge, for Sandy, and spread honey on it.

"He said you come from the Misty Hills—my uncle," said Lady Annette.

"I do."

"I've asked him about the hills. He puts me off."

Madeleine took up her own porridge. "The Misty Hills are less pleasant than most places to be lost in. If my father hadn't found him, his plight might have grown desperate."

Ignoring her own food, Lady Annette waved a hand in the air. "But it has the marvelous things—silver deer, and unicorns, and lilies made of mist. . ."

"Mo'ning lilies." Sandy smiled at her about a mouthful. "I picked 'em."

Lady Annette's mouth formed an o. "And the silver deer?"

"Lord Fergus saw them, certainly. He blames them for his going astray. Though I saw one on my way, and it did not lead me off the path." Lady Annette's gaze was rapt, and it was not as if she could hunt down Lord Fergus through the courts. Madeleine told her of the deer, and other stories of the mists.

"But you left it," said Lady Annette.

"I married."

Lady Annette looked wistfully at Sandy. Madeleine ate— white bread, finer than any she had eaten along the way—and wondered whether Lord Fergus's attempts to find Lady Annette a husband went as well, or as poorly, as finding her one.

"You must have loved him very much."

"I still do," Madeleine said. "What did Lord Fergus tell you?"

Color rose in Lady Annette's face. "*He* said I shouldn't talk to you about it, that it's hopeless."

With the sun overhead, light stole through the windows. Lady Annette having found some blocks, Sandy played in the corner.

"It will keep him busy while we wait for my uncle," Lady Annette said. Her lap held a gown she embroidered with poppies and daisies. "He is *very* busy. The queen relies on him—and two or three other noblemen—she can not rely on the ministers. It makes the court dull, all this concern."

Madeleine picked up some mending.

"You must have heard of the rebellion in Eastwyck. Fighting without so much as a by-your-leave to the king. For weeks!"

"King Walter is suppressing it?" said Madeleine.

Lady Annette looked troubled. "The queen sent for leave to send men. I thought she had authority to act; the ministers should have told her so." She brightened. "Though the king sent orders to gather men."

Necessary to suppress it, Madeleine thought. One could hope, and pray, for haste. God help the peasants there, but she could do nothing for them. "But Lord Fergus comes back before the depths of the nights?"

"Mid afternoon, unless something dire has happened." Lady Annette considered her latest daisy.

Madeleine mended. She could corner her godfather then. In the meantime, she remembered life at court. She remembered John wooing her—

She could smell the pool. It was not overgrown, but it smelled of water and the plants that grew there.

"It's over here." Madeleine held open the wrought-iron gate. The damp stone wall had moss growing on it, and next to it lay the pool, with its water lilies and the dark shape of fishes just visible in the murk of the water.

Lady Annette, holding the basket of bread, gasped. "I never knew. . . ."

"It must have gone out of fashion. Ladies would come while I was at court, to feed the fish and talk." Gentlemen would come to woo them. John and she had fed the fish. She said, "It will give us something to do while we wait."

Lady Annette sat by the pool edge. Madeleine crumbled bread and tossed the crumbs out. Fish rose, slowly, through the murky water. Some remained vague, swimming deep, not even gleaming. Others became clear, gold like a coin or the palest of sunrises, or like a red-gold sunset; their fins idly waved beneath the water. One tiny one, lustrous white with gold blotches, poked at the surface and nibbled at the bread.

"The queen has been busy since the king left," said Lady Annette. "Affairs of state." She tossed more crumbs. A red-old goldfish, larger than her hand, swam up to taste some. "The entertainments—there were more at my father's house. We were not driven to feeding fish there."

If the queen had kept up the entertainments, thought Madeleine, she would never have a chance at an audience. More crumbs brought up more fish: yellow gold and red gold and one a gold verging on white.

"A courtly amusement, feeding fish," Lady Annette said, scornfully.

"Many a lady has fed the fish here," Madeleine said. "It's stood since King Baldwin's time."

"King Baldwin." Lady Annette laughed. "So he did do something."

Madeleine smiled. A red goldfish sank beneath the greenish surface again. King Baldwin had been worse than King Walter. The nobles feared King Walter too much to run wild—at least, everywhere but Eastwyck—but King Baldwin had been too weak to restrain them.

Not that falling afoul of King Walter's whims was better than warfare. Both could kill.

Lady Annette glanced over her shoulder and scrambled up. "That was my uncle, he must have returned early. . . . I could have sworn. . . ."

They hurried, but Lord Fergus had left again before they reached the lodgings.

Lady Annette cursed herself for having thought they could amuse themselves for an hour. Sandy, startled by the noise, stared at her.

"If he stayed so briefly," said Madeleine, "he did not have time to talk to me. Best to wait for afternoon, when I could speak for a time." And hope for the words to persuade him.

A week later, orange sunlight slanted over the room. This day was too late. Lord Fergus could not speak with the queen, let alone arrange for her to do so.

Madeleine stood in the middle of the room. It was just as well that she had come through the Misty Hills; the time to go around was needed to persuade Lord Fergus.

She was no longer bone-weary every night, and no longer slept like the dead. Now, she remembered her dreams, which dripped with red.

"Has anyone *asked* her to pardon them?"

Lord Fergus stood before the mantelpiece, his gaze on it. His voice was a growl. "Do you imagine that the queen neglected to notice she can write pardons?"

"In all the disorder—possibly."

"Queen Katherine has plenty of time to notice it. The ministers keep as much work as they can from her. And she is no fool." He scowled. "Which is not true of you."

"*You* had not thought of it."

"You are as bent on your folly as the drunken young men who brag that they could deliver Lord Magnus by force."

Madeleine glared.

"No, you're worse than them," said Lord Fergus. "When I warned Lord Keith to watch his tongue, he did. *You*—you could foment war this way!"

"I could avert war this way," said Madeleine. "Do you imagine that only young hotheads think like them?"

Footsteps sounded outside the door. Lady Annette looked in. "Is he *still* refusing?" She put her hands on her hips.

"Considering whom you've gotten audiences for—and why—I don't see why you can't get Lady Madeleine one."

Something metallic clattered in the main chamber, followed by a wail. Madeleine bolted. Sandy sat on the floor, wailing. The poker from the fireplace lay beside him, and Madeleine could only glad that he had not gotten into the fire.

"Are children always—into things?" murmured Lady Annette, once Sandy's wails had diminished.

Madeleine nodded.

"I see why the nobles leave their children in the country." Lady Annette looked about the lodgings.

Too little space for a child, Madeleine thought. She kissed Sandy. One reason she had hired Rosie was that when they had met, John had worn mourning for his parents—but hardly been grief-stricken. She wanted to see more of Sandy than his parents had seen of John.

She wished it could have taken Sandy just a little longer.

Lady Annette squared her shoulders. "We shall just press our case again. The king is taking his time, gathering all the nobles he can."

Though no one knew how long that would take.

"Did you hear about the prison?" said Lady Annette, with sudden sharpness. "They've been put in the charge of Lord David of Bridgeton. A petty lordling, of base birth." She threw her hands into the air. "The king ennobled him not a decade ago, and many of the prisoners are of higher rank than he is."

Madeleine had known good noblemen with new titles, but did not want to quarrel with Lady Annette over it.

Then she wondered if the king had chosen Lord David to insult the prisoners.

"Morning, noon, and night," grumbled Lord Fergus as he led her down the corridor. "Had I known what a pest you would turn her into, I would have forbidden Lady Annette to speak to you."

Madeleine glided down the hall. She had hope, then, that he would yield. She wondered what he thought he could show her that would change her mind. Unless. . . her step faltered. John could have died of his injuries.

"Look, my lady." Lord Fergus flung open a door. A vast room glittered with mirrors and chandeliers—and jewelry, being filled with gaudy courtiers. Many of them wore strange, foreign styles; envoys, she guessed.

Not news, then, she thought with relief. He could have given news in the lodgings.

"Every one of them wishes to speak with the queen." He snorted. "The king reserved all foreign affairs to himself. When the Queen's Grace gave them audiences to tell them so, one returned, to be told twice. The rest could not be slighted with fewer audiences. So every day she must tell them the king has not returned."

Madeleine, too glad to care, looked at him. "She *could* grant my petition."

The castle hallways were quiet with morning: nobles lay abed with their hangovers, servants moved with care, to rouse no one, and the windows were too distant for any birdsong to reach.

The queen's servant climbed a back stairway, with Fergus following, and said, "In here, my lord."

The queen's antechamber, Fergus thought, past the formality. He felt the honor, though the queen could give nothing more than honor. He stepped in. Two windows left the room dim. The queen sat opposite, with her breakfast.

Fergus bowed deeply.

"I hope that all goes well with you," said Queen Katherine. "I have heard some tales."

"Madame, I doubt they reach the truth. My goddaughter came to court with her son."

"A boy much too young to be bound by the king's summons," said the queen. "He would hardly understand, let alone profit by the example."

"His father, my goddaughter's husband, is Lord John of Summerfield. Among Lord Magnus of Owlscourt's men— captive with him."

"I see." After a moment, the queen added, "She can not appeal to the king here."

Lord Fergus said heavily, "She came to appeal to you. She insists that the regent can pardon."

He could not have sworn that the queen breathed.

"I beg you to grant her an audience and explain that she has no hope."

The borrowed red gown swept the floor. The emeralds Lady Annette had lent her glittered on her hands—and, Madeleine supposed, on her throat. She looked a courtier and felt a fraud.

"Over here, my lady," said the servant, soft-voiced.

The door led into a walled garden, cool with morning. Fruit trees stood along the wall. Roses, still bearing dew, blossomed along a path of gray stone. It led to a pool. Before the waters, a woman sat. She was very young. Indeed, Madeleine realized, Queen Katherine might be younger than she was. Even beside her black hair, her skin was dark, and her face had a foreign cast. Her clothing was no more sumptuous than any courtier would wear from day to day, and she wore no jewelry.

Madeleine was glad of her time at court. She managed to curtsey.

Queen Katherine's voice was grave and even. "His lordship, your godfather, told me of your plight, and asked me to explain the impossibility."

Madeleine's mouth felt dry. Would the queen not even allow her to make her plea?

"I know the evil of what has befallen Lord Magnus and his men. So does Lord Fergus." Her mouth held deep groves to either side, and Madeleine doubted her guess of the queen's age. "Were it in my power, the pardon would have been issued before you had news of your husband's fate."

For all her time at court, Madeleine barely waited until the queen stopped. "But, Madame, if you know what evil this is doing to the king's reign—"

The queen looked coolly at Madeleine. The water behind her stirred, as if with the faintest of breezes.

"He appointed you regent to act, and not merely to obey," said Madeleine, but the words stumbled from her mouth.

"The King's Grace knows the ill will the orders incited," said Queen Katherine. "He does not deem it sufficient reason to alter them."

Not knowing what to say, Madeleine curtseyed. A bee blundered by her, and her stomach felt cold. A mark of favor, perhaps, to be received privately in the garden—but bestowed to soften that the queen could do nothing. "If your judgment does not match his. . . ."

The queen threw her hands in the air. "My judgment? A silly young woman's judgment? I do not understand affairs of state—I could not have overseen the treaty between this land and my father's." With a surge, she rose. Madeleine flinched, but the queen, spreading her hands, did not even glance at her.

"I could not know the laws of Darnien—though I studied them from the time that I knew I might become queen here. I can not judge whether jewelers are honest. How can I judge that the king is destroying the land? I have a weak, frail, *feminine* cast of mind. How can I understand affairs of state?"

Madeleine could do nothing more than breathe.

Queen Katherine's head sank. She sat, again.

Madeleine felt numb, but the queen did not order her out. She frantically marshaled her thoughts. "Why did the king make you regent, Madame?"

"I wish I knew," said the queen.

"Madame," Madeleine murmured, glad that neither servants nor courtiers witnessed those words.

"Consider Eastwyck. Men ought to be sent. Those fighting have no authority." Queen Katherine's mouth twisted. "As Lord Magnus of Owlscourt had."

Madeleine nodded.

"Yet—my lord husband gathers men to take them to the West Dales." Her voice turned plaintive. "He thinks I understand nothing."

A thought struck Madeleine. She felt like ice, but—John, she told herself. Even summoning up memory of him, she could barely speak. "Why, then, Madame, you may claim that you did not understand his wishes."

The queen looked at Madeleine as if not hearing her.

"*You* know that the king wishes you to ignore the troubles his orders brought." Madeleine tried to master her breath. She had yet to persuade the queen. "But what need is there to tell him so?"

Something almost approached hope in the queen's expression. "To defy him so. . . to set Lord Magnus free—and I would need to issue pardons, for everyone down to the men-at-arms. . . ."

Madeleine held her breath. The queen scowled in thought.

"Madame, the king has not forbidden you to buy some jewelry. Kings have lost their thrones for less." Madeleine drew a deep breath. Her heart she could not steady at all. "A loyal wife tries to shield her husband from his own folly. I would do as much for Lord John."

The silence lasted many breaths. Bees buzzed among the flowers, and Madeleine felt the sweat on her body.

Queen Katherine's expression took on a triumphant look, like a wolf that had made a kill—and then the expression was wiped off, as if with a cloth.

Her voice was wooden. "His councilors will prevent me. I can write the pardon. Were it delivered, the king could not retract it. Lord David—" She gave Madeleine a sharp glance. "A new creation, but Lord David would declare he had received it—if he had. But it must be brought to him, at the tower."

Madeleine's feet hurt. "Madame." She cleared her throat, and tried again. "Madame, I came here afoot, and in disguise. There is no reason. . . ."

Queen Katherine hesitated. "They have too much power. They will stop you."

"My brothers by marriage could not stop me. They knew that I was gone," said Madeleine. "My godfather has not shouted my folly to the court, and will not. Neither will his niece. You will tell no one of the pardons. They would hear after it was too late for them to act."

Queen Katherine bit her lip.

Madeleine whispered, "'God chose the foolish of the world to shame the wise, and God chose the weak of the world to shame the strong. . . .'"

"That," said the queen, softly, "is part of the coronation ceremony for the queen consort. 'Almighty God, Who does not despise the weakness of the feminine sex, but has chosen the weak of the world to triumph over the strong. . . .'" After a moment, her smile was serene. She held out her hand.

Madeleine bent to kiss it. The queen put her hands to Madeleine's head and lifted her face, to kiss her on the forehead.

Chapter 6—Messages and Arrivals

She had thought of doing it at night, but that the queen stayed awake late would be noticed. Even the ladies-in-waiting loyal to her—if she had any—were not always prudent in their speech.

Lady Lachina hesitated beside the writing table. "There are clerks about the court." Her voice was tentative, as if she tried to infuse her voice with the authority proper to a noblewoman instructing a woman royal, but young, foreign, and unaccustomed to this court.

Katherine picked her pen up. To stay up late would inspire another scolding, on her frivolous ways. "To undertake such a pious task with one's own hand—with my lord husband needing a guard on his own progress, I should have asked, long ago, that they pray for Heaven's aid upon us."

Lady Lachina drew away. So I should have, Katherine thought. She straightened the paper. Let the abbeys ring with prayers for Darnien—even if I conceived of these messages as a distraction from Lady Madeleine. She glanced at the doorway and the ladies-in-waiting who lingered there, and began her letter. Two or three would blind the women, if she did not act too suspiciously.

The uproar in the outer room, voices and loud footsteps, sprung up suddenly. Lady Lachina twittered that the queen could not be disturbed, but footsteps approached still.

Katherine made her voice ring. "Who goes there?"

A moment later, a man said, "Urgent news, Madame, for the regent."

"Come in." Her heart pattered.

In the doorway, a roughly clad messenger, not in royal service, bowed. "Good news, Madame. The treacherous Lord Ivo and his men have died for their rebellion!"

Katherine could not move. Good news, but— "The King's Grace sent men?" A surge of hope collided with indignation: the news was kept from her. She tried to squelch it.

The messenger did not meet her eyes.

Her mouth pursed.

"No, Madame. Lord Malcolm—his family and Lord Ivo's had long been rivals. The rebels attacked his home. And he— he has sent word, that if you wish to display the body as a traitor, he will send it."

"I see," said Katherine. She glanced at the letters. "Have the royal ministers been acquainted with the news?"

"No, Madame." He sounded surprised, as Lady Madeleine had been surprised with hearing of her true position.

She nodded. He was not a royal messenger; he would not know. Though he was not as weary as Somerled, she said "Lady Lachina! See to it that this man receives a meal and a bed. And summon the ministers in—an hour."

"Madame?" said Lady Lachina.

"What, leave my holy purpose?"

She picked her pen up. The only urgent matter was not one she could entrust to the ministers. A pardon for Lord Magnus and the men with him, with another that Lord David might prove that he had received orders to release them. Two more, for Lord Olgar, who held the men-at-arms.

She looked at her pen. A fifth one, for Lord Malcolm. She would advise him to keep it safe, unless needed. To reveal that he had received a pardon would argue that he needed one for wrongdoing, and not a great service to a fool of a king.

In the tiny chamber, Madeleine hummed. She still felt shivery with delight. Her dreams that night had not been bloody, but enough to make her blush in memory. For all that the pardon had to be delivered, she had gone to the chapel to thank God.

"Your son?" said Lord Fergus.

"Sandy comes with me." The clothing on the bed was the same clothing she and Sandy had worn before. "We would only have to send for him, afterwards."

She did not look at her godfather. He might think that she feared what the king might do to Sandy—true though it was. Lord Magnus would be safe not because of the pardon, but because he could flee to his lands, and Lord Fergus found this whole willingness to thwart the king uncomfortable.

"Papa come soon?" said Sandy from the doorway.

"We're going to Papa," said Madeleine. She looked at Lord Fergus. "Within an hour."

Behind Sandy, Lady Annette said, "I'll miss him."

Madeleine smiled. If Lord Fergus had married his niece off, Lady Annette would have been delighted with her own little ones, and not arguing for Madeleine.

"You would miss him anyway," said Lord Fergus.

Annette blinked.

"I will restore you to your parents' loving arms before the king discovers your part in the pardon."

He stalked off, and Lady Annette gaped at his back. "Off to the country," she sputtered. "He has done no fine job of finding me a husband here."

Madeleine remembered how court had found her a husband and smiled. "You might find a husband in the country."

"Some countrified stick-in-the-mud killjoy."

Madeleine wryly remembered John's returning to Summerfield covered with mud, which had happened more than once.

The road from the city was filled with peasants roaring over
how well they had fared, selling their produce. Sandy shrank
from them. Madeleine, hurrying him along the road,
wondered if they had drunk all their profits—at least, she
thought, glancing about, the ones loud enough to hear. Other
peasants seemed as wary of the braggarts as she was.

She began to reckon her story.

A trumpet sounded ahead. Madeleine picked Sandy up to
move from the nobleman's way. She pondered companions as
she stood in the grumbling crowd; she remembered garrulous
Ysenda and the pilgrims' generosity.

Her husband had been—was—in service, and had to travel
with his lord. She returned to his family for that time. That
would answer questions. Since the lands here were better
settled, she had no need to travel alone, except, perhaps to the
tower itself.

The noble's company tramped by. The nobleman himself,
thin and sour, glanced at the peasants. Envious? thought
Madeleine. Mere peasants could leave with their money before
the king's arrival. Nobles could not.

Her mouth twisted. Thin, pale, sour-faced—she thought
him the nobleman at the toll bridge.

"Down, Mama?" said Sandy.

The crowd thinned along the road. Madeleine lowered
him, but held one hand. Sandy stared about as if he had
forgotten their journey here.

She looked as well, and bit her lip. No merchants. No
pilgrims. Only peasants who had sold their wares.

"Lord in Bluefield," said one woman, drawing Madeleine's
attention. Bluefield was near the tower. "He struck the royal
messenger—the man carried a bruise for a week—"

Not so very furious, then. Madeleine kept her attention on the woman—a maid, talking with another. "And the king had his head cut off! He threatened to hang him!"

Madeleine felt chilled. The king had decided to give Lord Magnus a trial, but these women—and a third, an old woman stumped alongside.

She eased closer. It did not matter what they knew, but whether they would let her come.

"For striking a messenger?" said the other maid.

The first bobbed her head. "He *called* it treason. The man was a *royal* messenger."

A commoner, though, thought Madeleine. She was not certain. That news would spread over the court—but then, she had not listened to the tales. Thinking only of persuading Lord Fergus, she had not even mingled with the courtiers.

But, she reminded herself, she could not help that lord. She eyed them. The old woman faltered. The younger ones seemed not to notice.

"Good woman, are you well?"

The younger maid started. "Granny!"

"I'm fine, I'm fine." She peered at Madeleine. "I'll outlast the lot of you, young woman, whoever you are."

"I am leaving a noble household in Harthill, to join my husband in service to a lord near Bluefield."

The old woman's eyes narrowed. The maids whispered together. Madeleine thought that they would walk together, whatever they decided: the same road, the same time.

"Papa!" said Sandy. The younger maid smiled.

"You said," said the older, "there were too few of us, Granny Euna. You said it would be better if—"

The old woman snorted. "I know what I said, Peggy."

The ladies-in-waiting spread over the garden. Osla picked her place with care. Having such a tale was not something that happened often, and she did not want to miss the ears.

"I saw her leave," said Osla. "The queen spoke to Lord Fergus, Lord Fergus went to his chambers, and she left."

Lady Beatrix still perched demurely on the bench, as if she did not realize what Osla said. Osla lowered her voice still further.

"She was dressed like a peasant, and she left *alone*."

"Ladies don't journey alone," said Lady Beatrix, primly.

"You shouldn't be at court," said Osla, disgusted. Really! What husband could she get? No courtier would take a wife who could not pay heed to things; she might ruin his interests with a misplaced word. "You should have married Lord Alun."

Lady Beatrix looked at her with limpid eyes. "And abandon the Queen's Grace? She had only been married a year. Darnien was still new to her."

"I'm sure you were a great help," said Osla, tartly.

Lady Beatrix beamed as if it were a compliment.

If a catch like Lord Alun had swum into my net, thought Osla, I would not have been laggard.

The road wound through pasture. Granny Euna stumped along. Madeleine wondered how wise joining her and her granddaughters had been. Sandy meant that she could not walk quickly, but even with him, she could walk more quickly than Granny Euna. Peggy had found it easy to run ahead and find out where they might spend the night. And these women had not offered to help carry him. Her arms ached.

Despite the heat and dust, Peggy pelted toward them. "Soldiers ahead." She panted for breath. "Some from the castle, but others—"

Granny Euna thumped her staff on the road. "A good time to rest. Shade up there."

Madeleine swallowed. Then, joining might have been wise indeed. They walked under a towering oak, and Sandy plopped to the ground—and scowled. Smiling faintly, Madeleine lifted him and brushed away the acorns underneath. Sandy watched them bounce over dirt and roots for a moment, before he curled up and slept.

Granny Euna snorted. "You should stay. Send a message ahead. Lord knows there're fools enough who'd do it for fun."

Madeleine shook her head. "You are kind, but the lord is not there forever. If he leaves, I will be hard put to follow." She closed her mouth on the sour taste of having told only the truth.

A week after leaving court, a tower stood ahead: dark gray stone against green hills and a cloudlessly blue sky. Only the tower itself was visible; a hill hid the rest of the fortress.

She could have waited until the supplies came, Madeleine supposed, but she did not know how long the king would wait to bring his prisoners before the court. And there were dangers for a lone woman and child in a town as well as on the way. Bathing in rivers was perhaps safer than in bathhouses.

Her legs ached again. She had not dreamed at all on the road; she had been too tired, every night.

Sandy watched the pond beside the road. Madeleine hoped he would not express a fascination with the paddling of ducks there: two ruddy gold ducks swam across it, trailed by nine ducklings, fuzzy, speckled yellow and brown. Sandy pulled closer to her. "Mists," he whispered.

Madeleine blinked and looked again. It was midmorning, but wisps of mist still coiled on the pond. "Are they scary?"

Sandy tilted his head to one side. "Nooooo." He took her hand. "Stuff in mists."

Madeleine managed to speak firmly. "Then we should go away from them."

"Bad things. Keep Papa away."

Near noon, Madeleine stood on the nearest hill.

In the meadows about the fortress, scores of warriors formed companies as if preparing to leave. When the wind stirred—not often—a royal banner flapped. Bellowed orders punctuated the commotion.

Madeleine took a few strides forward, so that she would not be visible against the sky. Sandy continued, his wide eyes intent on the tower, and she snatched him up. He wailed.

"Shush!" she said fiercely. He stopped, looking puzzled. Madeleine looked at the companies. The sun beat down. The king might have sent them to fetch prisoners to the capital. Her tongue touched her lips. But she saw nothing to guard or convey prisoners—and they looked as if they went the other way.

To where the king was still on progress?

She drew a deep breath. If so, she wanted to arrive after they left. The general might seize the pardon and would bear the news to the king.

"Tower?" said Sandy.

"Later, dearling. When the men are gone." She gestured at the meadows. "Flowers?"

His face lit up. She lowered him to the earth. Sandy pounced on the field, to snatch at the yellow trumpet flowers. Madeleine sank to the grass.

The men arranged, and rearranged, their order. Every now and then, a singing bird flitted overhead, or Sandy returned to show her a flower, a stone, in one case a snail. As the sun sank, he came back, rubbing his eyes. "Don't *wanna*." His fingers tightened on blooms of yellow.

"Come here," she said, sweetly, and drew him into her lap, letting his head rest on her shoulder. After a minute, he slept, still clutching trumpet flowers.

The first companies began to leave. She smiled. They would not get far before nightfall. She wondered who was in command, and whether the king would regret putting him there.

She reached for the satchel, awkwardly, with one hand and tugged it closer. It lurched over the grass. Traveling, she had secured the pardon in the middle. Now, she fished it out, and laid it on top. She eased Sandy onto her arm, his head against her shoulder; he did not even stir. She slung the satchel's strap over her shoulder.

The companies still moved out. She waited. Only when the last man strode onto the road did she arise and walked down.

Sullen, Annette stood in the courtyard. No one else might pick her out in the crowds, but Fergus had to usher her out.

He only hoped that he had not already taken too long. Madeleine could not use the slippery magics of the Misty Hills, but still might have reached the tower by now. Once she did that—he had already heard rumors of her visit to the queen.

"What nonsense is this?" A nobleman's plumpness could not ease the sourness from his face as his travel-stained company waited by the gates. "I was summoned by the king."

"So was everyone else," said Fergus, under his breath. It would take at least a week before the news spread. Even then, nobles might fear to disobey. He would not leave, himself.

"The streets will be crowded," said Annette. "Difficult to get through."

"All the more reason to leave at once," said Fergus. "You will need every minute."

Some nobles stopped their gossip long enough to eye them. The last thing he wanted was more rumors. He gave Annette a desperate gaze.

"I'm not going to find a husband in the country," said Annette.

Fergus gestured at the sour noble still bickering with the guards. "One such as him?"

"He's married, uncle," said Annette.

"All the worse," said Fergus and escorted her to her horse.

She eyed the stables. "That woman's just arrived here, and you can't tell me that the king summoned her—"

If the woman had been an heiress, she would have received a summons. Fergus glanced over, and his mouth twisted. "She's from Eastwyck."

The last soldiers passed from the view given by the window.

Magnus turned back to the room. At least they went to join the king, rather than drag him and his men to trial. Though that brought little hope. The news of how the king acted on his progress only confirmed the king's caprices.

Leod moaned. His brother Phillip wiped his face. Magnus looked away. Leod, and perhaps Randall, would escape execution, no matter what the king willed. Lord David had done everything he could for them, but he had been right, two nights ago, to make that aid a priest.

His other men sat about the cell and showed little more liveliness. Lord John sat against the wall, his eyes closed. His arm still lay in a sling. Magnus rubbed his forehead. None of them, wounded or hale, had much strength to live.

The guards' calls, from the ramparts, reached him only faintly. He made out the question in their tones, and then a full phrase, "Who's that?"

Lord Magnus looked out. A woman—a peasant woman— walked down the road. She carried a child. "Who's that, indeed?" No man in the room so much as twitched.

More shouts came from the walls, and then from the courtyard. About the room, prisoners stirred. Phillip did not look up from his brother, and John did not twitch, but a handful rose to their feet and looked out the window by Magnus. Lord Gilbert whispered, "She's what it's about? Some peasant woman?"

The door clicked open. Lord David asked, "Do any of you know who is coming?"

Magnus could make out the woman's face, and so could shake his head. "Come look, men."

Groans of reluctance came from a man or two as they rose up, but even Lord John stood, though he was one of the last on his feet. When he reached the window, he stopped. His hand gripped the stone.

"What could a peasant like that have to do here?" said Sir Ualean. "With her betters?"

"She's my wife," said Lord John.

Silence fell.

Magnus considered a moment. Lady Madeleine. Had she been dressed as befitted her station, he might even have recognized her, but to have a name only deepened the questions: why had Lady Madeleine of Summerfield come to this tower? Dressed like a peasant?

"With our son." Lord John looked into the room. If his color had been bad before, it was ghastly now.

"If she came to see you," said Lord David, "she may do so. I had no orders to prevent—"

"She should not have come, there is nothing she can." Lord John looked at Magnus. "She should not have brought Sandy."

"Go," said Magnus. "A woman who traveled this far will not be put off."

Madeleine's feet slowed with every step. The guards were dark shapes against the sky, and they had shouted earlier, but now, she heard no hail. Sandy felt a heavier weight on her arm than he ever had before. Her tongue touched her lips. A peasant woman, demanding Lord David—Queen Katherine had not listed that among the reasons why she could not succeed, and Madeleine could not fathom why not.

She reached the gates. Within the courtyard, two men stood. Madeleine's heart seemed to stop. One was of average height, lean, his hair blond but darker and straighter than Sandy's—and then he looked up. Her heart hammered with certainty. John, though pale and with his arm in a sling.

The man with him called for the gates to be opened. They moved, with a faint creak.

Madeleine, wondering if it were too easy, walked in. The other man said to John, "I can let her see you for an hour or two—no more. She can not remain here the night."

John nodded. His gray eyes were flat and lifeless as he approached her. "My dearling, why did you come?" he said, his voice almost despairing.

Madeleine wondered how to tell him, how to touch him. He seemed further from her than when she first received the news.

"I could not believe it when I saw you coming—and with Sandy," John said. "You should not have come. You can do nothing here."

"My dearest," said Madeleine, her voice pitched as softly as his. "My dearling. I did not come here, first. So, there is something I can do here." She reached for the satchel and pulled out the parchment.

John looked at it. "What could you have brought? A pardon?" His despondent voice made the impossibility clear.

Her tongue touched her lips.

"No," whispered John. "You could not—I have lost my mind—am dreaming. A pardon, the king would not have...."

Madeleine also whispered. "I went to court to see the queen." She held the pardon out. "The queen's seal, see?"

John looked numb for a long, long minute. Then, with a sob, he threw his sound arm about her, his face coming to rest on her shoulder. Madeleine hiked up Sandy, and John reached out. The hand of his wounded arm touched the fingers of her arm that held Sandy. He trembled like a leaf. She saw no tears in his eyes, but his lips moved with no words emerging.

He had not let himself dream, she realized.

Sandy stirred, some flowers falling from his grip.

"A pardon for me?" John said, his voice shaking.

"Why," said Madeleine, unable to keep an undercurrent of laughter from her voice, "that would do the king little good. The land finds this *whole* affair contemptible. The queen, in her prudence, deemed that the only way to contain this matter would be a free pardon for all."

A shudder racked his body. "My gallant lady," he said, but his voice had lost what spirit it had had. Madeleine's tongue felt numb in her mouth.

"My lady," said a peremptory voice. The man who had stood with John met her gaze. His face did not look as commanding as his voice, but his tone did not change. "I know not what manner of paper you have there."

Lord David, she deduced. "It is for you. Look at the seal, first."

For a long moment, Lord David did not even stretch out his hand. He must have realized what the queen's seal meant. Then his hand moved, like an old man's, to take it from her. "This can not be," he whispered. "The king would never. . . ."

Madeleine felt almost light-headed. How long it would take to persuade them all? —but she had time now.

Sir Ualean grumbled that the woman only made trouble, that Lord John had married a fool, that his wife was wiser. Magnus's hands tightened on the window. He wished he had ordered Sir Ualean to silence when the old man began his whining. Lady Madeleine's voice carried to the window, but not clearly enough.

Lord David moved across the courtyard. Magnus realized that he came to the stairs to the tower, and he formed a coherent thought. He tried to suppress it. If he let false hope misled him, he would die of the pain.

In the courtyard, Lady Madeleine shifted her son. He forced his breath out. Perhaps she had won her husband's life. For that, he would praise God. Except—Lord David vanished into the tower—King Walter would not have granted a pardon for even a man-at-arms.

The door opened. Lord David stood there, with the paper in hand. Magnus could not read his expression, but it could not be entirely hidden.

"So, my lord, what did Lady Madeleine bring?"

"A royal pardon, my lord, for you, and all your men."

Lit up by hope or disbelief, pale faces looked up, all around the room.

"The king would not..." said Magnus.

"It is from the queen."

Magnus leaned against the wall before he collapsed. He closed his eyes. His vision was too blurred for him to see clearly, anyway.

The men from the tower pressed around, in the courtyard, as if they all had to see the pardon for it to hold. The guards muttered behind them.

Sandy stirred at the noise and peered about. "Papa come soon?" Then he stared into John's face, his expression as bewildered as John's was. His hand opened. The last flowers fell as he reached for his father. His weight lurched against Madeleine's arm.

Laughter came from Magnus's men about them—with more than a touch of hysterical relief.

John's hand brushed Sandy's cheek, and the boy's eyes widened.

"Shush, Sandy," whispered Madeleine. "Papa can't carry you."

Sandy's mouth formed an O. "Does it hurt?"

"A little," said John. "Not much."

Madeleine was ready to weep. What had befallen her John? She dragged in a deep breath. She *would* weep, if it were not for the fear that even that would not rouse John from his lethargy. If that happened, her heart would break.

Lord Magnus glanced over the courtyard. He was still the tall and broad-shouldered man, commanding in appearance—though his hair had grown more gray since last she had seen him. "We will leave within an hour."

"Sir Neil and his men are not long gone," said Lord David.

The sunset had already darkened to violet and crimson. Madeleine hoped the king's forces made better time than that.

Sandy wriggled in her arms. He was tired, far too tired, and should be asleep, but discovering his father would keep him awake a long time—perhaps even longer than the same discovery would keep her on her feet.

"You must go the same way," said David. "If you returned by the other, you would pass near the capital."

"Nevertheless," said Lord Magnus, "we leave tonight. Hiding in the woods would be safer than waiting here. If the right man arrives, he will not care for the pardon."

Lord David bowed his head, wearily.

"Have you stretchers that we might take? For the wounded?"

"Something might be done. Your weapons and money — the king had them brought here, too, so they might be fetched with you as evidence."

As Lord David left the room, Sandy yawned. For the first time, Lord Magnus looked perturbed. "My lady? You can travel?"

"I rested this afternoon," she said, "while the king's men were leaving."

Chapter 7—Escapes and Decisions

The scrap of moon lit the way no better than the stars. Trees, heavy about them, shadowed the road. Madeleine staggered along. Sandy lay like a stone in her arms. John walked beside her. He had given Sandy one last glance, by the torchlight, but said nothing.

"My lady." Lord Magnus's face was barely a blur in the darkness, and the rest of him was invisible. "Have you been carrying young Sandy much?"

Her arms ached. "He can not walk far," she said, almost in apology.

His hands slid about her son. She vaguely made out Magnus settling Sandy against his chest. Not a sound came from John, and Madeleine's heart sank.

Now and again, owls hooted, or leaves rustled, stirred by breezes or passing beasts. The moon sank, vanishing beneath branches for long stretches. Madeleine plodded along. She nearly stumbled over an unexpected root.

"You must have journeyed long," Lord Magnus said, "and quickly, to have reached the queen and then us."

Her thoughts felt muffled. "I. . . I came from the Misty Hills." She looked at him, forgetting that in the darkness, she could not read his expression. "I came through them. . . that was part of it."

"You still had far to travel."

"Two weeks. If this had been winter. . . ."

"Lord Gilbert!" called Lord Magnus.

A man loomed over them, even in the night.

"Carry the Lady Madeleine."

Lord Gilbert may have nodded, but Madeleine only felt him lift her off her feet as if she were as small as Sandy. She leaned against his shoulder, but did not sleep. Her thoughts moved in half-formed patterns, wondering how long Lord Magnus would travel.

After the moon had set, someone stumbled. Someone else called for another man and gave directions for John to be carried. Madeleine worried—John's injuries had not looked that grave—but weariness swept it away.

The cold had awakened him, and Magnus could not sleep. In the clearing, he could make out his men—and the woman and child. Lady Madeleine still slept.

Easy enough for her. She had delivered the pardon. Whatever heroic feats that took, she had done. His duties had begun. She had saved them but not defeated the king. The rumors that the lords who remained away had received warnings to—he had to learn his enemy there. And first, he had to get his men to their homes.

He sat up. Gilbert rose, lightly; he must have woken even earlier.

"Sir." He pitched his voice low. "Leod died."

Magnus dragged in a breath. He, like every other man here, had expected it, even without the journey. It still struck like the morning chill.

"May God have mercy on his soul," said Magnus.

Under the blankets, the ground was cold, but a warm lump cuddled under her arm, and Madeleine felt more heat beside her. The air smelled of pine. She opened her eyes.

Mist curled among the trees. Some still slept, but most of Lord Magnus's men walked about and spoke in low voices. John lay beside her. Her gaze was hungry on him. Even in sleep, his face looked worn.

"Lady Madeleine!" A young man bowed, courtly despite the grime. "We found a village—bought some bread and honey."

Madeleine smiled and tucked the blankets about Sandy. The mists were already melting.

The man looked at John. "Is he feverish again?"

Her heart nearly froze. She looked at the man, believed him serious, and laid a hand to John's face. Not heated, she decided. "No."

The man's shoulders slumped in relief. Madeleine's heart seemed to skip a beat. Had John been that ill?

"He's been better the last week," the man said, "but after last night—"

"Mama?" said Sandy, pushing back the blankets. Then, it was well into morning.

"Would you like some bread and honey, dearling?" she said. Sandy rubbed his eyes and nodded. Madeleine rose and looked about. Beneath the pines, men besides John still slept. One man slumped beside one of the prone figures. Then she noticed the blanket pulled over the figure's head.

"We didn't have much hope of Leod but. . . ." The man shook his head. "Lord Magnus's taking it hard."

Madeleine bowed her head. Eternal rest grant unto him, o Lord. . . .

"Honey," said Sandy, tugging on her hand.

The man dropped to one knee and said, "Come with Sir Oliver now—I'll show you the honey."

Sandy looked at Madeleine. She nodded, and he took Sir Oliver's hand. Madeleine closed her eyes again, to finish the prayer, and opened them to look for Lord Magnus. He ate with the rest. She walked across the amber pine needles. The men nodded to her. One gave her a wary glance, but she was too hungry to care.

Lord Magnus offered her bread and honey. She ate a bite and said, softly, "What happened to John? Sir Oliver said he was feverish."

"Without him," said Lord Magnus, his voice low, "there would have been no fight. A king's man came for me, sword in hand—the first warning we had. Lord John leapt in his way. He did not even have time to draw his sword. But the man had to knock him aside."

Across the clearing, Sandy laughed and ran. Madeleine looked at the bread in her hand.

"He bought us time to draw our swords. Not being struck down, I could command." His mouth set. "We fought. The king had to accept our surrender rather than slaughter us on the spot."

Madeleine glanced at John.

"It wasn't the blow so much as the fall. He never rose again for the rest of the fight."

"He was feverish after?"

Lord Magnus nodded. "Lord David did all that could be done for him."

The wounds were not what troubled him, thought Madeleine. John never took his duty to his lord lightly. She ate more bread and honey. It gave her reason to keep silent, but she tasted nothing.

"I hold him in all honor for his deed. As, my lady, I hold you. I will reward you both, if it lies in my power."

Madeleine would have been happier without the reminder that it might not lie in it.

He bowed. "Fortunate Lord John. When one has found a worthy wife, her price is far above rubies."

"I thank you," Madeleine said.

Her mouth felt dry. When John stirred, his sound arm rising between him and the sun, she ran to him. He blinked, and she smiled, trying to hide any doubt.

His hand brushed her face. "Good morning, my love," John said, but something in his voice deepened her fears.

The last mist burned away. The grave was freshly turned dirt. They had fetched a priest from the village, but all of them tried to avoid looking at it. Even Sandy hid his face in Madeleine's skirts.

Lord Magnus said, "My lady, you gave Lord David a pardon for me and my men—but not all my men were there."

Madeleine reached for the satchel. "The queen gave me two of each. This one for you, and your men with you, that you may have a copy as well as Lord David. This for the commoners who were taken, that you may free them —and another that you may produce if anyone challenges you while returning."

Lord Magnus took the papers in hand. After a minute, he looked up and at John, and then at the man they still carried in the litter—Randall, Madeleine remembered.

"An easy pace today," said Lord Magnus. "None of us could take more."

He strode off. Madeleine, glad to be free of that burden, looked around. John leaned on a nearby tree, so silent she had not noticed him. "Sir Neil," she said. "I saw him leave, with the men."

"He's gone to join the king. The West Dales are not taking the news kindly."

Madeleine nodded. Owlscourt was not in the West Dales, but it was near. Lord Magnus and most of his men had ties of blood and marriage, to the folk of the dales; John himself did, though none close. The West Dales had been independent long, and remembered it well, but still— "Unkindly enough that the king needs swordsmen? Does he fear revolt?" Her voice rose. "More than he feared Eastwyck?"

"He fears it," said John, his voice still flat. "As to unkindly. . . he ordered Lord Magnus to gather the men before charging him with treason for it."

Madeleine looked down. "I heard talk, at the capital, that the king would not get away with this."

John said nothing. Sandy laughed, and Madeleine went to fetch him.

The men urged them to the middle of the company, the safest place against attack. Sir Oliver offered to carry Sandy. "After all his running about this morning, he must be tired."

Sandy settled happily in Sir Oliver's arms, and then pointed at another knight.

"He has done enough for a boy so young," said Lord Magnus, with a smile, and then the smile faded. "Did you hear of my sons, or my daughter, while you were at court?"

"I did," said Madeleine. "They suffered nothing at the king's hands." She glanced about. "Nor has anything befallen the families of those who died or were captured."

Lord Magnus's shoulders slumped. "Thanks be to God." The men walked on with more eagerness.

Lord Magnus shook himself, like a horse shaking off a fly. "Did you hear of Eastwyck when you were at the capital?"

Madeleine told what she had heard. Lord Magnus looked graver by the minute.

"What did the courtiers think of this?"

"I fear I heard little at the court," said Madeleine. "I was not—" She spread her hands.

"We heard little in the tower." He snorted. "More of the king's progress. Had the tale about Lord Kyle reached court?"

"I do not think I heard it," said Madeleine.

"You would remember. Sir Neil *tried* to silence his men about it."

Madeleine tilted her head to one side.

"King Walter visited Lord Kyle of Belford, who has three sisters, and his wife, Lady Lilias, has two—all of them live at Belford. They played music in the garden, and the king complained of the noise. So they talked, and the king complained of the noise."

Madeleine lifted her eyebrows.

"They fell silent, and he complained that they haunted the garden like little ghosts. They retreated to their chambers, and he raged at their avoiding their guest." Lord Magnus shook his head. "That is why I insisted on leaving last night."

"The queen. . . ." She tried again, more firmly. "Queen Katherine thought that King Walter would not dare revoke the pardon."

"Let us pray to God that she is right," said John.

Madeleine's gaze went down the road. She would, but first, and firmly, she collected her thoughts for thanksgiving. All that she had prayed for at Summerfield was now hers.

At noon, Sandy insisted on walking, but before an hour was up, he was again ensconced in someone's arms. By evening, he slept there as they walked along a forest road.

A deer peered at them from the trees—a plain, brown deer, unlike the one that might have lured her from the path in the Misty Hills. They came closer. The deer bounded off.

"Camp here," Lord Magnus called. The sun was still well above the horizon, but the road dipped ahead of them, into a mire. The muddy lands stretched farther than they could travel before it set.

John sat on the nearest rock as the other men prepared camp. Madeleine felt lost and alone.

Sandy threw himself into "helping." The men smiled. Some of the dry leaves he gathered were used as Lord Gilbert lit the fire. After a moment, Madeleine asked Lord Gilbert if he would watch Sandy for a time. When Lord Gilbert agreed, surprised, she returned to John and took his hand. "Come, dear."

Bewilderment broke John's flat expression. She tugged and led him into the woods. As the brush blocked them off from the campsite, John said, "They will all know what we are doing."

Madeleine raised her chin. Her shawl slipped, and she pulled it from her hair. "We are married." She slid her hands over his shoulders.

John's mouth descended on hers in a kiss as delicate as a butterfly's landing. After a moment, he led her toward a mass of ferns, green in the shade. "There are," he whispered, "sixty queens, eighty concubines, and maidens without number. One alone is my dove, my beloved, my lovely one."

The smell of crushed bracken surrounded them. Madeleine lay on the ferns, and the mantle that John had spread for her, and he lay against her—their clothing still in disarray. Her hands smoothed his dark blond hair.

A piece of fern jabbed her back, through the cloth. Madeleine shifted. John stirred.

"Are you all right, my dearest?" she said.

"Better than I have been in a long time."

She looked at his face, wondering if they had caused his arm more injury, but it held only an easing of the dreadful despondency.

Not its disappearance. Madeleine knew not what to say.

John released a deep breath. "Thank you, my love. You almost make me feel a man again."

"My darling, what happened to you?"

"I heard. . . Lord Magnus told you. . . ."

Her hand rested against his head. "You saved your lord."

He turned his head, hiding his face against her shoulder. "I went down in the first moments—I struck not one of his foes. . . and was so wounded that they barely kept me alive until we reached the prison, even."

She put her arms about him. "My dearest, how could you think I would think the worse of you for that? You saved your lord's life."

His eyes closed, as if he feared she could read some passion in them.

She pitched her voice even more softly. "How could you think so?"

His face moved against her again. His voice changed. "I have been ill. And feverish." He looked up. His smile held a faint shadow of its usual impishness. "It is unkind of you to expect impeccable judgment from an ill man."

Madeleine laughed.

The sunlight had grown reddish when they straightened out their clothing. John picked bracken from her hair, making her blush. She had known what they would think. . . .

John rose and gave her a hand to her feet, but stood, after, holding her hand. "One thing."

Madeleine waited.

"Why did you bring Sandy with you?"

Madeleine looked at the forest floor. The reasons seemed flimsier than the dead leaves underfoot, but John's grip was steady on her hand. Hesitantly, she told him about his brothers. His grip tightened, but he showed no other sign of listening until she finished. Silence lasted for several breaths, after.

His voice was measured. "You thought they would murder him?"

"I thought they might—and I did not wish to risk Sandy."

John grimaced.

"And they came after me, telling lies."

He loosened his grip, and they walked back to the camp.

Sandy's laughter reached them before the talk. When they spotted him, a shadow against the fire, he hurtled across the forest floor. John went down on one knee, to put his sound arm about his son. Sandy threw his arms about John's neck.

"Easy with the arm," John said, but his voice was light. Sandy prattled about green lions in foreign lands. John held him as if he feared his brothers could reach across the land to strike Sandy down.

A horn sounded, echoing among the trees.

John looked up from the stream where he bathed his face.

Gilbert said, with a frown, "Not poachers. We should leave."

"And be taken for poachers ourselves?" John stood.

"Lord Magnus—" said Phillip. The other men looked uneasy.

"Has wisely tried to avoid attention," said John. His gaze went over the forest. "For us to flee would only *draw* the eye."

Then horses came through the woods, and they had no time to flee. The nobleman pulled up his horse and looked at them. At least his clothing was not rich enough for a great noble—

and his companions, milling behind him, were no more than knights.

"Who are you?"

A dozen explanations leapt to John's mouth. "Travelers, getting water," he said, meekly. Lord Magnus wanted them to escape to their lands in stealth. After he had failed him at the fight, he could not fail him in this.

The noble surveyed them again. "Strange travelers."

"There are many strange things in the land," said Gilbert.

After a moment, the noble's mouth drew into a thin line. "However did you break free of the king's prison?"

"The queen," said John, glad that Madeleine and Sandy were safely at the camp.

He scowled the more at John's words, but said only, "The *queen?*"

"She's regent," said Gilbert. "She pardoned us."

After a minute, the noble threw back his head and laughed. "Your Lord Magnus and you must be my guests this night. I must hear this tale."

John looked down, thinking of the tale that he would hear of *him.* He had, with no weapon in hand, taken on an armed man to defend his lord, but he wished, for a minute, that he had never wed. He would be free to travel the land as a knight errant, winning fame.

But when they led the hunters to their camp, Sandy hurled toward him, and he did not think on that again.

A week of walking brought them to the road's fork. One road headed north into woodlands; the other, west, bordering the fields. Though the sun was still high in the sky, Lord Magnus stopped the men. Madeleine glanced both ways, trying to guess their path.

The north road sank, and among the trees, one was red with autumn. Her mouth pursed. It must be a swamp, there, where the leaves always turned early, but even in the swamp, it meant that August was well begun.

"I must free the men-at-arms," said Lord Magnus, "but we have reached the end of the Misty Hills. The fastest way to our lands is north. Every wounded man will go, and many able-bodied, to protect them." He glanced at Madeleine and Sandy.

"Where will we gather again?" said Lord Gilbert.

"We won't."

The silence was deep until a breeze broke it, and then Lord Magnus's voice.

"We have a royal pardon—what else is needed? We need not act as if the king would demand our return to prison, and so gather together that he might take us captive together."

The silence returned.

"Besides, the king had—difficulties in the West Dales. We should prepare to show our loyalty with our aid."

Men laughed and talked of fighting, without speaking of who their foes would be. Lord Magnus moved among them, speaking to this man and that. John's hand descended on Madeleine's.

"Did you tell Lord Magnus why you brought Sandy?" he said.

Madeleine bit her lip. "They did us no harm before."

"Once they had emboldened themselves enough to act, they sent men after you. That must be the talk of the countryside."

Madeleine's head sank. The thought of returning to Summerfield made her almost queasy.

Sandy scurried off, toward a bright orange mushroom. She ran after, and his wails echoed under the trees. When she returned with Sandy, Lord Magnus and John stood together in silence.

"Come to Papa," said John. When Sandy wriggled, he put out his sound arm. "I told Lord Magnus that you had a reason to bring Sandy with you."

Madeleine yielded Sandy and felt the heat in her cheeks. She explained again. The story felt even more flimsy, but her fears did not fade.

Leaves rustled.

"I could dispossess them for defiance," Lord Magnus said, "but the king might claim that they were loyal to him. I do not wish to fight him over that. And, I would have to dispossess every lord who defied me."

Silence fell a moment. Sandy looked from face to face in bewilderment.

"Without that, I do not have reason enough to act against them. If my sister by marriage vanished from my home in the night—" Lord Magnus bowed his head. "I will send you with the news to my wife, Lord John. Take your wife and child. In token of your loyalty, remain my guest while you recover."

John bowed, awkwardly, with Sandy in his arms. Madeleine, almost sick with relief, curtseyed.

Chapter 8—News and Waiting

The river wound under the trees. A dozen red leaves floated down the dark waters. Downriver, they could see a scrap of tilled land. Lord Gilbert's deep voice boomed. "The border of my lands."

Madeleine drew a deep breath. The first lands under Lord Magnus's over-lordship. Faces eased, all about, even for the men who had traveled less than half of their journey. Sandy gawked, and Lord Gilbert swung him to his shoulders.

"Ford's this way."

At the ford, the fields spread. A castle stood behind them, and at the moment, they were not well-tended fields. Peasants clumped about the road, as if uncertain whether to greet them or flee.

Lord Gilbert splashed into the ford. Madeleine shed shoes and stockings and gathered her skirts; the water came half way up even Lord Gilbert's calves. John came up beside her, downstream, and kept a wary eye on her.

She remembered the gallant among the merchants' men, and glanced at his arm.

He smiled. "I could keep you on your feet."

They walked into the waters, on the river's pebbled bottom. The chill made Madeleine bite her lip and hitch up her skirts, but the pebbles did not yield too far underfoot.

The peasants grew sibilant with excitement. When Lord Gilbert rose from the ford, fright and doubt gave way in their faces. Many cheered. Some wept. Five ran toward the castle, hair, jackets, and skirts all flying on the breeze. The rest pressed around Lord Gilbert, and the air was full of questions.

Lord Gilbert boomed out their story. Sandy clapped his hands with glee. Madeleine climbed from the waters and let her skirts down. Everyone looked at her—Lord Gilbert was pointing. Madeleine stepped back. John put his arm about her, and Madeleine hid her face in his shoulder.

John drew her along the road, in the thick of the crowd and the gabble. Lord Gilbert let down Sandy, who scampered back to his parents, grinning. Someone produced a pipe, to pipe them up the flower-bordered way toward the castle.

At the castle gate, a lady peered through the ironwork. Lord Gilbert strode through the gate, took her in his arms, and kissed her thoroughly. She pulled away and babbled about feeding them, and how they would be lucky to eat rabbit, but did not step far from him.

Lord Gilbert's laughter rang. "My lady, these folk would find rabbit a feast!" He drew her out, presenting her as Lady Ceit, his wife, to this man and that man—even as she murmured about how to lodge so many of such high birth, many would have to sleep in the hall—and to Madeleine and John.

He said to Lady Ceit, his voice low, "These two receive a chamber, whatever their birth. No one will object."

Clean, if no better dressed, Madeleine descended the stairs with John. Sandy bounced about them.

Whispering drew her attention, and she made out the word "bandits." She faltered.

John strode toward the men. "What are you talking about?"

"Lord Dougal's lands," said Lord Phillip. "They've been plagued with bandits. The woods are full of them."

Madeleine felt chilled. If the widow could quell the robbers, she would have done it—and she was a widow, Lord Dougal having died in the attack. She gathered Sandy closer.

"Our duty is clear," said Lord Phillip. "Lord Magnus would have us hang these rogues at once."

"I doubt you need every lord here—"

"Trying to escape, Lord John?" said Lord Phillip.

"Do you think that these bandits are the only one who took advantage of the king's folly?" said John. "We must find them all."

"They should be put down. . . ."

John's mouth twitched. "How many men do you need? The bandits haven't got the king to aid them."

The agreement with that was raucous.

Their path did not lie that way, Madeleine realized. She and Sandy were safe.

She waited until John drew near and she could speak in a low voice. "With the lords gone, and so many dead, and no one to confirm their heirs. It must have seemed that law had died."

"Law has returned," said John. Sandy threw his arms about John's knees, and John rumpled his hair. She wondered why he looked a little sad.

In the antechamber, ladies-in-waiting whispered as they fussed with her clothing. The rustle of cloth drowned out the words. Katherine walked to the doorway. They fell silent. Lady Beatrix looked abashed; others looked furtive; none spoke. She let them dress her. They had never held their tongues before, no matter how malicious their chatter was. So, they now gossiped about her.

She would not plead for court gossip, like a nasty-minded woman rusticated by the king. Even if the king did not give her the respect due her station, she was the queen.

They laced up her gown, and she remembered Lady Madeleine. Shame might have nothing to do with their silence.

Her tongue touched her lip. She could not reckon the times. Too much could have happened. A bridge might have fallen, or rain made muck of the roads, slowing Madeleine; a messenger could have ridden all night with the news, speeding the rumor.

A woman took a comb to her hair, and Katherine braced herself against the tugs. Ladies-in-waiting retreated for her jewelry. Whispers came sibilantly back, just soft enough that she could not make out the words.

"Fewer ambassadors this morning," said a maid by the door.

Katherine let her breath out. Even the ambassadors might be reluctant to associate themselves with such a queen. But she had known that when she did it. She held out her hands. Her ladies-in-waiting slid rings on the fingers.

"And," said the maid, "ministers await you."

Katherine glanced in the glass. Every inch a queen— "Then I shall speak with them." She swept from the room. The ladies-in-waiting followed, without gossip.

Over a dozen ministers stood in the room, flamboyant in robes of office. Most wore the golden chains of their posts, as if for a coronation—or a trial.

"What is it, my lords?"

"Evil rumors have filled the court, Madame," said Lord Osgar. "We have come to have them refuted."

"What rumors, my lords? Do you imagine that I gossip with my maids?"

Lord Osgar looked taken aback, but another—Lord Roderick—said, "They concern Lord Magnus."

Katherine inclined her head.

"They declare that you had the man pardoned, despite his crimes!"

"Should I grant pardons to the innocent? Indeed, that would make mock of justice!"

Mutters ran about. A third man shifted his weight. Katherine did not bother to recall his name. "The king will be angry," he said, shrilly.

She lifted both eyebrows. "A show of clemency was important, to impress on the nobles the royal prerogatives." She touched her lips with her forefinger. "He had the man arrested, but you must remind them of the authority before you show the clemency, or they will think you weak."

"This show of clemency was ill-conceived, Madame," said— a fourth man.

"It is clear that attending court does not teach royal judgment to mere subjects." Katherine hoped her imposture did not show. "That is why the King's Grace appointed me regent."

Every man there had derided her judgment at one time. Now, let them try to claim that her judgment was sound.

"I sent it secretly to avoid warning the young hotheads, who might act rashly."

The men pulled back. One muttered, "We must let the king know."

Her stomach curdled. She wondered if King Walter already knew. It did not matter, after all, if she convinced the *ministers*.

By afternoon, nobles paid their respects to her before leaving. Rumors spoke of nobles even leaving without paying their respects.

Even in Lord Magnus's lands, they could not always find castles or monasteries to spend the night.

They woke in a pine forest. Sandy charged across the litter of amber needles toward his father. John grinned. Not that the camps were always uncomfortable; they had all slept well enough last night.

Sandy threw his arms about John's neck. "Lions!"

"Lions, then," John said, glad that Sandy had not specified *green* lions. Sandy pounced, they wrestled on the ground, and the smell of crushed pine needles rose about them. Sandy growled, and John growled back. Sandy laughed and threw his arms about John's waist. John sat up.

Madeleine had gathered their blankets. She straightened her shawl and looked at the other men. Only a handful still took this road. Some had reached their homes; many more had parted ways at one crossroad or another.

She said, in a low voice, "We will all part at the next crossroad. No one goes by Owlscourt."

"Lord Magnus," said John, slowly, recalling, "took his household men. And he—" He checked his memory. "Took all the men whose path would have taken them by Owlscourt, as well."

"No wonder he had to send us with the news," said Madeleine, her voice toneless.

John reached for his pack and slung it on. Lord Magnus believed in Madeleine's fears enough to protect them from Donald and Andrew. Even if John had done little to protect him from his foes. . . .

John realized that, where they clutched the strap, his knuckles had turned white. He released it. Lord Magnus did not need his services at Owlscourt, he thought bleakly.

Madeleine glanced at him.

John let out a long breath. On the other hand, his brothers had failed in their duty. Lord Magnus had right to more service from Summerfield, and John, none to complain of it.

The raindrops were so fine that Madeleine could not see them in the air, but they had fallen all morning and afternoon. Their shoes were covered with mud, and she felt cold and cross.

Sandy whined. They both had given up trying to quiet him.

"I think this is the last turn," John said.

I hope so, Madeleine thought. She made out shapes as they approached: peasants, leading a cow. They looked as dreary as she felt.

"Good folk, is this the way to Owlscourt?"

The peasants looked at John. One nodded. The other considered them longer, but without a word, they walked on with their cow, and soon were only dark shapes, moving through the rain. John and Madeleine, with Sandy clinging to her skirts, walked down the road.

"Pick me *up*, Mama," wailed Sandy.

Madeleine, too tired to argue, did so. Sandy leaned against her shoulder. Fields and the village emerged from the rain, and beyond them, the castle of Owlscourt. Madeleine let out a long breath. They did not walk faster, but they trudged on until the fortress loomed over them.

"Halt!" The word's echoes seemed to die quickly in the mists. "Who goes there?"

"Lord John of Summerfield, with his wife and son," called John. "And a message for Lady Elspeth."

A long moment later, the cry came back. "Lord John was taken with Lord Magnus."

"And released with him," said John. "Lord Magnus gave me a letter for Lady Elspeth's hands."

Muttering sounded on the ramparts, as if the men could not fathom what to do. One sharp phrase emerged: "get her hopes up." Madeleine shivered and stepped closer to John.

After a minute, the call came back: "Stand by the gates."

Madeleine gladly walked over and leaned against the stone. John stood there with his feet spread, as if bracing himself. Minutes passed, until Madeleine thought the sky darkened with advancing night. Then, within the courtyard, a door opened, letting out light and half a dozen people. One was a woman, hastily donning a mantle. Even by the torchlight, Madeleine could make out her auburn hair, and the pale fraught oval of her face: Lady Elspeth herself.

She walked under the gate. Her expression went blank. John bowed, and Lady Elspeth murmured, "I would hardly have known you, Lord John." Her gaze went past him, to Madeleine.

"May I have the honor of presenting to you my wife, Lady Madeleine?"

Madeleine tried to curtsey without waking Sandy. The curtsey was a poor thing—and Sandy stirred.

Lady Elspeth did not glance at the guards, or give orders about the gates. Her tongue touched her lips. "Your brothers told tales, Lord John, about your wife."

John laughed. It rang from the stones.

Clean again, Madeleine tightened the belt on her borrowed gown.

At the door, John said, "She let me give her the letter."

Madeleine laughed. "She had no need of it, with us here. We are a message in ourselves."

John smiled and sat on the chest at the bed's foot, but his good humor slid. "Lord Magnus sent word about preparations. For—because of the king. And about us twain."

Madeleine sat on the hearth.

"Lady Elspeth spoke of the nearer lords. The rumors of the pardon have spread, but to know that it was true—"

Outside the narrow window, rain fell, and it rumbled on the roof. The younger women sat forward with obvious excitement. The older watched Madeleine with more surreptitious glances. Lady Elspeth inspected the gown that she wore. She stood in the middle and felt awkward.

"Amber does not become you, Lady Madeleine," said Lady Elspeth.

Said one middle-aged lady, "How quickly might the gown be needed?"

"Lord Patrick—of Grimont—might come as soon as he receives news."

Madeleine's heart sank. Lord Patrick was of higher rank than even Lord Magnus or Lord Fergus—if she remembered correctly, he had royal blood.

Lady Elspeth tilted her head. "A blue dress. Blue for fidelity."

The youngest maid clapped her hands together. A white-haired woman, wearing black, left the room and reappeared with her hands filled with sapphire cloth. Madeleine remembered the dyes of the Misty Hills and the bales that the wool merchants had borne, and wondered where Lady Elspeth had bought the dye.

"Exactly the color, Dame Bride," said Lady Elspeth.

They draped the cloth on, fitting it to her. Rain drummed on the roof.

The clouds lowered, but not a drop fell. The castle ahead looked darker than the clouds. The flower-filled meadows managed to look dreary.

It was only the weather, Magnus told himself. He brought good news for the men there. About him, the men of his household, and the handful of lords he had kept with him, visibly relaxed, even as they walked through the village, where peasants were ragged and wary, and the chickens that scattered were few. They climbed the dusty road toward the castle.

"Halt there!" The voice from the gate was harsh. "This is a royal castle. You have no claims here."

He stopped. "I bear a message for Lord Olgar."

"A likely story."

Magnus's men stirred. Sir Conall stepped beside him, as if ready to draw in his defense. The wind picked up, bending over the grasses and flowers. Magnus shouted, "When a man can be imprisoned for falsely claiming a royal message?"

Silence followed. A couple of his men reached toward their swords before drawing their hands away. Remembering they could not storm the castle, thought Magnus sourly, as much as we might wish to.

Rain fell in splatters here and there; the drops were dark splotches, larger than coins, on the dirt. Magnus let out a long breath. With a faint clink, the machinery stirred within. The guards did not look out or speak, and the gate creaked open slowly. A hard-faced sergeant appeared in the opening and held out a hand.

"The message is for Lord Olgar," said Magnus.

"It'll get to him."

Magnus's voice hardened. He was afoot, but this man could not have taken him for a peasant. "For his hand."

"It'll get to him."

"I will show you the seal," said Magnus. Either Lord Olgar maintained the worst discipline among his men that any lord did, or every lord who complained of base-born upstarts had a case, when speaking of Lord Olgar.

The sergeant's gaze shifted. He glanced over Magnus's men as if gauging them for a fight. Magnus blessed Lord David for remembering the weapons, but wished he had brought more men.

"Show me the seal then," said the sergeant.

Magnus stepped under the gate to show the pardon's parchment. The courtyard behind held a dozen sullen armed men, weapons at ready. The sergeant, having brought neither torch nor lamp with him, squinted at the seal. "No noble's—"

"The queen's own seal, done with her own hand," said Magnus. "It is a pardon for the men you hold prisoner here."

"What nonsense is this?" The bellow reverberated down the stairs. From his clothing, the man descending the stairs had to be Lord Olgar; unkempt though it was, no mere knight, even, would dress that richly. His face was ruddy, but he did not look drunk at the moment.

Magnus could not keep his voice from sounding clipped. "A message for you, my lord. Your prisoners have been pardoned."

The men at arms heard that. They recoiled. Lord Olgar himself looked less aware than his men; he only stood, blinking. Then he scowled. "Only the king. . . ."

"During King Walter's progress," said Lord Magnus, "Queen Katherine acts as regent. Mark the seal."

The sergeant, and all the men in the courtyard, stared. Magnus felt glad to have his men about him. He met Lord Olgar's gaze as if there were no question of force.

Lord Olgar, slowly, took the pardon. He studied the seal before breaking it. Then he perused the paper for a long time, long enough that Magnus had to resist the impulse to reach for his sword.

Lord Olgar looked up with hatred in his face. "Sergeant, show these men to the prisons. Release the men into their charge." His gaze was on Magnus as if he expected him to play the errand boy.

Sir Conall stepped forward, the set of his shoulders belligerent. Magnus nodded. Conall followed the sergeant, and a dozen men followed him. Their footsteps resounded in the stairway.

Magnus met Lord Olgar's gaze. Try again to send me after your servants. Lord Olgar's eyes narrowed, but he did not speak.

Rain pattered, still drop by drop, but the stones turned damp in patches, no longer just spotted with wetness. Footsteps sounded again—of a single man.

Alone in the rain, Conall came across the courtyard. His mouth was grimly set, and the door stood open behind him— the door to the dungeons. They could be no more pleasant than any other dungeons in the land.

Conall reached him, close enough to whisper, but seemed to have no words.

Magnus, forcing himself not to glance at Lord Olgar (as if the man had any say in what he would do), said, softly, "How many of them live? And how many can walk on their own?"

"I think a quarter died. Another quarter can not walk on their own."

How many of the half could not aid another man? He should have kept more of the lords with him; he should have realized the greatness of Lord David's heart. "Show me."

Conall led him across the courtyard. The worst of it was that, whatever the storm, they could not stay the night. He would leave no man within reach of Lord Olgar.

"We will have to hire carts in the next town," said Magus. Conall did not twitch.

Torchlight flared ahead of him. He saw the first, gaunt faces. Food as well as carts. He walked down the last stairs. One of the ailing men, lying on the floor, had not been wounded when captured.

His jaw tightened. He had to preserve these survivors. He had to aid the widows and the fatherless children of the dead. He had to preserve peace and order. He could not climb the stairs and strike down Lord Olgar. If he committed any crime not covered by the pardon, King Walter would strike at once. Then *he* would have murdered the men.

A man-at-arms gasped, and Magnus looked over. His eyes had closed. After a moment, Magnus realized that the man no longer breathed.

May God have mercy on his soul, prayed Magnus.

A man rose to his feet, ahead of him, and steadied himself on the wall. "I can help."

"Who is *that*?" said Dame Bride. She peered out the window.

As the women rose, Madeleine said, "Did you stare so at my arrival?"

"We would have if we had known, Lady Madeleine," said Damsel Christie, "since you came in the rain, like this man in the mud—but it was dark."

The clash of weapons came from behind the walls. John had grumbled with the rest about the mire, but the week of rain had left the knights and men-at-arms eager to practice.

Her mouth pursed. Not eager to journey. Only an urgent matter would send any man on such dreadful roads. She followed the other women, to see the company of three, a knight and two servants by the looks of it.

"If Lady Elspeth doesn't know of him," said Madeleine, "he should be greeted none the less." The women looked at her, but when she turned to leave the room, half a dozen of the ladies fluttered behind her. They reached the courtyard, and saw no sign of Lady Elspeth.

The guards hailed and admitted the travelers. Madeleine curtseyed as the knight came into the courtyard.

"Where is the Lady Elspeth? I must speak with her, I am Sir Batair, and my right must be upheld—"

Madeleine raised an eyebrow. He had to have heard that Lord Magnus would return, and even with all the tales of bandits, his servants looked heavily armed. "We will tell Lady Elspeth of your arrival." She drew back among the women, into the building's shadow. Sir Batair did not follow them, but his gaze did.

"With all haste, too," muttered Bride.

"No." Madeleine had to struggle to keep her voice low, and she could not soften it. "Search for her slowly, and ask her to dally on the way. I will fetch the knights."

As she left, Madeleine suppressed the impulse to run. If Sir Batair knew how frightened she was, if Lady Elspeth came— once she turned a corner, and her footsteps would no longer reach the man's ears so easily, she gathered her skirts and ran.

She burst from the castle's postern gate and nearly into a mud puddle. On the wet grass, John and another man sparred, with wooden swords, but still, coming close was dangerous. She looked about. The men were mostly young; Lord Magnus had left a handful of men with Lady Elspeth, to protect Owlscourt. Madeleine bit her lip. Young and inexperienced, and they did not practice with steel; if needed, they had to get swords.

The other man sprawled in the grass. John turned and laughed. "Come to inspire your lord husband to new triumphs, my lady?"

"You must come," said Madeleine. "As soon as you have
your arms. You may need them. A knight came, and his men
are heavily armed."

Madeleine might have been wrong to send them for swords,
thought John. He climbed the stairs. Sir Batair's men had left
the courtyard; they must be with Lady Elspeth—God grant
that they were not late.

Lady Elspeth's voice reached them before they reached the
chamber. "I can not sign such a document without due
consideration."

The man's voice was not as distinct, but he sounded angry.

John touched Madeleine's arm and put her to one side, by a
window niche. "Stay out of the way."

Lady Elspeth's voice rang again. "Queen Katherine, in the
king's absence and after grave consideration, granted my lord
husband and his men a pardon. I would do no less than she."

John sprinted up the last stairs. Footsteps thundered after
him. He reached the doorway, and every gaze within turned on
him. Lady Elspeth looked gratefully at him. Her ladies-in-
waiting wrung their hands behind her; he wished that they, like
Madeleine, were out of the way. Sir Batair scowled. His men
looked indifferent, like hired bravos, but Madeleine had
spoken the truth of their weapons.

John did not stop until well inside the door, so the other
men might enter; there, he bowed. He heard footsteps behind,
but did not turn to see. "My lady! We heard of your guest."

Sir Batair's gaze turned poisonous. John moved his hand
toward his sword hilt.

"Sir Batair, you may receive our hospitality while you await
Lord Magnus," said Lady Elspeth.

After a moment, he bowed and refused it.

A handful of days had dried the mud, but not brought Lord Magnus.

In the walled garden, John lay on the grass. Rose bushes grew to either side, bereft of their flowers, but not their thorns, as if to protect them with added walls. Next to him, Sandy grinned. "Dragon."

John lifted an eyebrow—Sandy had grown fond of lions and dragons since Madeleine had taken him to Harthill—but he hissed. Someone walked through the garden, toward them, but not quickly. Sandy lunged. John wrestled with him before yielding. Sandy bounced as John gave fearful death gurgles.

Sandy swung his hands, hitting John's shoulder. John grabbed them. "None of that. A knight does not kick an enemy when he's down—not even a dragon."

Sandy pouted.

"Never," said John.

Madeleine came through the tangled rose branches, and John sat up. "Come give your dragon a hug," Sandy hurled himself into his embrace. He looked over the boy's shoulder at Madeleine.

Her voice was low but intense. "The guards have spotted Lord Patrick. He has a small company—came in haste. . . ."

John's mouth twisted. "We must ready ourselves, then." He had been a gallant knight who had rescued a damsel from her dragon of a father—once.

They ate in the antechamber, not the great hall. Then, it was no great feast, only supper, suitable for less formality.

"The queen," said Madeleine, not feeling hungry, "saw that ill will the arrest caused was far greater than the king had anticipated. She deemed a show of clemency best."

Lord Patrick lifted his wine cup. The candlelight glittered from it. Over its rim, he watched her as he drank. Madeleine modestly cast her eyes down and ate, a little.

He lowered the cup. "More than the queen knows. Every man of royal blood must have heard questions about the king's heir."

Madeleine's thoughts leapt back to Queen Katherine. She would have known if she were with child, but it might not have shown. The queen would not announce the news early. "God grant that the queen conceives soon."

"Woe to the land whose king is a child," said Lord Patrick. "At times in our history...." He shook his head.

"In the Misty Hills, we learn of the early days of King Leod's reign," said Madeleine, and hoped she sounded as grave as she intended. "But the sooner the heir is born, the sooner he will not be a child."

Lord Patrick snorted.

"From the same tales, we know that a child king needs only loyal men to prevent war."

After a minute, Lord Patrick glanced at John. "Is it true that he set Lord David of Bridgeton over you, Lord John?"

John's voice was cool and clear. "That is true. We were glad of it. Many of us might have died, had he made our imprisonment harsher."

Lord Patrick looked back a long minute. Madeleine wondered how close Lord Patrick was to King Walter by blood.

Chapter 9—Returns and Invitations

This shrine of St. Adelina—patroness of prisoners—was among the smallest churches Magnus had ever seen. Maples shaded and towered over the gray stone building.

Perhaps the pilgrims who had aided Lady Madeleine would visit this one. He took a step closer to it. He had had men in his service, for whom all he could do was pray.

People came in and out for their own prayers, and eyed him. Slowly, Magnus walked closer, hearing talk: of the king's coming south, of how the king had heard of the pardon, and struck the messenger. Magnus winced. In his own lands and among his own men, he could rely on the pardon; here, they could not stay long. He had living men in his service, and the dead men's widows and orphans to aid.

His eyes adjusted; the candlelight and handful of windows were dim beside the sunlight on the road. A score of his men were already in the chapel on their knees; some muttered their prayers. Prayers for the dead, in battle and in prison, prayers of thanksgiving for those still living—and prayers for continued succor.

Magnus knelt. "Lord," he whispered, "with Your justice endow the king, and Your Judgment the king's son."

By the massed candles, the cathedral gleamed, from gilt, or paint in scarlet and blue.

Katrine knelt. The cathedral was built of stone, but she knew it was not that made her feel so chilled.

"Lady Madeleine of Summerfield," whispered old William. "I knew she was no widow—"

Katrine folded her hands and prayed for anything that would stop up William's mouth. Did he want it known that they had aided Lady Madeleine? When they were poor peasants, with no great friends to aid against the king?

She looked up at the crucifix. St. Adeline was the patroness of prisoners as well as of widows. She would—leave Lady Madeleine's shell here.

The royal company rode through the greenwood. Somerled, surprised, rode toward them. He had guessed that King Walter headed north still, not east. But the banners were the king's.

King Walter must have recognized that Somerled wore his own colors; he pulled up his horse, stirring confusion among the riders who had missed the approach of a messenger.

They saw him, and the colors he wore, soon enough, and parted for him. Horses tossed their heads, or snorted. Men watched him with narrowed eyes. Drostan had said the king traveled with many soldiers, but he had not realized how many.

He dismounted and offered the letter, on one knee.

"What news does it bear?" said the king.

"The rebellion in Eastwyck has been suppressed," said Somerled. "A noble brought forces against it."

About, horses champed at their bits. For fear of meeting the king's gaze, Somerled did not look up. The faintest of breezes rustled leaves, but the sound came clearly to him.

"Then nothing will interfere with my plans for Michaelmas," said the king. "We will continue."

Somerled could only blink.

The king gestured for him to join the company. Somerled fled to the servants. They cursed and struck the mules to get them back on the road. Somerled noticed that the king had offered no reward. He wondered if that showed that the message *had* displeased him.

A cart lurched forward.

"You're a lucky one," one waggoner said. "When he heard of the pardon, he struck that messenger—and after he had that lord killed for striking one."

For the king to strike his own messenger was not treason, thought Somerled, wryly, with a touch of bitterness, but the waggoner, no messenger, already looked ahead.

"Have they got them back on the road *yet*?"

A wagon lurched, and Somerled glanced sideways at it. The wheels sank into the earth wherever it would yield; it was heavily laden. A man tromped along beside it: a stranger, and in that clothing, not a nobleman's servant. Somerled scowled. If he had to guess, the man was a stonemason, and at that thought, he picked out a dozen others.

His horse snorted. Somerled patted its neck and loosened his grip on the reins.

Abruptly, the woods gave way. A bridge, built of beige stone, spanned a gorge that held ferns and the echo of thunderous waters. King Walter pulled up his horse and regally contemplated the bridge. Every now and again, a horse stamped, juggling its harness, or a bird twittered in the trees, but the river made the only other sound. Somerled remembered Drostan's tale, of the gallows.

"These lands," said King Walter, "have been trouble enough. If you have no bridge to cross, you will not cross it to feud."

Somerled started. That bridge had taken long and cost much to build.

"Sire, your subjects will suffer—"

The nobleman who had spoken was young, and his kinsmen moved to silence him. The king gave him an amused glance. "They suffer from your feuds."

Somerled considered how few messages they carried about feuds, to or from these lands. He glanced at the king and pondered whether he could escape to warn the other messengers. They used this bridge when delivering royal messages.

In the courtyard, despite the chilly air, Madeleine stood with John and the rest of Lord Magnus's household. Only in the kitchen, where they cooked dinner, had desire not overwhelmed the chill—

A potboy, grimy with grease, peered out. An oath came moments before by a hurled spoon; it clattered on the stone, and the boy ducked back inside.

The small company walked through the open gates. Murmurs bruited about names, asking where Brian was, and Archibald, and other names that Madeleine did not catch. Her heart sank.

Lady Elspeth walked forward as if Lord Magnus had come alone. Madeleine could not tell whose arms went up first to embrace; she looked away. Lady Elspeth's murmur was too low for Madeleine to catch the words.

"For myself, well," said Lord Magnus. "I fear that I owe Lord David more than I knew. The other jailor—many men who survived the battle died in the prison."

Madeleine shuddered. Exclamations, of distress and fury, ran through the crowd. She looked from the company—at a gray-haired woman, her face worn, sobbing. A mother—or a wife, for many men-at-arms were not young—or, Madeleine realized, both. Then she could not look at her, either.

Madeleine thought she would learn to hate these meals in the antechamber.

"Lord Patrick does not mean to wait," said Lady Elspeth.

Madeleine stared at the venison on the plate before her. She sipped at the wine.

"Lord Patrick is the least of our worries," said Lord Magnus. "He will not get enough pledges of support to make him attempt to overthrow the king."

"Will any of them?" said Lady Elspeth.

"That," said Lord Magnus, "depends on the king."

And, thought Madeleine, the nobles. Who knew what they would take as pledges enough? They might think that others would rally to any open revolt. Worse, they might be right.

Lord Magnus glanced at John and Madeleine. "Do your brothers know about your fate?"

John nodded.

"I sent a messenger," said Lady Elspeth. "I also ordered them to send their wardrobes. They sent them."

"I will send another. Since they were—unable to aid me with Lord Peter of Waycross, they can deliver here the portion of the rents that are yours, while you serve me."

John bowed his head. Madeleine studied his face and felt cold. When they left the table, he whispered to Madeleine, "Any landless knight could do these services for him."

The night before, thunder had boomed, but the tempest had settled to a cloudy but dry day.

"The king! The king arrives!"

The messengers had arrived long before King Walter himself, but Queen Katherine's stomach churned as if she had

had no warning. By a window, she tried to convince herself that the crowds were smaller and less colorful than the last time King Walter had returned from a progress. Her gaze went over one band of apprentices, cheerful boys in bright blue smocks. It might even have been true.

"Madame?" said Beatrix.

Katherine rose. She could not pick out King Walter for the distance, but she would receive him properly, in the courtyard. She swept from the room. Her ladies-in-waiting exclaimed and scurried after, their skirts rustling until they arrayed themselves behind her. Along the way, courtiers bowed and curtsied. Katherine nodded to them; her tutors would be proud. She passed through the great hall, bedecked with late-blooming flowers, to the courtyard. Musicians, brilliant in their livery, stood by with gleaming trumpets. Smells of the feast drifted from the kitchens.

Katherine drew a deep breath. Nobles lined the courtyard, as they had the great hall, but—whatever was true with the commoners—these throngs were smaller. Once the tale had been confirmed, the nobles had swarmed from Harthill.

That would not please King Walter.

The musicians lifted their trumpets. The fanfare rang out.

As befitted royalty, for his entry into the city, King Walter had changed his travel-stained garments for scarlet and blue. In royal splendor, he processed into the courtyard. A groom taking his horse, he dismounted. Courtiers bowed and curtseyed like a field of flowers before a strong wind.

Katherine felt like a lone tree in a field, below a thunderstorm.

She acted properly, she told herself. When King Walter stood before her, she curtseyed. "Sire."

"Madame," said the king, bowing. He took her hand and drew her back to standing. She studied his face. He, perhaps, would not rebuke her before the court, but she could read nothing in his expression.

She remembered Lady Madeleine's face when she spoke of her husband. She kept her own face even. A match such as hers was the fate of princesses.

He stepped closer. His voice was low. "Indeed, a grand welcome, evidence of my subjects' loyalty."

Lord Patrick, thought Magnus, was not his only problem. He watched through a window. Beneath a threatening sky, a small company rode toward the castle. He picked out their banner in the gloom. Whitt—but it did not matter. Another inheritance to be confirmed. With how the last lords had died, these were not formal courtesies.

"Better they should grumble to me than to another."—but he rubbed his forehead. Lady Una, her eyes red with weeping, had offered fealty for an infant grandson. Both the child's father and grandfather had died in the king's attack. "Good Lord have mercy on us all."

"My lord?"

Magnus turned to the servant by the door. "Bring the wine up, Neil, and send for the clerk."

He walked down the stairs, which were darker than usual. The courtyard even managed to seem bright as he emerged. He drew a deep breath. The men had to be confirmed, and the land restored to order.

His own knights appeared swiftly, without a summons. Guards hailed the arrivals, and the names came in a flurry. Magnus caught Ranulf, Arthur, and Sim before he lost track of them. From the north and east—by Lord Patrick's lands. They rode into the courtyard with a clatter and dismounted there.

"My lord!" Arthur swept a bow as their horses went into the stables. "We came in all haste, and together, to guard against bandits."

"Necessary, nowadays," said Sim. "One never knows *where* an attack might come from."

Young, hot-headed puppies. They had not seen the men-at-arms in the dungeon. They had not returned to his lands from there, burying a man every night for a week. They had only their own griefs and not an endless stream of the bereaved. Yet they acted as if the injury was theirs alone.

An older and wiser head should not show himself flustered. Not to mention that if he ever loosed his rage, he would never manage to stop it up again. "Come inside. We may speak easier, without the threat of having it—dampened."

A few of them laughed. They followed him to his great chamber, where he sat, and the clerk already waited, with pen in hand. Sim stepped forward to recount what lands his father had held. Magnus's clerk noted them. Magnus held out his hands, and Sim dropped to one knee before him, to give his oath.

As he accepted fealty from the third, thunder boomed. Rain hammered on the roof, and rainwater gurgled down. He raised his voice. When he received the last oath, the rain still pounded, and the clouds held no break. The men would have to stay the night. If the rain went on, they might well have days to foment their grievances.

"My lords, let us retire to the great hall. My lady will be delighted to receive you."

As they went down, Lady Madeleine, looking damp, walked up and curtseyed. "My lord? The rain caught Lady Elspeth and some of her women in the garden. She directed her ladies to receive your guests, and hoped they would accept her humble apologies."

"No man would dream of denying the noble lady," said Arthur. He bowed. Deeply. "My lady?"

Magnus had seen that bright eye on Arthur before. "Lady Madeleine, may I present Lord Arthur?" Arthur bowed, even more deeply. Magnus added, "My lady, I have not seen your lord husband this morning. I wished to speak with him."

Arthur looked only slightly taken aback. Magnus hoped that he had not overcome his scruples about married women. Madeleine spoke of the armory. "I will have to see him later, then." He turned to the other ladies, and the rest of the men.

Most of the young men chattered as if mindful that these women were young, fair, well-born, and unwed, but Sim returned to Madeleine as soon as the introductions were done, to speak of the pardon and the king's folly.

Madeleine's fingers clutched her skirts as if she wished to flee. "It was the queen who—"

"Aye, the queen." Sim drowned out any other talk. "The queen, and not the king! There's lawlessness—the consort, not the monarch."

Did the man wish that the pardon had not been granted? Before his own liege lord, whom it had saved? Not an hour after pledging his loyalty?

"Lord Sim," said Magnus, coldly, "King Walter has the authority to appoint when he wills as regent."

Thunder boomed when Sim opened his mouth. Moments later, he said, "A proper king would have granted it himself—if he had ever committed such folly!" He spoke more darkly. "We could have a proper king."

God in Heaven have mercy on us all, thought Magnus.

The other men drew back, leaving a passage between them.

Magnus spoke as softly as he could without the rain drowning his words. "Whom do you propose, as this proper king?"

Sim's hand went to his sword hilt. "After all the men he's murdered? First get rid of this one."

"Get rid of this one, and we will find ten thousand. They will tear the land apart. The law would suffer worse than it does under King Walter."

Sim looked about resentfully, as if he expected support. Magnus followed his gaze, to daunt anyone who would try. Curse not the king, not even in your thought, he thought.

In the solar, dark with evening, Lord Magnus paced, his shadow interrupting the orange firelight. "The fools."

Madeleine pulled out another stitch. Sandy ignored his toys and peered up at Lord Magnus. Lady Elspeth's graciously permitting Sandy to be underfoot might not be all to the good. Lord Magnus, she told herself, had had to entertain those fools all day the day before. He still had to fear what they might dream up on the way home.

Those thoughts did not steady her stitching.

He stopped by the fireplace. The low fire cast orange light and dark shadow across his face. "We can not hold the king's authority at naught. If they mind the deaths, how many more do they want to die?"

"You could have refused the pardon," said Madeleine. Her voice was tart even in her own ears. She tried to make it tarter. "You did not *have* to accept it. You knew the king's wishes as well as the queen did."

Lady Elspeth laughed.

The next morning was clear and bright. From the ramparts, Magnus watched as a small company escorted a woman through the mire. Their banner was of a knight who had defied his summons. Magnus studied her with care. Lady Madeleine had told him that Lord Donald and Lord Andrew had received a messenger. If he knew who had sent those messengers, he would know his enemy. But he doubted that this lady would tell him.

She huffed as a groom helped her dismount, and waddled to stairs. Not the treacherous lord himself, but Lady Morag, his wife. Magnus scowled. Baird had not died, in the fight or in captivity, as so many good men had, but Lady Morag wore black.

Magnus felt his mouth twitch. It did not *have* to be for Baird, he reminded himself. When Lady Morag curtseyed in the doorway, he had smoothed his face out again.

"My lord, I have come for justice."

Magnus raised his eyebrows.

"My lord husband was *murdered*." She paused for a breath. "Lords returned to their lands, filled with contempt for law. They murdered my husband over land—they arrived in force, he had no chance—"

"Which lands?" said Magnus.

She froze.

"Redwood, I suspect."

Her face contorted. In his absence, Lord Baird must have leapt to seize lands. However vague his claim to them, he had thought that no one would contest it.

For once, that he could not impose justice on the faithless lord meant nothing.

When the summons arrived, the ladies-in-waiting chattered furiously about gowns and jewels.

Katherine did not, even as they combed her hair and slid rings on her fingers. Walter visited her, nights, for a husband's duty rather than speech, but sooner or later, he would speak to her by day. Even with conversations falling silent wherever she went, she knew that he had struck the messenger whom Lord Olgar had sent. Young women whispered that the messenger was lucky to live. She wished she knew whether the older women were wiser than to think it, or to say it.

"I suppose that will have to do," said Lady Lachina.

"It would not do for me to be late," said Katherine. The ladies-in-waiting blinked as if they had forgotten she could speak, but trailed her down the corridors to the king's.

King Walter stood gold and crimson in his robes. She would guess that his attendants had been as nervous as hers.

He rose to greet her. She curtseyed. His bow was deep, and he spoke evenly. "I have considered Michaelmas."

Michaelmas, thought Katherine. Even having summoned her, he would not ask about the pardon.

She inclined her head. A thought with a sting as sharp as a wasp's said that his ministers had told him her reasons, and he had no need to speak with her. She kept her face steady. The ministers had feared to speak with him, too. She could not hope that she would never face the evil hour.

Regally oblivious to her thoughts, he said, "I will not remain in Harthill. I will appoint Lord Osgar to the regency."

"Another messenger," said Damsel Christie, from the window.

Madeleine looked up. She could not see the messenger, only treetops yellow with autumn. Only Damsel Christie would find another messenger interesting, after all that Lord Magnus had sent and received these last weeks.

Said Christie, brightly, "In royal livery."

For a moment, Madeleine thought her heart had stopped. Then it hammered.

Royal livery might not mean anything. The king might have sent a message having nothing to do with the pardon. He might even have given some favorite leave to send a message thus.

Her heart would not steady.

Madeleine put aside her sewing. A royal messenger should be greeted. She hurried down the stairs and reached the courtyard as the messenger passed the gate. A groom approached, but no one else. Madeleine bit her lip.

Lord Magnus emerged from the other tower as the groom took the horse's bridle. Servants cluttered the shadows by the door, and Madeleine stepped over to ask whether anyone fetched wine. A flurry of motion broke out.

Lady Elspeth appeared, and Madeleine assured her that a servant went for wine. Lady Elspeth gave her a distracted smile. Madeleine pulled out of the way, into the shadows.

Lord Magnus, walking toward the door, paused by her. "It appears that I will offer hospitality to the king."

Madeleine's hand clenched on her skirts. Perhaps Lord Magnus should not have sent his men to their lands. "When?"

"Michaelmas."

The messenger vanished into the great hall.

"A grand feast, with nobles from all over the land. The King's Grace will bring several from court—including one Lord Keith."

Who had talked of freeing Lord Magnus by force. Madeleine nodded. King Walter had summoned nobles to watch the trial and executions, but whatever he intended with this feast—it could not be that. She hoped. "May St. Michael defend us from evil."

"I shall have to summon some of my lords. It will not be cheap, however it goes." After a moment, his mouth twitched.

"Lords Andrew and Donald of Summerfield, and their wives, certainly."

Madeleine swallowed. "Will the king bring the queen?"

"No. And—he will appoint Lord Osgar regent."

Madeleine felt chilled. She hoped that both the absence and the appointment were caused by a fear that the queen might miscarry. But the queen had not thought of the pardon.

"Do not look so downhearted, my lady," said Lord Magnus. "Here lies a chance to placate the king—to protect my lords and men, and the widows, and the fatherless."

"Does he seem—appeasable?" said Madeleine.

"He did not seem likely to capture me," said Lord Magnus. "Perhaps enough flattery will make him forget."

Lady Elspeth inspected Madeleine's gowns, and the jewelry spread over the coverlet. "It will do. *If* you plan wisely."

"Sandy?" Madeleine whispered.

Lady Elspeth paused. "There is a small manor nearby. I sent my children there when they were too small and we had many noble guests."

Madeleine nodded meekly. Another strange place for Sandy, but he would be far from the king.

They went down the stairs. In the courtyard, Lord Magnus spoke of hunting farther from the castle, to leave the nearer animals for hunts when the king arrived. One knight grumbled that he should demand the beasts. Mutton and beef would grace the table as well as venison.

"In need," said Lord Magnus, "the peasants can drive their beasts from raiders who destroy their crops."

Moonlight lay in diamonds across the blanket, and lent nothing color. Madeleine's hand fretted the blanket.

"I wonder how long we will have our own chamber," said John, from the shadows beside her.

"It depends on how many nobles come. And how soon."

"And after—" John's fingers traced her arm. "I thought of returning to Summerfield. I can not remain away forever."

Madeleine sighed. John had talked like that before obeying Lord Magnus's summons. She considered whether to tell him that she was almost certain that she carried a child again—but it would be unwise to distract him with what lay before them.

Her voice sounded thin in her own ears. "Lord Magnus would not give you leave to go until after Michaelmas. He will need your aid in the hunting."

John groaned. "Madeleine, I did nothing that any landless knight could not have done."

"You saved his life as well as I did," said Madeleine. "You were the first to move—"

"I was not the last. Other men took blows meant for Lord Magnus. Some died."

Madeleine bit down on a sigh, before it could make John more stubborn. If he pointed out that anyone else might have appealed to the queen, as she had, she would hit him. She *had* saved Lord Magnus, just as John *had*.

She glanced sideways. John lay without stirring. Perhaps returning to Summerfield would lift this cloud. She leaned over to kiss him.

She woke in the night, gasping in the darkness. It was not like the bloody dreams of John's execution. She could remember only that it had been dark and bewildering—and she was shaking with fear.

John grunted. The moon had long set. She could see nothing, but he was warm beside her, and as she fought for breath, he shifted toward her. Her hand touched his arm. With another grunt, he stiffened into wakefulness. "Madeleine?"

She silenced him with another kiss. That dream she did not want to speak of—or even remember. After a minute, his arms came about her.

Chapter 10—Preparations and Gathering

Banners flapped in the wind as the first nobles arrived, and the ladies whispered names. Several of the men, Madeleine could place from the banner. Others she remembered from court. One....

"Lady Elspeth? My godfather arrived."

With a smile, Lady Elspeth dismissed her. Madeleine hurried down the stairs. In the courtyard, grooms rushed to take horses, and men churned about. Still on the stairs, she looked over the faces.

Lord Fergus's gaze went over the crowd. His voice rang. "Lady Madeleine." He walked toward her, and his companions followed. Madeleine descended.

Lord Fergus kissed her hand and presented her to the lords with him. In all their greetings, none commented on her presence at the court, months ago, or the pardon. Lord Torin said that he had danced with her at court, before her husband had danced her away from him.

Madeleine smiled, but the words came with difficulty; she had lost the knack of court. "I can see that Lord John broke your heart with his deed."

"Good thing his wife is not here to hear *that*!" said another. The lords laughed and walked toward the hall to greet Lord Magnus.

Lord Fergus touched her arm. "You are well? And happy?"

"Very happy, and very well. My lord husband has recovered from his injuries."

"Be glad then. Beware of trying more."

A warm welcome there. As if she could not feel the danger in her bones. She curtseyed, and Lord Fergus went with his companions. On the stairway back to the women's room, she stopped and went, instead, to the nursery. She stopped in the doorway to watch Sandy crowing over his toy knight.

Madeleine felt another smile answer his. Then she recalled that Sandy would turn three while King Walter was here, and Sandy was not. Her smile felt fixed even as Sandy talked of a green lion.

She heard soft footsteps behind her. John, behind her, leaned on the doorframe as he watched Sandy.

He said in a low voice, "Have you heard the news from Eastwyck?"

Madeleine felt a flurry of incoherent reactions and then an insane spasm of hope: King Walter had gone to fight and could not come to Owlscourt.

Sandy's knight charged over the stones.

"The rebellion was put down. By a noble named Lord Malcolm."

Madeleine's heart sank. Her thoughts could not come clear. She could not wish Lord Magnus's misfortunes on another, even if it might keep the king from Owlscourt. "Pray God that the king does not make him suffer for it."

John walked forward to pick up and hug Sandy. "You're going on an adventure, soon, like a knight. . . ."

Sandy put his hand in his mouth. "Green lions?"

"Maybe, maybe—did I tell you the story about a knight who saw a lion and a dragon fighting?"

Sandy's eyes widened. John told him how the knight came to the lion's aid and ever after, they had adventured together.

"Lady Madeleine!" A boy at the door bowed. He breathed hard. "Lord Magnus wanted you—"

"What happened?" said John.

The boy looked between them. "He said a nobleman wished to hear how the pardon was granted."

Peasants brought in the harvest. With Sandy perched before him, John rode on a narrow track between the fields. The manor stood on a hill, with a pond before it. Sandy wriggled and exclaimed over the swans. As they reached the gate, the old knight who held the manor came forward. His lady wife, as gray-haired as he, came with him, to take Sandy. The knight assured John that they had received Lord Magnus's orders.

Simple enough, thought John, exchanging some pleasantries, and watching the lady smile at Sandy's exclamations.

The knight glanced at the sun. "Will you stay the night?"

He could still travel for a few hours, this day, but John nodded. Once he left this manor, he would have to travel until late to find shelter for the night, and it was not as if Lord Magnus needed him back.

Sandy yawned, enormously. "I had a chamber readied," said the lady, and carried him in. John and the knight remained in the sunlight. John let his breath out and looked about. They would be harvesting in Summerfield, too.

Before one hut, an old, twisted peasant sat. A crutch lay next to him, but he whittled. About him, children played with painted wooden animals.

"Does he make those?" said John. The knight gave him a strange look. John pointed, and his expression not changing, the knight nodded.

"It will be Sandy's birthday in a week," said John.

The knight blinked. After a moment, he smiled. John walked down from the manor house. A dog yapped at him. The children grew wide eyed. Some pulled back, clutching their toys. The man's eyes only narrowed. John told him that he wanted an animal from him.

"A lion," he said.

The man's eyes narrowed further. "A fancy lion?"

John glanced at the children's toys, to be sure, but some were painted. "Green," he said, knowing what Sandy would say to any other color.

In the chapel, Madeleine knelt. Outside, the air was cold, but the bodies packed within turned the chapel stifling, and the perfumes were not equal to their task. Though, at that, the nobles could still crowd in the chapel. The king would arrive in two days, and more nobles came with every hour. Soon, Owlscourt would hold more than would fit in its chapel.

It was nearly time for the service. She closed her eyes to collect herself.

"Lord Malcolm's not coming to the feast," said a noble behind her. Madeleine drew her breath in and tried to ignore the gossip.

The priest intoned a psalm. "Lord with Your justice endow the king, and with Your judgment the king's son. That he may govern Your people with justice, and Your oppressed with right judgment."

Madeleine opened her eyes to look at the priest.

"He shall have pity for the poor and the lowly."

Madeleine closed her eyes and bent over her hands to pray. May Almighty God have mercy on and guard His fool of a priest. The priest intoned on. Madeleine bit her lip. Why couldn't she hope? "From violence and extortion he rescues them—" He could, if he wished. By God's grace, if he wished to, King Walter could administer justice.

Or he could die, and his heir could administer it.

Her fingers tightened about each other, and she prayed for justice, however given.

At the service's end, Madeleine moved as slowly as the crowd. Lord Magnus emerged at her elbow. "Lady Madeleine? Some lords wish to hear how you obtained the pardon."

Again. Madeleine nodded, but bustle arose near the gate, spreading through the courtyard. She grimaced. Another nobleman. At least, it no longer mattered how large his retinue was—the servants slept in tents—but she wondered if this one, too, wanted to hear the tale.

Lord Magnus had not moved. She wondered about the rank of those he was bringing her to, but followed his gaze across the courtyard. He had the advantage of height, but heads moved enough that she could see. The newcomer was Lord Peter of Waycross.

Any reconciliation had to include the king's favorite, but Madeleine stepped back.

As if her movement had awoken him, Lord Magnus started to cross the courtyard. The crowds, fixed on Lord Peter, shifted reluctantly. The nearest lords greeted Lord Peter with no more words than they had to. Lord Peter himself was jovially effusive. After all, thought Madeleine poisonously, what could they do to him?

"Jackanapes," muttered a young knight. "Ought to pay the price for his knavery—"

Madeleine did not even turn to see who spoke before she spoke. "Who will bear the price for *that*?"

John's horse splashed through the stream. As it climbed the other bank, to the road that paralleled the stream, Owlscourt appeared ahead, however little that meant. Madeleine was there, but he doubted he would so much as speak to her for many a day.

Hoof beats came from behind him. Knowing that any guest was likely to outrank him, John pulled up his horse. He made out the banner: Lord David of Bridgeton. John did not urge his horse forward. Lord David's men muttered and stared as they passed him.

Lord David pulled up his horse. "My lord, are you not one of Lord Magnus's men?"

John gave a half-bow. "John of Summerfield, my lord. Returning to my lord's castle."

Lord David's expression flickered. "It is good to see you hale again, Lord John. Join us for the rest of the way."

Would be hard not to, thought John. He kicked his horse's side. After a moment, Lord David said, "Your lady wife—she did not find the journey too taxing?"

"Easier than arriving at the tower," said John, "with all the men who would carry Sandy part of the way."

His manner brightening, Lord David asked about the gathering at Owlscourt.

They reached the first tents. Mutters began, and the sidelong glances at Lord David, whose liveliness slipped. John kept his smile. It was an effort, but if his humor slid, men would conclude that he was angry with Lord David—who had saved his life.

The gates loomed ahead, and they rode under, through shadow and back to the sunlight.

Lord Magnus appeared there, as if Lord David equaled him in rank. As the stable boys took their horses, he grasped his hand. "How was your journey, my lord?"

In the courtyard and about the gate, the mark of favor was noted. A few nobles seemed mollified; perhaps their eyebrows went up, but their expressions eased. Others grumbled harder.

Lord Magnus turned to greet John. "Lady Madeleine is in the rose garden, with Lady Elspeth."

John nodded and wove his way through the courtyard and sardonic comments on how well Lord David had served the king.

He reached the garden gate. Madeleine was within, he thought, but no refuge. He felt a sudden sickness with the whole affair.

In the royal garden, Lady Beatrix sat in the corner, for all the chilly breezes and the dreary brown that fall had brought. Hiding here meant that she could hide that she was crying and could not stop. Queen Katherine never left her chambers; Beatrix could only wonder if King Walter *had* ordered her to stay there. No one attended court, and courtiers who were trapped here did not even attend Lord Osgar. The entertainments were less than if they were mourning the king's death. And she felt *so* lonely.

She sniffed. Lord Osgar harrumphed about how no one courted his favor, but he never *thought* about how dreary the court was.

"My lady," said a firm voice, coming from among the barren flower bed and the leafless branches. In surprise, Beatrix looked up. It *was* Alun—and after she had refused him—and her traitorous heart leapt at the thought of escape.

He bowed. "You are as lovely as ever."

She felt the tears welling. She did not know what to say. A glance at his grave face, and she blurted, "I do not know if the queen *can* free a lady-in-waiting from her service, now."

At the words, she could not hold the tears back. Alun sank to one knee before her, took her hand, and after a moment said, "Beatrix, you must stop. You will sicken if you cry like this."

Which drew new tears. She dashed them away with her free hand. Alun rose to his feet, keeping his grip on her hand to draw her up. "You must come in. It's too cold, and this— wasteland will not make you merry again."

Beatrix obeyed. She felt too weary not to, and once he shut the door on the cold, the warmth *was* pleasant. They garnered curious glances and greetings. Lord—Keith said, "You will not see me much longer. Off to this Michaelmas feast."

He had cut it fine, though Beatrix, leaving after the king. She would never be so foolhardy. She stepped closer to Alun.

"I did not think you had business there," said Alun.

"The king—invited me." His mouth twisted. "I was angry enough at first. But to stay here, under that jumped-up knave who held Lord Magnus's men? Not high enough to hold nobles, but high enough to lord it—" Lord Keith snorted. "He's too fond of letting people lord it over us."

"That was Lord *Olgar*," said Alun, "not Lord *Osgar*. Of old and reputable family, is our regent."

"You're doing nothing except protecting yourself," said Lord Keith, and Alun merely met his gaze.

Beatrix drew a horrified breath. Disputes over the regent— the countryside would be even drearier, and Lord Osgar could rusticate a mere lady-in-waiting. "Oh, Lord Alun," she gabbled, "I feel cold. I must have taken more of a chill than I thought. Please, can we get to the great chamber? There will be a fire."

Alun, urbanely, ushered her off before her thoughts cleared—and shocked her. If she had kept her wits about her, she might have discovered treason against the queen. A loyal lady would support her mistress.

Then, even more shocking, she thought that loyalty to the *queen* was what a lady-in-waiting owed. Lord Keith had not intimidated anything against the *queen*.

She was glad when they reached the hearth. The fire burned from a vast bed of jewel-red coals, and she could devote herself to warming her hands.

John looked at the tents—minor nobles were camping with the servants—and the sour set of his mouth spoke for him.

"He has to be somewhere," said Madeleine. "He would not leave Owlscourt without King Walter's leave. Even outside the Misty Hills, he has never enjoyed hunting since he was lost."

"You can speak with your godfather later," said John. "Lord Fergus may not *know* anything more."

"Then he can tell me so," said Madeleine.

John's voice slowed. "Lord Magnus asked me to attend him, before noon."

Madeleine hesitated, glanced about the tents, and picked out a blue tunic she had seen before. "There! You can leave me with my godfather while you attend Lord Magnus."

"Such secretiveness," said Lord Fergus, as Madeleine drew him over by the woods. "It can only lead some men to reflect that I aided you in obtaining the pardon."

A stride from the trees, where they could be clearly seen, Madeleine stopped. "What could be more natural than a goddaughter, bereft of her parents, seeking out her godfather?"

Lord Fergus snorted. "You aren't bereft of your *father*." But he spoke low enough that she could ignore it.

"I must know what threats you know of, that I and my lord husband face. Or his overlord faces." Lord Fergus twitched at that addition, and she met his gaze. "He and I have no protection but Lord Magnus."

After a moment, Lord Fergus said, heavily, "I know only that King Walter asked after the woman who obtained the pardon. How much he learned—Lady Annette had already returned to her parents, and he did not question me."

Madeleine stared into the forest. She would dream that night, she knew it.

Trumpets sounded on the road. She stiffened. All about the camp, courtiers stirred like a bee hive warming to day. The castle gates were thrown open, and shouts rose to hail the king.

Like flowers opening before the sun, thought Madeleine dryly.

In the small room that Lord Magnus had managed to reserve for himself, John tried to look unconcerned. His back was to the door, but his ears strained. Lord Magnus had not much time to deal with Donald.

Footsteps sounded, and he could gauge the distance of each one. The door opened, and Donald glanced about the room. His gaze fell on John. He blinked as if surprised, and then his mouth tightened before he looked at Lord Magnus sideways.

He stepped inside, holding the door open. Andrew followed him in, shut the door, and stood, silent and twitching, behind Donald.

"Is Lady Madeleine well?" Donald's voice was deep, calm, resonant. "I know we are all deeply in her debt, but. . . ." He spread his hand. "To leave in the night—and to take young Alexander! I feared her grief had turned her wits."

"She feared how fast rumor would spread," said John. "And the fewer who were involved, the fewer who could be punished."

Andrew flinched, and words flooded from his mouth. "It was a worry. With the marriage articles, the king's rage might have left us unable to support even our own wives."

Behind the desk, Lord Magnus shifted his weight, without taking his gaze from Andrew. "May God be thanked, it came to naught."

John watched his brothers, looking for any sign of treachery. Donald was unflinching, Andrew had always been nervous about nothing—perhaps Madeleine's fears had touched him, but John was still glad she had taken Sandy with her.

Trumpets blared outside, and shouts followed. Lord Magnus rose, his face calm, as if this were not an interruption. "The king is arriving. We must greet him."

John almost felt relieved.

Royal foreriders reached the courtyard. Magnus walked toward the gate. Up and down the road, crowds cheered the king. That gave him time; King Walter would linger to listen. He did not dally, even when looking for Elspeth. She stood at the gate, and he breathed a sigh of relief.

The king's horse came down the road. King Walter smiled at his beloved subjects. A weedy man, with hair of nondescript brown—even royal traveling clothes could not make this man look like a murderer.

Magnus felt his mouth tighten. He forced himself to smooth it out. He had his duty to those men who had survived, and the widows and fatherless children of the dead. It would protect him from the king's anger, but it was also right. His gaze slid over the men behind King Walter. Among their number, Lord Olgar smirked.

His bow paused only a moment.

The king accepted a groom's aid in dismounting. "It is well to see you obeying here."

For the want of words to answer that, Magnus bowed again.

Chapter 11—Festivities and Disputes

Lady Elspeth said, "More wine for the side table."

Madeleine curtsied—not deeply, not in this crowded back corridor, but even so her hands brushed others. She hurried for the wine cellar.

The single lamp cast more shadows than light. Madeleine hesitated on the stairs, but the steward, grumbling, came out from the casks and looked up at her, his face catching the light. He glared. "For that Lord Olgar again?"

Madeleine blinked. Like the rest of the women, she had eaten in a side chamber, not the great hall. "Lady Elspeth ordered it."

The steward promised the worst wine, but went to draw it. Madeleine retreated, into the barely brighter corridors, and went down them, past the great hall. Despite herself, she peeked in. Lord Olgar's face was more flushed, and his gestures clumsier, than those of the men about him. She hurried on.

Christie caught her before the door. "Is it true, about the arrests? And the hangings?"

Madeleine drew a deep breath. "The King's Grace took a firm hand with bandits on the way here."

"They said some were innocent. . . ."

Madeleine glanced at Christie's wide eyes. Did she think her own lord guilty? "Come, let us go to the solar."

She led the way. Besides, you could not follow the king's path by gallows. The king had indulged in ill-advised clemency. as well, rumors spoke of how a bandit who committed murder the day after his pardon, and how he died when the lord's men went to seize him. The king had raged.

They reached the solar, and the women chattering within. Madeleine drew a deep breath. The king had not actually punished the lord's men, but she would be glad when he left.

In the gloom, the great hall resounded with snores, of those too lowly to sleep even five or six to a chamber. Madeleine eased her way after Lady Elspeth, toward the stairs. The sleepers were still of high birth, to sleep indoors. She did not want to wake them.

At the stairs, they walked more quickly. There, no one slept—now. Madeleine wondered whether that would be true if it rained.

A window let in scraps of starlight. Lady Elspeth paused. Her voice was low. "Lord Olgar will drain our wine cellar."

"He is fond of the bottle." Madeleine lowered her voice still further. "With the frosty welcome—"

Lady Elspeth sighed. "The king will note it. My lord husband—but the worst offenders are not subject to him."

And his own men were none of the most obedient. The, thought Madeleine tartly, how could they be? They were only men and not angels.

The huntsmen moved about the forest. The trees were green and yellow; here and there, one was scarlet, or held scarlet leaves on one bough while all the rest were green.

The morning air was chilly. The king's voice carried through it. "In King Adair's day, his men defended a stock of wood disguised as Prince Leod to the death. Their only thought was to get the prince away."

John walked swiftly. He had not lost the knack; despite the dead leaves underfoot, red and orange scattered over the brown carpet from the last year, he could hear the king.

"They knew what loyalty was in those days."

Prince Leod had been in danger, thought John, because traitors killed King Adair his father. Though the lord who saved him served loyally as regent, he too was treacherously murdered a few years later. Prince Leod had to hide in the Misty Hills for years while a usurper reigned.

Such loyalty.

His breath was a fog before him. John went over dew-laden grass, to ask if Lord Magnus should join the beaters.

Lord Magnus glanced at the king, who showed no signs of shifting a foot. He spoke in a low voice. "With the king this eager to hunt? They need no help."

John's shoulders slumped. The beaters were not so close as to hear the king. Lord Magnus cast him a sardonic glance. "You may tell the beaters that they need not scare off the game."

John bowed. At least the walk would keep him warm, and buy a moment's peace. He strode off, finding the men in the brush and delivering the message to each in turn. They all looked rather chilled.

In due course, he walked back toward the main hunt. Dew had soaked his boots, and his breaches past the knee. From the silence in the brush, the king still showed no signs of wishing to hunt. He stamped his feet, trying to keep some warmth in them. Lord Magnus had worried about whether they could rouse enough game to satisfy the king. He should have worried about whether he had meat enough without the hunt.

And whether, thought John, we will freeze to death. He walked more quickly; he could see no one, with the voices ahead were hidden by a bush fiery red with autumn.

King Walter's voice rose petulantly. "I will not have such insolence."

John edged toward him. The bush ceased to hide the scene. A man stood pale and mute before the king, and John could not have moved. Lord Peter of Waycross did not seem to notice, his gaze intent on the king.

"I should dispossess you. . . ."

John, feeling pale himself, looked about. Ahead of him, another company of men stood; some of Lord Magnus's men and some of the visiting nobles, they glanced at the king and muttered.

John eased his way toward them. "What did Lord Peter do to offend?" he whispered.

Several shook their heads.

"We should tell Lord Magnus," said one knight. "If the king is offended with Lord Peter. . . ."

John thought of asking King Walter for the disputed lands and shuddered. He would not divert the king's rage like that, not for Lord Peter. From the silence, no one else wished to.

"Lord Malcolm has it best," muttered another knight.

John rifled through the last weeks' rumors and messengers. Lord Malcolm. Then he winced. "He is not here?"

"He plead that he had to take care of his land."

"I heard," said a nobleman, belligerently, "that he didn't sound very pleading."

He had raised his voice. The king glanced over, and they fell silent, like children whose tutor had arrived.

Even this early, and in this cold, idling knights and squires filled the courtyard.

Besides that, the breeze reached the rampart, and she could see. Madeleine stood with her hands on the stones. The hunting party emerged from the woods. She leaned forward to look for their quarry; the kitchen would need to know. What she saw was that the hunters seemed subdued.

King Walter rode in their midst. His voice rang. "There were more beasts in the Misty Hills! And that Simon! Thinking that a hunt for his betters was his own amusement!"

They had a deer, and the venison would need to be prepared for the table. Madeleine descended the stairs. John came across the courtyard to her.

"Did the hunt go well?"

John took her in his arms and whispered as if using endearments, though that would deceive no one who saw his face. "Lord Peter of Waycross angered the king during the hunt. King Walter threatened to dispossess him."

Madeleine's mouth popped open. She managed to ask. "Why? Did anyone hear *that*?"

"No one. Perhaps even Lord Peter doesn't know." His arms tightened. "And—after that, one Sir Simon was ordered from the festivities because he killed that deer."

"Fortunate Sir Simon," said Madeleine.

Behind the castle, John stood with the other knights on the practice field. Dinner had come and gone, the sky showed orange, and the air there grew chilly. Soon, it would be too cold even considering the king's absence from the field.

Someone rode down the road.

He scowled. If the rider wanted hospitality, he had chosen ill. "A messenger?"

"A royal messenger," said Sir Conall. "Best if he gets greeted fitly."

John, and half a dozen others, followed him into the courtyard, half empty from the cold, with the nobles crushed inside. Those still out of doors gave them curious glances.

Minutes inched by.

The messenger's horse stamped against the stones, under the gate. Sir Conall gave the grooms their orders, and they rushed to take the man's mount.

Conall stepped forward. "Sir?"

"I have a message for the king," said the man, without enthusiasm.

"I will bring you, " said Conall. The man took a paper from the saddlebag and followed him. In the courtyard, John wondered what sort of message would frighten its bearer so. The man looked tired enough to be glad of his journey's end.

Calum, a young squire, stared up the stairs. "I never heard that King Walter was frugal with messengers."

John's gaze went up the window, where the king sat with his great nobles, where the servants fetched the finest wine.

An outraged bellow came from that room. John jumped. All across the courtyard, startled gazes went to the window.

"ARE THE WEST DALES STILL A KINGDOM?"

The king's voice went on, but lower. Nobles hurried down the stairs, as quickly as they could without making more sound than a mouse.

Lord Duncan of the West Dales, descendant of kings, would be a king, if the West Dales had not been taken into Darnien. The source of the message was clear enough. John straightened, carefully kept his hand from his sword, and brooded. After what befell Lord Magnus, reaching for his sword might be just, however imprudent.

Someone stormed down the stairs. The footsteps resounded as if the attempt was to make them loud, rather than to avoid the king's notice.

John stepped into the shadows.

King Walter burst into the courtyard. His step was
unsteady, as if drunk, and he glared about as if ready to strike
down anyone who spoke. The messenger darted down the
stairs behind him; John could see no signs that he had been
struck, but relief had not added much color to his face.

The king's fingers tightened on the letter. "This—
insolence! To answer a summons with a demand for a safe
conduct?"

John's mouth dropped open. He could not dream of a way
to better offend the king—any king. Though, especially a king
who could not be relied on without it.

The dinner stirred with rumor. Lord Duncan's name rose
again and again. Madeleine considered as she drank. King
Walter spoke of how wise it had been to take Sir Neil's men
with him, when he went near Eastwyck.

Madeleine put down her cup and realized that Gilliane
watched her. She had drunk rather more than was wise. Her
cheeks were flushed like apples, and her hand was unsteady as
she lowered the wine cup. Up and down the table, ladies
glanced at her before looking away and chattering. Nichola
stared at her plate with a fascination that the food did not
inspire.

"Madeleine," muttered Gilliane. Nichola did not look up,
but she stopped eating.

"Magdalene would be more to the point," said Gilliane, her
voice still low but laden with anger. "Obtaining the queen's
pardon. Which favorites did you *really* petition?"

Casting doubt on the legitimacy of the queen's children was
treason—unquestionable treason. Rumors of queenly favorites
had inspired specious claims to the throne, and war.
Madeleine's mouth went dry.

More eyes turned on Gilliane, even Nichola could not feign eating, but Gilliane herself did not look away from Madeleine.

She leaned forward. "How, after all, does a woman obtain such a favor? Except, of course. . . ."

Madeleine felt the color draining from her face. Words leapt to her mouth. "Are you well?"

All about, ladies smiled, or smirked. Gilliane's eyes narrowed in anger.

"My lady Gilliane!" Lady Elspeth hurried over, with two of her ladies. "If you were not well, our gracious lord king would not demand that an ailing woman attend the feast."

Gilliane looked on the verge of letting words spew from her mouth, but Lady Elspeth clapped her hands on Gilliane's arms and drew her from the table.

Nichola quickly took another bite.

Madeleine, unable to collect herself so easily, looked about. Nobles and knights stared after Lady Elspeth and Gilliane. Others muttered. At the head of the room, the king stared, his face fixed, at Madeleine and no other.

Madeleine looked at her plate. She had eaten little, and did not know how much she could choke down. He had not harmed Queen Katherine, she reminded herself.

With tales of clemency and gallows all about, that did not reassure.

In the kitchen, Lady Elspeth looked over the pastries. An elaborate crowned lion, the centerpiece, stood on the table.

"As fine as any at court," said Madeleine.

"I doubt it will appease the king."

"He came to show that he had accepted the pardon," said Madeleine.

"Or test the waters," said Lady Elspeth.

She left. Madeleine wished that Lady Elspeth had not reminded her. She closed her eyes. However the king distracted from the great feast, it was Michaelmas. Saint Michael, Archangel, defend us in battle. Be our protection against the wickedness and snares of the devil. May God rebuke him, we humbly pray, and do you, oh prince of the heavenly host, through the power of God, thrust in Hell Satan and all evil spirits who wander the world seeking the ruin of souls.

Servants came for the pastries. Madeleine left, passing through the courtyard, into the garden. There, she stopped within the gates. Rose bushes veiled her from the ladies who talked within. She drew in a deep breath. The flowers were gone, but the air smelled of greenery and earth.

The gate opened behind her. Madeleine turned. Andrew glared at her. "Don't think you've gotten away with it."

Madeleine looked at him.

A loud laugh came from the garden.

Andrew's face contorted. "John was a traitor. The king was entitled to seize his lands."

"The king will not seize them," said Madeleine.

Andrew looked sly. "He might yet. The marriage articles for our parents' wedding were confused. We could petition the king to—simplify them." Andrew leaned closer to her. "We have already petitioned the king."

Madeleine did not move. Her thoughts hunted for an escape. John had complained of the agreement himself, but she would not stand aside while Donald overrode them for his own benefit.

"John and you are not high in the king's favor, are you?" Andrew smirked. "Lord Magnus can hardly help you there."

"But who will help you?"

Andrew blinked.

"The king is not pleased with traitors, nowadays. On the hunts, he's grumbled of them. Will he favor two brothers who turn on the third?"

For a moment, Andrew stared at her. Then his gaze darted about, as if seeking an escape.

Madeleine smiled. "Perhaps you can save yourself. Perhaps you can tell him that Donald led you astray....."

Andrew yanked the gate open and bolted.

Madeleine, no longer smiling, latched it again. Betraying both his brothers would not endear him to the king, even if the king were not touchy about betrayal.

Again, laughter came from behind her. She sighed. If King Walter broke the articles, Lord Magnus and Lady Elspeth would keep them in service. They would survive. So would Sandy, and—she touched her waist—so would any other babe.

The clear morning was again chilly. A score of noblemen and knights stood about the courtyard. John drew in a deep breath. The air was fresher than the quarters where Lord Magnus's knights slept—twelve of them in a small room—and so he would wait here, even if there was nothing to await. King Walter had never left hunting to this late and still gone. His councilors had sounded severe, with armloads of petitions.

Donald sidled along the courtyard. John scarcely dared to breathe. When Madeleine had told him of Andrew's threats, he had hinted to Donald that his plan had its dangers—a gallant act, he thought sourly—but had seen no sign that Donald had listened.

Donald vanished into the building.

Minutes later, a loud and angry voice emerged from the master chamber. A councilor hurried down the stairs and asked after Andrew of Summerfield.

In the spate of denials, someone said, "John's his brother," and people pulled back from him. The councilor looked down the path to him.

"I am serving Lord Magnus," said John. "My brothers slept outside—I do not see them—"

The councilor grumbled and walked through the gates. After a moment, more noise came from the master chamber: footsteps echoing down the stairs. King Walter emerged, Donald pale and uncertain in his wake.

"Where is that man?" King Walter snarled. "This Andrew of Summerfield?"

One noble said, "Your councilor went after him."

King Walter's gaze settled on John. "You. You are their brother."

John bowed. One of the men you arrested on false grounds. The husband of the woman who thwarted you. He prayed for anything to distract the king.

The king flourished a paper. "Do you know what this says?"

"No, Sire." He could guess, but that he would not say.

"Your brothers think to take your inheritance." His eyes narrowed. "They said something of an heir. . . ."

After a long moment, John knew that the king awaited his speech. Nothing else would have driven him to speak. "My wife and I have been blessed with a son. They are both childless."

The king snorted again. The councilor reappeared at the gate; Andrew, looking green, followed him.

"It is not enough," said the king, "that you treacherously attempt to deny your brother his lawful inheritance. You then sneak around, trying to betray each other."

Andrew and Donald gaped at each other. After one piercing moment, John studied the flagstones. Whatever he and Madeleine urged, nothing would have happened if they had not betrayed each other. They had drawn the king's attention more than Madeleine and Sandy could ever have. Except, with the king now glaring at his brothers, John felt more sympathy with their fears than he ever had before.

"I will not have such treachery tearing my land apart." King Walter looked about. "Lord Daniel, take these men into charge. Deliver them to the tower."

John looked between his brothers, unable to feel anything, but he felt the color draining from his face. The king had no grounds for that arrest. All about him, the murmurs agreed as Lord Daniel obeyed.

John let his breath out. After what he had done to Lord Magnus, the king had little grounds to call another man treacherous; then, looking at the king's red face, he thought perhaps that was what had driven the king.

Lord, have mercy on us all, he prayed.

The sky was clear, and the sunlight filled the courtyard, where Donald and Andrew stood in chains.

Madeleine pulled back, further into the shadows. She wished for that peasant shawl again; she could have hidden her face with it. They had conspired against her and John, and their children—whether they had meant Sandy's life or not— but they looked as bewildered at Sandy at some whimsical order. She remembered how she had feared Donald when she fled for the pardon. She could not fear him now.

By the gate, Nicola sobbed. She doubted that would soften the king's heart, but Gillian's bitter words rose, asking how King Walter could commit such treachery. Madeleine turned her face away. However capricious the king was, that would harden his heart. She could not even try to protect Nicola by quieting her. Gilliane would take any attempt at comfort as gloating, and in her rage, might harden the king's heart still further.

Madeleine stole to the chapel, to pray for delivery from injustice.

The candlelight was dim besides the lights from the windows. Peaceful—Madeleine drew a deep breath and felt a stir of shame. For the sake of peace, they submitted to the king's caprices. She could have submitted to the loss of the inheritance. She and John would have suffered no more than if John's father and grandfather had drawn up sensible marriage articles. Lord Magnus might even have granted them lands.

She let her breath out. Too late for that. She genuflected before the sanctuary light and went to pray.

Once again, King Walter lingered near the back of the hunting party; another man would have been left behind, but other huntsmen still took the chance to play the courtier.

John glanced back now and again as he strode through the wood. This time, King Walter had not complained as other hunters had felled three beasts; John suspected that he had disappointed the men. Perhaps—perhaps the king grew reconciled to the pardon. They could hope.

A shout came from ahead. The hunter sounded more shocked than pleased. Babble followed.

John ran toward the noise. Had they stirred up wolves, or even a bear? Those would be noble quarry, but dangerous.

A clump of men stood about, looking as stupid as sheep.

"What happened?" said John.

The men gawked at him, and said nothing. Conall stood woodenly in his way until John put a hand to his arm to shift him aside.

Behind him, a body lay, face down, on the ground. Hair covered what little of the face would have been visible, and the cloak slumped about the body, but John thought: Lord Olgar. The arrow sticking out his back was clear enough. From the dark red of the blood, and the amount pooling on the earth, they had nothing else to do for him. Except—

John managed a croak: "We must send for Lord Magnus." He swallowed. "Send the news to the king." As one man moved, John tried to pray, Eternal rest grant unto him, o Lord.

. . .

He stared blankly at the body. He was dead; no further revenge was needed.

"One Sir Batair came to me." King Walter stood before a fiery red tangle of vines, as if the leaves were a tapestry in his own castle.

Magnus inclined his head rather than say anything.

"Impudent wretch." The king snorted.

So King Walter would not take Sir Batair's case, as he had Lord Peter's. That was a relief. Magnus inclined his head. "My lady wife told me of him."

A cry came from ahead. Magnus started and wondered if there were trouble.

The king seemed to have not even heard. "He complained of Lady Elspeth! That she dithered about justice with the plea of her husband's absence!"

Elspeth had justly denied Sir Batair's plea, but—Queen Katherine had acted in her husband's absence, and Elspeth would have his head if he said anything that might harm their children. "My lady wife always acts with due respect."

"My lord! My lord!" A lord charged through the trees. "Lord Magnus!" He stopped and gulped. Magnus wondered if he had noticed the king before. "Sire. Ahead—" He gestured at the trees.

"If you have lost your tongue," said King Walter acerbically, "we should see for ourselves."

The lord nodded. "This way." He set out. King Walter already followed, and Magnus's stride matched his. They reached a grove where hunters spoke in low voices. Something lay in their midst.

Magnus scowled. The last time Conall had looked like that, he had just come from Lord Olgar's dungeons.

A nobleman started. Silence fell as the men saw the king and, bowing, pulled back. A body, an arrow in the back, lay face down in the leaf mould. Magnus put together the clothing and the body's appearance: Lord Olgar had died here.

He felt the color draining from his face. This was an accident. This had to be an accident. Even if he learned who the murderer was, he could not punish him, and admit that Lord Olgar had been murdered.

Half a score of his men stood about. Their faces were set. His only reassurance lay in that none had suffered personally from Lord Olgar's viciousness—that he knew of.

King Walter was bone-white. His eyes shifted, his gaze darting about as if a glance could strike down the murderer.

"A thousand pities that I was not here," said Lord Magnus. "I think Your Grace would rather have the killer of so faithful a servant than the conversation of any man."

"My Lord Magnus," said another lord, "you are quick to condemn, when this unfortunate man was struck down by an arrow, and not a spear."

Magnus tried to calm his hammering heart. If other nobles thought as he had—but this man was not his own.

"What do you mean, Lord Torin?" said King Walter, clipping out each word.

"It is clear," said Lord Torin, "that Lord Olgar wore no bright colors in his hunting garb. Rashly shooting arrows is blame-worthy, but you are ready to treat this as murder!"

"A stray arrow struck down Lord Olgar—may God have mercy on his soul," said another. "An unfortunate mischance—"

Not with this crowd about Lord Olgar, thought Lord Magnus. King Walter looked ready, not to point that flaw, but to rage at them as murderers.

"I fear you mistook me, Lord Torin," said Lord Magnus. "I wish to rebuke the killer for his folly. No one wishes to condemn falsely, to treat imprudence as if it were murder." He spread his hand, indicating King Walter. "The king wishes for nothing but justice to be done."

Murmurs of agreement ran about the men. One man said that King Walter would not blacken this festivity, a proper occasion for clemency, with a rigid insistence on justice. King Walter looked from man to man. He looked more enraged by the moment, but his tongue was clearly tied by the implicit accusations of rashness and injustice. Though he had not let such charges sway him on the road—Magnus prayed that all the nobility would join in the matter, if only to uphold their own prerogatives, and that the unity would convince even the king.

He prayed Queen Katherine was with child. With the king this close to acting rashly, he needed an heir. For now, he could only delay the day of that need.

"Did any man mark the archer?" said Magnus. When silence and annoyed glances answered him, he said, "Then every lord should warn his men, of the perils of rashness. Any man could have been this—unwise."

Flint-like faces looked back at King Walter's gaze.

King Walter inspected each in turn. Magnus did not doubt that if he saw any flinching, the king would seize them all on charges of murder. But it seemed that the king had underestimated the fury of the nobility, and that, this time—this once—he realized he could not withstand them all.

"A faithful servant indeed," whispered King Walter. "A man who sent me news that my foolish young queen had withheld."

"Did you see how Lord Peter looked?" said Lord John, pitching his voice low. Sunlight, passing through the leaves, splattered itself against his face in the empty grove; the hunting party returned with the body. "I do not think you will see him on the hunt again."

They could not lag far behind, they would be needed at Owlscourt, but—"I marked how the king looked," said Magnus. "For all his gratitude, I would not have liked to be the messenger that Lord Olgar sent."

Lord John's voice went lower. "I thought of Lord David."

Magnus considered the faces he had seen. A guard for Lord David—"More than that," he said heavily. "A guard on the king. If I speak of the need, he will declare that Lord Olgar was murdered. But the guard is needed."

After all their preparations for the king's arrival, they had more preparations, and in haste. Madeleine stabbed the cloth with her needle.

"Mourning," said Lady Elspeth. A pale line was sharp about her mouth. "Mourning—his funeral will not even be here—the King's Grace has ordered the body returned to his lands, as if he had heirs to bury him, as if he could be buried with his ancestors!"

"But," said Madeleine, "you can not want him buried on Lord Magnus's estate." Everyone looked at her. She smiled. Perhaps she was fit for a courtier after all. That had been a pretty piece of equivocation; it gave Lady Elspeth pause.

The women returned to sewing. Madeleine was intent as the rest. Lord Olgar could be buried with his ancestors, but the nobles would object, even for a newly created lord. She held up a gray dress. With black ribbons, it might be fitting.

If the king grumbled that the ribbons could easily be snipped off—she would have to endure. It would be a lie to contradict him.

Two days later, in brilliant attire, the lesser guests gamed and talked in the great hall, nominally in hope that the king would grace them with a summons to the master chamber. Madeleine picked her way through the room.

"Heartless," said one knight. "First he plunges us in mourning, as if this Lord Olgar were his brother. Then he forgets him."

Heartless indeed, thought Madeleine. King Walter had moped over Lord Olgar's death in the funeral and the rest of the day, plunging the court in gloom for a mere nobleman. An old man had laughed, and King Walter struck him across the face, drawing blood with a ring. The next morning, the king had acted as if Lord Olgar had not died, shedding his mourning and asking courtiers why they were so glum. He spoke no more about the killer. Even Lord Keith and his fellows seemed perturbed by that silence.

Madeleine sidled past the knights, toward the stair way, where Lord Magnus had summoned her.

The afternoon sunlight lay placidly over the room.

Magnus wished that he had not had to tell Elspeth first, and disturb her peace, but Madeleine was in her service. And Elspeth had the right to sit in the corner while he met Madeleine as well—he glanced sideways at her.

She met his gaze. "This can not be good."

Footsteps sounded on the stairs. In the doorway, Lady Madeleine curtseyed.

"Close the door, my lady," said Magnus. His voice was harsher than he had intended, but he could not ease it. "The King's Grace wishes to speak with you, in a private audience."

He thought she flinched, but the woman who had won the pardon was made of stern stuff.

"Concerning what?" she said.

Magnus thought of the pardon, of Lady Gilliane's wild charges, of Lord Donald and Andrew's petition. He said, "I do not know."

"I see." Lady Madeleine inclined her head. "I will see what I can do to placate him."

If she could calm the king, she would put him again in her debt, as deeply as she had when she obtained the pardon. Magnus thanked her. She left.

Elspeth let out a long breath. "The poor child. God bless the day she eloped with Lord John—but it was not as fortunate for her as it was for everyone else."

"Have you seen her with her husband?" said Magnus. "A more blatant encouragement to defy your father and run off with your lover, I could not imagine."

A wry smile touched Elspeth's mouth.

Madeleine walked toward the stairs to the master chamber. She was not as grandly dressed as for her audience with Queen

Katherine, but even in the gaudy company in the great hall, the glances at her were puzzled. She reached the stairs and climbed, leaving the crowds behind.

She took a step, keeping her gaze fixed on the stone, and thought, I do not want to do this. She still took another. Lord Magnus had looked gray but certain as he told her, and like John, she owed Lord Magnus her service.

She climbed to the top of the stairs. Reluctantly, she looked up. A servant leapt to open the door.

Lord Magnus's spare chamber had been hung with new tapestries, woven from richly dyed thread. Carpets covered the stones of the floor; despite occasional ink stains, they were so red and violet that Madeleine was afraid to step on them. A clerk perched behind a tiny desk. His pen scritched over paper. The king, twisting a ring on his finger, stood by the window, looking out.

Madeleine curtseyed anyway. King Walter twitched, as if he had seen her from the corner of his eye, but did not turn. Light glinted across the room, from his ring. She tried to calm her breathing. The clerk scribbled on. Finally, with a grunt, King Walter looked at the doorway.

Madeleine curtseyed again. All that mattered was that she give King Walter no weapon to wield against her, or her husband, or her overlord.

"You are Madeleine of Candlewood." He gave the ring another turn. "That lies in the Misty Hills."

Madeleine could not move for a moment, but the words held just a hint of a question. "There I was born and raised, Sire. I have not returned since I wed and became Madeleine of Summerfield."

King Walter chuckled. Madeleine felt cold.

"I hunted in the Misty Hills this spring," said the king. "The dangers are—embellished."

The Misty Hills were notoriously enchanted. Madeleine considered the tarns of madness, the hawk, the Dead Men's Bells, and even the dragon. They were less dangerous than this audience. Then she remembered the pilgrims. "Many tales exaggerate."

King Walter nodded as if she had agreed. "I must know more about the hills."

Madeleine could not stop her breath from growing shallow. Whatever his purpose, she could not trust his honor.

"Well, Lady Madeleine? Tell me of the Misty Hills."

Madeleine curtseyed a third time. "I beg your pardon, Sire. I was trying to recollect my past, to answer fittingly. I am a poor, foolish lass, and it has been a long time—" She hesitated. He might have learned, from Donald, that she had vanished into the Misty Hills. "—since I lived there."

King Walter's voice was snappish. "I wish to know about the Misty Hills."

What does he know already? she wondered. Some things everyone knew. "They are always covered with mists. Some charms and tricks will cause the mists to thin—"

"I know *that*."

"Oh, ah—" She scrambled for words and realized that being flustered made her look foolish. She drew a deep breath. Another thought told her, sharply, that a foolish woman might not give sensible answers. "Er—oh, Sire, you have been in the hills, you know that much."

He gave her a baneful glare.

"There are beasts in it that can vanish into the mists."

"I've *seen* them."

Gold, she thought. He might know that, but he might not, if his guides had taken care. "There's dragons, too."

The king snorted. "So they say. Have *you* seen one?"

"Ah—" One. When I was passing through the Misty Hills, to fetch the pardon. She looked down. "It was at night. . . ."

The king's snort held more derision this time. Only terror
kept a smile from her face—and she had not - *lied*. She had
not *said* that she had imagined it.

"I need to know about the Misty Hills."

"Sire, I will gladly answer your questions," Madeleine said.
"My nursemaid told me many tales about the perils of the hills,
when I was small." She looked at him with wide eyes. "Many
young men laughed at them, being ready to show themselves
bold, but young men can be foolish—"

"There are paths in the Misty Hills."

"So there are," said Madeleine. As the king watched her, she
heard the pen scratching. She had forgotten the clerk. She did
not glance at him now. "Do you wish to know something
about those paths?"

"They're enchanted, aren't they?" For the first time, he
stepped from the window. A stride away, he studied her.

"Some are," said Madeleine slowly. She had told Nichola of
them. Earlier, she had told women at court. Whatever he
thought of women's folly, he might heed womanish gossip.
"On some of them, it takes much longer, or much shorter, to go
from one place to another."

"I need to know *all* about them."

Despite his soft voice, she flinched. "Some maids said that
walking on one would reveal to you your husband. But my
mother said it was superstition, and I was not even to learn
anything of these paths."

His hand slashed through the air.

Madeleine pitched her voice with care, to soft meekness.
"Sire, if you have questions, ask and I will gladly answer. But
the lords of the Misty Hills, who could answer you far more
rightly, are your subjects."

"Conceited knaves. Expecting *me* to obey their *servants*."

He spoke softly enough that Madeleine decided she could
pretend to have not heard. If he had defied his guide when in

the Misty Hills—she had not known how bad his judgment was. "There is much loyalty there." She sifted through history to pick her words. "The folk of the Misty Hills hid King Leod from his foes for many years."

She shut her mouth. They had hid him from the crowned king at a time when the laws of succession were less than clear.

The king glared. Perhaps he remembered his own comments about loyalty in King Adair's day. Madeleine felt the urge to babble, to break the silence. She pressed her lips together.

"I need to know the Misty Hills. You have doubtlessly visited many a place there."

"Fewer than you might think, Sire, and with an escort. Nowhere in the realm do maids of gentle blood travel without escorts." She widened her eyes. "I could tell you about the morning lilies, but I fear that would not interest you."

He scowled, half turning from her. "Morning lilies?"

"Flowers in Misty Hills grow up like mist in the morning— if you touch them, they dissolve like mist. An amusement for children, but not a fitting matter for a king."

His lip curled. "I need to know the lords there, and how many men-at-arms they have."

She could have laughed. There she could tell the truth. "The lords are enrolled in the rolls of honor, that much I know, but as for the men—no one would have bored me with such dreary matters." Her mouth twisted. John insisted, from time to time, but her father never did. She bit that down.

King Walter looked thoughtful. Madeleine shifted her weight, and he glanced at her. "You will stand here as long as I wish."

Madeleine curtseyed again. "An honor, Sire."

King Walter waved her off. Madeleine curtsied a last time and fled. She had not distracted him from his plans, whatever they were. She hurried down the stairs and almost wished that she and John were not returning to Summerfield. They would hear of the king's next blow sooner at Owlscourt.

Half way down, she leaned against the wall's cold stones, longing for the peace from before Lord Magnus's summons. Memories—riding through flowering meadows, lying before the blazing hearth in their room, laughing at antics of Sandy's—stirred until they roused nausea. Such moments might come in the future, but always and forever, she would remember that the king could strike at any minute.

She wished she could find John to weep on his shoulder.

Chapter 12—Departures and Questions

Madeleine angled across the courtyard, toward the chapel.

King Walter stormed down the stairs, and she cringed against the wall. Without glancing about, he called for squires. "I have a dozen messages to send. Within an hour."

Squires bowed. Madeleine wondered how she had inspired this; though he had not seemed angry when she had left, no one else had gone up the stairs since then. The king summoned another clerk. As he returned toward the stairs, he glanced past Madeleine as if she were not there.

A hand brushed her wrist. "Over here," whispered John. Madeleine let him draw her over. He put his arms about her. "What happened?"

Madeleine wrapped her arms about John and told him.

At his silence, she said, "I did not know what else to do. I could not deliver the Misty Hills into King Walter's hands."

John shook his head. "I would not deliver your father or your brother to the king's mercies, not if my life depended on it." His jaw clenched. "Or my brothers' lives."

A gust bore yellow leaves across the courtyard. The grooms readied horses for departing nobles—among them, Lord Fergus.

Madeleine crossed the courtyard.

He pitched his voice low. "Good morning, Lady Madeleine. It appears the king is reconciled with Lord Magnus."

"Good morning, Lord Fergus." She spoke as softly. "I fear that he has been distracted from Lord Magnus. He sent for me to ask of the Misty Hills."

Lord Fergus twitched. "The more fool he."

"He has visited them—at least once."

Lord Fergus's mouth tightened.

"You marked the messengers he sent. King Walter might notice if I sent my father a message. If you—" He had spoken of her father's regretting the estrangement; he must have spoken with her father. She looked imploringly at him.

He raised his voice. "Come, goddaughter, let us go into the chapel, out of the way."

She went before him. The dimness of the chapel engulfed her. Lord Fergus shut the door and glanced about, but no worshiper knelt at any altar. "What happened?"

She told him, shortly. "And that is all I know." After a moment, she added, "Little more than I told you in the courtyard, I fear."

He scowled. After a minute, he said, "You will leave soon?"

"For Summerfield. John is fetching Sandy even now."

"God grant that you enjoy peace there. If you do not, you can not come to me at court. I return to my lands. The king might remember Lady Gilliane's charges."

Madeleine grimaced. Only one man could be the favorite in Lady Gilliane's story—and having an affair with the queen *was* treason. And nothing required that he remain. The queen had no more need of wise councilors. "God grant that you enjoy peace at your lands."

Afternoon sunlight warmed the air as they rode over the hill and into Summerfield itself. After only a few days of journey,

they were home. An orchard stood ahead of them, on a
northerly slope. Peasants gathered fruit there.

"Apple!" shouted Sandy, from his perch before Madeleine
on the saddle. He looked hopefully at his father. "For b'fday."

John laughed at such cunning and dismounted. Gilliane
and Nichola, subdued, also pulled up their horses. Madeleine
considered the weather, the prospects of trouble ahead, and
whether she should tell John about the baby now, or as soon
she could get him away from Gilliane and Nichola.

Peasants gathered around John and implored news of Lord
Donald and Lord Andrew, and the king, and Lord Magnus.

Madeleine's heart sank. Not now, she thought.

In the evening, they arrived. Gilliane, her expression hollow,
dismounted before the groom took her horse's reins. Nichola
moved more slowly, staggering until a maid took her arm.
Madeleine waited for them to vanish into the great hall.

"Come inside," said John, holding Sandy. "It's cold."

"A moment," Madeleine said. She walked to the garden
gates. The rosebushes, lacking their flowers, still stood.

John looked over her shoulder. "You thought Nichola
might have had it done?"

"She sounded—" Madeleine let her breath out with a rush.
"That was when I knew they thought of you as dead." She
lowered her voice. "And I thought of you as dead, as well. I
had nothing to blame in them."

Sandy rubbed his eyes.

Another servant came through the door. "My lord? A
message—"

John stepped aside with him. They spoke in low and
hurried voices. Looking at the house, Madeleine stood in the
courtyard. Had Gilliane left a woman in charge of the

household? Even if she had—they had returned, and from the
way Gilliane had stalked off, she had not retrieved the keys.

John scowled and handed Madeleine Sandy. "I will have to
leave in the morning. Justice."

Madeleine nodded, but her heart sank. Gilliane had
complained that there had been too much work for two.

He kissed her, and they walked inside. The servants,
gathered in the great hall, watched them. Gilliane stood still.
From her expression, a servant had asked a question she had
not answered. Her gaze darted about as if seeking an escape.

Her gaze on the flagstones, Nichola wrung her hands.

The rumor could have reached Summerfield by now,
Madeleine thought, but the servants turned at their entrance,
and hope dawned on many faces. Madeleine's heart skipped a
beat. If the rumor spoke of the brothers—

"Lord Donald," said John, "and Lord Andrew have been
arrested by the king."

Anxious murmurs went through the hall. Nichola, with a
sob, fled. A maid glanced at Gilliane and hurried after Nichola,
and the others stirred.

Her face pale, Gilliane looked at John and Madeleine. As
the servants withdrew to their work, she said, "This is *your*
fault. You drew the king's eye to Summerfield."

John shifted his weight, Sandy looked at her with wide eyes,
but Gilliane glared as if she were entitled to a response.

Sandy leaned against Madeleine's shoulder, and Madeleine
said, "The traitor's wife and child?"

"Yes!"

"We were that before I went to court. What were you going
to do, before I ran off?"

Gilliane's expression contorted too rapidly for Madeleine to
read it. "How did you—" Then, with a ragged breath, she fled
after Nichola.

Now she knew: she had been right to fear. She could not triumph in the knowledge.

An aged woman caught at John's sleeve—Janet, Donald's old nurse. Her eyes were already wet. "Is there hope?"

"There is always hope," said John, but his voice held little.

Janet looked at Madeleine, her eyes pleading for a better answer.

"They—are only prisoner," Madeleine said. "The king has not threatened to try them for a crime."

John looked between them. "For now," he said, gently, "I will have to take Donald's place, in seeing to your care."

In the morning, Madeleine ate a solitary breakfast; John had left. A maid reported that Gilliane had yet to emerge from her chamber, and Nichola only asked for food.

Madeleine brought Sandy into the solar; the lighting was better for sewing than in her chambers. He plopped down by the window. Where the sun cast a square of light, he put his wooden knight to the floor. He put aside his green lion—but then, he had played with it for weeks. The knight he had not seen since she carried him from his bed, any more than she had seen the shirt she had worked on, and took up again.

Sandy's knight hopped over a hearthstone. ". . . the dragon goes hiss, hiss, hiss—go 'way, knight, 'cause I'm gonna *eat* this lion. . . ."

A gasp from the doorway startled Madeleine. Nichola's eyes were enormous. Madeleine's hand froze on her needle. It had not been long since Andrew's arrest, but Nichola might know if she was not with child.

Madeleine pitched her voice gently. "The solar is pleasant."

Nichola looked as if she expected Madeleine to seize her, and hurried off. Madeleine looked at her sewing. Gilliane was not there to disapprove. Then, Andrew might have told his wife why he had betrayed Donald as well as John. Her fingers tightened on the needle.

"Papa come?" Sandy stood by the window, his knight ignored in his hand. She hurried over.

A messenger, in Summerfield livery, dismounted in the courtyard. Her shoulders slumped. "No, Sandy, he won't." A messenger from him was message enough: he would be gone longer.

John's horse leapt ahead, through the bushes red with autumn. If the thieves got to the stream—he did not think that Lord Paidean would protest the intrusion into his lands, but catching them on his own lands would be better.

Panicky voices rose ahead, and John scowled. How foolish did they intend to be? His horse leapt from the trees, and John saw the three young fools, and the four cows they had stolen.

One thief reached for a spear.

John drew his sword and struck him down; he had left himself wide open. Blood spouted. The man, gaping, fell first to his knees, and then on his face, to lie there in a pool of red. The other two thieves looked too boggled to move.

John pointed the bloodied sword at the surviving thieves and shouted for his men. The thieves did not twitch.

The peasants burst from the trees and gabbled. Irritated, John turned away. "Bring the thieves to their punishment— and the dead one to his grave." He withdrew to clean his sword. The peasants converged, except one.

He pulled off his cap.

John gave him an annoyed glance.

"My lord? There's talk in the village, that young Maud was carried off five months ago by Harold."

"If someone brings the case before me, I will hear it and do justice," John said wearily.

Stubble filled the fields. Fergus thought the harvest had been abundant. "That is my brother's house," he said to his companion. Another day's journey would bring him to his own lands, and Lord Jockan had only a little farther to go. He had been lucky to meet him after returning from Candlebrook.

Lord Jockan glanced at the stables. "Looks like another guest."

Fergus followed his gaze. A stable boy led a single horse inside. The horse did not look familiar to him, but with only one, it was not a *great* guest. Though he and Lord Jockan— even with their attendants, even this far from rebellious Eastwyck and Owlscourt where the lords' absence had allowed lawlessness—had traveled together against bandits, a traveler had arrived alone, or brought only men-at-arms, afoot.

"Foolhardy," said Fergus.

Annette, drably dressed, met him at the doorway. Her mouth was pursed. She would not find a husband that way, he thought.

"A visitor came looking for you," she said.

"For me?" repeated Fergus, stupidly. Lord Jockan gave him a glance, and Annette looked impatient. He collected something of his wits. "I would have thought he would have come as a wooer."

Annette's smile contorted her lips. She greeted Lord Jockan and led them through the great hall to the great chamber. There her mother, Lady Dolina, entertained a dark young nobleman, who rose as they entered. Dolina presented him as Lord Malcolm. Lord Jockan started. Fergus hoped that he mastered his own reaction.

"I heard," said Lord Malcolm, looking at Fergus, "that you had something to do with Lord Magnus's pardon."

Fergus's heart sank. Lord Malcolm was not Lady Gilliane, but his words reminded him of her. "Favorably, I hope."

Lord Malcolm's smile was not pleasant. "Between the nobles who left court when they heard of the pardon, or after the festivities at Michaelmas, I have heard much of you, my lord."

Fergus nodded warily. Dolina gave orders for ale, but he did not glance at her. He had not lingered at Candlebrook for a return message. He wondered what Lord Thomas had heard, and thought.

In the great hall, autumn light flooded the crowd.

The woman before her was young, but the case was grave. On the dais, Madeleine sat in the chair, trying to ignore the empty seat beside her. At least Gilliane and Nichola both stayed in their chambers.

"Harold and Maud must appear before me," she said.

"She would never have agreed," said the woman, Maud's younger sister. Her voice came light and fast. "Never. He carried her off by force—"

"Nevertheless, they must appear," said Madeleine. She wondered if the woman's confidence was ignorance, or if this were an attempt to deny a dowry. Five months after the event, indeed. Donald or Andrew could have heard the case.

After a moment, the woman curtsied.

"Her family may come to court, and if the case goes against Harold, bear Maud home."

The woman's smile looked grateful. Madeleine felt how strained her own smile was. She could not say that she prayed that the delay would bring John home. If he returned, she could watch while John offered Maud the choice of a ring or a sword. Or she could sew in the solar; John's shirt was not done.

Trees towered to either side; red and gold were brilliant among the green, and beneath the gray of the lowering clouds. The clouds had darkened as they rode, John thought, but the forest gave way to pasture.

"The village," said a man-at-arms.

John looked. Harvest was in; few peasants moved about the fields. A young man, dressed in his finest, as if to go wooing, strode down a path. John looked away. The days in prison flooded back. Nobles, even traitors, were beheaded rather than hanged. Nevertheless, he thought that if the case were brought, and he ordered Harold's execution, he should watch it.

As he rode, and the men at arms walked, they saw more peasants. Old women spun by the thresholds, but few young ones; the children that ran about were small; only a handful of men gathered about the alehouse. But it did not look, except for the want of people, as if some plague had struck.

John pulled up his horse before the first cottage where a woman spun. She blinked with rheumy eyes. He tried to gentle his voice. "What had happened?"

"Gone to the manor, my lord." A small child scurried up, seizing her skirt, to stare at John from that shelter. "To hear the complaint."

"What complaint is that?"

She wound the thread. "They brought Lady Madeleine a complaint 'bout Harold and Maud."

The hearth fire was low, but still gave as much light as the open doors.

Madeleine sat rigidly, in the chair. Far more than the crowd of before—it seemed that half the village had come. Harold, tall and square-shouldered, helped a dispirited Maud stand before her. The loose dress could not conceal the swell of her belly. When her own child had not stirred—Madeleine tried to reckon. The baby could have been conceived after Harold carried Maud off. From the murmurs, Maud's kin had not known of her child—and, Madeleine reminded herself, carrying a child left some women dispirited.

"Here is my wife, the mother of my child." Harold's voice rang. "However they slander me."

"The law is clear," said Madeleine.

"You do not perform this once in a decade."

Such impudence, and she could only wonder why. "It is, however, done."

"How is my marriage alone called into doubt?"

"It has been," said Madeleine. "No doubt you are glad that the slanderers' tongues can be silenced."

"No lord offered *you*—"

Madeleine stiffened. Half a dozen men-at-arms put hands to sword hilts. Even Harold faltered to silence.

"Stand back from Maud."

When Harold looked to hesitate, a man-at-arms loomed over him. He pulled away; the man-at-arms shadowed him, and she noted him, to commend him to John. She took the sword and ring in hand. Some noises came from the courtyard, drawing peasants' glances, but Madeleine was too caught by the cold weight of the metal. She took the ring in her right, the sword in her left, and held both out to Maud.

Without a flicker in her expression, Maud took the sword. For a moment, she fumbled with the weight. Then she held it steadily, without meeting Madeleine's gaze.

Madeleine blinked, once, twice. Only the muttering stirred her.

Harold stiffened. All about, there were murmurs and sidelong glances. The sister looked radiant—but Harold found his voice again, however ugly it was.

"You wouldn't dare. . . ."

Her mouth was dry. "Men," said Madeleine, "seize him." Her heart hammered as she sat up straighter.

A figure appeared in the open door. The peasants were intent on her, but she kept her gaze steady, until John walked out of the sunlight, and ceased to be a shadow.

"What happens here?"

Starts spread through the crowd. Peasants scrambled from John's path. Harold did not stir. Neither did Maud—though her sister darted over to her. John walked toward the chairs.

"The matter was grave," said Madeleine, "we could not delay it—but you must hang this man."

John reached his seat and took it. Swiftly, she explained. John nodded. "Hang him, provide her dowry from his estate—" He glanced at Maud. "And provision for the child."

Harold huffed up. "No man offered *Lady Madeleine* the ring or the—"

"This Michaelmas, her godfather could have accused me before the king," said John, "but that he already knew what she would choose."

Madeleine smiled.

Mother would approve of the court at Darnien, finally, thought Katherine. Among the seated ladies-in-waiting, every head bent demurely over sewing, and every pair of lips was meekly shut, without gossip or foolish chatter. No lady-in-waiting even asked leave to play a lute, or to sing, though that might be permitted under her mother's watchful eye.

Her gaze went toward the window. When she first arrived, her Mistress of the Household had warned her of differences between the courts. She had heard women giggle over her since. This conformity to Elphshenian custom was not to please her—Lady Beatrix gave her sympathetic glances and doubtlessly thought herself bold for it—but, like the rest of the court, they had seen how rarely the king spoke to her and knew how reluctantly he visited her bed.

She supposed that she should inform King Walter that she thought she was with child.

The sky over the harbor was dark blue, dotted with stars. Katherine studied it. She had heard tales of foreign wizards. Her tongue touched her lips. The gossips fell silent about anything whenever they realized she could hear. The wizards might have nothing to do with her.

She looked at the cloth she was neglecting to sew. God in Heaven have mercy on them all, it meant ill ahead for someone.

A clamor in the corridor stirred all her ladies, like leaves on a pond when a stone was thrown in. Before the noise was clear, King Walter stood in the doorway. As the ladies leapt up to curtsey, Katherine laid aside her sewing for her own curtsey.

King Walter bowed and dismissed the ladies. They left like petals blown off a rosebush. Only when they had vanished down the hallway did he turn to face her. "Are you with child?"

Queen Katherine's heart jumped. A moment later, she said, "I believe so."

By firelight, Madeleine combed her hair. Horses clattered into the courtyard, and she went to the window. John dismounted. He must have settled Harold's estate, then. She glanced at the sky, where the sunset had darkened to crimson, and wondered how late he had left. She went on with her hair, more slowly, to wait.

She heard his footsteps soon; he must have only left his horse at the stable and climbed the stairs, but he walked slowly. Madeleine pulled on the comb awkwardly, trying to keep her gaze on the door without staring.

The door opened. John walked in, his head bent and his shoulders slumped.

"Dearling?" She lowered the comb.

"I'm tired," he said, without looking up. His mouth twitched. "I hanged a man. And you were not, indeed, offered your choice—"

Madeleine flinched. "I didn't—"

"That's what Harold said of Maud. And you are in my power." He met her gaze. "That woman—Maud—was five, six months gone with child. Even if she conceived the day he carried her off, Donald or Andrew could have done justice."

"Perhaps—word did not reach them."

John ran a hand over his face. "And what word is not reaching me?"

Madeleine rose to put her arms about him. Moments later, she could only suggest bed.

As he undressed, John said, with sudden savagery, "The king would never have dealt with such matters. Why do they—" He threw his clothing to the floor.

"On his progress," said Madeleine, "the king—rendered justice on peasants."

"And so every wise man fears that innocence won't save him, and every fool thinks he will receive mercy!" He crossed the floor toward their bed. "I do not want to think on it!"

Later, while John slumbered, she stroked back his hair from his face and tried to reckon how many months ago she would have delighted in this return to Summerfield. . . .

No, even with John's being alone to deal with troubles, the lands held more tumult than when she had left. He was right in thinking the king's whims spread throughout the land.

Her arms tightened about him. And she would not spare the tumult if it were the price of the pardon.

The wind sent scarlet leaves cascading over the rose bushes where all the leaves were brown. A horseman arrived, in the courtyard. Not John, of course.

Madeleine let her breath out. She thought she felt a wriggle, and swallowed. She should have told John about the baby when they left Owlscourt, or even after Harold's execution, any time when she had a chance to speak.

The messenger spoke to the groom who took his horse. When the groom answered, he scowled and spoke again. This time, the groom pointed to the garden.

Madeleine's hands clutched her skirt. Not an ordinary messenger—he did not wear livery, and his clothing was fine enough for a knight's. She tried to remember, and she had seen him at Owlscourt, in Lord Magnus's service. John had done much for Lord Magnus and *not* received the reward Lord Magnus promised him, or her. To be just—she squelched the thought that Lord Magnus had had no chance. For too long, she had not seen John. She did not *want* to be just.

The messenger came through the garden gate and bowed. "Lady Madeleine. Lord Magnus wishes you and your lord husband to come to Owlscourt. Lord Patrick awaits your visit."

Madeleine knew the breeze was cold but could barely feel it. "Lord Patrick? We have met him. . . ."

"Lord Magnus said—Lord Patrick was likely to come to Summerfield if you did not come to Owlscourt."

The wind sent leaves tumbling past her, and tugged at her skirt. "I fear my husband is busy about the estate. Between the king's visit, and his brothers' absence, there is much to be done."

The man inclined his head. "His lordship sent me to act as your steward."

That much haste? thought Madeleine. "I will send a messenger."

Chilly rain and yellow leaves hit them even beneath the gate, blown in by the stiff breeze. Sandy, rosy-cheeked, looked out with eagerness.

John eyed the clouds. "What a charming day. The only blessing is, no one wants to go to war in this weather."

The evening before, the trees had held most of their leaves. Now, all but a few leaves formed a golden and scarlet carpet. Madeleine let out a long breath. "John, with all the last weeks, I have not found a better time. . . ."

John raised an eyebrow.

"I'm with child again."

After a moment, he grinned. "We made Sandy when we were fleeing your father and sleeping in haystacks. Perhaps we should have tumbled in the woods more often."

She could not return the grin for long. Another baby would be another to face the king's wrath—which gave them more reason to stay in Lord Patrick's favor.

Sandy babbled about the leaves, trying to snatch them whenever the wind blew them close enough.

The roads were not good, and John would not ride hard. Though the journey only took three days, they reached Owlscourt by evening, with Sandy already asleep before his father.

Lord Magnus came to the courtyard to greet them. Even by the evening light, he looked haggard. As the grooms led the horses away, and a maid took Sandy, he said, "My lady, did anyone tell Lord Patrick that you came from the Misty Hills?"

"No. . . I do not think so," said Madeleine.

Lord Magnus grunted.

"My lord," said John, "is Lord Patrick waiting on us?" He sounded more weary than their journey would explain.

"He is. This is all the private speech we shall have until he is satisfied."

Madeleine felt as tired as John. "It is known that I come from the Hills. The rumors flew for months after we ran off."

"Lord Patrick asked," said Lord Magnus. "Come inside."

"So there are marvels in the woods indeed?" said Lord Patrick. "Not just legends?"

"My lord," said Madeleine, "the mists never fail. Once you were within the hills, a charm might reveal the sun for a moment, but no more."

She was glad that Sandy, ensconced in the nursery, could not babble his account.

Lord Patrick snorted. "Mists destroy nothing. I have heard of *monsters*."

"Dragons?" said Madeleine. "Pools that drive to madness? Monsters that form out of the mists to attack and vanish when the traveler defends against them? Paths that lead through the Hills in a day—or never end?" She paused. Lord Patrick did not look ready to disclaim them as fairy tales. Sourly, she wondered what he had already heard. "They're all true."

"The king talks of using such marvels, since men have failed him," said Lord Patrick.

Madeleine felt bewildered and afraid.

"He confers with foreign wizards about the hills." He lifted a wine cup. "While he was at Owlscourt, he sent messengers for them. Now the court teems."

"I do not think that *foreign* wizards are likely to be much aid." She could not keep the pride from her voice. From time to time, a wizard would think the Misty Hills were a bird for plucking. Some had escaped with their lives; one or two, with even their wits.

He looked over the cup. "The rumor speaks of a wizard called Morgan."

"I know little of wizards," said Madeleine, but—from time to time, folk did leave the hills. Wishing to be a wizard might be one reason.

Morgan was a common name there. She jerked her gaze back to Lord Patrick. He looked smug.

The meal on top of the journey had left her weary to the bone, but Lord Magnus brought them both to his lodgings. They came. The talk might be needful. Madeleine settled in the chair. And—she could not have slept.

"The Misty Hills," said Lord Magnus.

"I could ask," said Madeleine, slowly. "In Candlebrook—I would meet Lord Fergus's escort there, to go to court. I was known there. It's not *in* the hills."

John came up to her. Firelight made his face as gold as his hair, and his hands fastened on the back of her chair. "We will soon know what the king plans: when he does it. Even if you learn of a runaway named Morgan who wished to be a wizard, you could not learn what the king plans—or how to foil it."

"We could learn enough to warrant an eye on the Misty Hills," said Lord Magnus.

John inclined his head. Madeleine realized that no service Lord Magnus asked of him would be refused, after having fallen so early in the fray when they were captured. She swallowed.

Lord Magnus pondered the fire. "Many a lord might aid me. Perhaps even lords of the Misty Hills." He shifted in his chair. "Such as—Lord Thomas of Candlewood?"

"He might," said Madeleine. The clarity of her voice surprised her. She looked at the fire. If she fell silent now, she would never speak. "We had best leave at once, if we wish to return before snowfall." The chance was small that snow would fall, or be enough to block their way, but it was not her place to decide. If he deemed it not worth the risk—she would not have to speak with her father.

"In the morning," said Lord Magnus. She could not make out his eyes in the shadows the fire cast. The flames snapped, and a log settled, deeper in the ashes.

"Lady Elspeth will be honored to take Sandy in her care while we go," said Lord Magnus.

Madeleine said nothing. Bad enough to have hauled Sandy across the land, in quest for the pardon. With winter drawing near, for him to remain safe and warm was good.

"And I have looked for other things while administering justice. Nobles disobeyed my call."

John nodded.

"Lady Gilliane has kin in Lord Peter's lands. All the lords who disobeyed had kin there, by blood or marriage."

Madeleine sighed and looked into the orange flames. Neither she nor Lord Magnus could do anything about that. Perhaps they could do something about the Misty Hills.

Mists, gray with evening, wound about the leafless trees, the stubble on the fields, the gate ahead of her, and the peasant leaning on it; a handful of lights like candle flames floated in it, barely visible with the evening. She knew that mist, she had seen it for many years. Even with the lights, she could talk. No one trusted Angus with secrets, but he had stayed in Candlebrook while she lived far from the hills.

"A dire thing, my lady." Old Angus shook his head. "Young Morgan was always a fool. Came from Gryston. There was chatter enough when he ran away."

Madeleine's stomach felt as if she had swallowed ice. Gryston lay in the heart of the Misty Hills. Morgan would know everything.

"And he's doing *something* fer the king. There's a tower in the hills."

Madeleine scowled. What good was a tower that could not watch? Why would anyone build one? Then she remembered. She had even seen that tower once; Jasper had showed her.

"No one has ever gotten close enough to lay a hand on it." Her voice was thin, and she could not strengthen it. "My nurse said it was a glamour, to lead a wicked man astray."

"Our Morgan has laid hand on it, and more. They brought in—things. Food. Blankets. Candles by the ream. But no swords or spears or arrows—they have magic for that." Angus grinned, like a gargoyle. "Not finding it as easy as he likes."

But, hard or easy, he was succeeding, thought Madeleine.

"Cussing about the candles." He waved his hand at the gleams about them. "Don't like them one bit."

She quietly thanked him and wandered along the cottage-lined road. To lead wicked men astray—her nurse had been right. The cold had come early, all the cottages' garden plants had turned dead and brown, she might have been right about the snow, but Lord Magnus decided rightly. They could learn what the king was about: imprisoning someone in the Misty Hills.

"Madeleine," said John gravely, from between two buildings. A chicken squawked its outrage as he emerged.

"John." Madeleine paused until he came close enough. "Lord Magnus should not remain here. The stories are all the same—and if the king wishes to imprison someone securely, the most likely victim is neither you nor me."

She could not read his face. Desperately, she wished she could.

"I doubt it's Andrew or Donald," said John.

Even if it were—they could do nothing for either of his brothers, now. Madeleine put her arms about him. "You must help me persuade Lord Magnus to leave here. He is in danger."

John laid a hand to her face—warmer than his mantle. A smile teased his mouth. "If Lord Magnus wastes the effort you spent in rescuing him, I shall begrudge him that."

A ghostly candle flame flitted across the road.

A low fire shone on the inn's upper room. The windows were closed against the chill and the candles, and the solid oak door was shut, but none of them spoke above whispers.

Lord Magnus sat by the fire. The shadow his chair cast covered half the room. "How did you send word to your father of Sandy's birth?"

"I sent a message to this inn." Madeleine huddled in her mantle. "Told the innkeeper to hold it for him, or for Jasper. My brother."

"We will leave such a message—and go." He looked into the fire. "I have to deliver the tax money to the court within a month—or send a deputy of noble birth." His voice was slow but resolute. "John. Of all the men under me, you are the one who knows the most about these affairs."

Madeleine closed her eyes. A forlorn thought managed to hope that John would return before the snow grew severe; then, ordinary sense forced her eyes open again.

"An honor to do this service for you, my lord," said John. His voice was neutral, but his expression was not.

Your overlord is blessed with you, for your loyalty and service, thought Madeleine.

Chapter 13—Taxes and News

The sun was brilliant, but a chilly wind came down the streets. It blew past the gates behind the castle, where the taxes were delivered and stowed away. John stamped his feet. At that, the day had grown warmer since dawn.

"Lord John, anything more?"

John glanced at Lord Magnus's men. "Be at the gate at dawn."

The dozen men bobbed their heads; most dispersed to the taverns; two led the mules toward the inn. He let his breath out. Their task was done, but he had to pay his respects to a dozen lords at court. Only by leaving tomorrow could he avoid having to attend the king and queen. He headed around the castle. The streets seemed to hold fewer people than whenever he had been at court, though it had not felt that way when they delivered the gold.

At the gate, he scowled. The courtyard lacked the usual bustle. A dozen servants hurrying through, half a dozen glittering lords and ladies, and a handful of guards did not leave the courtyard empty, but he had seen more people there when he arrived in the gray dawn, after a great festivity had kept everyone up late. Cold or not, it was noon. He did not think winter could bring this decrease.

He walked through the gates. Then, he had never been to court in the wintertime before. A lady said something to a lord, and both darted indoors. He could not take that door; he walked on, toward the doors by the great hall. The greater lords would lodge nearer the royal presence, and he had to attend to precedence—start with Lord Gavin of Hawkehill.

"Who knows why the queen is so dreary?" said a fine lady. Her voice rang across the courtyard. "It can't be because the king is angry with her. It relieves her of his presence."

"Perhaps she's increasing," said another lady, hopefully.

"With all these wizards about?" said a lord. John stopped at the doorway, in the shadow. That comment made no sense, even when the lord went on to say, "They're here for the queen."

"Nonsense," said a lady, shrewishly. "They fetch a spell of fruitfulness from the Misty Hills. Once they get it, *then* we can speak of whether she is increasing."

You are eavesdropping, John told himself. He walked inside.

Perhaps the vacant courtyard had been the weather. Candles and lamps kept the crowded corridors bright. Except for the servants, few walked quickly. Courtiers glittered and filled the air with their gossip and the scent of perfume.

"Really," said one lady, "Phillip should not have roughed up those men." She waved her fan. "Just because they carried out the king's orders."

"But, my lady, they *were* in the king's service," said another woman, her red mouth set in hard lines. "They knew what their orders were likely to be."

John's mouth hardened as he edged his way past that clump. Just what they needed: offending the already capricious king.

"And now," said the first lady, "his father has lost lands. He could have lost them all—"

John let his breath out and walked on.

"No, no, no," said a shrill voice. "The king wants the treasure in the Misty Hill to hire mercenaries. Why would he care about the roads?"

"To send his men over the roads," said another.

John could not pick out either speaker in the crowd, but that hardly mattered when the rumors were so wild.

The antechamber was not crowded, but the servant ushered him to the inner chamber. There, Lord Gavin sat alone, with a cup by his side. John bowed, and Lord Gavin nodded to the servant, who poured mulled wine for him.

The honor, John reminded himself, was for the name he had come in, not himself; he need not look for ulterior motives.

The servant handed the cup to John, who sipped it gratefully. Even the corridors had not completely warmed him.

"Have you heard anything in Owlscourt considering the West Dales—and Lord Duncan's defiance?" said Lord Gavin.

John shook his head. "Beyond that he demanded a safe conduct? That we knew at Michaelmas."

Lord Gavin mused, "Lord Duncan still remembers when the West Dales were another realm, I fear." He drank some wine. "Had you heard about the queen, back in Owlscourt?"

"No, my lord." His heart seemed to pound, not faster, but harder. "The last news of court to reach us was when the king came." He lowered the cup.

"She is under arrest," said Lord Gavin.

John started. The wine sloshed in the cup.

"Whatever is said, she is. Her chambers are guarded, and she never leaves—not even for Mass."

"Perhaps she is ill?"

Lord Gavin snorted. "She has been seen at the window. She looks better than she did at Midsummer—not this year's, the last's—when she *was* ill. King Walter insisted that she attend the festivities." He sat back. "Besides, he plans to send Queen Katherine off, under guard. No one knows where."

John felt chilled. When he left, he could not stop for any snow. "Has he consulted with a foreign wizard, by the name of Morgan?"

"How did you know about that?" After a moment, Lord Gavin scowled. "And what does it matter?"

Keeping that secret would benefit no one except the king. "Using magic, King Walter is preparing a prison in the Misty Hills."

For a long moment, Lord Gavin contemplated the wine within his cup. John shifted his weight, keenly aware of how long he had traveled. First to Candlebrook, then back to Owlscourt, then to court. . . . Lord Gavin gestured him to a chair. "Sit, sit."

John sat.

Lord Gavin lowered his cup. "Rumors say the queen is with child. God grant that she is. Even if the king repudiated her— and the bishops would not allow it—who would he marry? No king would let his daughter wed him. And—you have noticed how thin the court is?"

"Some," said John. "I have never been here in winter."

Lord Gavin's voice came fast and low. "Nobles are sending their marriageable daughters away. Some even say so. Not just the great noblemen, either—even the petty ones, when such a marriage would insult every great noble in the land. The king will want a new queen if he puts away Queen Katherine, but no woman wishes to be her." His voice deepened. "If he sends the queen to the Misty Hills, that would explain the rumors of a dragon."

John drained his cup. Rumors, rumors, rumors. He put the cup on the table. Then, Madeleine had told Lord Patrick that those of dragons were true.

Long after the service was over in the dark chapel, Magnus
knelt before the altar. All Souls'. He had done little enough for
the men who had died in his service. He heard muttering
behind him about how long he had been there, but he did not
stir, and the people left.

The few candles still lit barely illuminated the crucifix.

Magnus bent his head over his hands, praying for the souls
of the dead, praying that John's duty at court would go well,
that he would have no more men to pray for this time next
year.

Then, if John did his duty well and returned with news that
there was no escape from King Walter? No escape from
treason?

Magnus closed his eyes and prayed for the strength to do his
duty. And for John's safe return, so that he might know what
his duty would be.

Queen Katherine sat by the window. The early morning
courtyard held a confluence of courtiers. They already grew
drabber than summertime, as mantles covered their court
finery, but she did not sit for the view. If she remained still
enough, the ladies sometimes forgot her presence and repeated
stories. Her tutors had never instructed her in the need to be
more quiet than a mouse, but in the next chamber, women
arranged clothing and chattered, and necessity instructed well.

"Lord Magnus had to send *someone*. How else could his
taxes arrive?" said one woman. "How many men does he have?
He was likely to send someone who had been arrested."

"Lady Madeleine's husband," said another, older voice—
Lachina, Katherine guessed. "Lord John of Summerfield was
not merely a prisoner—and is no fool. He leaves within an
hour."

Queen Katherine's gaze went over the courtyard. A fair-haired man emerged from the castle, to meet a company of men-at-arms. Their colors were unmistakable: Lord Magnus's men. She turned her attention back to the nobleman. Young. Handsome. She would not have noticed him among a crowd of courtiers, but Lady Madeleine had.

The groom held Lord John's horse, and he mounted.

Go back to Lady Madeleine, she thought. Make her happy. May God grant that you twain live to see your children's children. Her fingers bit the window frame. I do not wish that my sacrifice be in vain.

Lord John surveyed the castle's windows. His face was grim. Then he led his company out.

"Oh," she whispered, "oh, that I had wings like a dove; I would fly away and be at rest." Her mouth trembled. For it was not an enemy that reproached me, that I could bear; neither was it he who hated me that did magnify himself against me; then I would haven hidden myself from him, but it was you, my equal, my guide, and my comrade. We took sweet counsel together, and walked to the house of God in company.

She turned from the window, not to listen more closely to the women, but to find the priedieu, and kneel.

"Wise of him to wait until her third month," said Lady Elspeth. Her voice was brittle. "It lessens the risk of her miscarrying. And his only heir—he must take care."

Madeleine's hand touched her waist. She was beginning to show; the queen would not, not yet.

The baby wiggled, and her mouth tightened.

John stood before the fire. He had shed his mantle, but the snowflakes in his hair had only started to melt. "She might be safer there. The king has raged, every now and again, about her folly. He has not struck her, but servants have gone about with bruises. In the Misty Hills, the queen and the babe will be out of easy reach."

As if the Misty Hills were harmless in themselves.

"This is my fault," said Madeleine.

Silence followed for a minute. A log shifted in the fire, sending a ribbon of orange sparks crackling up the chimney.

John said, "The queen chose to grant the pardon."

"The king thought she was a fool before," said Madeleine. "He had told her so. He left power in the hands of the ministers, because he thought her understanding weak."

All of them looked at her.

"She told me that, at great length, when explaining to me that she could not grant a pardon. I proposed to her that she grant it. When the king complained, she could tell him that she did not understand that he did not want it. This is my fault."

She looked away, out the window. Against the pale gray of the sky, snowflakes were dark specks. They did not fall thickly, but after falling for hours, they showed no signs of ending. John had had to come through them, bearing the news.

She let out her breath slowly.

"The queen," said Lord Magnus, "is a woman of excellent understanding. She granted the pardon to preserve the peace in the land. There are always risks in such acts."

"There are more risks in what the king does," said Madeleine. "And most in the land thought there was nothing to be done for *you*, my lord."

"There was little that could be." About his mouth, the lines were deep groves.

Madeleine looked at him. Her mouth set in mulish lines; she did not will it, but she could feel her mouth setting and did not resist.

Lady Elspeth took a stitch. "What, Lady Madeleine, would you have done differently if you had know what would happen to the Queen's Grace?"

Her voice was light, as if indifferent, but Madeleine turned her face away in despair. She could have done nothing else. John laid a hand to her arm.

Lord Magnus said, "A rescue by force—Lord David would have had to kill us all, but you rescued us by stealth."

By law, thought Madeleine, drearily.

"If King Walter imprisons Queen Katherine in the Misty Hills, we may see what stealth can do."

Madeleine let her breath out. Lord Magnus knew that he proposed rebellion, that at Michaelmas, only the number of nobles who would have witnessed it had saved him. But—the king's folly might destroy the land.

Lord Magnus looked at John. "Your lady wife's knowledge of the Misty Hills may be needed. If the queen must be taken away, we can hardly do so without a woman to attend her."

John met his gaze. "My wife is also with child."

"The rescue must do no more than a breeding woman may endure, or it will be no rescue."

John inclined his head. "A true knight will rescue ladies from peril."

Trees stood darkly about them. The thick mists, more gray than white, added little brightness to the scene. Queen Katherine studied the narrow track; that was better than seeking monsters in every coil of mist. She had seen rabbits that had not fled into the woods, but merely vanished as the company approached.

She swallowed. Even not looking up—King Walter had intimidated that he had a destination prepared for her, but she had heard tales of the Misty Hills before this.

Earlier on the way, people had come to stare. They had stayed many strides from the company and not even muttered. Here, even they had vanished. Then, she told herself, she had seen neither flocks nor fields for some time.

A bird called, and Lady Osla jumped.

"Just a bird," said Queen Katherine. Her voice was queenly, even now. Her tutors would be proud.

Lady Osla cast her a mortified glance and turned her attention back to the road. Katherine let her breath out. Her ladies-in-waiting grumbled about missing the gossip of court.

They were not thinking ahead. They would miss more than that. Katherine fixed her gaze on the dirt on the path. Her tutors had instructed her on thinking ahead. At the moment, it seemed only an added torment. Her escort would be as unmoved by her agony as by her regal bearing.

Young Lady Grainna whispered, spitefully, "We're bringing her to a prison and she still plays the queen."

Katherine suppressed a smile. King Walter could not uncrown her.

He could, however, strip her of her attendants. All impulse to smile faded. They were gently bred ladies. Their families would resent their imprisonment. The ladies might resent dismissal to their homes, away from both the pleasures of court and its young bachelors, but whatever happened, no one would heed them, and they would be ladies-in-waiting no more.

None of them seemed to have realized that yet.

The road opened out into a meadow. At the far end of it, a tower stood: a plain gray tower with a single door and a single window visible. Mists wreathed it. About her, the men's shoulders slumped in relief.

Katherine contemplated it. That tower could not hold her, and all the women attending her. She let out her breath.

A man came to hand her down. She was a queen, and the daughter of a king and a queen. She would show them how a queen acted when persecuted.

Lady Osla and the others started to dismount. The captain of the men-at-arms shook his head. Startled protests rose about her.

"The Queen's Grace can not be unattended!" said Lady Lachina.

Katherine smiled sadly. The King's Grace will know that I have been chaperoned to this tower. All the ladies looked shocked, but did not attempt to dismount. Lady Beatrix started to cry.

Katherine looked at the plain gray stone. The king did not think that ordinary means sufficed to contain her.

The door opened, as silent as the mists about it. A man emerged. He wore dark gray wizard's robes, set with sigils in dark red; Katherine could not be sure that those sigils were embroidered in. The robe swept the grass as he come toward them. The captain addressed him as Morgan, and she drew a deep breath.

Morgan bowed at her. Young for a wizard, but his eyes were dark and fathomless. "You must know the magic of the tower, and how you can live here."

Her head held high, Queen Katherine permitted him to show her the kitchens. No wood lay by the stove, but it heated when certain things were done. Morgan was as impeccably smooth as any of her tutors, but despite the lesson, Queen Katherine was glad that a queen had to know how to cook, in order that she might see to the kitchens' being properly run.

And then Morgan left the kitchen. Queen Katherine followed him to the hallway. He withdrew from the tower, the door closed, and the key turned in the lock.

She watched the door for a long time.

I carry the royal heir, she thought. He can not mean to leave me here forever. Her hands clenched into fists. If I were to bear a child unattended, even if the babe and I survived, no witness could swear that some peasant's brat was not stolen from the cradle.

She felt a movement in her belly. She swallowed, wondering if it was, indeed, the child, and turned. Behind her, the stairway coiled up the tower.

Slowly, Katherine climbed it. She had seen windows, high on the tower. Would watching the company go only increase her misery?

She found an upper chamber. A bed lay before her; beside it, there were books, and a lute, and cloth, enough to make the baby's clothing. She would only go mad for the want of company, not for the want of anything to do.

She looked out the window. Her ladies-in-waiting were being shepherded away. They looked stunned, and then they vanished into the mists. They would have to return to their families. Katherine put her hand to the stone of the window's frame. There were worse fates. Their parents might fitly praise God for their daughters' safety—and the escort vanished into the mists as well, except for a few men-at-arms, who lingered by the wood's edge.

The wizard Morgan still stood in the meadow. His gaze went over the tower, past the window, and he smirked. She tilted her face away. Yes, you have me captive; I can not escape from here; I have no magic to pick locks. But she could not bring herself to look away entirely.

Morgan's hands moved. Something took shape in the air before him. Katherine's mouth went dry. After a minute, she could make out a leg, covered with scales, and then a broad shoulder. Slowly, a head rose out the misty form—an enormous head. A mouth gaped wide enough to swallow her whole, with teeth larger than swords. Two enormous eyes peered about.

A dragon shifted in the meadow.

Katherine tore herself from the window before she died of fright. Her heart hammered like a drum. After a minute, she managed to think that her mother had not told her how a queen behaved when guarded by a dragon, but that witticism did nothing to calm her. With a moan, she collapsed on the bed, unable to think, unable to pray, unable to stir.

When she finally arose, the light from the window showed that evening was near. The mist lay thick in the air. The dragon coiled about the tower. Its eyes were closed, but then an eyelid twitched. An eye, as deep as a pool and as easy to drown in, looked at her.

She looked away. Fortunate Lord Magnus, who had only execution to face.

As stiff as a wooden doll, Lady Osla walked through the queen's chambers. If someone noticed her here, the king might remember the queen's ladies-in-waiting and pack them off to their parents.

She glanced at the wardrobe; it still held Queen Katherine's gowns. She shivered. They might be safer at their parents' homes. Or—Lord Alistair had been attentive over the music last night, and Sir Tomas, the day before in the garden. Neither one was a *grand* match, but the court had grown so money-grubbing that among the great, a fair face might win a seduction, but never a marriage. Either man was grander than anything she could find once rusticated; Lady Beatrix would regret her loyalty now. Osla retrieved her sewing and left quickly. She would not find either man in the queen's chambers.

"My lady!" The man who shouted ran up to her, panting, and she recognized a servant's clothing. "My lady, the queen's ladies-in-waiting. . . ." He looked about.

"Sir," said Osla, "tender maidens keep to our chambers when not required. Of a certainty, you would not be admitted there."

The man colored. "You are needed."

Osla raised an eyebrow. No servant could order her about, but she did not know who had sent him.

"An ambassador wishes to speak with you."

Her heart sank. No man she wished to speak with, and then she felt bitterly cold. "An ambassador from—Elphshen?"

The servant nodded. Osla imagined King Walter's reaction if she spoke to this ambassador and shook her head.

"But, my lady—"

Osla tried to walk away. The man stepped between her and the door. A servant! She raised her hand to slap him.

"My lady, he speaks of *war*—and only a lady-in-waiting can assure him that the queen is well and healthy."

Then he will ask how we last saw her, and pry until he learns of the dragon. . . . "Sir, if you imagine that I will speak with a strange man alone—to spread gossip about my good mistress, no less—you mistake me entirely!"

She stormed off, but flight down the dark corridor did not let her flee her thoughts. The ambassador would sneak about until he spoke with some lady-in-waiting. The king would hear of it. She would be sent off with the rest—guilty and innocent alike—with no more ado than if they had let themselves be seduced.

After all the offenses she had seen, where the courtiers had been permitted to remain at court!

She fled to the privacy of the cold garden to weep.

The evening darkened. Lord Magnus's men filled his great chamber. A council of war, Madeleine thought. Lord Magnus paced as if he were the only one there. The knights pulled back to give him room and muttered among themselves.

Madeleine looked at the hands she kept folded in her lap.

"Alone, unattended—her father could declare war for this!" Lord Magnus slammed his hand against the wall.

Madeleine flinched. But to rescue the queen—however capricious King Walter was, he would respond to that.

"She could miscarry. She could die in childbirth. And there would be no witness to the child's birth. The last thing the land needs is rumors that the babe King Walter presents as hers is some farmer's brat." He turned from the wall to glare as if they were all guilty. "There is not even a man acknowledged as the king's heir, should the babe not inherit."

"Is there any way to determine King Walter's heir?" said Lady Elspeth, dryly.

Lord Magnus drew a ragged breath. "War, once he dies."

John snorted, though he looked pale. "What is to be done?"

"Get her out," said Lord Magnus. "From that tower and to safety. There is no choice."

"That *would* be treason," said a knight.

"And war," said another.

"If we attacked the king's men, yes," said Lord Magnus. "But he has sent no men to the Misty Hills to guard the queen. The king must have set magical wards."

Queen Katherine had saved her husband. She had to save the queen. "A dragon," said Madeleine. What else had her carefully evasive words betrayed to King Walter? From the corner of her eye, she saw others looking at her, but she was intent on her memory. "He spoke of a dragon, and there are dragons in the Misty Hills." She glanced over the knights. Many looked away. "I can not bring many men safely through the Misty Hills."

A knight's eyebrows drew together. "You don't want to give their secrets away."

"I would have brought my lord husband and Lord Magnus back through the Misty Hills if I could have," said Madeleine. "Do you think I wanted to spend a fortnight walking from the tower?"

She turned to Lord Magnus. "I will need gold." She hoped that Morgan's magic meant that anyone could reach the tower, and not just the master of the spell, or they would need a miracle. Bad enough that the dragon had to be faced; that, she could master with enough gold.

"The king must have food brought there," she said.

"He made arrangements," said Lord Magnus, "but the folk of the Misty Hills do not talk of them."

"They will be furious," said Madeleine. "They might help secretly. The Mists hide much."

They might help—once she told them what Lord Magnus, another outsider, had planned. Just as Morgan had put the king's plans in place. Pleading for the aid would not be pleasant.

"Whom should I send with you?" mused Lord Magnus. "Besides Lord John."

John bowed. Madeleine glanced over. It would be improper to send her and not him, and from the set look on John's face, he still believed he must avenge his honor.

Madeleine opened her mouth and shut it again, and then wrenched her thoughts away. She could not protect many, but breaking into the tower might require force, and they might meet the king's men. Her teeth closed on her lower lip.

She looked out the window. The clouds were darkening, more with advancing evening than from thickening. But that in itself showed that winter was coming, and time was short.

"Whomever you send," she said, "we must go afoot. Horses from outside do not take to the Misty Hills."

"I could send men to bring the horses back, once you were within the hills," said Lord Magnus.

"That would draw attention. Once he hears, the king could send men to guard the queen—far more men than I could bring through the hills."

The great hall held nobles who strove to play dice, or sing, or chatter, as if all was normal. Alun surveyed them until he picked Beatrix out.

She looked frail and worn. Alun's indignation mounted. Queen Katherine could have dismissed her ladies-in-waiting when King Walter imprisoned her.

Her eyes grew large as he approached, but when he took her hand, she rose. Alun drew her off, out of the hearing of the hall. "Whom do you have to ask for leave to marry, now?"

Beatrix paled, and Alun felt exasperated. Languishing about the court was no help to the queen. Her parents had not sent her to court to frighten off wooers. And had he not been a faithful lover for four years?

"I've—" she whispered, "—been afraid to ask."

Before, he had ignored the fear in the chamber, lurking in the nervous chatter, but her words had made that impossible.

Beatrix managed a feeble smile. "Some are afraid that we *all* will be sent away if King Walter realizes that her ladies-in-waiting are still about."

"If you left to marry," said Alun, "one day a child of yours might serve the queen's child." The thought clearly pleased her, and he reckoned for himself whom she must ask.

The trees were so thick that despite the loss of their leaves, they blocked the view with tangles of trunk and branches. Somerled leaned forward as the village came into view. A petty place, but the royal banner flapped over an alehouse.

He kicked his horse's sides. With a snort, it jogged forward. The villagers might be glad to be rid of the king. It might benefit the queen if the king were distracted, though that was no business of his. A royal messenger never thought about royal concerns—except to reason where the king stayed.

As he rode down the village's road, the guard's hail came swiftly. He answered. Minutes later, a royal minister appeared by the alehouse doorway to beckon like a servant. Somerled followed him to the king.

King Walter, seated at a table, looked up. Somerled proffered the message.

Without reaching for it, the king said, "Do you know what this contains, good man?"

"News, sire, of treachery." When the king did not stir, he added, "In Darfeld." The king continued to stare. Somerled uneasily remembered Benneit's death and how the Eastwyck rebels had been put down.

The king—finally—took the letter and called for his ministers. Somerled bowed and retreated. If he had lingered, the king might have reached for a coin, but he felt no impulse to remain. The king's voice rose within, calling out orders about soldiers and supplies.

Two ministers emerged, talking. "It's good to—you, you're the messenger. The King's Grace will have you accompany him until he needs you for a message."

Only a few more days, thought Madeleine. Sandy slept, snuggled beneath the blankets, with his knight and green lion.

Even on the muddy road, the hoof beats were audible. Madeleine rose from the bedside. A messenger dismounted in the courtyard—at this hour. Madeleine fastened the shutter against drafts and hurried toward the courtyard.

Lord Magnus descended the stairs ahead of her; he looked back and gestured toward his chambers. Madeleine curtseyed and fled back up the stairs.

Sewing by the fire, Lady Elspeth looked up. Madeleine had time only to mention a messenger when the door opened. Lord Magnus entered, with John on his heels.

"Another revolt," said Lord Magnus. "Lord Oliver has declared himself king." A smile twisted his mouth. "The king is not the only member of the royal family to suffer caprices."

Lord Oliver, thought Madeleine, was even further from King Walter than Lord Patrick was—and there was reason to doubt the legitimacy of his descent.

"The king," said Lord Magnus, "has set out to put down the revolt. It seems the lords about Lord Oliver are rising to help the king—and the king has yet to complain."

Lady Elspeth said, "Has he made a claim beside his blood?"

"Injustice. A cousin of his complained to the king of how her guardian abused her wardship. The King's Grace dispossessed her for disloyalty."

Madeleine winced. But—the revolt would distract the king for only a short time. Lord Oliver could not have that much support.

"We must move in the morning," she said. It would be before Sandy awoke, she thought, and shivered.

Chapter 14—Paths and Wolves

Beneath the mist, feathers of ice spread over the pool's dark water. Pines stood beyond, and Madeleine's breath was white on the air before her. She remembered how long she had hunted for the path during the summer and let her breath out in a sigh.

She pulled her mantle closer, against the wind. The brush will have died back, she told herself; the path will be easier to see. "I left the road a little ahead of this."

The other two men Lord Magnus had sent, Sir Bernard and Sir Henry, watched her.

John surveyed the hillside. "Isn't this the path we came out?"

Madeleine nodded. Winter had changed it from then. "If you see anything. . . ." She walked on. The frozen ground was hard underfoot, but the pines blocked out the worst of the wind. She remembered: the stream did not emerge from the woods either. She wondered what happened to it, if it, like the enchanted paths, flowed endlessly and reached nowhere—she strained her ears.

"How far do we have to go to find this path?" said Sir Bernard, sounding less disgruntled than exhausted.

"Not far," said John.

"Shush," said Madeleine, almost before she realized she had heard something. When Sir Bernard muttered, she glared at him. The faint sound might not be the stream, but she could not be sure, either way. "Follow me." She gathered her skirts to get a better view of her footing, and climbed.

The forest floor was even lumpier than the road, and the leaves were slippery from melting frost. Mist wreathed in long tendrils over equally intricate roots. She walked with care, and stepped on roots where she could, to keep her footing. Once, she slid, and John leapt to grab her even before she knew she was falling.

Both Sir Henry and Sir Bernard walked behind them. "All this and a dragon afterward," said Sir Henry. "Never heard of anyone who's even *seen* a dragon."

"I have," said Madeleine. "A dragon came up to where Sandy and I slept, one night in the Misty Hills."

John flinched. Both the others looked warily at her.

"And you—" said Sir Bernard.

"Gold," said Madeleine. "I could not kill the creature, but I had laid the gold to keep off any such magical creature of the mists."

"We're here to rescue the queen, not to kill the dragon," said John, quietly. "Gold will suffice." There was a white line about his mouth. Sandy, with his knight and his green lion fighting a dragon, was like his father—but Madeleine felt more grieved than amused.

They walked on. Madeleine wondered what Queen Katherine felt, to have the dragon lurking outside her window, and then they reached the hilltop.

Before them, the valley lay swathed in mist. Halfway down the slope, the trees were dim shadows, and the valley that held the stream was invisible—if she had heard it correctly.

"Anything could lurk down there," said Sir Henry.

"Not quite," said Madeleine, "but many things do, including some that the gold would be little protection against. I only went this way before because Lord Donald was a great danger." Before that, if John and she had not taken this way, her father could have, and so separated them. Still—their flight had looked different in the summer's greens. Now, their folly astounded her.

Sir Henry looked gray. "Lord, have mercy."

Madeleine walked down the slope. John's hand slipped under her elbow to hold her steady. Lord, have mercy on us, indeed, she thought. Even in winter, they could pass through the forest more quickly than she had with Sandy, but she and Sandy had done nothing more than pass through.

"It is fortunate that the hills prevented your capture," said John. "Donald would have taken your entering them as final proof of madness."

Madeleine managed a smile.

The stream emerged from the mist. It glittered black among the pale brown of the dead leaves. Clumps of ice clung to the stones. Madeleine stopped by the bank. The ground was harder than ever beneath her feet, with all the ice embedded it. The water was shallower than it had been in the summer, but she and Sandy had not faced the cold once out of the water. "Now we must cross."

Sir Henry groaned. Sir Bernard looked disapproving—of Sir Henry, she thought.

John's mouth twitched. "We won't freeze to death for a little water." He put one arm about Madeleine's shoulders and scooped her up with the other arm beneath her knees.

Madeleine leaned against his chest and put her arms about his neck as John tramped into the water. "*I* won't freeze to death for a little water," she whispered.

"Ah, but I like doing this," he whispered. Madeleine tightened her grip.

Sir Henry and Sir Bernard splashed after them and climbed out as John put Madeleine back down. "We're going to have to keep a good pace to keep warm," said Sir Bernard, and then, sharply, "What's that?"

His voice startled the deer. It leapt away, a dark gray shadow in the mists. Sir Henry went for his spear.

"A deer," said Madeleine, sharply. "Even if a mist creature."

"It led Lord Fergus astray," said John.

Not him, too, thought Madeleine. "Is that a reason to *follow* it?"

The deer, thought John, had led Lord Fergus astray.

He kept his gaze on Madeleine. If the other knights saw him hesitate, they would take fright.

Besides, staring about was useless. The beasts did not swirl about in mist. They emerged, or they vanished, entirely.

A bird twittered, somewhere in the jagged branches.

He let his breath out. It had been spring when last he ventured here. Nearly summer, with the trees in leaf, and the birds far more profuse. . . the mists encircling the leafless branches looked different.

A rabbit skittered through the dead leaves. They were wet and already moldering, and the sound was low and muffled. The rabbit vanished into the brush.

They emerged from the firs, but even with the trees leafless, the mists were little brighter. They would camp, Madeleine decided. She muttered the thinning charm. The sun gleamed faintly, just over the nearest hills. She thought the Dead Men's Bells had grown here, but if so, the winter had put them all away.

"Here, tonight, I think," she said.

Without comment, the men lowered their packs. She went to John, and they talked of food.

Sir Henry emerged from a hollow, his arm laden with dead wood. Madeleine walked over to where Sir Bernard scrapped the leaves from a patch between trees, to help him. For them, a fire would not be the danger that it would have been for a lone woman and her child, and the night had been cold enough during the summer.

A thick layer of moldering leaves hid the dirt, and at first they uncovered roots, but after a handful of minutes, Sir Henry laid wood on bare earth and pulled out flint and steel.

Madeleine rose. John pulled out their food.

"An easy passage," he said. "You and I had to outrun that boar, at least."

Madeleine slid one hand down his arm. "You can walk through most woods without being attacked, most of the time. The Misty Hills are the same, except for the *manner* of creature that may endanger you."

Sir Bernard fed wood to the fire. Smoke curled up, thick and black. Madeleine scowled. Had Sir Henry found damp wood? He had known enough not to lay the blaze on tree roots.

Then long arms uncurled from the mass of the smoke.

Her tongue numb in her mouth from horror, Madeleine leapt toward the blaze. Sir Henry and Sir Bernard gawked without moving. From the woodpile, she grabbed a branch to poke the logs apart. The flames subsided as the cold air damped them, but did not die. She glanced at the dead leaves about the dirt; she could not let this fire spread.

The creature swelled; it was no longer so black, but that did not console her. Eyes formed in the dull gray, bright orange embers that glared at her. She crouched and poked the logs further apart. Flames sank, until her stick began to smoke. She buried it in the ash, hoping to smother it.

John appeared beside her, water bottle in hand. Madeleine, afraid of what steam would do, grabbed his arm. "Just a little."

John nodded and threw a handful of water on the flames. Steam puffed up, swelling the creature. Madeleine bit her lip. It looked paler than before, but did that mean anything? John, grim-faced, spread more water over the higher flames. The creature grew still larger—but, Madeleine realized with a rush of relief, no more formed. Pale talons at its arms' end grew no sharper.

"There's water in the firs," said Sir Henry, coming back to life.

"NO!" Madeleine whirled so quickly that the breeze stirred the fire. "Use the water bottles." She bit her lip. If the water was not enough, they could beat out the fire with blankets. She did not even want to think of what the water from the tarns of madness would do to the creature.

Scowling, Sir Bernard threw more water on the blaze, and the talons reached for him, to pass through his arm. Madeleine breathed a sigh of relief.

Sir Henry eyed the firs.

"Go after those pools," said Madeleine, "and you will not return sane. Even touching the water is dangerous."

"Everything in these woods is dangerous," Sir Henry muttered, but he did not move.

Long minutes later, Madeleine stirred the damp ashes again, seeking any spark. At least, with the care they had taken, the fire had not leapt to a root, to burn underground to a tree.

"Now there's just the matter of water for *us*," said Sir Henry, his voice hard.

"If we can't go back, we must go on," said Sir Bernard. "But if there's no water in the Misty Hills. . . ."

Madeleine tried to remember the next spring.

"There's water," said John. "We drank from springs along this path, Madeleine and I."

"But," said Madeleine, "it's down the path." All three men looked dispirited. Her shoulders slumped as she inspected the mist. The moon would set soon, after the sun. "I don't think we should sit about here, where the smoke...."

Sir Bernard rolled his eyes. Sir Henry grumbled about monsters. John looked up from the food he was packing and, to her surprise, smiled. When they were on the path again, he whispered that they would obey her now.

Madeleine smiled, but that smile faded quickly. The mists were touched with scarlet and orange, and growing dark. Creatures could lurk in the mists, Sir Henry was right there. Ahead of them, a clearing was filled with grass; staying there might be better than trying to go further. They would reach water early the next day.

Brush rustled. Madeleine glanced to one side, wondering for a moment if it were wind. Eyes and teeth glinted. "Wolves!" she shouted.

In the sunset light, they glittered fiery colors. Their fangs bared, they looked at her: only two of them, but that was only two misty wolves.

John's left hand was on her arm. She went behind him. She had to see: the men could fight, but that would not drive off these wolves. John's right hand already held his sword. Sir Henry and Sir Bernard's swords glittered behind her. Her chest tight, Madeleine rummaged for the gold. Better to camp here than to fight these wolves to go on.

A wolf snarled and leapt. Sir Henry's sword passed through the body, and its claws raked him. Sir Bernard attacked, his blade grazing the wolf's head, and drawing blood, but moments later, his second strike passed through as readily.

Behind her, something struck John's sword. He must have seen that he had parried the wolf's attack—a misty bite was nothing fearful—but that would not drive the beast off. Her fingers clenched the gold. She could trap the misty wolves inside a circle of gold with the men, but she could not hold them off.

Her mouth felt dry as a bone. Sir Bernard drove the wolf off from Sir Henry, but his blade had Sir Henry's blood on it as well, and John gasped as his wolf got past his guard.

Evening, thought Madeleine. Misty creatures attacked in the evening because the fuller the light was, the more form they had to take lest they dissolve into nothing—she looked ahead. The clearing had more light than even these trees.

Madeleine took a handful of gold, to have ready, and shouted, "Follow me!" She sprinted down the path, ignoring her legs' painful reminders of how far she had walked that day. The wolves snarled, but it took them a moment to look up, and the men did not move. Her heart hammering, Madeleine cast a circle of gold around, as large as she dared.

John bolted after her. Even by the sunset, his face was ashen. The second wolf turned on Sir Bernard and Sir Henry, and they fled.

"Inside the gold!" Madeleine called. She prayed that none of them knocked coins astray. If the wolves got inside—she did not have time to complete that thought when John reached her, and the other two men pelted after. One coin flew aside. Madeleine grabbed another and threw it as the wolves charged.

Growling, the beasts circled them. Madeleine swallowed. "They will have to stay more substantial, here in the light. Only in shadows can they be half here and half mist."

John stalked to the edge. "They can attack anything that reaches over the gold, can they not?"

"Yes," said Madeleine.

John feinted at the nearer wolf. It snarled but pulled back.

Sir Henry groaned.

"Let me treat your wounds, before the light goes,"
Madeleine said. They had cloth for bandages—though, she
thought as she tore that cloth, they had been fools enough to
not bring torches.

The wolves circled around one, twice, thrice. John's sword
lashed out and struck one in the shoulder. Blood gushed.
With a final snarl, the wolves dissolved into mist.

John looked at his sword. The blood had dissolved as well.

Madeleine's mouth twitched, in spite of herself. "The blood
didn't last when you pulled the sword into the circle," she said.
"The solar properties of gold prevented it."

Sir Bernard snorted. She saw no blood on him, but John
had gasped. "Your wounds as well, my lord husband. The
misty wolves are wolves like any other—they have gone for
easier prey. If we wish to go for water. . . ."

All three men groaned, but she did not see distaste in their
faces.

"We'll be at the end of the path tomorrow," said Sir
Bernard, hopefully.

"Easily, if we were just leaving the Misty Hills," said
Madeleine. "But we may spend more time hunting for the
tower than getting to the right part of the hills."

I will have to ask, she thought. They could not wander,
hoping to find the way. The king would not be distracted long.

A bird twittered in the trees. Madeleine pulled her shawl
closer against the evening chill. Much *it* cared, she thought
bitterly.

Chapter 15—Dragons and Escapes

Clouds lowered. Somerled eyed them. The threatened rain, or snow, did not justify seeking shelter. And he was unlikely to find shelter closer than Thansport Castle.

His horse leapt the narrow, ice-clogged stream and climbed the hill. Lord Oliver had been put down, and the king had praised the lords who had done it. If rumor were true, he had never complained of Lord Malcolm; the queen's pardon might have been wasted there.

The horse reached the hilltop. Snowflakes, few but fat, drifted on the valley and the dark gray of Thansport Castle, where Lord Duncan lived. The king was even willing to deal with Lord Duncan—willing to preserve the peace.

The queen was still in the Misty Hills. That, he did not want to think on.

At his urging, his mount leapt down the road, toward the stables. The few peasants out of their cottages hurried home rather than glance at him, but when he reached the gates, the guards hailed him from the parapet's shadow.

"A royal message."

One snorted. "Our lord's sent the king *his* message."

"I've the safe conduct," said Somerled.

Silence reigned. A gust bore snow past Somerled. So agreeable was the king that he assented to Lord Duncan's unreasonable claim—and from the sounds, here too the king conquered. Lord Duncan would obey. All went well for the king.

His horse stamped a hoof, but Somerled felt light-hearted. The queen might be free by springtime. If she bore a son, the land might know peace for many years.

The peasant women did not gossip with her, any more than her ladies-in-waiting had. By the upper window, Queen Katherine strained her ears. Most of the rough chatter was complaints about the load, but some news drifted up. About an heiress disinherited for complaining of her guardian.

She remembered the guardian who had, months earlier, lost his lands as well as the guardianship. She glanced across the room to the prayer book. Perhaps issuing the pardon had not been foolish in any sense. If she had fallen afoul of the king for other reasons, she would have suffered no more because she had refused to free the prisoners.

A shout from downstairs drew her attention again. One peasant pointed at the flecks that were dark in the mists.

Katherine smiled sadly. At least they scrambled with the supplies and did not abandon her at once; at least King Walter would punish them if she lacked the food.

Snowflakes fell. Between her and the ground, where the sunlight fell on them, they gleamed white. The men and mules had barely vanished in the trees when the snow ceased, without so much as garnishing a blade of grass.

The dragon settled about the tower. She thought it slept.

The mists darkened with evening. Madeleine looked tired. More tired than their journey would account for—this day had been unmarred by monsters—unless she found this baby more wearying than carrying Sandy.

John's mouth tightened. She looked for the place to leave the path and find someone to tell them about the tower.

The road to the tower led through Candlewood—through her father's lands. He stepped closer and touched her hand. For a moment, a smile brightened her face.

He smiled back but said, "Who will we speak to?"

Madeleine looked weary again. "Ina, I think. Her house is a little apart from the village."

"Won't she gossip?"

"If a score of peasants see us, half will gossip. Some might even tell the king's men."

"Dear Lady Madeleine." Her hands still grubby from her garden, Ina took Madeleine's hands and kissed her cheek. "Looking so like your dear dead mother. So like Lady Sorcha."

Sir Henry and Sir Bernard waited outside the grove where Ina's cottage stood. John stood behind Madeleine. Madeleine felt them there, but she knew better than to urge haste on Ina.

"I heard that you had been in the Misty Hills earlier this year, but I didn't believe it—to pass through like that, without a word."

"I was in haste, Goodwife Ina," Madeleine said. "Did you not hear what happened to my lord husband?"

"Disgraceful business." Her dark eyes assessed John. "Especially with this young man putting a baby in your belly."

"This one was conceived afterwards," said Madeleine, trying to sound grave.

Ina scowled. "You had a child. That was what they said: a child came through the Misty Hills with you."

Had she seen someone as she came through the Dead Man's Bells? "I bore John a son three years ago. I brought him with me, through the hills. I did not wish to leave him behind. Not when his uncles had claims to his lands."

"Ah, yes, those wicked uncles who tried to disinherit your young man." Ina patted her hand. "You did well by your lord husband." She still narrowed her eyes as she looked over Madeleine's shoulder to John.

Madeleine licked her lips. "Not so well by the queen."

To her surprise, Ina nodded. "A disgraceful business. I told the king's men so myself."

Madeleine flinched.

"I offered—the queen *will* need a midwife—and they would hear nothing of me! The king's guarding her away like she was made of gold, and he has a dragon—" She looked at Madeleine. "A *dragon* guarding her! And he thinks his wizard's going to keep it from eating the queen. Forever! If I had been Morgan's mother, I would have paddled his bottom for talking 'bout wizarding—stopped him *before* he ran away." Ina shook her head. "Boasting about using some little charms we all know, but better, and backwards. He even tried to say that gold doesn't stop the creatures because it's like the sun! He was a knave and no mistake."

Was? thought Madeleine.

Ina's voice turned sly. "But the king didn't get everything his way. Morgan's dead."

Behind her, John moved, sharply. She dragged in a deep breath, trying to guess what that death meant for her—and then she collected herself. "God have mercy on him."

"Someone killed him in his sleep—he was fool enough to sleep in the Misty Hills. Proved he didn't know everything he thought he knew. The king was fit to break rocks for hours." Ina chuckled. "He wanted to do more to the hills. Seems he's not getting more than a prison for his queen."

"But he did get a prison for the queen," said Madeleine. "Because she pardoned Lord Magnus. She saved my lord husband. And the land will be at war without an heir—"

"There's always war. Never comes in the Misty Hills. You will be safe here—your lord father would never turn his daughter away, or her husband or child."

Madeleine fought to speak with dignity. "I would have no lord husband, were it not for the queen. I thought loyalty was regarded here. You yourself told me about hiding Prince Leod." When Ina made no answer, Madeleine pressed on. "And you are a midwife. You went to aid her yourself."

Ina's voice turned heavy. "There's nothing to be done, Lady Madeleine. Your lord father has words for the king, but only his own men hear them. And heed my words. I caught you when your mother bore you, and I learned a thing or two in the years before. . . ."

Ina had never approved of Lord Fergus. Madeleine wondered what she would say if told that she reminded Madeleine of her godfather. "Is the king not having food sent to the tower?"

"That he is." Ina tilted her head to one side. "There's a dragon—I told you."

"Nothing that gold won't restrain," said Madeleine. "It's not as if we have to kill it to get to the queen. Getting to the tower will be the hard part."

The wrinkles on Ina's face deepened with her scowl. Madeleine met her gaze and fought against blinking.

Ina heaved out a sigh. "I suppose you're so stubborn you would find out the truth. They got a spell—makes the path to the tower short enough to go on. A couple of bold lads have run up to touch it, while they put the food in, so it is possible."

Madeleine nodded. That sounded simple enough.

"The dragon sniffed around to scare them off, if they stayed," Ina said. "You'd need the king's treasury to hold that one off. And Old Peg's Todd had to stay there three days, 'cause the path went away. Near starved."

"We shall rely on that," said John. "Without that time, we could not rescue the queen; we can not fight that company." He let his fingers rest on Madeleine's shoulder. "When does the next company go?"

Ina eyed him for a moment. "Tomorrow. And you're taking your lady wife with her own little one there."

John slid his arm about Madeleine's waist. "Whom else could I bring? Should I bring the queen through the woods, unattended? Even if I *could* bring her."

Ina smirked.

Mists twisted among leafless brush, beneath the maples' bare branches. It blurred the hills with its thickness. Madeleine stirred. Even if it had held them there another hour, she should have asked Ina if the mists had thickened in truth.

A pair of ordinary gray squirrels skittered through the dead leaves, but nothing else moved.

Be with us, o Lord, Madeleine prayed, for we are in trouble and need.

Sir Henry jerked his head toward the path. They pulled back, into the shelter of the nearest hill. Men and mules plodded along the frozen path. One man sang a traveling ditty. Another cursed a mule and thwacked it.

The footsteps faded. John listened and nodded. They hurried alongside the path, just close enough to keep the track in sight. Branches jabbed their clothing and snagged Madeleine's hair. Her heart hammered.

They came over a slope and stopped, barely still beneath the trees. Madeleine had never seen this valley before. Dead grass, brownish and low, spread between them and the tower. Thick firs covered the slope behind it, shadowing the land, and a darker shadow lay before them, behind the tower. Men unburdened the mules, shouts rang, and a plump middle-aged woman, dressed like a peasant, sat by doorway. She watched and swung her foot—proof that the king had not lost all sense of propriety.

Madeleine's mouth twisted. Queen Katherine's father would still not approve.

High above them, in the tower's window, a second woman sat. Misery lay over her bearing, visible even at this distance.

Madeleine's gaze moved back, to the darker shadow. The dragon sat, still. Its shoulders reached higher than the doorway, and its black scales seemed to fade into the mists. A man stood before it, with something glinting gold in his hands. The dragon watched with unblinking eyes and latent power. Its gaze flicked back and forth, over the company, the grass, back to the trees. It can't see us, thought Madeleine, and then the dragon stirred. She slid deeper into the woods.

"The firs, to hide," said John, his voice low. "When they leave—" His face was grave, but his eyes were bright, and his hand rested on the sword hilt.

In the afternoon, the forest lay silent. The men and mules were long gone, the dragon had slithered back toward the tower, and they never had heard any sound from the queen.

Gold glinted in Madeleine's hands as she handed the coins out. "If the dragon comes too close to you, lay the gold all about, so it would have to pass the circle to reach you."

John did not even glance at his sword as he took the coins. Sir Henry looked skeptical, but held out his hands like the others.

"Now, let us go free the queen," Madeleine said. She took a deep breath, filled one hand with gold, took a coin in the other, and headed out to the grass and the tower.

The dragon's nose greeted them at the forest edge. Madeleine tossed her coin so that landed between them and the dragon. It sniffed, and Madeleine edged her way toward the tower, tossing a coin each time the dragon seemed ready to lunge. It tracked them, its dark eyes fathomless and intent. Sir Henry muttered to Sir Bernard, but Madeleine did not heed him enough to make out the words.

They emerged from the woods. Madeleine saw no sign of Queen Katherine at the window, but the queen would come to the door—and if not, they had brought an axe.

The dragon followed her gaze. With a hiss, it rose up, until its head reached the level of the window. It turned, tightly for so large a beast, and darted toward the tower. Moments later, the dragon had encircled the tower. Its scaled body wrapped around the base twice over, hiding the door. They had no ladder—and, even with the gold, she would not have dared climb over the dragon. Its head slithered over its scales to look at her. Its expression was unreadable.

"Now what do we do?" said Sir Henry, giving unforgivable voice to her own horror-struck thoughts.

Queen Katherine must have heard something. She stood at the window, her fingers clenching the stone. Her face was set in dreadful lines, of hope dashed in the instant of its birth.

"We wait," said Madeleine. Her voice was clipped, and she could not restore it to normality. "The dragon will not—is not likely to rest here forever." She found herself remembering that they had brought only food enough for four or five days.

They had torches, Ina had provided that much, but they bedded down in the forest, waiting inside gold on the cold earth. Now and again, an owl hooted. The dragon had not stirred.

"Magic," said Sir Henry. "No telling what manner of beast it is, or how long it can lie there."

Madeleine wished she could contradict that.

"If it left to eat, the queen could escape."

Sir Bernard was too polite to speak, but she could read his agreement in his movements. And she was not certain of John. "It is a misty creature," she said. "Like the wolves, it can come and go, but can not cross gold."

A flame leapt up, glowing orange.

"That's it, then," said Sir Bernard. Madeleine looked at him sharply. AS if he were familiar with the Misty Hills. "In the morning, we attack it. The wolves could feel our blows, and the dragon will feel them, too."

John glanced toward the tower. "If it vanishes?"

Sir Bernard grinned. "How can it keep us from the door then?"

Madeleine sat like stone and felt stupid.

In the morning, the mist lay thicker than ever. Madeleine murmured her sun charm. The mists barely thinned. She repeated it. A silver circle, faintly brighter than the mists about it, appeared long enough for her to guess that it was midmorning. The instant she let the charm drop, the field was again as dim as dawn. "Morgan did something to the mists."

"He did something to the monsters," said John. "That is the important part."

Madeleine dropped to her knees to pick the coins up. Wolves might attack them again, and the men were already intent on the dragon.

The last coin slid into her pouch. Madeleine knelt a little longer on the hard ground, contemplating the dead leaves before her. You, she told herself severely, are glad that they can bring the dragon down and rescue the queen.

She rose. The tower window was empty. Then, the queen had no reason to rise early in the morning.

The men drew their swords, which glinted a little in the light, and advanced. The dragon had not twitched a scale since taking up its position. Madeleine's fingers tightened on the gold. "In You, O Lord, I put my trust; let me never be put to confusion. Deliver me in Your righteousness and cause me to escape; incline Your ear and save me. Be my strong tower—" she winced "—a fortress to keep me safe...."

The men came within striking distance. The dragon lifted its head and seemed to concentrate on John. The baby wriggled. Madeleine thought she would choke. Lord Magnus would not permit John's widow and fatherless children to suffer—and she tried to stifle that thought.

Sir Bernard's sword flashed. The blade drove through the dragon's scales as if they were of air—or mist.

Madeleine bit her lip.

Sir Bernard struck again. John and Sir Henry brought down their swords. Sir Bernard put a foot forward. It landed on the scales, not through them, and he struck at the flesh beside it.

The dragon, Madeleine realized in horror, could partly dissolve, and partly remain.

The sword bit into scale, drawing blood, and then falling through air. Sir Bernard fell forward at the surprise. A claw snatched him before he struck ground. More blood spurted as the dragon hefted him into the air. John's sword hacked at the claw, and Sir Bernard started to fall.

Madeleine ran down the hill, her hand clutching the pouch to keep the gold from spilling. Sir Bernard fell heavily on the dragon's scales. With a contemptuous flip of its coils, the dragon tossed him aside and reached for John and Sir Henry. John threw himself backwards, parrying. The dragon did not catch him, a gout of crimson blood flowed from its claws, but Sir Henry cried out as the claw sliced him.

"Break free!" Madeleine shouted. Sir Henry staggered back; the dragon had wounded but not caught him. She threw the gold blindly about, until the coins spread through the dead grass like out-of-season trumpet flowers—nothing so neat as a circle, but shadow dragons could not pass gold. The men staggered within, and the dragon looked banefully at her. She glared back. It still kept them from the door.

Something moved at the window. Queen Katherine looked sadly down at them. Madeleine's tongue touched her lips. Then she shouted, "Can it understand us?"

"Yes," called the queen.

The dragon almost looked smug. Madeleine turned away.

Sir Bernard was not even looking toward the tower, or the dragon. Half-sitting, half-sprawled on the earth, he moaned.

"Lie still." Madeleine reached for the satchel. If the knights died—she did not stop to think on whether John could rescue the queen alone, her hands were moving so quickly, but she could not stop glancing at the dragon.

The dragon bled: its claws, where John had struck it, its side where Sir Bernard had. Blood flowed over its scales even now. Madeleine tightened the bandages. Sir Bernard flinched, but the wound was deep enough to need the bindings.

She glanced at the dragon again. Perhaps the blood oozed, but the flow was still thick. The dragon moved more slowly, as well. If the men could only keep it substantial long enough to hack it to pieces—the dragon, like any other misty creature, relied on vanishing to escape harm.

"Vicious creatures," Madeleine muttered. Blood did not quite seep through the bandage she had put on Sir Bernard. She called John over to hold down the bandage and turned to Sir Henry.

The mists were even thicker, and darker, than they had been at dawn. Morgan *had* done something with the mists, and here, perhaps, made it the strongest. Madeleine tore the bandages.

Mist wound itself between her and Sir Henry. She scowled at it. If only, if only. . . and she remembered Ina's words. Her hands stopped. Even Sir Henry's "My lady?" could not rouse her from her thoughts. Morgan reversed some spells. One charm thinned the mists—Morgan must have thickened them. Madeleine pronounced the charm. For a moment, the grayness grew lighter. Then, she had lightened the mists that morning.

She thought as she bound up Sir Henry's wounds. Sir Henry gasped from the tightness; Madeleine, without loosening the bandage, sat back. Cast twice, the charm had done better.

The dragon peered at her. Losing blood had not dimmed those sharp eyes. Beneath the scales, muscle shifted.

Madeleine gestured to the men, to come closer, and spoke in a low voice. "Remember the wolves?"

They nodded. Sir Henry and Sir Bernard looked puzzled. John looked worried.

"You will know when to strike."

John drew his sword. He stood inside the gold coins, but between her and the dragon.

That will not help, she thought. She closed her eyes, and heard Sir Henry and Sir Bernard shift their places. She hoped their wounds would not hinder them.

Deliver me, O my God, out of the hand of the wicked, out of the hand of the unrighteous and cruel man. She opened her eyes. Queen Katherine stood at the window, but her head bent, she no longer watched. Madeleine recited the charm, over and over.

The mist paled at the first charm, and then grew paler, turning dove gray. Madeleine nearly stumbled over her tongue but went on. The dragon reared up to loom over them, but it did not gather for attack. The mists around it grew pearly gray, then white.

The sun was a silver glow overhead, a featureless moon slowly growing too bright to look upon. With a snarl, John leapt to the attack, his sword glittering. The dragon lashed out, its claws going to snatch, but John parried one blow, Sir Bernard beat off the second, and Sir Henry got in a solid blow on its shoulder.

Madeleine's tongue nearly tripped over itself. The dragon could not pass the gold, but its movement jostled the earth enough to make her balance uncertain. She sat, hoping that would make it easier to concentrate. The mist thinned no more, but she could not stop. She could not find out how long it would take Morgan's spells to return, not when John and the others struck and parried, and the dragon feinted about.

Then the dragon was gone.

As the wolves had been, thought Madeleine. She recited the charm once again, as the men lowered their swords.

Queen Katherine screamed.

Jolted, the men looked about. The dragon's claws emerged from midair about John. One came so near his sword arm that he could not lift the blade. Sir Bernard and Sir Henry struck. Blood flowed for an instant before the dragon vanished. All three men fled back to the gold.

"Gone," said John, between panting for breath. "For a moment. It's not like the wolves. It's been spelled to guard the queen. As long as it lives—" He looked about.

The mists darkened. Madeleine murmured the charm again, and the glow returned. The dragon could dissolve entirely, and reappear. It could no longer both strike and vanish at once, but sudden attack would be enough, if it could attack at any time—and, as well, evening was coming.

"As long as it. . ." John paused.

Before she could speak, John raised his sword and stepped out of the gold. The white mist light made his hair glitter, and his face was set.

Madeleine's throat choked, and the charm faltered. Gray encircled him. From it, the dragon's maw emerged, gaping dark. The dragon intended to swallow John whole. . . .

Madeleine gabbled the charm, unable to stop. John drove his sword forward, into that open maw. He leapt back, dragging the blade with him. Blood splattered all over him. He gasped in pain. The dragon, a moment later, roared and reared back, all its coils shifting in agony, and blood gushed.

Sir Bernard dragged John into the gold. The blood vanished, but beneath where it had struck, John's skin showed red like burns. The dragon thrashed. Blood sluiced from its mouth, and its wild sprawls seemed to be dying down.

"Sir Bernard," said Madeleine, "ready the ax."

Sir Bernard nodded and eyed the tower door. The dragon gave a gurgling scream. Its coils slammed against the earth. The ground shook, and the wind gusted by, nearly knocking them off their feet, but the dragon did not rouse again; it lay against the earth, still bleeding, and making a choked, piteous noise. Madeleine wondered if they should finish it off, and then glanced at John again. He stood without faltering, but he made an incautious move and gasped in pain. No, the dragon could die on its own.

It shifted, or perhaps that was the weight falling. The flow of blood had slackened.

Sir Bernard strode from the circle and struck the door with the axe. Good solid oak, thought Madeleine. It would take some time to come down. He continued, the blows resounding in the meadow. A narrow gap opened in the wood, and it opened, large enough to see in, and then the door fell into a pile of broken wood on the floor. Sir Bernard lowered the axe.

Queen Katherine leapt up from the stairs and threw herself across the gap, to wind her arms about Madeleine's neck and sob.

"We can't leave at once," said Madeleine. They sat in the kitchen. The tear tracks were still visible on the queen's face. Madeleine tried not to glance at her every other moment. "We did not learn how to come here on our own; we followed along with the supplies. We shall have to await their return."

"So," said the queen, "they will come here *while* we escape." Her words were steady; Madeleine was glad. "But—should we not at least leave the tower?"

Madeleine thought of spending more cold nights without shelter, and quailed.

"With the dragon dead," said Queen Katherine, "with the door smashed—they will know at once."

"We will leave," said Madeleine. "On the morning that they come."

The queen frowned.

Madeleine said, quickly, "Madame, we heard that some boys came after the men who brought your food. One even said he was caught here."

After a moment's consideration, the queen said, "I saw some odd shadows between such visits, but nothing I could be sure was human. I dare say such a boy would not have ventured too close to the dragon."

Madeleine smiled. Certainly not close enough to touch the tower.

If the king had moved—Somerled glanced warily at Lord Duncan. He had brought message to the highest nobles in the land, but never before had he served as a guide. Nobles did not ride at a messenger's speed, or hunt about for the end of the journey. Grizzled like an old bear that had gained cunning what he had lost in strength, Lord Duncan glared at the road.

"The king's banner." One of Lord Duncan's escort pointed. Somerled could not make out the device, but who else would be at such an obscure castle? Except the lordling himself, and too many people milled about for that. As Lord Duncan's escort formed about their lord, Somerled fell back. Let Lord Duncan impress the king with his state; he had not impressed Somerled with his coins.

The guards' hails were answered, and the company trooped in. The king himself came to greet Lord Duncan; even in the face of Lord Duncan's truculent men, his words were measured, and his bearing serene. Somerled sidled toward the kitchen; there being no message, there would be no reward. Food and drink, he could get, if he acted quickly enough.

Inside, a spit boy asked, "Is that really Lord Duncan?" Somerled nodded. The cook bellowed for spiced wine and sweetmeats. Somerled slid over to the hearth for warmth. The kitchen's servants eyed him, but they must have recognized a royal messenger's livery—now. They might not have a week before.

Besides, they readied the king's food. Throwing him out of the kitchen was, like feeding him, less important.

A back door opened next to the hearth. A short stairway led to the lord's private chamber, where the king stood. Somerled turned away, smiling. Not the state the king was accustomed to. He wondered how long the king would suffer it.

A royal page ran down the stairs—Somerled pulled back—and called for the wine. The cook swore at the servants, even as one gave a tray, with cups and flagon, to the page. Up the stairway, Lord Duncan stood before the king.

"TREACHERY!"

Somerled started. The page jumped back. Cups and flagon fell; wine cascaded, crimson, down the gray stone. At the top of the stairs, the king held a bloody dagger. Blood, redder than the wine, spurted from Lord Duncan, who held no weapon. Somerled's breath came fast and shallow. If Lord Duncan had dropped a weapon, the sound would have echoed louder than the tray.

His face contorting, the king stabbed again as Lord Duncan reached for his sword. Treachery? thought Somerled. If Lord Duncan intended treachery, he would have had his blade ready.

Guards, grimfaced, burst in to surround Lord Duncan with swords in hand—grimfaced but not surprised.

Treason, thought Somerled. The kitchen servants swarmed, gaping, about the stairs. Somerled staggered away. He reached the door before his thoughts stuck together: I delivered the safe-conduct with my own hands to Lord Duncan. May God have mercy on him. He stumbled into the sunlight. May God have mercy on his soul.

In the courtyard, servants ran about. Guards glared, ready to strike. White-faced, Lord Duncan's men stood with swords in hand. "You!" One stepped forward, toward Somerled. "What happened here?"

"Treachery and treason," said Somerled, croaking out the words. "Lord Duncan is dead—murdered." Hands tightened on swords. The royal guards, by the gate, were not enough to overwhelm this band; the king had kept back enough men to ensure Lord Duncan's death. Some of the men looked ready to stab him. Somerled was not certain he blamed them. "The king has men enough to slaughter you—and keep the news from the heir."

"Lord Ewan," said one, older than the rest. He glanced at the gate. "Lord Ewan will avenge this—if he hears."

Somerled drew into the shadows, where the fight might not reach him, where the king's men might forget that he spoke to Lord Duncan's men. The coin that Lord Duncan had given him, petty though it was, burned in his pocket.

"Stop there!" shouted a guard, but Lord Duncan's men did not falter. Not until swords clashed, and they had to fight rather than flee.

After sharp moments, Lord Duncan's men took their wounded and fled. Treachery and treason, thought Somerled. The king did not order you to tell them, and foiling his plans is treason. His stomach heaved. He turned aside to retch.

The king emerged. His clothing was splashed with blood, guards surrounded him, but as he demanded the traitor's men, he moved easily, as if unwounded. He saw the bodies at the gate and shrieked in outrage.

Somerled pulled back again. Not the kitchen, he could not eat—the chapel. He darted to the door and took sanctuary.

The gloom smelled of candle smoke and incense. Somerled tried to steady his breath. First of all, to pray that no one had noted his speaking with the men. He saw the tabernacle candle, and clumsily genuflected. The coin Lord Duncan gave him could pay for a mass for the lord's soul.

With a jerk against the blankets, Madeleine woke.

Thoughts fuzzily fell into place: she was wrapped in blankets, not trapped in thick, wet mists. She sat—in the tower. If the king's malice caused her being here, still, it did not envelope her like a dark mist—

Morgan, she thought. But Morgan was dead.

"May God have mercy on his soul," she whispered. A faint scent, foul, hung on the air; the dragon was dead. She lay back, letting her breath out. The king's men would know that before they reached the tower.

All the more reason, thought Madeleine, to sleep now, so as to wake then.

The firs offered little protection from the wind, but they stood in that shelter. Queen Katherine stared into the distance. Madeleine inspected her with care: the queen had regained color these days, but Madeleine was still wary.

Queen Katherine was about a month less gone with child that she was. She must have conceived just after the king heard of the pardon. Madeleine slid her hand over her waist.

"Madame!" called John.

Without a word, the three of them hurried beneath the trees, to join Sir Henry and Sir Bernard. Her heart hammering, Madeleine tried to listen. They walked on the path until something was heard, ahead. John led them over the nearest hill. There, they waited, and waited.

Noises slowly grew distinct. Mules moved slowly, and men swore. One cursed not only the mules, but also some wolves. At least, thought Madeleine with spiteful pleasure, they were not the only ones being troubled by the creatures of Misty Hills.

It seemed a long time later when John gestured toward the path. He glanced at Madeleine and offered his arm to the queen.

The path was easier going than the brush, but narrower than many paths in the Misty Hills. Even leafless, branches poked at them until Madeleine wondered that all the oaths had been directed at the mules.

Then a sound came from behind them, so indistinct that Madeleine could not even be sure that it was a shout, let alone whether it was in shock or outrage. Without a word, they hurried.

As soon as we can, we have to leave this path, Madeleine thought. It will make it harder for them to follow us.

The darkness of Ina's cottage smelled of dried herbs. Madeleine lingered by the door.

"I do not like this," said Ina, over Sir Bernard's wounds. "Drag her about the country—how can your noblemen protect her from the king?"

Madeleine kept silent. Ina's carping did no harm. Quarreling with her would do no good.

"Depending on how much your tongue wags," said John, leaning on the doorway. "You *know* who took her. Others may guess—"

Ina snorted. "You think no one will recognize her?"

Madeleine looked outside. Queen Katherine sat under the trees on a stool; having banned her from the sickroom, Ina had dragged it out for her.

And if Ina wanted to quarrel—"If she miscarried or gave birth without witnesses, the trouble for the kingdom would be greater," said Madeleine.

"The king will be after you."

"King Walter asked me about the Misty Hills, at Michaelmas. I evaded him, and he had recourse to Morgan." She smiled. Her mouth moved stiffly. "The king is already after me."

But she had other things to consider: the paths from the forest. Andrew and Donald might have told King Walter of the path she had escaped them by, but there were others. One took only two days, and, like that path, came out in Lord Magnus's lands; indeed, it came closer to Owlscourt than the path that took but a day. She let her breath out. She had never been down it, but Jasper had told her of it.

"Best to leave soon," she said.

"Don't want to scare the queen with the candles?" said Ina.

"Do you think the candles worse than a dragon?" said Madeleine.

Chapter 16—Escapes and Paths

A stream babbled through rocks and clumps of ice, down the slope. Madeleine climbed alongside it. When Jasper had told this story, she had envied him.

"What are you looking for, Madeleine?" said John.

"My brother told me. . . ." She climbed over a rock. Water streamed from a crack in a great oak, pouring through the gnarled roots. Behind and to either side of the oak, the earth was dry. "That."

Queen Katherine picked her way over ground hard with frost and studied the oak. "What is the meaning of that?" she asked.

"The Misty Hills hold many marvels," said Madeleine. "No one knows the meaning of them all."

John snorted. "You would be safe betting a large sum that there's a story behind this one."

Madeleine spread a hand. "This far from Candlewood— Jasper did not hear the tale when he passed by here."

Sir Bernard said, "How much longer in the Misty Hills?" Though his wounds were healing, he looked gray.

"Less than an hour," said Madeleine.

"How far did we go into the Misty Hills, anyway?" said Sir Henry.

Said Queen Katherine, frigidly, "It took me an hour to reach the tower, when my lord husband's men took me there. From the other side of the Misty Hills."

Sir Henry turned even grayer than Sir Bernard.

Madeleine wondered if Morgan had told King Walter of the paths, if the king had heard of the rescue and sent men to hunt for them.

Then, she thought, we go back into the woods. They had food enough to try again.

"Madame," she said, "do you know where the king stays?"

"In Blackwyd," said Queen Katherine. "At least, he intended to when he delivered me to my guards."

Near the Misty Hills. Madeleine bit her lip as they walked on. The king's men could make more haste than a company with two injured men, and two breeding women. Her baby kicked.

Her thoughts moved more slowly than their plodding. Once they left the hills, two roads led to Owlscourt. One wet by the Misty Hills. The road and hills parted way two days' journey from the castle itself, but for a long time, they could hide in the hills if need be.

Madeleine only hoped they did not need to hide in snow.

At the slope's bottom, a stream flowed between the ice. John stepped forward to help the queen over the water, and then Madeleine . They climbed the next hill.

Through the trees on the slope, they could see open fields, covered with stubble. No mist wreathed about them, and no one walked along the road—no one to spread the news of a company from the hills. Madeleine's shoulders slumped in relief. "Let us see how far we can get before sunset."

"To shelter, I hope," said Sir Henry.

Madeleine glanced at the low, gray clouds, promising rain or snow. She, too, hoped.

"One wonders that he dared come that far," said King Walter, jovially. His voice rang over the great hall.

Somerled, at the lowest table and lucky at that, brooded over his dinner.

"With his men that fickle—fleeing at the hint of trouble." King Walter chuckled. "Much good they would have done, if he had only faced robbers."

Somerled looked into his ale cup but did not see his reflection. He was safe. The king had convinced himself that they had fled from cowardice; he would not look for treachery.

The hall's doors opened. The king glared, but the messenger walked up to the high table, where he dropped to one knee and held out a letter.

He looked gray, thought Somerled.

King Walter glanced at the seal, scowled, and broke it. Somerled had thought the hall quiet before. Now, it was still. He did not dare drink, or put down his cup.

King Walter's lip curled. "Even *wizards* fail me."

In the cottage, firelight reached only a stride from the fireplace. Where the queen sat, it shone brightly enough to show how worn her face was. Snowflakes melted in her hair. The old grandmother curled on the other side of the fire. Madeleine and the men huddled behind the queen.

Madeleine was so tired that she ached. Walking through the hills, and then along the hills, had been wearisome, but then this storm had come—she doubted that the queen even noticed the meanness of their lodgings.

In the shadows, away from the blaze and strangers, the peasant children peered, and whispered to each other.

"Nice lady, for a foreigner," said the grandmother.

Madeleine closed her eyes. Lord Magnus could not hide the queen for a day. A foreign woman of high birth—even the meanest peasant knew the woman was the queen.

She opened her eyes to look at the peasants. For all their generosity, she would take care not to let them know what road their guests left by. She swallowed. There were—hunting lodges and things.

She drew nearer the fire. The queen touched her hand and whispered, "We *have* escaped the hills."

The next morning, the road wound on, but only a few hours into their travel, John lingered. Madeleine looked back.

John hurried down the hill, though the road was muddy with melted snow. "Men," he said. "On horseback."

Snow plopped wetly from the tree boughs, leaving behind bare branches and green needles. Sunlight lay slantwise across the field to their left. To their right, the mists coiled on the hillside.

"The king's?" said Sir Henry, sounding too weary to care.

"The livery is wrong," said John.

"We hide nonetheless," said Queen Katherine. "You might have been mistaken."

For a moment, Madeleine thought of hiding from men who had come to their aid, but John knew Lord Magnus's livery. She led the way up the hill. The snow did its best to soak their boots.

"What colors did they wear?" she asked.

"Green and gold."

Madeleine scowled, and said, "Lord Patrick." The others looked at her, but said nothing. She wondered whether Lord Patrick sought only to prosper under the king, they reached the hilltop, and she looked ahead. The mists were not thick enough to conceal, but she saw a thicket of brush. They hid in its bare branches.

Queen Katherine touched her arm. "Lord Patrick—does he want to be king?"

"He—is of royal blood, Madame," said Madeleine.

The queen did not speak again. The approaching horses could be heard, though not distinctly, on the muddy road.

After the riders passed, they waited before they emerged.

After two days of warm weather, the road was a mire. Madeleine was too weary to care about anything as John haggled with the peasants over a place to spend the night. Queen Katherine's head was bent.

"A good tea, my lady," said the maid. "Good for the blood when a woman's carrying."

Madeleine could smell the herbs, but shook her head. She had no wish to risk herself on a hedgewitch's lore.

"Then for the other lady?"

Madeleine glanced at Queen Katherine's still slender form. "How did you know she was with child?"

"His lordship's men looked for her." The maid's eyes were guileless. "Lord Patrick's men. They said the king wanted— they went that way."

Madeleine tried to decide whether going that way would take them too close to the men. Then, if they took another route, that would say that they were hiding from the king's men—as if the peasants were ignorant of that.

Wind picked up, over the fields. One peasant assured John that it would snow by morning. Madeleine closed her eyes.

After the snowy morning, Madeleine could only hope that it would conceal their tracks. Beneath the noon sun, snowmelt formed puddles on the still frozen ground. Madeleine's legs were soggy and chilled. The queen leaned on Sir Bernard.

Hoof beats sounded on the road. Madeleine let out a long breath. It formed mist on the air. "Into the hills," she said.

"If the monsters attack again?" said Sir Henry.

Madeleine gestured toward her pouch.

Sir Henry huffed. "*Before* we find a place to camp?"

"If the king's men attack, it will not matter whether we have camped." Madeleine walked off the road.

The snowfall had not been deep, leaves broke through the whiteness, but leaves and snow alike were slippery. She took care with her steps, heard the slowness with which anyone followed, and glanced back. John picked the queen up and carried her up the hill. She walked with even more care.

At the top, she saw that the valley was filled with thick mist, but she did not need to see. She had never been in this part of the hills before, and looking would have revealed nothing to her—except, perhaps, a path.

Valley, Madeleine told herself. Go downhill, and you may happen on the water. You can follow a stream as well as a path, and then follow it back to escape the Misty Hills.

Sir Henry groaned. "More of the damned mist."

Madeleine walked down without glancing back. She heard footsteps, however slow, behind her. Lord, have mercy on us. Christ, have mercy on us. Lord, have mercy on us.

"I saw them here!"

The voice rang from the road. Madeleine looked back. Sir Bernard, and John and the queen, were still visible on the height. They had to lose the king's men quickly.

An arrow whistled through the air. John and Sir Bernard hurried.

"They had to have seen I had the queen," said John. His face and the queen's were as white as the snow underfoot. Queen

Katherine did not look as if she could walk. Without a word, Madeleine walked on. The mists alone might hide them.

Another arrow whistled. She heard a grunt of pain. From over the hill, came a curse and a tirade that they should not waste arrows on shadows in the mist.

But the arrow was still stuck in Sir Bernard's shoulder.

Madeleine could only be glad that he had not cried out, and that the arrow held back the blood. They would have to draw the arrow out, bind the wound, and try to prevent fever— later. Footsteps came up the hill.

Foul language came with them, cursing the fools that Lord Patrick had wished on them. Madeleine winced but did not hesitate. If the king killed his heir, Lord Patrick's case would be that much the stronger. She gathered her skirts to watch her step the better and glanced at Sir Bernard. She wished she could speak, but Sir Henry followed her gaze and eased back to stand beside Sir Bernard.

Madeleine's breath formed little puffs of mist. When the ground leveled, she could walk no faster; the ground was too slick. John took an awkward step, and Madeleine reached out to steady him.

A sound came through the woods. Madeleine flinched, and felt John's start through her hand. The sound came again. A deer, she realized. If only it would lead the men astray.

A harsh voice called, "What monsters do these hills have?"

"*They* went through the hills," said a second voice.

"*She's* from the hills—the witch."

They knew whom they looked for, but no footsteps sounded. Madeleine held her breath.

"It was only a deer!" said a third man, in disgust.

"Only a deer? Lord have mercy, Torcall's lied to us!"

Madeleine frowned.

"Claiming to be from Harthill! He's from the Misty Hills, able to tell what all the creatures are."

The second man spoke again. "Does the king know you came from the Misty Hills?"

The footsteps sounded again, heading away. Madeleine could have wept with relief.

The pool spread, black water and feathery ice vanishing into the mists, and its banks were muddy puddles. Madeleine could hear the water flowing from it, or to it.

A guide. She hoped that they had walked straight since entering the hills, but who could be certain? A stream had to flow somewhere.

Nearby, the stream gurgled between a handful of boulders and under bits of ice. She picked her way through the brambles toward it, to the stones.

"We must tend your wound, Sir Bernard," she said.

John lowered Queen Katherine and, with an arm about her, helped her sit on the nearest boulder. He looked weary. The queen sank down, in spite of how cold the stone had to be.

Sir Bernard sat on the next stone, and Madeleine surveyed the wound, which the arrow staunched. Yanking the arrowhead out would cause the blood to flow again. Leaving it in would cause fever.

Madeleine set her mouth and put her hands to the arrow. Sir Bernard stiffened. She broke off the shaft, and he winced. She pulled the bandages out, to have them ready to clap when the arrowhead was out.

"We can return to the road from here?" said John, sounding gray.

"We can," said Madeleine, "but we won't."

She had not realized what she would say until she had said it, but though everyone else stared at her, it was clear.

"If the king has men enough to find us there, he has men enough to find us wherever we emerge. On top of that, he knows we would return to Lord Magnus's lands."

The snow scrunched under John's feet. "His men can not be everywhere at once."

"Neither can we," said Madeleine. "We can not tell where is safe. With Sir Bernard's injury, we can not flee even as fast as we did this time. We have to hide, and the only way we can be sure of hiding is to stay in the Misty Hills."

Madeleine drew a deep breath. Even moments before, she had managed to avoid thinking of what that meant. "We must go to Candlewood, and throw ourselves on my—Lord Thomas's mercy. The lords of the Misty Hills are no more friendly to those from outside than their folk, but he is my father."

Her throat felt dry. Her gaze went to John, still the proud young knight who had dared the hills to free her. She was no prodigal daughter either, ready to confess to having sinned against God and her father. His refusal to sanction their match had been unreasonable and his hopes of a great match, stubborn vanity. She would bring that husband and his unborn child under Lord Thomas's roof. If she could, she would corrupt her father into treason.

No, Madeleine thought, not treason. It is not treason to protect the kingdom and the king himself from the king's folly. She had persuaded Queen Katherine. She could hope to persuade her father.

"Are you certain of your welcome?" said Queen Katherine.

Madeleine flinched. "It will be better than any other place we could reach."

Sir Henry snorted. "We have spent days wandering when hours would have taken us there. You did not think so—"

"They passed it," said John. "Bringing food in, and coming out. We could not have gone directly there. They would have seen us."

She had not thought of that, but Madeleine kept serenely quiet.

Madeleine glanced sideways. Queen Katherine walked, slowly, alongside John. She looked ahead before the queen could notice. The stream widened into another pool. This one verged on a lake, but before that, a path ran alongside it. The mud had been churned up, and the ice broken, by someone coming along the path. Within the last day—the ice had not reformed.

Following it would get them somewhere.

Two or three paths took a day's journey through the hills, or two days, in this weather. Others were quicker than the distance would seem to warrant. Madeleine studied the path. An ordinary path could take them through the hills in an ordinary length of time. Unless they took an endless path, or a snowstorm struck them, they would find Candlewood within a week.

There, Madeleine told herself stoutly, she would find a healer for Sir Bernard, who looked worse every day, and whose loyal service to Lord Magnus deserved a better reward. She stepped on the path and walked south.

Mist contorted ahead of her. Madeleine stopped. Behind her, she heard swords being drawn, but as it took form, she stood still. The creature rose up too high for it to be a wolf. It stood on four legs, when a bear would be that tall only on its hind legs. Then the stag looked at them.

John moved, behind her, as if to lay a hand on someone's arm, and whispered, "It's all right."

The stag looked mildly at him and dissolved into mist again. Madeleine let out a long breath. It was a sign of good luck, or so the peasants said. She and John had seen it when they had fled her father.

"Madeleine," said John, "is the stag said to have a sense of humor?"

Madeleine blinked. "No."

After a moment, John said, "Is it said *not* to have a sense of humor?"

Too bewildered to speak, Madeleine shook her head.

"Well, I'm wise to it. Twice it appears to predict good fortune just when we're in trouble. It has a sense of humor."

Sir Henry and Sir Bernard looked sour, but Queen Katherine laughed.

In the evening gloom, the path wound through more trees. Madeleine watched for puddles and patches of ice. Checking the footing helped distract her from the knowledge that Candlewood lay only an hour or so ahead—or so the peasants said them, however truculently.

Water opened, up ahead: a stream that moved so slowly that Madeleine could not tell which way it flowed. The path went along it. She looked for the stepping-stones, and stopped. She could just barely make out, through the mists, a bridge.

"What's that?" said Sir Henry.

"A bridge," Madeleine said, the words coming woodenly to her lips. Built of gray stone, it arched over the waters. Lichens encrusted it, and moss now brown with winter. Beneath them she could make out carvings: strange faces, with leaves instead of hair, and gaping mouths.

"I never saw anything like that when I visited the Misty Hills before," said John.

A foolish thing to say when they wanted them to cross the bridge—when peasants had directed them here and, by the footprints, used the path themselves. The bridge could not be an illusion that would throw them into the waters, though it might have other perils.

"The Misty Hills," she said, "are a place full of marvels." She looked to either side. The stream vanished into woods and mists and showed no signs of being shallow enough to ford. They could not afford to lose the path through fear of the bridge.

If they did, they would not arrive at Candlewood. . . .

Before she could lose her courage, Madeleine climbed over the stones, braced for an outcry or some magic. At the other side, she stopped, feeling foolish.

Night approached. The air grew chilly, and with Candlewood lying ahead, lights glowed all about, like ghostly candle flames. Queen Katherine clearly thought it beneath her dignity to stare, but weary though she was, she glanced about. Even John seemed fascinated. Madeleine stared into the trees, trying to pick out the manor house.

None too soon for Sir Bernard, she told herself, or for Queen Katherine. She merely wished that she faced another dragon at the path's end.

"Hey there!" The voice was belligerent and young.

Madeleine stopped. When she had left, she had known the servants, but those words gave her little to go on. She let her breath out. And new servants would have come, since.

She called, "We came to visit Lord Thomas."

"Ha!"

"Who's there?" called another voice.

"Calling on Lord Thomas? At this hour? Strangers with a likely story, that's who."

"It's Lord Thomas's place to decide," said Madeleine. "Or Lord Jasper's. Who are you?"

"Why, my lady, his servants," said the second voice, emerging from the gloom. The candles' light cast distorting shadows, but Madeleine saw enough.

"So you are, Ian. Is my father home?"

For a moment, as Ian blinked, Madeleine dreamed that her father was elsewhere and she could rest before his return.

Then Ian said, "Yes, my lady, he is."

"I must speak with him." A breeze fluttered the candle lights, as if they were true candle flames. Madeleine shivered.

In the great hall, the fire blazed. Before it, servants told stories and roasted nuts. The rest of the room, even the stairs leading to the lord's chambers, lay in shadow.

Ian pulled the door shut, with a thud. A manservant looked up. "Huh?" The other servants glanced over before they had pushed back their hoods.

"Lady Madeleine!" Little Helen looked at her—except that the kitchen maid was no longer little. Madeleine doubted that she were still a kitchen maid.

"Did your husband turn you out of house?" demanded one manservant.

"No," said John, with equal ferocity, stepping up beside her. Goggles of astonishment followed, and murmurs and glances at Queen Katherine.

"Sir Bernard needs aid," Madeleine said, trying to keep her voice from sounding thin.

Old Beitris shouted orders, and the maids scurried. Ian walked through them, to the stairs. Queen Katherine approached the fire, and the servants pulled back, whispering; Madeleine followed and warmed herself.

John slid an arm about her waist and glanced at Beitris. "A good woman?"

"She gave you that posset for your headache," Madeleine said. "She has always medicined the people of Candlewood."

Helen appeared at her shoulder, giggling, to congratulate her on her young man and the little one. Other servants surged forward with well wishes, and one pushed a mug of mulled cider into her hands. She sipped gratefully at it. Servants asked if she had heard of that horrible thing, that the king sent Morgan to break up the enchantments of the Misty Hills. He was dead now, but the mists were *still*. . . .

Madeleine's mouth twisted, but she went on drinking. Not a word about outside the hills, though they had to know what threat John had faced.

She glanced at the stairway, again and again. It seemed a long time before Ian reappeared, climbing down the stairs. "My lady Madeleine." His words silenced the hall. "Your lord father wishes to speak with you." He glanced over at John but said nothing more.

John shifted his weight but did not rise. Madeleine drained the mug. Across the room, Sir Bernard cursed as Beitris prodded his shoulder. The noise echoed.

Madeleine walked to and up the stairs. Talk broke out as she reached the top, but she could make out no words.

"In his private chamber," said Ian.

Lord Thomas, of course, would not make a public spectacle of their meeting. Madeleine walked through the outer chamber. Ian did not follow.

The firelight was dim behind her. Lamplight from her father's private chamber did not spread far from the open door.

She reached the threshold. The lamp on her father's desk shed a pool of light, surrounding it and him. Her father sat there, his head bowed over the papers before him. From the way his shoulders hunched, he was not reading.

She stepped inside. When he did not stir, her throat felt too clogged for words.

Lord Thomas sighed and looked up, revealing the lines on his face. Perhaps the lamplight cast shadows that made them look deeper than they were, but there were more than when she had fled with John.

"Daughter."

"Father."

"So you have returned—with your young man."

"With my lord husband." Neither he nor she moved. She dragged in a deep breath.

His gaze flitted down to her waist. In this light, her traveling clothing had to conceal the thickening. She laid her hand, protectively, over her waist. His mouth twisted.

"And not my husband alone. The other woman with us—"

He looked away, but sounded exasperated. "I heard rumors about Lord Magnus, but to go this far...."

"What if the queen had died in labor for the want of attendants?" Her voice surprised her with its fire. "Much good a fine match would have done you then, if the land erupted in war. It would be sooner rather than later, with the king growing more capricious by the day. Unless you think that his imprisoning the queen was an act of wisdom."

He sat back. "No. His latest was, if anything, worse."

Madeleine felt uneasy. "Lord Oliver?" she said.

"Lord Oliver was put down, and King Walter did not even have to execute him—he died in battle." He spread a hand. "Before that, Lord Duncan of West Dale demanded a safe conduct to meet the king."

"I heard that," said Madeleine.

"The king granted it. When he arrived, the king had him conducted to a private chamber—and struck, shouting of treason. His guards finished the man off."

Madeleine looked at him, blankly. One insanely calm thought pointed out that the guards might have believed the cries and feared for the king—but she thought them part and party to the murder. She let her breath out.

Her father pointed to a chair. "You look weary. Sit."

Madeleine took it.

"He had a wizard who let him into the Misty Hills," Lord Thomas said. "The hills we took as the guardian of our freedoms."

"Didn't the wizard die?"

"He died." Lord Thomas's voice was sad. "But where there is one, others will follow."

Madeleine drew a deep breath. "I am glad I did not make a grand match. Escaping court might be difficult—Lord Fergus thought he was fortunate to get away. Despite Morgan, it is harder to harm someone in the Misty Hills than at court."

Lord Thomas snorted.

"King Walter's favor can not be relied on—and would not outlive him. God willing, guarding Queen Katherine could grant us favor in the highest circles, far more than any match I might have made. If more wizards come, having such favor would be a good thing."

"So it would," said her father, heavily.

"They might be brought—wizards—if there is war over the throne."

He nodded.

Madeleine, tempted to babble on, bit her tongue.

The lamplight flickered. Her father sighed. "Child, had you come and asked for shelter, I would have received you—without reason, without excuse, without even an apology." Lord Thomas turned to face her. The light slanted across his

face, etching out the groves. "And, if a stranger offered reasons
of such excellent prudence why I should shelter him—I would
shelter him."

He rose. "Of a certainty you are safe here."

Madeleine stood. His arms came about her. She laid her
head to his shoulder, dangerously close to weeping.

His voice rumbled through his chest. "Your young man—
this John—he is good to you?"

"Very good. We have been happy." She swallowed. "You
meet him when he wooed me. Did you think that he would be
cruel to me?"

Her father put her back and looked into her face. "In spite
of his kin? Even here we heard of their striving to disinherit
him."

"That was only the last months. And whenever was I a great
one for gossiping with other ladies?"

Lord Thomas put his hand to the curve of her cheek.
"Young Alexander? They said you brought him through the
Misty Hills, when you went to the king."

"Lady Elspeth of Owlscourt has him in her care. I had to
bring him before—"

Her father looked considering. Madeleine leapt ahead,
before he could realize why she had had to. "John is here. Lord
Magnus sent three men to face the dangers, but he could not
send me without my husband. Bad enough that only one
woman attends her, and she of my birth."

Lord Thomas snorted. "A royal lady-in-waiting. The place,
I would never have dreamed of." He looked about. "The maids
must ready this room for the queen. I suppose she will wish to
go to bed at once."

"Father, we have slept in the peasant huts. And the queen is
so weary she will not notice the maids, once abed."

"Should I tell her, tonight, of Lord Duncan's death?"

Madeleine considered. The queen was tired, but. . . . The fire crackled. "I do not think she would be pleased if such news was withheld from her."

Chapter 17—Waiting and Messages

"Queen or no queen," said Nessa, "she hasn't seen thread like this!"

Her children peeped at Madeleine. Then, few of them could remember her—and two, Madeleine could not remember. The open door let in the chill, but also the sunlight, on reds, blues, and violets.

Madeleine inspected them gravely. With no clothing for either baby, they needed thread. Besides, she and the queen had nothing else to do.

"Dyers from the Misty Hills sell their threads," she said.

"Not like mine," said Nessa, and gave a price.

Minutes later, carrying thread and fewer coins, Madeleine walked toward the hall. Snow fell through the mist. The manor emerged from the mists, and the dark forms of the outbuildings became distinct.

A shrill voice said, "Is that the queen?"

Madeleine blinked. Nessa's Ebby, only a baby when she had left, stood at her elbow and stared. Wearing an old blue dress of Madeleine's, Queen Katherine stood in the doorway, and the wind blew snowflakes past her.

"It is," said Madeleine quickly and walked over.

Queen Katherine inclined her head regally. "I was looking for the chapel."

Madeleine showed her the way through the snow. Ebby did not pull back until Madeleine looked at her. The last thing a weary woman, months gone with child, needed was the curious. Ebby vanished into the mists like a squirrel.

Madeleine pulled the door open. The chapel's quiet surrounded them. The air smelled faintly of smoke and candle wax; only the tabernacle candle glowed, red from the glass. Genuflecting, Madeleine kept a wary eye on Queen Katherine, but she knelt and rose easily. She followed the queen to the altar rail, where Queen Katherine sank to both knees and murmured, "I will praise You, Lord; You have rescued me. . . ."

Her voice faded as her head bent over her hands.

A stride away, Madeleine knelt to pray silently: And have not let my enemies rejoice over me.

A long minute later, finished with the psalm, Madeleine looked up. The crucifix hung ahead of her. She could barely make out more than the cross.

Madeleine closed her eyes. In You, O Lord, I put my trust; let me never be put to confusion. Deliver me in Your righteousness and cause me to escape; incline Your ear and save me. Be to me my rock and my refuge, my strong tower. . . .

Queen Katherine walked into the hall. As Madeleine came in behind her, Beitris caught her by the arm. "Sir Bernard," she whispered. "He's going to live, belike, but that arm. . . ."

"Will he lose it?" Madeleine whispered back.

Beitris pondered a moment—an answer in itself. "He's not going to use it much."

Madeleine nodded and hoped that the queen would not need his sword arm. "Look after him." She hurried on.

The great hall was chilly, the fire still banked for the night. Queen Katherine paused. "You went to buy thread?"

Madeleine gestured at their skirts. "Madame, these dresses I left when. . . I left. I left nothing for babies."

Queen Katherine looked considering. Lord Magnus had, no doubt, chosen women to attend her, women of higher birth than Madeleine, and knowing what to do—

"Fortunately," said the queen, "my mother held that a queen must be able to oversee the sewing properly."

At the top of the stairs, the queen said, "Is the mist always this—close? The king said he had done something—had Morgan do something—to it."

"Morgan did something to the mist," said Madeleine. She did not say that the queen would have found them close before the spells.

Snow gleamed over the fields. Here and there, Magnus could see stubble that broke through. He sighed and looked over a peaceful scene. In a peaceful land, it seemed. Lands restored to their lords, outlaws suppressed, and even young fools muttered less—unless the snow hindered the tales from reaching him. His window did not look over the road.

Footsteps sounded, light and rapid, on the stairs. Magnus turned. In the doorway, Elspeth looked so pale that he took a step toward her.

"Men are coming," she said. "In royal livery, and armed."

He strode toward the door. She hurried him to the window on the stair, to see the company.

"To arrest you again?" whispered Elspeth.

He touched her cheek. "With my men too far-flung to be all caught, and ready to rage?" King Walter, perhaps, did not consider that Owlscourt lay beside the West Dales; many of his men had reason beside his arrest. "I think you should return to your ladies."

Elspeth flitted up the stairs. Magnus went down. If he had thought, he would have directed Lady Madeleine—elsewhere. Somewhere.

In the courtyard, he ordered the gates opened, and the company rode in.

Their captain pulled up his horse and said, "Where is she?"

"What woman are you seeking?" said Magnus. "And by what right?"

The captain scowled. "The Queen's Grace."

"Has ill befallen her? I had heard that the King's Grace brought magicians from far lands to protect her."

The captain's mouth set in hard lines. Magnus met his gaze. His own knights shifted behind him, and he raised his voice. "Take the king's men over the castle. Show them everything they wish to see."

He wished he could not imagine reasons why these men had reached this castle, but Lady Madeleine's company had not.

Katherine sat by the window. The fire crackled, and Madeleine sat by it. Katherine felt a draft's cold finger touch her and knew the fireside would be warmer.

She did not move, though shadows formed about her. She had seen the candles the night they arrived, even if weariness had kept her from more than a glance. She should not have let herself be frightened of them the next night. *This* night, she would see them.

Out of the corner of her eye, she saw yellow flare.

Slowly, she let her breath out. Like candle flames on invisible candles. Nothing so monstrous as the dragon. More slowly, she turned her head.

They glowed—here and there, shifting through the trees. Katherine swallowed. They moved no faster than a man could walk, and at the steady height, like a man holding a candle.

"Heh," said Ian. "Come two days ago, I've put you to work on the foaling. . . ."

The stables were dark and warm and smelled of hay and horses. John admired the gray foal. For all that the horses of the Misty Hills could endure their magics, they looked like the horses outside. "As if you needed the aid. A fine colt."

Ian barely twitched, but John thought he was pleased. "Nor even Lord Jasper. He went off, knowing it was near time, but knowing I was here. When he's all but promised the foal."

They left the stable, into the glowing mists. Loud voices sounded before the house.

"So soon?" Ian said. "To look at their foal? Promises are one thing—"

Two youths came about the house. Their clothing was better than a peasant's, no worse than what he might wear himself if riding on some task, and they resembled each other greatly.

Ian muttered, "Sons of Lord Haral of Kineford. Lady Sorcha's cousins."

Twins, surmised John; not full grown, and their heights matched. He nodded to them. They stared back. One, his hair a trifle darker than his twin's, said, "They said the colt was back here."

"It is," said John. "I just saw it. I am John of Summerfield, Lord Thomas's son-by-marriage."

The youths looked away, as if trying to guess what to say, but a minute later, presented themselves, the speaker as Derek, and his brother as Ninian.

Then Ninian said, "You were the ones who brought the queen here."

How fast the news flew, said John. "So we were."

"Not fitting," muttered Derek.

"Quite unfitting," said John, "to hold the queen prisoner like that."

Ninian took a step forward. "What's the king going to make of this?"

"I commend your loyalty," said John. He glanced between them and wished he knew their tempers. "Doubtlessly, you have no choice but to obey him in all things."

Their glares grew poisonous. Derek said, "We don't grovel before the king."

John's eyebrows shot up. "I find it hard to believe that two gentlemen fear the king—but it must be so, if loyalty does not drive you."

Ninian scowled. "You're meddling."

"The king unleashed his wizard on the Misty Hills," said John. "The very mists have been touched. Is this—not meddling?"

Their expressions remained truculent.

"Lady Sorcha," muttered Ian, "always had manners."

"I knew that the king had ventured to the hills, before, but I thought little of it." Lord Thomas lowered his wine cup to the table. It glittered in the firelight, though the fire burned low. "He was hunting."

Madeleine remembered the king's complaints at Owlscourt and went on sewing. Queen Katherine tilted her head to one side, listening.

"He came to the northern parts, far from here, so I did not have to mark him. There were no rumors of his caprices then."

"Did he not lose his guide, and get lost in the mists?" said Queen Katherine.

Madeleine, not turning her head, listened.

Lord Thomas nodded. "Many a lord's done that, though. Too many to mark. Lord Fergus did."

"You might have found the king," said John, standing by the fire, "as you did Lord Fergus."

"He's not Lord Fergus for gratitude." Thomas glanced at the queen. "Not even when he was not noted for his whims."

"He is a king," said Queen Katherine. "When kings are known for their generosity, they are often overthrown. Taxes must be high to supply munificence and those who receive it take it as their due." She sat back. "So far from earning gratitude, he may stir resentment that he did not give again."

After a silent moment, John crouched to lay another log to the blaze. Orange flames licked it.

"And, for me to find him would have meant he wandered far." Lord Thomas shook his head. "Too far. The king's death without an heir would be bad for the land. Imagine if he should vanish, and no one could prove whether he died."

A log in the fireplace gave a loud crack, and sparks flew up, bright orange dots in the smoke. The noise pulled Madeleine from her vision of the king's vanishing. She shivered.

Beneath the ice, Graybrook's babbles were muffled.

Jasper's horse leapt it easily; his attention was on the manor house ahead. Even through the mist, he could see dark shapes moving about it. He rode closer. Grooms led off horses.

Visitors, thought Jasper. He rode up and handed off his own horse. He stayed a moment to study the others. Fit for young noblemen; perhaps they were just hunting, and had stopped to greet Lord Ross and Lady Isobel. He walked toward the hall.

"It concerns you," came a voice, touched with malice. "You are about to bind yourself to that house in marriage."

"We pledged our honor. We have sealed the betrothal," said Lord Ross. His voice was calm, but the answer came quickly, as if he realized that some defense was needed—as if he might not do this, were his honor not bound.

Jasper stepped into the room. A youth stood before Lord Ross. Lady Isobel stood in the back of the great hall; she glanced past her father and the youth, at Jasper. The youth started and turned. Though he bowed when Lord Ross presented Jasper as the son-by-marriage, he added without pause, "I must be off, on my hunt."

"Good fortune at it," said Jasper. The youth left, calling for his horse.

"What was he speaking of?" said Jasper.

Lord Ross did not look at him.

Lady Isobel, color in her cheeks, said, "The story is that your sister rescued Queen Katherine and brought her to Candlewood." Her cheeks grew more pink. "Serves the king right. Thinking he can ignore the prerogatives of the Misty Hills."

Madeleine, thought Jasper. Madeleine is at Candlewood. He drew a deep breath, to steady himself. It would hurt Isobel if he left at once. That was the only thing that kept him.

"That young rogue claimed to have seen them both," said Lord Ross. His voice was slow and heavy. "Bad enough what the king did, but he merely set the tower in the hills. He did not meddle with the estates."

"Meddle!" said Lady Isobel. "Is that what will befall me after my wedding? You will find my presence here *meddling*?"

He ought to say something. He ought to try to calm his overwrought bride, he ought to point out they could not trust rumor, but he stood and thought that the story might be true.

"She defied the king's wickedness—" She turned to Jasper.

"I have not been to Candlewood," said Jasper, "or I would have brought the tale myself."

"What are you doing?" said Drostan.

Somerled looked about the tiny room. He had shared it with seven other men, though they were seldom all here at once. He thought he had everything of his own. He slung the bag on his back. "Urgent dealings, for my family."

Drostan's eyes narrowed. Somerled tried to meet his gaze steadily. King Walter might not realize that he came from the lands east of the Misty Hills, and that he had neither gone there nor gotten a message from there—but such things could hardly be kept secret from other messengers.

"It must be urgent," said Drostan, "in this weather."

"My father has spent too long on looking for a bride. Unless I go to look over his shoulder, he will get nowhere."

Drostan's mouth twitched. After a moment, he said, "You are a royal messenger."

"I was. I already have leave to go."

Drostan stood in the doorway, blocking it.

"I delivered the safe conduct into Lord Duncan's hands," said Somerled. "With my own hands. "

"You are not accountable for the messages you deliver," said Drostan.

"I've taken coins for them," said Somerled. He shifted his bag. "Besides, do you trust every lord in the land not to blame the messenger?"

With a grimace, Drostan stepped from his way. I'm not, thought Somerled darkly, the only messenger who thinks so. You are right; many of us are abandoning our post.

"Have you heard about the Misty Hills?" said Drostan. "You're going near there."

Somerled's heart stopped before hammering. "About the queen?"

"What other news would come from there? They say she's been taken from the tower."

Nothing, thought Somerled, would distract the king from that. Courtiers would be wise to flee at once.

With a few days of rest, the queen had recovered her color. In the window seat, she watched two red birds flit through the snow-laden branches and ignored the sewing in her lap.

Madeleine inspected her own. She could sew enough for two babies. She smiled fondly. Being a lady-in-waiting in court would be beyond her, but here, as long as she attended Queen Katherine by day, and slept in the outer chamber by night, propriety was served. Their evenings might be sparse, with only Sir Henry, her father, and John—Beitris having threatened Sir Bernard with a dire fate if he rose from his bed—and their days filled with needlework, but they managed.

Queen Katherine took a few desultory stitches. "Your brother—Lord Jasper. Your lord father said that he was not here, but did not say why."

"Courting," said her father from the doorway. "He had some work about the farther estates, but I gave him leave to go on when he was done." He bowed. "Madame. A Lady Isobel of Graybrook. The betrothal has been concluded, but not the marriage articles."

Lady Isobel—Madeleine remembered a thin, dark girl, with an eye for fine needlework. Then, she thought with a smile, Jasper probably had no high description of John.

"What glad news for your son and your house," said Queen Katherine. "May they live to see their children's children. Are the discussions going well?"

Lady Isobel, Madeleine noted, was no grand match. She managed to avoid being petty enough to say it aloud.

Hoof beats sounded outside. Madeleine rose to look. She blinked. Lord Thomas had not sounded as if Jasper had enough time to do his tasks, venture to Graybrook, and find his way home again.

Still, he had hardly changed a hair. The groom took his horse, and he looked over the house. She doubted he could see her in the shadows.

She turned back to the room. "My brother has returned. He could answer you himself."

The queen smiled. All her regal grace could not save her from looking eager.

Just inside the great hall, Thomas stood with Jasper. Warning him, thought Madeleine as she came down the stairs. Jasper nodded every now and again, and glanced at the upper chamber. She went down the last steps.

She saw nothing of John. Then, when John had come to Candlewood to woo her, Jasper had met him.

The voices fell silent. Then Jasper said, "Madeleine." He put his arms about her, and kissed her cheek. She kissed him back; his face was still chilled from the wintry air. Then he stood and looked into her face—as mute as she was.

Their father came beside them. Jasper glanced away. "I heard of—your arrival."

That would explain much. "The queen wishes to meet you."
Jasper's eyebrows lifted. Madeleine smiled wryly. He had
not considered how dull Candlewood might look beside a royal
court. "Come, I will present you."

Someone moved by the hearth. Thinking it was John, she
looked over. A servant tended the fire, and Madeleine let out
her breath.

The queen asked Jasper about his intended bride until the
mists outside grew gray. John's arrival had had Jasper greet
him, but Queen Katherine was not thus diverted from their
talk.

Madeleine picked out a green thread.

"No, my sister did not wed here," Jasper said.

Madeleine blinked and looked up.

"She and Lord John had met at court. That was where he
wooed her."

He won me here, thought Madeleine, when he braved the
Misty Hills for me.

"They met here, and left to marry. It was the talk of the
land for a month or so." Jasper's gaze shifted. "My lord father
maintained that she could have made a grander match."

"It would not have mattered," said Madeleine. "I wished to
marry John."

Jasper twitched. "She sent us news of the wedding, and of
her son's birth, but nothing more."

"You sent us no news," said John.

For a moment, the crackle of the fire broke the silence. A
log sighed, settling deeper into the ashes.

"I would have sent news of my wedding," Jasper said.

Queen Katherine glanced between them, and raised an
eyebrow. Madeleine's stomach roiled.

Jasper said, "Tell me of Sandy. Who does he favor?"

"John," said Madeleine. "His hair is fairer and more curled, but the servants at Summerfield assure me that John's hair darkened." She smiled. "And that he chattered as little. A boy of few words, Sandy."

Jasper returned the smile. "I would like to see him."

"You would have been welcome at Summerfield," said John.

The silence that ensued was so deep that Madeleine heard the swish of the snowflakes against the windows.

"Ah," said Jasper.

Madeleine's tongue touched her lips. She had not thought John this angry, still.

John's voice grew colder. "You did, after all, manage to send her a dowry, and not cut her off without a penny."

Lord Thomas looked older than a minute before. "Madeleine did not even leave a message. You were gone before I returned, and the servants would never have dared open such a letter."

The fire burned on. Snow swished against the windows. After a minute, John inclined his head. "That was not the impression that we had, my lord."

In the fire, a log sighed.

"Sandy," said Queen Katherine, "is with Lady Elspeth now, but it would be well if he were not. After my lord husband violated a safe conduct, I grieve to say that even a child might not be safe."

"We have not even concluded how to tell Lord Magnus of your safety, Madame," said Lord Thomas. "Sending someone to fetch my grandson would be a greater danger. Any token could reveal the messenger to the king's men."

"I'll go," said Jasper. "I need no token to identify me." He smiled. "I promised Lady Isobel that I would bring her the truth; I could pass by there, and be on my way."

Madeleine sat up. No one looked ready to dissuade him. A glance at his face quenched any desire of hers to try. "I would not take the path I took to reach Queen Katherine. Lord Donald knows I vanished into the hills there."

Water gurgled beside the snowy path. The stream was still visible in places: black stretches of water between the snow-laden ice, as it babbled from beneath the oak's roots. Jasper smiled. On the right path, at any rate. His smile faded. Even if the king's men might know about this path. In the warmth of Candlewood, he had thought the speed worth the risk.

It was too late to take another.

His hand went to his throat, to the medallion of St. Michael. Isobel had been somewhat quieted by the news, but without a word to discourage him, she had given him the medallion.

The mists gave way, and Jasper rode out of them. Along the road, as far as he could see, no one moved, nor even any beast or bird. His breath forming small clouds on the air, he turned his horse along the road. It was as snowy as the path and little wider.

Two days later, the warmth of the afternoon turned the road into muck. The sunlight came through hazy clouds, and his horse's legs were covered with mud.

Jasper was glad of that when he saw the men ahead. They wore livery. Flight would draw their attention, but grime would hide the gray hide of the Misty Hills. He and that company rode slowly toward each other.

They hailed him. They drew no weapons, but never had their hands far from them.

Jasper pulled up his horse. "Is the bridge still good?" They looked warily at him. "They said it was in the last village, but with the water from the snow. . . ."

"It's good," said one man, surly. "You seen anyone along the road?"

Jasper paused. "Peasants driving their cattle."

Another man cut in. "Gentry."

He glanced among them, over their gear—no gentry among their number. "What is the meaning of this? Hectoring the gently born?"

"Looking for the queen," said one. His fellows glared at him.

"And what are you doing here?" said the first man.

Jasper set his face in disdain. His heart hammered. If he betrayed himself as Madeleine's brother—but he could tell the truth. "If you bandy about the name of gentlewomen, your tongue might get cut out one day." He straightened. "I am fetching my poor sister's child—the child she bore after running away with a young man. If you ask my name, I will cut out your tongue now."

The other men chortled.

"What is the meaning of this?" said Magnus, pulling up his horse on a snowy road.

The king's men looked banefully at him. Magnus looked back. It had to look like a chance encounter, and not a plan crafted with care after he heard the news. The leafless trees were dark from snowmelt dampening them, and every man's breath was white in the air. He glanced at the prisoner. Phillip looked back at him. "What are you doing here with a lord of noble birth? In chains?"

The captain straightened. "The king commissioned us—"

"To search for the Queen's Grace!"

"This man struck one of my men! That's treason!"

Magnus's heart beat harder. He could not even hint that he had heard why. Invading the women's quarters—that was reason enough for anger, even if Phillip's brother had not died in the prison. "So is leaving your task. You were commissioned by the king to do that, not punish malefactors. The King's Grace may hold that he punished you on his behalf."

The consternation on the captain's face gave him hope. He pressed on before the man had time to think. "I will hold this man. I am a jailor of suitable birth. The king will approve."

He prayed that they would not find the queen. Besides her safety, the king's displeasure with failure would make him overlook the illogic of a punishment before the crime.

But while they yielded up Lord Phillip, he still did not know where the queen was. Whether she was safe, and safe from discovery. Lady Madeleine might have led him into folly.

"In the women's chambers," muttered Phillip.

Magnus laid a hand on his arm.

In snowy fields, Owlscourt stood ahead. Jasper was glad that he did not have to venture to Summerfield. He kicked his horse's sides. It barely needed the urging to move more quickly to the gate.

The guard hailed him. Briefly, his name jumped to his mouth, but King Walter might have men here. "A message for Lord Magnus."

A breeze poked at his neck. Slowly, as if ill-oiled, but silently, the gates opened. He rode in and felt no surprise at

seeing armed guards. Then he glanced past them. Lord
Magnus stood on the flagstones. He let out his breath, and it
was white on the air. He dismounted. A stable boy took his
horse and hurried off. No one else approached.

He walked to Lord Magnus. "My lord, I bear you a message
from my sister and her husband."

"Is she all right?"

Not Madeleine, Jasper guessed. "Yes."

Lord Magnus raised his voice. "Come in." In the shadows
of the doorway, he spoke again. "And your sister, and the
men?"

"Sir Bernard was shot by the king's men. His arm will never
be the same, but he is unlikely to die."

Lord Magnus shook his head. "With Lord Duncan of the
West Dales—and more things—I begin to worry that the
tower might have been safer."

Jasper snorted. "My lord father has taken her under his
protection."

The stairs were dimmer than even the cloudy outside, and
he could not make out Lord Magnus's expression. "He got her
into the Misty Hills."

"With Morgan's help," said Jasper. "Morgan paid for it."

Lord Magnus said nothing more, as they climbed six steps.
Then his voice emerged from the dimness. "You can speak
freely, here, but the news of your arrival will spread."

"News does," said Jasper.

Laughter—a little child's laughter—pealed from the room
ahead of them. Jasper stopped, without thought of kings or
queens or rumors.

Lord Magnus sounded amused. "Go see your nephew."

Jasper climbed the remaining stairs, barely noticing that he
was brushing by Lord Magnus as if the man were a servant. In
the room, a dark-haired woman, of middle years, knelt by a
blond boy. Jasper heard Lord Magnus saying something, but

did not make out the words. The woman moved back. Jasper
went down on one knee besides Sandy.

"Good evening," he said.

Sandy looked wary. "G'evening." His hands tightened on
his toys: a wooden knight, a wooden green lion.

"I'm your Uncle Jasper."

Sandy scowled. "Haven't got an Uncle Jas-per. Got an
Uncle Donald, and an Uncle Andrew. . . . they're gone."

He favored John indeed, thought Jasper. "And I came.
Your mama asked me to bring you to her."

Sandy turned the lion over in his hand—and then he
grinned. "Carried off by wicked uncle."

Jasper leaned forward and kissed the boy's forehead. "In the
morning," he said and rose. By the doorway, Lord Magnus
stood with another man. Jasper raised an eyebrow.

"Lord Phillip," said Lord Magnus. "My—prisoner."

Jasper flinched.

"The king's men ransacked the women's quarters at his
castle. He awaits the royal judgment for striking one." Lord
Magnus met his gaze. "Can you safely bear Sandy away?"

"The Queen's Grace does not think him safe here," said
Jasper. "I can say that my sister ran away from home, and I am
fetching her son." His mouth twisted. "It's even true."

The evening grew darker. Perhaps he should have waited, but
Candlewood was too near.

Sandy crowed and reached for the snowflakes. Jasper
tightened his arm around the boy's waist. Sandy wriggled.

"Dragon!" He pointed at a shadowed bush.

In spite of himself, Jasper looked. The bush's branches were
plain. "Not a dragon," he said, with a low laugh. Their

approach made the branches lose any hint of draconic shape. "I don't think you've ever seen a dragon."

Sandy bobbed his head. "Mama slept. Dragon looked at us."

Jasper's arm tightened about his nephew again. He was glad that they were not that far from Candlewood.

Beside the game, a candle burned. Its light did not reach far. Neither did the firelight. The queen sat with sewing neglected in her lap. Sir Henry and Sir Bernard wordlessly moved the pieces. Even John sat by the fire and said nothing.

No news had come since Jasper had left. Not even of other things about the land.

Madeleine sighed. A chess piece clicked against the board. She inspected the tiny gown. She had forgotten how small newborns were.

"Unca Jasper, down!"

Madeleine dropped her sewing. She had missed not only the sounds of the horse, but Jasper's climbing the stairs.

John already moved from the shadows. Sandy hurtled across the room. John dropped to one knee, and Sandy threw his arms about his father's neck and boasted of how his Uncle Jasper had brought him through the woods, and the candles, and how he had seen a dragon.

Madeleine glanced at Jasper. He said, his voice low, "A bush."

Madeleine walked over. Sandy turned his head to bestow a kiss on his mother. John sat again, with Sandy in his lap. The queen sat still and watched them. Sandy wriggled around and smiled. "Ev'ning," he said. The queen smiled, regally, graciously.

Jasper warmed his hands by the fire. "Madeleine, Lord Magnus had more news: your godfather lives in peace and safety on his estates."

"That *is* good news," said the queen.

Jasper turned from the fire. "And—the king is not taking this disappearance graciously. His men are searching everywhere, in Owlscourt and elsewhere."

In the pause, Madeleine heard footsteps on the stairs—slow and deliberate movements. They had matters that, if less important, were more pressing. "Come here, Sandy."

Sandy, only mildly perplexed, let her take him from John. She turned to the door.

Lord Thomas came in but no closer. He watched Sandy, his face half hidden in shadow.

"This is your grandfather, Sandy."

Sandy scowled. "Grandpa's *dead*."

"You have two grandpas."

Sandy's hand went to his mouth. For a moment, Madeleine could not look at her father. Then Sandy smiled. "Like uncles!"

Chapter 18—Festivities and Alarms

The smell of the cooking spread from the manor house's kitchens, where cooks labored at sweet puddings and spiced cake. In the valley, where the cottages clustered, snow lay on their roofs, and smoke curled from their chimneys.

Madeleine looked past them, to the forest. Peasants gathered at its edge, and children ran about and laughed. The first ones already wandered into the forest, to gather ivy and find the Yule log.

"We'll have to walk quickly," said John.

Madeleine looked at the way. Dried-out plants and brown flowers still poked above the snow, but the footing was uncertain.

She smiled in mischief. *If* they walked that way. "Follow me." She went to their right, into a pine grove. The needles were thick and amber-colored underfoot.

John, after a grunt of surprise, followed. "You showed me this one on May Day."

Madeleine laughed. The pines went down a slope where gray rocks pushed their way through the needles and roots. John took her arm. Madeleine leaned on him. Hill doves tolled among the trees as they reached the slope's bottom.

John looked up it. "We will return across the fields."

"Of course," said Madeleine. "The way to bring back the Yule log." Despite herself, her smile faded. Fetching the Yule Log and the ivy was a politick act on her part and John's. It showed that all was well.

A small girl came toward Madeleine. Her hands were full of ivy, and she wore an ivy crown. She smiled broadly and held out a second crown. Madeleine bent over. The girl crowned her, over her veil. Madeleine straightened carefully, lest it fall off, and the girl ran off, giggling. All about the forest clearing, other women donned their ivy crowns as they caroled.

John straightened the crown. "Does this mean we have sufficient ivy?" he said in her ear, his breath warming it.

The sleighs' wood had vanished beneath their green burden. Madeleine stamped her feet; that knocked off some snow, but nothing could warm her toes. "One hopes so."

A whip cracked through the air. The oxen lugged the log across the snows. "With that monster," said John, "Candlewood will be warm for a long time."

They joined the songs "in honor of the Prince of Peace." Madeleine sighed. Peace. Peace in the realm, peace in her life—John reached out to take her hand, and she smiled again. She had peace in her family.

Oxen hauled the log through the village and up to the manor house. Lord Thomas greeted them at the doorway, and servants produced eggnog that Madeleine seized on with gratitude.

"A fine start to the season," said John. Madeleine kissed him.

At the top of the stairs, the queen stood. Her gaze was steady. Madeleine realized that Queen Katherine had watched them—not the revelers in general, but her and John. She colored, and found herself remembering that the queen had conceived after she had granted the pardon.

From the whispers about, the cooks outdid themselves, even for a Christmas feast. Once or twice as they presented a dish by the flourish of two trumpets, Katherine thought that they would celebrate Lent early for the want of spice, but the results fit the feast. She ate meats, puddings, comfits—

Then the dinner was done. Servants attacked the lower tables to clear them aside. Others handed about candies to the high table, and to the peasants.

Katherine leaned forward. "Do you have entertainers, my lord?"

"Sometimes, Madame," said Lord Thomas. "Not as much for Christmas. We celebrate by dancing." He glanced to the side. "Musicians, of course. Between the dances, mummers, but the dances come first."

"What are the dances that must be held?" There would be such tradition, at Christmas time. She suspected it would be adhered to here more strictly than at King Walter's court—or even her father's.

Lord Thomas spoke slowly, "The first, in honor of this high solemnity, is that the lord of highest birth dances with the lady of highest birth." He paused as the last table vanished, and the musicians moved into place. "If Lord John were the eldest son, and not the second, he would be the lord of highest birth, but as it is. . . ." In a less grave man, she would have thought his expression anxious. Peasants and servants glanced at the high table. Lady Madeleine studiously did not look at her. "No one would wish the lady to dance if. . . ."

Katherine inclined her head. "If the dance is stately, I think that a most fitting tradition, and well worth keeping."

The music went on, evenly.

Her father and Queen Katherine turned through the measures. Queen Katherine stepped awkwardly more than once, but her father moved to match her.

Her father led the queen back to the high table, and the next dance was to begin: another measure of the one the queen and the lord had danced. The handful of knights that held their lands from Candlewood rose, and servants and peasants stirred. Sir Bernard and Sir Henry looked awkward. Two daughters of knights, young and giggling, ran over to them, and they proved too discomfited to refuse. Madeleine's gaze went over the gathering figures. Even young children joined in. When she was here, she had yet to fail this dance since her feet could trace the measures.

"Are you fit for it?" John murmured.

Madeleine rose. He led her to the gathering couples, who put them at the head of the dance. The music struck up, and Madeleine stepped into the measure.

I wonder how the king celebrates Christmas, thought Madeleine. Then the measures drew her in, leaving her no time for thought. When that dance was done, Jasper laid claim to her. Only for the third did she plead weariness, and join the high table again.

After that one, dancers pulled back. Mummers swept out onto the floor: St. George in white with a red cross, wielding a wood sword and wearing a preposterous helmet; the princess in patchwork finery; her father the king crowned in ivy; the doctor in his long black robe, with his bag; the dragon in green, with a long tail. Madeline smiled. Some of these things, she had seen when she was Sandy's age.

Sandy sat up, even from his pudding, and said, "Dragon!" pointing with his spoon.

Madeleine uneasily wondered how much he had seen of that dragon, that night.

Sandy watched, rapt, as St. George and the dragon fought, and the dragon fell to the ground, writhing, and shouted, "Help, help! A doctor, a doctor!"

St. George, being a true, gallant, and chivalrous knight, held his shield over the dragon until the doctor had cured him with some absurd potion from his bag. Then they fought again.

Sandy's eyes were wide. Queen Katherine leaned forward to whisper to Madeleine, "It's as well that the dragon could not speak. Otherwise, your husband and the other men would have revealed themselves as ungallant knights."

St. Stephan's Day dawned clear and bright. The frost had formed, wherever anything was bare of snow, but it was not that cold for a December day. No hale young man had an excuse not to pay the Christmas calls.

John glared at the frost. They had not talked, but Lord Thomas's son by marriage should go with his son.

"I do not think it wise," said Lord Thomas behind him.

John tensed.

"Why not?" said Jasper. "You forgave Madeleine."

"It would remind all that the queen is here."

"Should we act abashed?" said John.

Lord Thomas turned to face him.

"Her presence gives them no grounds for offense. We should abash *them*, if they try to shame us."

Jasper grinned.

The hall at Bramblebrook was larger than at Candlewood, and ivy festooned every inch of it. Jasper glanced at the track. Visitors had beaten the snow into the frozen ground. He wondered how many of them still remained at Bramblebrook.

John looked at him. Jasper said, "Lord Allyane keeps a fine table—and cellar. We'll see many a young lord here."

"Not entirely sober?"

Jasper nodded.

"Then, once we are past here, the worst is over."

Jasper hoped he was right.

They rode up. Stable boys took their horses though Jasper could see how little room was left in the stables. A portly man, of middle years, appeared in the doorway. Laden with ivy garlands himself, he waved a great cup in the air. "Come in! To good ale, good food, and good cheer!"

He beamed widely enough to vouch for the last, and his face was red enough for the first. John glanced at him and then at Jasper.

"Not the lord," said Jasper. "His uncle, Olewer. Who never misses a chance at ale."

They reached the doorway. The gathering filled the great hall. A shout of laughter reached them.

Sir Olewer lifted his cup again. "To good Lord Jasper of Candlewood!" He took a swig and turned, unsteadily, toward John. "And to—" He peered.

"My brother by marriage, John of Summerfield," said Jasper.

Olewer stared at John. Then, looking if not more sober, at least more solemn, he lifted the cup again. Jasper wondered whether it was a toast to John, or a response to shock.

Inside, the air was warm from more than the fire. Jasper was not astounded that Sir Olewer had remained by the open doors. At least, though Ninian and Derek looked at them, they did not seem on the verge of resuming their quarrel.

He nodded to the nearest man he knew—Sir Rory, who still looked sober. "Have you seen Lord Allyane? My brother by marriage and I must greet him."

Sir Rory glanced at John and raised his cup.

John inclined his head. "I can hardly drink Lord Allyane's ale without his knowing me."

"Why not?" snarled another man. "You brought the king upon us without knowing us."

John raised his eyebrows. "My name is not Morgan."

Some men smiled. One said, "Lord Allyane was by the fire."

Jasper nodded and headed off, with John. He greeted half a dozen men, presenting John, drawing glances, but went on. When one youth assured him that ice wolves had been seen about the villages, he hesitated only a moment, asking, "Have they been harrying the sheep?"

Sir—Cuthbert laughed. "When have they not? Why should we wait for what we know is coming? It's not so mild a winter that they will content themselves with deer!"

"They never content themselves with deer," said another knight. "No matter how mild the winter."

"A hunt is in order," said Sir Cuthbert.

Jasper inclined his head. "I must go greet Lord Allyane."

"So you must. He's by the fire." His gaze went to John, but he did not ask his name. John bowed, deeply. Cuthbert, coloring, looked away, and someone laughed.

Near the fire, Lord Allyane sat with wine-cup in hand. He blinked not at all at John and offered them the ale. "Finest ale in the hills! Drink it here, so you will not taste the lesser brews!"

Jasper smiled. Fine though the brew was, he doubted that he or John would get that drunk. He drank some, glanced about the hall, and felt a hand on his sleeve. After a blank moment, he knew that someone tried to draw him away from John.

Reluctantly, he went. Only when they were strides away, hidden by a clump of young men flirting with Lord Allyane's daughters, did Jasper manage to turn and see—Sir Chrisdean.

Sir Chrisdean looked past him rather than at him. "So that's whom Ninian talked of."

"My brother by marriage," said Jasper.

Sir Chrisdean looked at him. He did not seem drunk, but Jasper did not doubt that, Christmas peace or none, a fight might be in the offing. He took another drink of ale. Better here than at Candlebrook, with the queen and Madeleine.

"I didn't think you were—pleased with what happened the last time a stranger came to your manor," said Sir Chrisdean.

"So we were not," said Jasper. "I just met my nephew. A sad thing, when we rashly commit ourselves to courses that will last for long after. It pleased my father to be able to reconcile with my sister." He raised his ale cup. "Then, I suppose outsiders are not welcome in the Misty Hills now, after the king and his wizard. Morgan was as good as an outsider, doing such things." He shook his head. "Though Ninian still seemed to fear the king."

Sir Chrisdean scowled.

"With Morgan gone, I am surprised to see such fear of the king about. Is there another wizard about?" He cocked an eyebrow. Sir Chrisdean looked ready to retreat—and prepare another attack. "A wizard I have not heard of?"

"Wizard?" said another man, sharply.

"Not that I know of," said Jasper, "but—why else would so many lords about the Misty Hills dread the king's wrath? They have no aim except to please him."

"We are the lords of the Misty Hills!" roared a man—in the crowd, but so large that Jasper could see him. Hew, Jasper remembered. Talk quieted. "We obey the king's lawful commands, because we are his lords, and not from fear!" He lowered his voice ominously. "And as for his unlawful commands. . . ."

He looked about the room. The silence was broken with roars of agreement, many a lord and knight clapping his hand to his sword.

Jasper breathed a sigh of relief. John stood at his shoulder. John glanced at Hew and pitched his voice low. "Can he compel them?"

"He's only a knight, a lord's cousin—and more bluster than fight," said Jasper. His mouth twitched. "But he's done better than that. He's convinced them. They will not go back on their word."

"Just as long as none of them consider expelling the queen a lawful command."

John's mouth was harsh. Jasper remembered he had been one of the prisoners—and remembered Phillip.

The clouds were bright, and the snow gleamed.

A Christmastide visit, thought Malcolm. Is there anything strange in that? He surveyed Owlscourt's battlements. And he was a lone rider—where, after all, would he find new men?— but he should look harmless.

The guards responded to his hail, and the gates opened into the chill. He rode in, handed off his horse, and noted how few horses stood in the stable—but he had seen travelers leaving Owlscourt for Christmas greetings elsewhere.

All to the good—he needed few witnesses.

A servant ushered him up a stairway. Lord Magnus stood in the doorway to greet him. "A far way to come to bear Christmas greetings."

"Not as far as all that," said Malcolm. "I have not returned to Eastwyck since—" He spread his hands.

"Lord Fergus sent me word," said Lord Magnus. He stepped back. In the chamber, a lady sewed. Malcolm raised an eyebrow.

"I have no secrets from my lady wife," said Lord Magnus.

Malcolm bowed. "I spoke with Lord Fergus. He was reluctant."

Lady Elspeth took a stitch.

Malcolm decided that Lord Magnus did not intend to answer him. "I have heard that he was reluctant in the matter of a pardon."

"He did not believe it possible," said Lord Magnus. "Nor did I. Even when I saw Lady Madeleine had brought a paper to the tower, I did not believe it a pardon."

Malcolm snorted. "Because you had not thought of the queen. Now it would do you no good."

Lord Magnus's eyes narrowed. Lady Elspeth laid her sewing in her lap. That blow had drawn blood.

"There is the question of how long the pardon will stand."

"My lord," said Lady Elspeth, "this is treason. At Michaelmas, King Walter feasted in our hall. He accepted our hospitality and did not attempt to void the pardon."

Malcolm snorted. "I have a pardon myself. Queen Katherine also sent a warning against letting it be known without need. A sage, prudent, and judicious princess."

Lord Magnus poured a cup of cider. Malcolm let his breath out. When Magnus held it out, he reminded himself it was an offer of hospitality. Mulled cider, welcome warmth against his hands—he drank no more than a sip, against drunkenness.

"Some of us," said Lord Magnus, "lament the sufferings of Eastwyck—but still have things that they might lose."

As if his sister were dead. "Beneath this king," said Malcolm, "you *will* lose them."

"In a civil war, we could lose them as well."

"Though the queen is with child?"

Lady Elspeth's voice cut in. "Let the poor woman bear her babe before you crown it." She picked her sewing up. "You will need every moment to prepare."

Malcolm glared at her. If the king had acted against Lord Ivo at once—he had lost good men in the fight.

Lady Elspeth sewed again. "I dare say you know much about the temper of the land. Queen Katherine may need the shelter of your knowledge, if she is to be regent for her child."

On St. John's Day, Queen Katherine looked out the window. "I did not know that you expected visitors."

Madeleine rose. "It's Christmastide." Then, she had never been to court at Christmas. The custom might not hold there.

"They visit at Harthill, to be sure, but do your young men fare over these hills and snows, to but visit?"

"It would be strange if we had none," said Madeleine.

It would be worrisome. Before, some years, no one had come until St. John's Day—once or twice, even Holy Innocents—but she would have preferred visitors yesterday. But five young men drew up their horses in the morning light, horses too fine for peasants. Though their faces were red from the chill, they laughed as the grooms took their horses. Her heart hammered as she wondered whether they were drunk. "I will greet them."

She walked down the hallway and the stairs. Ian hurried toward the door.

By the fireplace, the maids did something involving seeds and bowls of water. She ought to rebuke them—or perhaps not, not being the mistress of the household. A maid giggled. Madeleine looked away. Her mother had always rebuked the New Year's Day fortune-telling as superstition and nonsense, and Madeleine had never joined in.

Then, she had never wanted so much to know what the future would bring.

The door opened. "Why, good folk, no one to greet us!" said a nobleman. "When we have come to wish you a merry Christmas, and blessings on the New Year!"

"My lords!" Madeleine called.

The first noble bowed. "My lady!" he cried, as jovially as if he had not complained, or she had been deaf. The others bowed after him. Ian glanced at Madeleine and then at the dumbstruck maids. His mouth moved: Send for Lord Thomas. Maids scurried off.

"My Lady Madeleine!" said the last man. "We have come to wish you God's blessing on you and yours, and your father and his, and the queen and hers, this New Year!"

"And a thousand curses on the king," said another.

The fire crackled clearly in the silence. *He's* drunk already, Madeleine thought. His companions looked abashed, but he peered about the hall.

"The queen," said Madeleine, "is within the antechamber." She walked toward the stairs, and they followed.

The New Year's Eve mists were dark, though not yet dark enough to summon the candles. John's breath formed more mist on the air as he and Jasper rode toward Candlewood. Their horses' hooves clattered on the frozen ground, but they did not speak.

It would be unkind to Jasper to try, thought John in amusement. No one had cared what he had to say. Jasper had had to do all the insinuating.

They came over a hill and could see Candlewood. Jasper let out a long breath. Torchlight shone from the open door and revealed the guests within. A groom took horses. The lords of the Misty Hills were not evading Candlewood.

"So your sore throat had bought us something," John said.

Jasper smiled wryly; the torchlight cast strange shadows on his face.

"The king," said John, "will be furious. He will get word of the defiance."

"Just as well that so many support us—even if it will make the king *angrier*."

It might not be possible, John conceded, to make the king more angry. He remembered prison, awaiting trial—they rode down the hill, and the grooms hastened to take their horses. Laughter came out of the hall, and they went in.

The queen held court by the fire. "Indeed, my good lords, I did not know how strange the Misty Hills were. The tales did not match the truth." Queen Katherine smiled. "Everywhere else, dragons *crave* gold."

"A sparse court this Christmas," said the innkeeper at Candlebrook.

John drank his ale. Jasper's voice rose outside, over the horse he was buying, but he did not need him, and they might need the news. "More sparse than before Michaelmas?"

The innkeeper lowered his voice. "People left when they heard of Lord Duncan's murder." John cocked an eyebrow. The innkeeper leaned toward him. "Royals left. Without the regent's leave."

John's tongue touched the mug. For other courtiers, going without leave was ill-mannered, but a courtier of royal blood had to ask. "That must not have pleased him."

"Lord Osgar was fit. . . ." The innkeeper shook his head.

John, not having meant the regent, lowered the mug. "Did no one tell King Walter?"

The innkeeper snorted. "Some lord told him right off—'bout a rival. King did nothing."

Young Simon, Ina's grandson, burst into the upper chamber. His face was ruddy from the cold. Queen Katherine raised her eyebrows, but the boy was oblivious, his words rushing out. "Gran sent me—riders—not friendly." He threw his hands in the air. "Coming here."

Queen Katherine said, "The Christmas visiting is over? It's not yet Candlemas."

"We can not celebrate so long here," said Madeleine. She felt sick. This late, it was not a Christmas visit.

"They don't *look* like visitors," said Simon. "Leather and weapons and grim faces. They looked like war!"

Madeleine stood. "I have to tell my father."

Queen Katherine's eyes narrowed. "I should order them back. They will obey their queen."

"Madame," said Madeleine, "if they mean you ill—giving them any order will put you in their power. I will speak with my father."

She fled the chamber. The servants looked startled. She saw no one but servants—and Sandy, playing before the hearth.

Sandy should not be there, in the midst of a fight. Those who would oppress a breeding woman—her baby wriggled, and her mouth set. Breeding women.

"Ian!" she called. "There are armed men in the woods. Fetch my lord father. If there's time, my brother and husband."

Motion by the fire made her blink. In the shadows, Sir Henry and Sir Bernard had sat at the draughts board. Sir Henry rose, and Sir Bernard pushed back his chair. Two knights, thought Madeleine. They could not quibble about Sir Bernard's injuries. "Helena, Will, Beitris, summon the men-at-arms."

Sandy's hand went into his mouth. Madeleine tried to
gentle her voice; she did not want to frighten him. "Sandy,
come here."

Sandy held his knight. He slowly took his green lion, and
even more slowly rose. Perhaps she wanted to frighten him a
little, but he walked across the floor to her. She snatched him
close. Sandy gave a startled squeak. Madeleine forced herself to
slacken her grip.

Mists, gleaming whitely, curled about the trees, their bark dark
by wetness. The snow was white beneath. John picked out
tracks on it. Small birds, squirrels, and rabbits had crossed it;
once he found deer tracks; but it showed no sign of wolves.

He cast a little farther about and heard the horses in the
woods. Looking up revealed nothing of riders. He pulled
against the trees to conceal himself. Then he chided his own
cowardice. Neither the king nor any noble, like Lord Patrick,
could freely send his men within the hills.

At least, he hoped they could not.

Then he picked them out, and their armor and weapons.
Men of the Misty Hills, they rode toward Candlewood. John
followed through the trees, stepping with care through the
snow. They could not mean well, when they were armed like
that. His heart beat harder.

The riders came out into the fields of Candlewood.

Lord Thomas's voice boomed across the snow. "What do
you here?" He stood in the doorway, with Jasper and other
men behind him. John let his breath out in relief; they had
received warning.

The lead rider pulled his horse up. "What do *we* do?"

John stopped. The manor house was defensible, which
meant he had no way to reach the defenders. His hands

clenched into fists. He could leap into the fray when it broke out. Perhaps fighting would conceal someone crossing the fields—and Lord Thomas would need him. The company outnumbered the men at the manor house, many of whom were no more than men-at-arms.

The rider shouted. "Who is bringing the king's rage down upon us all? Who have done nothing to offend?"

"So, you fear. . . ."

The leader's hand chopped through the air. "None of your quibbling." He rode forward. His horse's hooves crunched the snow. "The woman you shelter is as much a stranger here as the king—and has less claim on us."

John's tongue touched his lips. Even with his aid, a fight might be doomed. He wished for a tenth of the men that had pledged to stand against the king.

"So you have come to bravely deal with two women far gone with child," said Lord Thomas.

Men hunted wolves nearby; that was why Lord Thomas had asked him to see if the wolves hunted Candlewood sheep. John gave the company a wary eye again, but the stables were not in the manor house itself. Traveling through the Misty Hills was difficult enough, he could not chase these hunters afoot, but if he could get himself a horse. . . .

He eased his way through the woods, and then, his heart hammering, into the stables. Horses snickered, but no stable boy spoke. John looked about. No one moved.

He knew little of the hills, and had never traveled through them alone. As befit a loving brother by marriage to a stranger to the hills, Jasper had never let him out of sight during their Christmas calls, and he had fled with Madeleine, years ago.

Neither could guide him now. He could not even venture to the village. He would be seen, and the peasants might not even know what he needed. Some never left their village.

A horse stamped. John headed down the stalls, for a mount. He hoped to draw men back here to a fight, perhaps to their deaths, and he feared the Misty Hills. That was folly—and worse than folly, when speed was needed.

Jasper had chosen his horse before, and it was in its stall. He saddled and bridled it, and led it from the stable. He could not gallop off, when they had enough men to chase him, and so he inched into the woods. Voices rose, and he heard hooves on snow. It hid the noise he made. He did not look back; it would slow him.

Within the woods, he mounted and clapped his heels to the horse's sides. It leapt out at a good pace. The road spread through the woods before him. Christmas visitors had trampled snow until the way was clearer, and John heard no one following. Pursuit, at least, he need not fear—though he might return to find Candlewood a burnt-out husk, and Madeleine and Sandy's bodies in it.

He could ride faster. He laid the reins to the neck, and the horse sprang out, over the snow.

Snow leapt from a branch and into John's face. Wet and chill, it clung. He shook, trying to get it off. The horse snorted, and John patted its neck. Then things moved through the trees like clouds of smoke.

No, nothing so harmless. Black eyes glared at him, teeth were as sharp as broken ice, gray pelts were lank with fur clumped together like icicles, and the wolves, for all their heaving sides, glared banefully at him.

His horse tried to pull back. Those wolves were being hunted, thought John; the hunters were close. He yanked his horse's head around and clapped his heels to its sides as hard as he could. The horse leapt forward, whinnying, and alongside the pack.

The wolves snarled, the nearest one nipped at his boot, but they did not turn to pursue. His horse was still frantic, but with the wolves behind, John only had to keep it to their track—and then he heard the hunting horn. He breathed a sigh of relief. The hounds and riders came through the snow toward him.

"Good Lord Almighty! What are you doing, meddling with the hunt?"

"John of Summerfield," said another. "Knowing nothing of the Misty Hills. Don't you have *wolves* out there?"

At least, they had pulled up their horses. Their breath, and their horses', added to the mist.

"Not all wolves walk on four legs," said John. "Not all of them seek sheep, either. Men are attacking Candlewood."

He looked about. The looks ranged from annoyance through anxiousness, to outrage. A horse tossed its head.

"I thought the men bold enough to hunt the wolf would be the best to fulfill their oaths and aid Queen Katherine."

"Where's Jasper?" said a man, sharply.

"At Candlewood," said John. "I came alone."

"Through the Misty Hills?" This man spoke in a deep voice. "Do you not know the danger?"

"There's danger enough at Candlewood, for the queen, for her child—for my wife and children! What sort of knave would *care* for the danger?"

"The wolves," said a man, darkly, "must be hunted."

"Hunt them, then!" said John. "If I stay to quarrel, such of you as think the men more important than wolves will not arrive in time. We have no hope unless we leave at once."

His gaze went about the faces. For one fearful moment he thought he would return alone, that his ride had been wasted, when he had thrown away any chance of aiding Candlewood to make it. Then men began to nod.

Some did not; no more than half the hunters followed, and others set out after the wolves again, cursing the interruption. He could only hope that he had drawn enough.

The horses loped through the woods. With a steady pace, they passed hill after hill, each one echoing the last, until they burst from the forest, and Candlewood lay before them.

The manor house was surrounded. Torches blazed about it: orange, and fearfully close. Their leader still harangued Lord Thomas, but he intended to fire the house. All about John, men shouted and lay the reins on the neck. His heart hammered as they galloped across the snow, and he tried to pray. God grant that the fool *not* fire the manor house in desperation.

The leader turned toward them. His face contorted. A man moved toward the house, torch in hand. Though the horse could not be accustomed to combat, John drew his sword and spurred his horse. The torch came around, as if the man thought to use it as a club, and John struck. The horse shied from the blood and the fire, but the man fell, blood reddening the snow. The torch melted snow and drowned itself, the orange flames guttering out. The man clutched the wound. John fought to master his horse. All about him, the huntsmen drove back the torch-bearing men.

"YOU FOOL! Sir Cuthbert, do you know what harm you are doing?"

"Protecting a lady from an oppressor?" The knight sounded young and determined. "Lord Haral, you are in no place to criticize anything *we* do."

Lord Haral clenched his hand into a fist. "What would the king say of this? Bad enough to shelter the queen—do you wish him to know that you are keeping her here by force?"

"Do you wish the king to know that you are usurping his authority?" shouted John. Every eye turned on him. "The king has authority over the queen. You have none. And you threaten his heir. For this, he could *kill* you."

"He wouldn't—" said one man.

John laughed. It came out even more harshly than he intended. "He *ordered* Lord Magnus to do what he arrested him for."

Lord Haral's face contorted. "He would not. . . ." And then he reached for his sword. His men fell back. Sir Cuthbert drew his sword and dismounted.

A shout came from behind the house; then, smoke. John dismounted in haste to bolt over. There, men were already beating out the fire. John turned back.

Lord Haral, bleeding, knelt in the snow. Sir Cuthbert spoke gravely with Lord Thomas; John heard mention of patrols. A small figure hurtled over the snow. "Papa!"

John dropped to one knee and caught Sandy's charge. The arms clasped, with the ferocity of fear, about his neck. John patted Sandy's back and whispered. When he rose, his son in his arms, Madeleine stood by the doorway, smiling tremulously.

Near the man he had felled, someone called for a priest. John looked at the blood and hoped a priest could come in time.

Chapter 19—News and Beginnings

Snow covered the dried grasses and muffled the dips and rises of the land. Cold seeped in the window, the drafts fresh but bitterly chilly.

Madeleine sighed. The raiders had never returned, but now—Christmas had come and gone, the withered ivy had been thrown away, the Yule log had burnt up by Candlemas, and the flat winter landscape rolled before the window. She found the winter almost as wearisome as the queen did.

Queen Katherine took a few stitches by the fireplace. She ought to join her.

John and Jasper hunted wolves. The young men had pressed for John even more than Jasper. She supposed that was a good sign, and she did not, exactly, envy them the tramping through the snow after those creatures.

A bird jumped across the snow, leaving a trail of tiny footprints. The wind blew over it, and snow skittered, starting to blur them. A woman plugged toward the house; she was too bent over and wrapped up to be easily identified. Madeleine leaned forward. The woman reached where the house sheltered against the wind. She straightened.

"Madame, Ina is coming—to see to our health, no doubt."

Queen Katherine almost brightened.

"Both of you are fine," said Ina. The air smelled of herbs she gave, to strengthen their blood. She eyed the door. "Is Lord Thomas here?"

"No," said Queen Katherine.

Ina hesitated. "When will he be back?"

"We do not know," said Madeleine. "He and Lord Ross are discussing the marriage contract."

Ina looked hopeless. "Then, Lord Jasper, or Lord John?"

"Hunting wolves," said Madeleine.

"What news, Ina?" said Queen Katherine, commanding.

Ina flinched—as if it had not been obvious—and eyed the queen. "There's talk of a stranger. Madame. Half the folk think he's a king's man—dressed like a noble, and looking for Candlewood. After the king's meddling!"

A noble, thought Madeleine.

"I hope he knows what he risks." The queen looked pensive. "Do they know his name?"

"No, Madame," said Ina. Then, "He's a stranger."

"We will need some," said Madeleine. "The nobles of the land will want better witnesses than a midwife of the Misty Hills about the child."

Ina's face set in sulky lines.

"And," Madeleine said, "you might have to go to court."

"For months," said the queen. "To testify again and again."

"My father," said Madeleine, "would insist on it."

Ina blanched. "I'll send Simon."

Lord Ewan of West Dales knew what the king might do when angered. Queen Katherine had to concede that.

Madeleine glanced out the door again. Mist hovered over the snow, and thickly. She could not see the village, but two dark figures emerged from the woods. They approached, became two men against the whiteness. One was Jasper. She looked at the other. Lord Ewan, though a grown man, looked younger than Madeleine would have guessed. She wondered how old Lord Duncan had been.

They reached the door. She curtseyed. "Welcome to Candlewood, Lord Ewan."

Lord Ewan bowed. "Greetings, Lady Madeleine."

Madeleine inclined her head and led the way. At the foot of the stairs, John stood; he bowed deeply, drawing a glance from Lord Ewan, and brought up the tail of the small procession. As surrounded as his father had been when Lord Duncan was murdered, Lord Ewan did not flinch.

Madeleine drew a deep breath, proceeding down the hall, and through the ante-chamber. With Lord Ewan here, King Walter's case that they had conspired would be strong. May God have mercy on them all.

She opened the door to the master chamber. Queen Katherine contemplated the fire, but she had sat facing the door.

Lord Ewan's voice caught. "The queen?" Madeleine nodded. As if collecting himself, he said, "She seems very—sad."

Madeleine thought that he was thinking how lovely Queen Katherine was. Her gaze went down. Young men might succor a helpless queen out of chivalry. As long as Lord Ewan kept it to himself, it might draw him more strongly into the queen's party. From the corner of her eye, she watched his gaze. She did not think he even noticed her father.

Queen Katherine lifted her head. Madeleine walked over to stand behind her. Lord Ewan bowed, stiffly. Madeleine's gaze went to the floor again. The king had put an end to Lord Duncan, but his heir was like him, and more angry.

The man reached for his sword. Madeleine stiffened. John and Jasper reached for theirs, but his hands settled on the clasp of his sword belt. Queen Katherine's expression did not change, but Madeleine saw the tension in her shoulders.

Lord Ewan removed his blade, scabbard and all, to toss it at the queen's feet, and sank to one knee. "Madame. I have come to pledge my sword, my loyalty, and my lands, to your service, and to that of your child."

No one so much as breathed. After a moment, Madeleine's fingers tightened on her skirt. Open treason. She glanced through her eyelashes.

Lord Ewan let out his breath. "May God defend the right."

"There is still the king," said Queen Katherine.

"He who breaks oaths expects others to break theirs. What regard would my father's murderer have for my pledge?" He met her gaze. "With such a king—it is a knight's duty to protect ladies from oppression. A lord of the Misty Hills took young Lord Alexander of Summerfield from Owlscourt. It takes little reckoning to guess where they might have gone."

Were there any doubt, thought Madeleine, the visit of a great nobleman, young and in mourning, to Candlebrook would settle it. She did not feel much rancor. The folk of the Misty Hills were not *that* close-mouthed.

Queen Katherine's voice was cool. "The dangers that might lie ahead can not be averted by one lord's might."

"The land has other lords," said Lord Ewan.

"So there are. Some will be needful, to bear witness to the birth of this one. . . ."

Lord Ewan blinked. Madeleine suppressed a smile. Before all else, to put down King Walter, they needed a king.

"The land faces evil times if doubt is cast on the heir."

"Such lords can be found," he said, warily. "If. . ." He glanced back at Lord Thomas, and Jasper. "If they can reach the place of the queen's confinement."

"Something can be arranged," said Lord Thomas.

Sandy's laughter rose from the snowy garden below, making Lord Ewan start.

Lord Thomas said, "Let us speak. You must be our guest this night."

So they would conspire, not against, but for the king, so that his heir's legitimacy would go without question. Madeleine supposed King Walter's gratitude would not overwhelm them.

"It would be too dangerous for Lord Ewan and Lord Magnus to speak." Sir Bernard moved stiffly toward the fire, carrying his wine cup in his left hand.

Katherine considered him. She did not think he carried the cup to remind her what he had suffered in her service.

"But Lord Magnus must hear of what Lord Ewan intends."

Lord Ewan watched him with narrowed eyes.

"If the king ventures to Candlewood, it will be in such force that two swords will give you no aid. Sir Henry and I can carry the news. You will gain more from it than from our presence here."

Madeleine's mouth twisted. Katherine agreed with her. Still, his argument was sound. "That would be best."

Murmurs of agreement came about the room. That, Katherine decided, settled the matters before them. She glanced at Lord Ewan. It was never safe for a queen to have courtiers overtly admire her. In some ways, it was less safe for her, without the king's regard to protect her. Then, in some, it was more safe, because the king's charges would be viewed as wild. She could not throw away so useful a thing as a lord who earnestly desired to serve her. She smiled at him.

"Lord Ewan goes out as he came," said Jasper, "or it would be too clear where he went—but you two will need a guide through the hills."

Sir Bernard flinched. Sir William said, "Candlebrook—"

"You can not be linked to Lord Ewan," said Lord Thomas.

The queen watched the two knights follow a peasant into the trees.

Madeleine picked her sewing up. "Just as Lent begins—part of our penance, to do without even that much company."

The queen laughed. "You spent many a year with little more company. If this ends happily, you can come to court."

Madeleine bit her lip and smoothed out the cloth. "I do not think I would wish to, Madame. This life is not pleasant, but it is the fear and the waiting that brings it about."

Queen Katherine looked at her.

"Besides, your regard would inspire envy in ladies of greater birth. That would be unpleasant. It might make life more difficult for your child."

Queen Katherine blinked and looked into air as if rapt in the political implications.

Madeleine sat by the window. Late snow drifted down. There were pains in her belly. Behind her, the queen talked lightly with Jasper, about Lady Isobel, about the king and the news from Candlebrook. King Walter had ventured to the port, to speak with foreign wizards again, or so rumor said.

Jasper said, "No one besides Morgan ever left the Misty Hills to become a wizard."

No telling what Morgan might have taught anyone else, Madeleine thought. Then she gasped. The snow outside was too thick to wait. If Ina did not come at once, she might not come in time; they had to send for her.

Her fingers tightened on the window frame. At least John had taken Sandy with him, when he and her father had gone to a nearby manor. She turned back to the room.

"He intends something," said the queen. "He's gone too far in his plans to permit my escape."

Madeleine opened her mouth, but a pang silenced her.

"At the court," said the queen, "I would have heard half a dozen things, if I had to eavesdrop like a scullery maid."

Madeleine took a step toward them.

"Madeleine!" said Jasper.

"Send for Ina," she said.

The queen went pale, but her voice was firm. "And send for Lady Isobel, as you said." Madeleine stared blankly at her. "I have need of a lady-in-waiting."

We should have thought of that, thought Madeleine, but they had no time. "Send up a maidservant first."

"At once, Lord Jasper," said Queen Katherine. "I have never borne a child."

Jasper left. Outside the room, he ran.

The queen urged Madeleine toward the bed. Madeleine shook her head. "Your bed. . . ." She gasped, forgetting what she said. The queen eased her down.

"I should stand as much as I can bear it," Madeleine said. "I remember that much from Sandy."

"Walk, even," said the queen, soothingly. "I learned that much of delivering a child."

"I should not stay here. I should go to my own bed."

The queen laughed. "In the outer chamber? Your father has no back stairway. I would have to pass through your birthing chamber to leave this one." She smiled. "Your lord husband will have to shift for himself."

Another pang struck Madeleine, hard enough that Queen Katherine's chatter could not distract her. She clutched the other woman's arm, silencing her.

Dawn, through the mists, lightened the room. Lady Isobel cooed over little Edane. Edane waved her hands, and Isobel pulled back her auburn hair as if she feared that Edane would find the color too fascinating and grab it. "She's tiny."

Madeleine, lying sore but triumphant, put her arm about her daughter. What, after all, needed to be said?

"The queen is arranging the christening feast. She ordered me out of her way." Lady Isobel smiled wryly. "I did not know that a lady-in-waiting's duties were so slight."

The clamor of moving tables came up the stairs.

"She seemed bored before," said Madeleine. She lowered her voice. "I thought it was that she did not have all the people of court about her."

Queen Katherine reappeared by the door. Isobel started, but the queen did not notice. "*That* is settled. 'Twill not be a *grand* feast, but it will be suitable."

"We are not *grand* folk, Madame," said Madeleine, "despite the honor of your presence... and it is Lent."

The queen smiled. "We keep Lent at court. The festivities will not be too grand." She sat by the bed. "Edane—your mother was Sorcha, and Lord John's was Fenella...."

Madeleine laughed. "My mother wanted a second daughter to name for her mother—and failing that, a granddaughter."

The queen touched Edane's cheek. "I suppose I do not have to name the babe for King Walter, if it is a boy."

Madeleine flinched. Naming a prince or princess was always a fraught matter. "Alexander, or David—both were great kings of this land, who ruled in peace."

Queen Katherine smiled. "Alexander, like your son?"

Madeleine colored.

"If I did not call the little prince Sandy, it might happen that no one noticed." Edane cooed. "David would be—provocative, with Lord David."

Obeyed the pardon, Madeleine thought with a sinking feeling. "Did anything—happen to him?"

"He was well enough last I saw him." She sat back. "They said that Lord Magnus greeted him fondly, at Michaelmas."

"He did everything he could for Lord Magnus's men. He most likely saved Lord John's life."

"King Walter raged about it," said Queen Katherine, sounding smug. "Even his own creations defied him." Her voice slowed. "That he could not even stop the troubles in Eastwyck."

Madeleine's start reminded her that she had just given birth. "Did he even try?"

Queen Katherine shook her head. "He complained that Lord Magnus had forced him to arrest him."

Madeleine tried to think of something to say to that.

"I heard," said Lady Isobel, softly, "that he said he should dispossess some lords. His lieges feared him less than Lord Magnus's feared him."

Queen Katherine nodded slowly. "He would. Why else would Lord Magnus's men obey him better?" She looked out, as if staring through the wall. "Now, he blames something on me. I do not know what, but he has found something."

Edane yawned.

John looked at Candlewood. Mists coiled, in the gloom. Sandy bounced before him on the saddle. He lunged toward the floating candles—enough that John kept one arm firmly about his waist—and burbled to his grandfather.

Despite Sandy's chatter, Lord Thomas also studied the halls.

A servant ran toward them. "My lord, my lord! My lady is lighter of a hale little daughter—"

Thomas smiled, and dismounted without even reaching the house. John, his heart hammering, saw stable boys coming. Trusting them to take the horses, he took Sandy and ran after his father by marriage.

A woman appeared at the top of the stairs. Lord Thomas hailed her as Lady Isobel, sounding surprised. She beckoned. Sandy's eyes went wide.

Queen Katherine sat in the outer chamber, on the bed he had shared with Madeleine. He hesitated. She waved him on.

Madeleine lay abed, and the cradle stood beside the bed. John tried to steady his breathing—he could not calm his heart—but Sandy wriggled, and tiny hands went up. John went to stand over his daughter.

Sandy said, "Small!"

Edane, as solemn as her brother, waved her hands. John lowered his son. Sandy stared a moment longer and scampered off to the hearth. John touched his daughter's fingers and went over to kiss his wife. His heart slowly steadied. She looked less worn than after Sandy—who was sending his knight and lion through the mists where horrible monsters that lurked in them. Madeleine looked at John.

"He listens when the servants tell tales," said John. "We saw nothing horrible in the woods."

"And the dragon," said Sandy, "- *smelled* all around the stones where the princess was. . . ."

Long minutes later, with Edane asleep, they settled about the fireplace. Madeleine, abed, looked drowsy but not asleep.

"We spoke of names for the prince as well as for Edane," said Lady Isobel. "Madame has all but decided that a prince should be named Alexander, but a princess is another matter."

Alexander—oh, King Alexander, John thought, but great though he had been, perhaps not the best name for a prince. He smiled. "Leod strikes me as most suitable."

"*Leod*!" said Lady Isobel. "He was a good king, but fought incessantly." She sat back. "As well, it would be unwise to remind the land of King Gillis the Usurper."

"Naming the prince Alexander would do that," said John. "Alexander was Leod's son, named for his stepfather and regent."

"Leod would be provocative," said Queen Katherine. She looked wistful. "Hiding in the Misty Hills. . . ."

John's mouth twisted. "I wonder if there is any rhyme or reason to what enrages the king. When a child is born, he will act." Or so we hope. Then we can act against him, and fail or succeed, but wait no more.

Madeleine shifted. "King Walter may come to the Misty Hills and get a dragon to eat him." She yawned. "The consequences of his folly would fall on *him*, for once."

Lord Thomas sighed. "If a dragon ate him, there would be neither body nor witnesses to prove his death." His mouth twitched. "And every lordling would search for him, and need guides and hospitality."

Silence fell. John envisioned how many of those lords could die as well.

Queen Katherine sighed. "I shall consider a name for a princess."

"Marjory was a great queen," said Madeleine, impishly.

The queen drew her finger over Edane's wrist.

John smiled. "King Alexander's mother." King Leod's wife. The daughter of King Gillis the Usurper. King Gillis had offered her to Leod, to lure him from the Misty Hills, and failed. Three years later, he had tried to marry her to a bridegroom justly known as the Spider King, and Princess Marjory had stood on the betrothal to refuse him. Whereupon Leod had carried her off and married her. The name was not, perhaps, that prudent a choice.

"Perhaps I shall," mused the queen. "She brought peace to the land, after division had torn at it. A better legacy no one could wish for a princess."

Lady Isobel helped Madeleine into the blue gown. They should have made the bodice looser, thought Madeleine. Edane slept in her cradle. Madeleine checked the blankets against the draft.

"Up and about, and just in time for Holy Week," said Lady Isobel.

Madeleine smiled. In the room, she had been up and about for a week, but the four weeks were up that day. "How bad is the mud?"

Isobel picked up the veil. For a moment, she looked at it as if dreaming of the day she would wear one, but then she said, "Most of the snow melted last week, the mud is subsiding."

Ah, well, thought Madeleine. Isobel covered her hair, and they left. Below, the great hall hummed like a beehive. John waited by the doorway, with Sandy bounding about, and she took John's arm. Outside, the peasants gathered about the church. On the steps, Queen Katherine smiled radiantly on Madeleine.

There, Madeleine knelt. The queen would find herself here in due course—they hoped. If the news of the birth did not enrage King Walter so much that Queen Katherine had to be moved before she was churched. And that, only if the queen survived. If either the queen or the babe died—that was too unpleasant to think upon.

And now, her attention should be on her own survival.

The priest lifted his book. "As it has pleased Almighty God of His goodness to preserve you in the great peril of childbirth, you shall therefore give hearty thanks to God, and pray.

"I will lift up my eyes to the hills
From whence comes my help.
My help is in the name of the Lord,
Who has made the heaven and the earth."

The firelight did not reach far from the inn's hearth. Ewan stood by the door while his man Roban haggled with the innkeeper. He could see the faces about the common room only as pallor in the gloom.

Then, with his men about him, he had little to fear.

Some men, sitting about the fire, looked back at him. One rose to his feet. He carried a sword—gently born.

His men shifted about him. Old Villean stepped between him the fire. Ewan grabbed his arm. Sworn to the queen, he could not risk a private quarrel. He drew a deep breath and reminded himself of that lovely, wronged lady as the man approached. He came close enough that no one else could mark his voice. Ewan could make out his face but not place those dark features.

"Lord Ewan. I am Lord Malcolm of Eastwyck."

Ewan's heart jumped. The queen had pardoned this man. "As soon as my man secures a chamber—" but Roban looked away from the innkeeper, nodding. Ewan's thoughts raced, and they climbed the stairs to the small, dark room, and his men lit three candles they had carefully brought. Ewan sat and offered Lord Malcolm a seat.

Lord Malcolm said, "The king can not be abided long. Every day he remains on the throne, we are in danger."

Queen Katherine, Ewan reckoned, would not be delivered for several months. But Lord Malcolm's face was set in harsh lines.

"You of all men should know that—better even than Lord Magnus."

"But not as well as you," said Ewan, coldly. "Do you intend to have a sovereign still in his mother's womb?"

Lord Malcolm leaned forward. "Can this prince protect us from King Walter's folly? Could even Queen Katherine? Queen Fenice came from Darnien, knew our customs and laws—yet she never thwarted King Michael. What hope has this foreign princess to thwart Queen Fenice's son?"

"Queen Fenice," said Ewan, "was a mouse with no thought beyond her sewing." How dare this knave compare Queen Katherine, queenly, anxious to protect her child and the land, to King Walter's mother? Queen Fenice would have submitted if King Michael had killed her son. "Queen Katherine will stand for her child's rights."

"Much good will that do the rest of us."

"When you hold a pardon from her own hand?"

Lord Malcolm surged to his feet. Ewan's men reached for their swords. Lord Malcolm did not glance at them. "A pardon for—my crime?"

Ewan met Lord Malcolm's gaze. "I have sworn to support the queen. Do you wish me to be as foresworn as King Walter?" His heart hammered. He wondered how he managed to stay seated.

After a long minute, Lord Malcolm dropped back in the chair.

"A man without fear of King Walter," said Ewan, "might aid her." Lord Malcolm's expression was poisonous. Only for the queen would I suffer this, Ewan thought.

"*What* is the queen doing?"

"Having a care to her child," said Ewan. "The land needs witnesses who can attest that the child is indeed the babe she bore. A man who does not fear the king would swear to the truth."

Lord Malcolm's expression sunk into resentful lines. Ewan reached for the wine. Lord Malcolm would betray no one to the king, but that was his only reassurance—thus far.

Spring flowers lined the meadows. Beneath the mist, white lambs gamboled about the ewes. Beneath the trees, peasants gathered at the tables where the wedding feast was set.

Madeleine sat by the manor house and nursed Edane, watching Sandy cavort with the peasant children and (she smiled) grow as grubby. Jasper and Isobel, in their wedding finery, sat surrounded by garlands—though Jasper was not one whit more radiant than John in plain and travel-stained clothing on *his* wedding day.

Queen Katherine came over by her. "It is traditional that the queen's ladies-in-waiting be unmarried."

Madeleine's eyebrows went up. "But, Madame, there are no courtiers here. How could you lure an unwed lady here? With no prospect of marriage?"

Queen Katherine smiled. "A queen must abide what she faces. King Leod abided by having a knight for his guardian."

Edane stopped nursing. Madeleine fastened up her dress again.

"Only a few months," Queen Katherine whispered, but Madeleine heard. Only a few months until Queen Katherine had her own, and the king heard of it. Prince Alexander's birth, or Princess Marjory's, would draw some response from the king.

Chapter 20—Returns and Plans

A steady drizzle came through the mist. The day was dark. From the window, Madeleine could, just, make out the white wild roses; they had bloomed early this year. Edane nursed like a piglet. Before the fireplace, John and Sandy played lions.

"*Green* lion," said Sandy. "And I'll be the knight!"

Simon ran down the path from Candlebrook. His face was so white that her smile faded. Some news, or someone, had come.

Jasper left the stables. Simon ran to him. After a minute, Jasper walked with Simon toward Candlebrook. Madeleine scowled.

"Dear?" said John.

Briefly, Madeleine told him. "But why would Jasper—?"

"To bring someone here?" said John.

"The king is returning to the hills," said Lord Magnus, from beside the fire. His boots still carried spring mud, and his face was bone-weary. The windows were dark with night. No sounds came except an occasional owl hoot outside.

"No one thinks he was pleased with his foreign wizards, but no one dares speak to him of it."

Madeleine laid Edane in her cradle. All the rest were so intent on Lord Magnus that no one noticed her. With the servants gathered in the great hall, the private chamber seemed as isolated as the tower had, but there, they had plans for escape. Queen Katherine's pregnancy was far more advanced; she would be delivered within a month or so, but not yet.

"Nobles are frightened to have his progress come to their lands, and it is not just the expense."

He paused. The fire snapped, and the coals settled. Nothing else moved. Lord Magnus's gaze settled on John for a long time, until John shifted.

Words came from his mouth as if he had to force them. "Lord John, I regret that the one piece of justice he attended to was beheading your brothers."

Color seeped from John's face. Madeleine, glad John was already sitting, came up behind him and laid her hands on his shoulders. He seemed not to notice. His lips moved silently.

Lord Thomas's voice came, solemnly, from the shadows. "May God have mercy on their souls."

Madeleine realized that her hands shook. She closed her eyes. Eternal rest grant unto them, o Lord, and let perpetual light shine on them. Her fingers tightened on John's arms. O God, Creator and Redeemer of all, give your servants departed this life remission of all their offenses, that they may obtain your pardon and so enter into the fullness of eternal joy. We ask this through Christ our Lord.

She opened her eyes. John had not stirred. Madeleine sat and put her arm about him. She felt no warmer herself.

"Why?" said Jasper. He looked shocked.

After a moment, Queen Katherine said, "Or did he give no reason? I know he gave them no trial."

"His reason will not strengthen his reign. He blamed your escape on them, Madame. He said they lied to him."

John shuddered.

Madeleine's voice sounded distant in her own ears. "They must have told him where I vanished into the hills. I thought of that. We came by that route, but we left by another."

She felt like ice. She had not thought what might happen.

And if she had?

She let out her breath. She would not, could not have chosen otherwise. She still did not know if they had conspired against her and Sandy when John was a prisoner, and she had killed them. "Gilliane? Nichola?"

"To them? Nothing," said Lord Magnus. "The steward I sent governs the land in peace. I sent word that if they asked for their dowers, either to return to their families or to retire to a convent, they should be granted them, but until then, they should abide in peace."

"Even so," said John, his voice creaking.

Madeleine found herself thinking that Gilliane had been married too long; a childless widow would not remarry. Perhaps Nichola—some man might believe that she was not barren.

"If they had done so at once," said Lord Magnus, "the news might have reached me, before I left—but perhaps not, the roads are slow with the mire."

"They would not," said Madeleine. "They would fear to draw the king's attention."

In the gray morning, peasants and servants whispered. Kneeling in the church's first pew, Madeleine heard the word brothers. She shivered. And sin, when it is full grown, gives birth to death. She bent her head over her hands. John wore old mourning, borrowed from her father, just as she wore a dress of her mother's, but his grief would have been clear without it.

She closed her eyes.

John said, drawing her attention, "I must speak with the priest, about a fun—"

A funeral. Except that there could be none.

"The priest can hold a service without the bodies," she said.

The priest entered, and she attended to the service, but afterwards, lingered while the others left. She looked about, at the crucifix, the sanctuary light, the statues, but she could not compose her thoughts.

Her stomach growled, and she left. Breakfast would be served in the antechamber.

She entered as the porridge was served. Lady Isobel looked up at her and said nothing. Madeleine sat and took the porridge and honey. After a moment, Lord Magnus spoke. She ate.

"No one knows when to act against the king. They fear to be dispossessed." He glanced at Queen Katherine. "Having avoided a battle over me, the nobility hope to avoid one altogether—and King Walter is not pleased with me yet."

Sandy's voice came from outside. "Don't cry, papa."

Madeleine shut her eyes. They had told Sandy of his uncles' death, but she did not think he understood.

"I do not know what the king is about," said Lord Magnus, "but he sent word to the nobles, as he did for my trial."

"A summon to Harthill?" said Madeleine.

Lord Magnus shook his head. "To the Misty Hills. To Candlebrook."

Simon peered through the brush and over the brook and the candles gleaming over it. His mouth formed an O. Edward *had* seen the noblemen—dozens of noblemen—and they walked about in the evening. One waved his hand in the air; something *enormous* glittered on a ring.

The voice rang over the water. "Whatever possessed the king to summon us *here*? His message would be more fitly delivered at court."

Edward hadn't known *that* when he boasted to Ebby, thought Simon. For a minute, he pondered—but Edward would come back, to be the first to. . . to. . . to let the noblemen see him, instead of sneaking about.

Simon grinned. *He* would do it first.

"Do you wish to defy him? Lord Haral did." The voice was harsh. "The king was not jesting when he threatened to dispossession."

Simon slid forward, as sneakily as a wild cat.

"He *said* we are outside the Misty Hills—but look at those." The man gestured at the candles, barely visible in the evening light. "They come out of the hills. Who knows what evil they bear?"

Simon giggled. *Afraid* of the candles? He reached the brook side.

"You! Boy!" A nobleman glared at him. "What are those lights? Come over here at once!"

Simon darted away. He had shown himself, and he was not going to tell *them* anything.

"I'll show you to behave with such insolence!" The nobleman splashed into the brook. Simon ran, heard a splash, of a man falling into the brook, and ran on, laughing.

"He didn't dare chase me!" Simon beamed at Lord Thomas. He hopped from one foot to the other—too excited, Madeleine thought, to notice that he was in the lord's private chamber.

Lord Thomas sighed. Simon eyed him.

"I forbid you to do that again," said Lord Thomas. "We do not need young noblemen tramping through the hills."

"That'd be silly," said Simon.

"If every nobleman behaved wisely," said Lord Thomas, "the land would be better than it is." He turned to Queen Katherine. "I must squelch this folly."

"Go at once," said Queen Katherine.

As he left, Lord Magnus sat back. "They did not speak of why the king summoned them, but someone might know."

"Who to send?" said Madeleine. "The servants could not speak with nobles. Their servants may not know." If their masters did—but the nobles feared the king. "After Michaelmas, few nobles would not know me or John; you were well known before then."

"I could go," said Lady Isobel, diffidently.

When Queen Katherine said, "The child saw no woman among them," Isobel eased.

The queen continued. "Lord Jasper might not be known. Or Lord Thomas."

"Are there any nobles from the Misty Hills?" said Lord Magnus.

"No," said Jasper. His eyes narrowed, like a hawk awaiting the chance to strike. "Some went to court when you were arrested, my lord, but now, it would be seen by the rest of us, and we remember Morgan."

The silvery deer looked through the vines at her. Madeleine wished it would lead some nobles away. For all the mud—and the spring showers had lasted long this year—many had arrived in a month.

The deer bounded away, noisily, through the brush. Then, she had no reason to think ill of the nobles, yet. The king had yet to propound his decisions to them.

Two peasants emerged from the trees; their arms laden with firewood, they were talking. One, chuckling, said, "Should have heard 'em about the brook."

Madeleine arched an eyebrow.

The peasant bobbed his head. "My lady—all the candles bobbing about—you'd have thought they never saw anything like it before." His dark eyes were as bright as a bird's. "Don't they have wizards out there?"

"Wizards," said the other. "But not the Misty Hills."

Nobles filled the pastures and village of Candlebrook. They milled about the inn where the king stayed—a crowd somewhat less brilliant than they would have been at court.

Thomas strode through the crowds, as if looking for someone. Not a pleasure jaunt, he thought, even if they dressed as if hunting. The few women were doubtlessly heiresses, or guardians. Like the men, they glanced past him.

A stir spread from the inn. As faces turned toward it, an upstairs window opened. King Walter himself looked out. Thomas tried to look solemn and insignificant.

"Lords of the land! We have summoned you here to witness the punishment of treason!"

Thomas let his breath out slowly. Lord Magnus was hidden within the Misty Hills. From the murmurs about him, everyone else had noted his absence. Thomas studied the king's face. Lord Duncan had been murdered. Lord Ewan—he considered for a moment, but the nobles would have heard of such an arrest.

The king looked over the crowd. Mutters fell to silence, however ungraciously.

"The Queen's Grace has betrayed not only the allegiance she took on with her marriage vows. She permitted the escape of traitors. She defied and escaped her just punishment. She will suffer for such treason!"

Mutters broke out anew. One lord whispered, "Isn't she breeding?"

King Walter looked out, as if he could stare into the hills. "She hides in the Misty Hills. Even as we brought her into them, we will bring her out again."

Nobles shifted. Hoping he would not be noted, Thomas eased his way through. The king's plans were plain enough. Their only hope was that Morgan's magics were less than the king thought—and that he escaped to bear the news.

"She shall suffer forthwith!"

Before, Thomas thought, she bore the child. About him, others spoke of how that was against the law, and whether the king thought he could find another bride.

Thomas's gaze went across Lord Ewan. The young nobleman's face flickered, but only for a moment.

We may need you yet, thought Thomas. At the crowd's edge, he sidled toward the trees. No one cried after him. He fled.

Sunlight came through the leaves to dapple the floor, but they huddled in the private chamber as if a storm raged outside.

"The nobles won't let him," said Lord Magnus. "They will not let the king destroy his heir."

Madeleine tightened her arms about the nursing Edane, who wriggled. No one seemed much convinced by Lord Magnus's words; to judge by his dark eyes, not even Lord Magnus.

Lady Isobel rose. Her auburn hair shook over her shoulders like a banner. "He will not stop with taking the queen from the hills. Once he has treated the Misty Hills so, we will have no safety." She glanced about as if defying them. "My father will shelter the queen at Graybrook."

Madeleine looked at Queen Katherine. Though she wore a voluminous gown, her pregnancy was obvious. Under the best of times, travel to Graybrook took hours. The queen could not ride, and no cart could traverse the paths.

Ina would have to come, just in case the babe had to be delivered on the way.

In the garden, Sandy squealed. Madeleine closed her eyes. It would not be wise to bring Edane or Sandy. Ina would have to find her a wet-nurse.

"Never had to deliver a baby on a path before," Ina grumbled as if they had willfully chosen this way.

Thorny brush nearly overgrew the path. Madeleine pushed back a branch. Ina stumped through. Madeleine rolled her eyes and held the branches for the queen. Lady Isobel reached past Queen Katherine to take them from her.

Madeleine drew a deep breath of the air, smelling the greenery. Birds twittered. Hooves beat on the trail behind them, and she whirled about. John must have heard it as well. He stood with his sword half-drawn in the midst of the bushes—where a horseman would have a harder time reaching him. She swallowed. Even against a lone horseman, John would be unlikely to do more than buy them time before he died.

A shape became clear through the mists. Then a gray horse came into view. Moments later, Jasper pulled his steed up. "The king's already at Candlewood. He's coming this way."

Madeleine felt the color seeping from her face. She stepped closer to Queen Katherine.

Jasper's gaze went past John, to Madeleine. "Beitris took Sandy and Edane out to the village; they are fine."

"How did he know?" said Madeleine. "How did he know she was gone *without* searching the village? Or which way to go? There are a dozen paths."

Jasper looked downcast. A bird sang, in cheerful indifference, during the silence. He glanced at John, and Madeleine remembered how his brothers had died.

"Let us go," she said. "It could have been a peasant."

"There's a fork ahead," said Ina.

"The left fork leads to Graybrook," said Lady Isobel. "If we women take the queen by that, you two can set another path, to mislead them." When the men said nothing, she said, in exasperation, "The king brought men enough to overwhelm you both—and you have to go with John, Jasper, to guide him."

"In the Misty Hills, you need a guard," said John.

"I have traveled from Graybrook to Candlewood without being attacked," said Lady Isobel.

"I have gold, as well," Madeleine said. "The longer we wait, the less likely it is that we will have a choice."

John came up beside Madeleine. Their fingers brushed together for a moment, and she thought she would weep if he said a word, or offered to kiss her.

Isobel slowed as they approached the fork. She kissed Jasper farewell and watched after him until Madeleine touched her arm. Queen Katherine and Ina already picked their way along the verge, out of the mud.

"I think I'm with child," Isobel whispered as they went after them. "I didn't tell Jasper."

"It would distract him," said Madeleine. "He needs his wits about him." Jasper and John would not merely mislead the king; once he found them, they would feign that the queen went on, and guard her pretended path. "You did the right thing."

Isobel nodded, but her face was despondent. Madeleine prayed that she was right. The baby would be a comfort to Isobel and Lord Thomas, if. . . .

She spoke in a hurry, trying to distract herself. "I did not tell John about Edane until after Michaelmas. I could not distract him, either."

Madeleine peered from behind a fir. Despite the mists, she could count the company on the valley's other side. Only a handful, she assured herself. The king had not managed to get a large company into the Misty Hills.

She could not permit herself to feel grateful that John and Jasper survived. She could not even take the time to wonder how the king's company knew which path to follow.

She wished that wolves had found the king—hungry wolves.

The leading man lifted something. Even in the mists, it glinted, as the charm to quell the dragon had glinted. He gestured to his men, and they moved. Madeleine flitted, through the trees and mists, to her companions.

They awaited her in a grove. The queen sat on a boulder, Ina grumbling nearby.

"King Walter is following us," said Madeleine. "He must— this quickly, he must have picked the right way."

"Should have kept the men," said Ina. "They could fight and hold them off. You know how they protected young King Leod from his enemies?"

Madeleine grimaced. The fight, protecting a wooden stock, that King Walter had praised. Worse, Ina might even be right: such a ploy might have better protected the queen's escape.

Too late now, Madeleine thought fiercely. "There's another path ahead."

"The king will follow us," said Ina.

"An enchanted path," Madeleine said. "If we can not throw him off our trail, our only hope is some creature will *take* him off." Was enticing the king to his death was as much treason as killing him?

"There's tarns of madness up there," said Ina. "Think you that you can get him into one?"

"What is your way to save the queen?" said Madeleine. "He's using Morgan's magic. . . ."

Her heart seemed to stop. Morgan's magic. Morgan's magic, based on the mists. Her hands went to the gold. "Hurry," she said, her voice constrained. The king had already found them here. "Let us leave here."

"What are you up to?" said Ina.

"I'll tell you as we go."

Mists roiled about them. The rose bushes were thicker with thorns than with flowers, which could only help. Queen Katherine sat on a blanket, with Lady Isobel and Ina beside her. Madeleine laid the golden coins about in a large circle. Every now and again, she looked about. They could not see the path from here. It was unlikely that the king, or anyone else, would see the gold's glint.

"Now," said Madeleine, "we wait."

"We have waited months," said Queen Katherine. Her hand went over her swollen waist.

Madeleine looked at the dead leaves of the forest floor. Her breasts ached, reminding her of Edane. "I do not think that it will take months for the king to miss us, or find us."

"How can we tell?" said Lady Isobel.

Madeleine straightened. "I will go look."

Lady Isobel opened her mouth.

Madeleine said, "I saw the talisman and would recognize it."

She hurried into the woods. Her drab traveling clothing, duller than the hide of the leaden deer, could hide her among the trees. The land about was lush with undergrowth that could shelter her. She cast along the path. If she kept her eye out, she would spot the king's company before they saw her.

The valley appeared ahead; she saw nothing of the king's company. She hid behind a bush to wait.

"Another path up here!" bellowed a man hidden by mists. She held her breath as they emerged: a dozen men, armed, and from their movements, wearing armor.

King Walter produced his talisman with a flourish. His men stood about him. Moments crept by, longer than the last time she had watched. Slowly, his body stiffened, until he lowered the talisman, and said "Which of you fools meddled?"

Madeleine felt ready to sing for joy. Not now, not now— but soon. I will praise You, Lord, You have rescued me, and have not let my enemies rejoice over me.

The king's voice rang. "It worked an hour ago. It does not work now. *I* did nothing, and there's no one but *you* about."

The men shrank back.

"I see." His eyes narrowed. "You—none of you—will claim the blame because it falls on *all* of you! Frightened by shadows, you knaves conspired to avoid the Misty Hills—and your duty to your king!"

Madeleine's mouth went dry. If his men abandoned him, if she could find Jasper and John, they could overpower the king. Her fingers fretted her skirt. Then... they could....

The men retreated among the trees. One looked about, and directly at the bush.

"We did not do it, sire. It was her!"

His hand pointed to Madeleine.

Chapter 21—Flights and Perils

She could not run back to the queen.

Madeleine managed not another coherent thought as the men shouted, the king gawked, and she scrambled back, but that thought ruled her. She had to lead the king from the queen, as John and Jasper had tried to.

Perhaps she could lose them on the path.

Perhaps not, said another thought.

She fled down the hill. Staying would be folly as great as trying to win a pardon from the king. Shouts rose behind her, and the sound of footsteps, but she could not look. She hoped that the king's men had had enough of his folly, but even a few could take her down.

Brush sprung up ahead of her. Madeleine barely kept her footing as she turned. She fled up the slope opposite—as if she could outrun her pursuers.

"Damned knaves! Call this *service?*"

Perhaps the men fell back. Madeleine's breathing came so harshly that it drowned any sounds of pursuit. The king might try to force them to follow instead of chasing her. She might have time enough to escape, and then—his magic found Queen Katherine, not her. That thought put a burst of speed into her legs. She reached the height of the next hill.

Before her lay a cliff. Air appeared, strides ahead, and nothing but air until the forest floor, far below. Right and left looked passable. She fought for breath. Right would lead back to the path, and surer footing—and the tarns of madness lay that way.

She dragged in the deepest breath she could. The tarns lay among firs. She ran right. Firs were dark, and their shadows hard to see through. Enough to hide in? She picked her way between tangled roots. She would learn; she had no other hope.

"Damn you scoundrels! That frightened of a lone woman? I will bring her down myself!"

Madeleine's foot slid on leaves. She barely caught herself before she fell down the hill. Her hands came up, filthy and scrapped, with blood showing, but she could only run faster. It's only the king, she told herself, one man alone.

A roar came from the hill top. Despite herself, Madeleine looked up. The king stood dark against the mist's whiteness. He carried a sword, even if he had yet to draw it. Alone, he could overpower a lone woman. She wished the king's men *had* come. They could not make her fate more certain; they might have aided her against King Walter's madness.

She broke for the path. So long she had spent evading him. Even at Owlscourt, she had eluded his questioning. She could escape once more. She ran on the path. Her breath came so harshly that she could barely hear her heart hammer.

The footsteps behind her fell further back. Madeleine risked a glance over her shoulder. The king slowed even as the firs emerged from the mists. Madeleine leapt ahead and, the instant she stood among the firs, slowed.

She told herself that she wanted to keep the king from hearing her footsteps, but her blood pounded in her ears, and her breath was so loud that he would hear *that*. She walked with care, through the grove. Her eyes adjusted to the dimness. After a moment, she picked out the sunlight, pearly in the mists, that marked the first, round pool. Blue flowers sat serenely on the unrippled black waters. That would unnerve him. She drew her shawl more closely about her, to keep her

face from showing pale in the dimness. God grant that the
tarns would unnerve him, and let her go free.

"Damn you, woman," grumbled the king.

Madeleine held her breath, hoping to pass unheard. The
light flash on his drawn sword.

"Worse than Lord Magnus. He was open. You slithered
into the court to suborn *my* queen."

Madeleine looked ahead of herself, to avoid catching his eye;
in this gloom, even the whites of her eyes would draw notice.
She tried to pray, hoping that the tirade sprang of frustration,
and he would fall off soon, but the king advanced into the firs.
Madeleine waited.

He did not come toward her; her hiding had done that
much good. He reached the pool and stood, blinking against
the light. He would not be able to see her in the shadows, and
her breath came out against her will. Muttering, he shoved his
sword back into its sheath, as if it were too awkward to carry.

Madeleine looked away. She had escaped him.

For what? said a cynical thought.

Her heart hammered again. She had escaped him, to let him
escape and attack again. Her hand clenched her skirt. In many
places in the Misty Hills, nobles and peasants alike hated the
king's presumption. They would hide the queen, and use gold
to protect her from the magic.

Her fingers tightened. Meanwhile, the king would run wild
in the land, attacking anyone innocent, from the peasants to
the highest nobles. *She* was safe, she could protect John and
their children, but the folk of Summerfield lay in danger if the
king was enraged with her. And Lord Magnus, and all his
lands, and Lord Fergus—and Lady Annette, and the pilgrims
and merchants who had helped her on the way. And other
innocents. The king had shown no restraint thus far, except
for pure fear of power.

The nobles might stop him, she told herself.

They had not yet. Except at Michaelmas, where they had been gathered in force—and even there, they had only thwarted him in one plan. He had soon had another.

The king started around the tarn. He moved slowly, as if he could inspect the gloom despite the radiance he stood in.

He might lose himself in the mists and die, just as her father had feared. Her nails bit into her palms, even through the cloth. That would be worse. Queen Katherine could not uphold her child's claim with no proof of his death.

The tarn lay placidly before her—the tarns of madness. Ina had taunted her with them.

Madeleine swallowed. In the waters, King Walter would go mad. In long enough, he would turn simple-minded and harmless, a puppet king, under some regency or another.

First, she had to lure King Walter into the tarn.

Madeleine strode out. "Sire!" The word echoed from the waters; the firs swallowed it up, silencing it.

After a long minute, King Walter looked up. He studied her for another minute. "You."

Madeleine stood. That would infuriate him.

He whispered, "You traitor," and drew his sword. Both sounds carried over the water. "Perhaps I will not execute the queen. *You* led her astray."

"Ingrate." Madeleine surprised herself with how cool she could keep her voice. "Your queen preserves your reign from your folly. That word is more suited to those who egged you on to arrest Lord Magnus."

"I needed no counsel to see what was needed." He shifted his sword. Light glinted from it to the tree trunks about.

"Then you were a traitor to yourself," said Madeleine. "If you wished to leave your throne, you could not have done much better."

His lips pulled back from his teeth. "My queen is too much a fool to see her own folly, and that she should guided by her betters. You are another."

Madeleine widened her eyes. "Why, Sire, how can a fool be to blame, when involved in matters beyond her understanding?" Angry past thinking, she reminded herself. If he *thought*, her plan would end in disaster. "The one to blame is the one who involved the fool and worse, did not blame himself."

The king hefted his sword. "Once you die, she, free of your influence, will be willing to be led."

Madeleine did not know how she spoke, with her mouth so dry. "First, you must kill me. Then, you must find her. The Misty Hills sheltered King Leod when he was young."

His mouth twitched.

"With the loyalty you yourself praised. We can shelter your lady queen and your heir, as well."

"Do you not know that Morgan gave me powerful magics?" He flourished his sword. "Over even your precious Misty Hills? They thought to defy my summons to the queen's trial."

With care, Madeleine made her mouth twitch. The king might have magic enough to bring the Misty Hills under his mastery, but she did not need to let him know that. "Morgan could not even preserve his own life."

That struck, but he still looked more disdainful than angry. She looked over his shoulder. The king glanced back. Madeleine made her voice drip with sarcasm. "Your men—do you think they will enter the Misty Hills willingly, however you brag of Morgan? Even when you are with them! And do you propose to play the guide rather than the king?"

The king all but snarled at her.

Angry, but not furious, Madeleine thought, and cast about for something to enrage. "Why, the Misty Hills cover an extent as great as the West Dales."

The king, his sword flashing in the light, started about the tarn. Nimbly, Madeleine hurried the other way. She kept the water between her and the king. At least the round pool made it easy to judge. He broke into a run. Madeleine fled, praying that he would not realize why she kept to the pool.

He stopped, suddenly, breathing hard. Madeleine stopped so abruptly that she swayed on the water's edge. She must not fall in, she must not. . . .

"You wretched whore. You think you can govern my lands through my queen, who should obey *me*."

Madeleine raised her head. "I could do better than you."

The king stepped forward, to the verge of the pool. But not in.

"Don't go in the water," Madeleine said quickly.

The king looked at her with such consideration that she knew that Morgan had not warned him about it—but she still had to get him *in*. She had to convince him that the tarn was a danger to *her*, not him.

He lifted another foot, and she screamed, "Don't, don't!" The cry died in the trees.

"Foolish child," said the king. "I *know* the water is harmless." He waded in.

Her heart in her throat, Madeleine fled, but she glanced back. Perhaps Morgan had warded him. Perhaps *he* did have nothing to fear from the waters. But his expression changed before he was knee-deep in the tarn, as if his thoughts were changing.

She did not stop and no longer looked back. If it worked, she would know soon enough. She stumbled over a root, caught herself on a tree, and hurried on.

Another pool emerged ahead of her. Madeleine paused. The mists hid the pool and the king from her. She could only hear her own breathing and heartbeat. She leaned on the nearest fir despite the bark's roughness and struggled for calm.

Even when her breath eased, and her heart slowed, she could hear nothing from the king.

A bird sang. Madeleine pushed off the tree. She could not leave the king. He would wander off and never be found.

She returned to the tarn. The king had almost managed to climb out the other side. Soaked to the shoulders, he stood knee-deep in the waters, his sword lowered, his face blank. The blade was damp. He had, foolishly, not kept it out of the tarn.

She stopped strides away, out of easy striking distance. "Put up your sword, sire." Telling him to come out of the water could wait until that was done.

He looked at the sword as if wondering what it was. After a moment, he said, "Was going to. . . ."

"Put the sword up," said Madeleine. "When you remember what you have to do, draw it again."

The king's face brightened.

Chapter 22—Disputes and Conclusions

"This way," said Madeleine. She did not dare touch the king when he was still damp, she wondered if anyone should even when the clothes were dry, and she had to bring him with her.

At least, his bewilderment had not slackened, and he followed.

"This way," she repeated, and walked over the next hill. Roses blossomed ahead of her, white in the white mists, and Madeleine sighed in relief. "Madame!"

All three women looked up, and all three paled. The queen looked ready to faint.

Madeleine turned to the king. "Stay here." He bobbed his head. She hurried to the other women and, in a low voice, explained. Queen Katherine could not stop looking at the king, but he only looked curiously back at her.

For a long minute, silence followed her story.

A squirrel scolded from the nearest tree, and Queen Katherine let her breath out. "Are we nearer to Candlewood or to Graybrook?"

"Candlewood," said Lady Isobel.

Queen Katherine started to her feet. Madeleine hurried to help her.

Sunlight turned the mists luminous. The king walked obediently along. Isobel hummed under her breath.

The king's men appeared out of the mist. Isobel gave a little shriek. Queen Katherine stepped back.

The men gawked, looking from Madeleine to the king, to the queen, to Ina and Isobel. One reached for his sword and hesitated.

"Help the king," said Madeleine. "He fell afoul of the Misty Hills, and must be protected."

The king smiled at them. After a handful of wary glances, they obeyed, perhaps because she seemed to know what she was about, but —they obeyed. Before they could think again, Madeleine walked off, down the valley and back up the other side. They would reach the fork soon, but they could not go after John and Jasper. She did not trust her command to last if they had to turn about.

Two figures came through the mists. The king's men reached for their swords. A moment later, John and Jasper appeared, both pale.

"They can guide us," said Madeleine, quickly.

After a hesitant moment, glancing at the king, who hummed merrily, the king's men moved their hands from their swords.

John raised an eyebrow, and Madeleine smiled. Jasper's mouth twisted into a smile, as if he knew he could not ask. That was true enough; she could not hesitate and give the king's men a chance to think.

Isobel appeared at her shoulder. "I'll explain to them."

Madeleine nodded. Isobel drew the men off the path. As Madeleine led the company by, Isobel spoke in a low voice.

Moments later, Madeleine heard another set of footsteps. She glanced back. Only John followed. Jasper and Isobel stood in tight embrace. It broke even as she watched, but she could not bear to look at them. Patience, she told herself.

John still kept a wary eye on the king's bewildered men, but Madeleine paid them no heed. In her father's house and with men who would defend her, she did not fear them. Her voice low, she explained to her father.

"I will fetch him new clothing," said Lord Thomas. "And dispose of what he wears—"

"Don't burn it," said Madeleine, sharply.

His mouth pursed. Then he nodded.

The queen leaned on Jasper as she came into the hall. "Mistress Ina, you had best not leave." She paused. "And, I think those witnesses. . . ."

Out of the shadows, Beitris rushed to help her. The king's men looked wildly about, from the queen to the king.

"Leave the Misty Hills," Madeleine said. "Go to Lord Ewan of the West Dales. Tell him the queen needs witnesses."

They gawked at her.

"The queen—and the king—need the message to be carried," Madeleine said, acidly.

"My lady," said one, "it's through the Misty Hills."

Jasper's voice carried across. "I'll go with them. You attend the queen, Madeleine."

Madeleine considered as her brother left. With Ina and Beitris, the queen needed little from her. First. . . . She looked about for a maid.

"Go to the village and fetch me Lady Edane," she said.

They emerged from the mists: a small company, but once she picked out Jasper and Lord Ewan, Madeleine realized that Lord Magnus was perhaps the least of these grim-faced magnates. Even standing at the window where they could not see her, she felt her heart hammer.

Her father went to greet them. He did not seem perturbed. She turned away, envying him.

Abed, Queen Katherine wore only a plain shift, and her hair lay unbraided and loose on the pillow. She glanced at Madeleine. "They are coming?"

"They are here," said Madeleine. With Ina and Beitris hovering and Isobel sitting by the fire, she went to the door. Behind her came the sound of rustling sheets, and then low voices.

It seemed a long time before she heard the footsteps on the stairs, and before those footsteps turned into men. With the lights behind her, she must be a shadow; they eyed her as if half expecting a creature of the Misty Hills.

She curtsied. "My lords." She stepped back.

Though breathing hard, Queen Katherine sat propped up on the bed, as queenly as if it were a throne. She nodded as Lord Ewan presented the men to her, even when he called one Lord Malcolm of Eastwyck. Madeleine swallowed. One was lower in birth than Lord Magnus, then.

"Good my lords," said the queen. "I trust that Lord Thomas informed you of the king's state."

Lord Malcolm said, "We saw him."

"Then you know that he had need of a regent, to hold this land in peace, for him and his heir." She stifled a gasp and fixed them all with her gaze. "You will witness that this babe is that heir, and then you will act." She had to pause, now and again, but she had her orders ready.

Candles danced about the trees.

John watched the path, but the men he escorted, both of them royal ministers, were more intent on the way than the candles. The nobles who had petitioned Queen Katherine for leave to depart, as if she were already regent, had dared the hills, but they had gawked.

"Folly," muttered one. He eyed John. "And the King's Grace is captive here."

"The King's Grace is not well," said John. "We would not distress him."

"Or so you say," said Lord Tavish. "A doctor—"

"You will see for yourself," said John.

Lord Roderick caught at Lord Tavish's arm and gestured at the path. John's eyes narrowed. He watched the councilors as they traversed the path and entered the hall at Candlewood.

In the private chamber, the queen lay abed. The men made their bows, warily. She nodded to Lord Ewan.

"The Queen's Grace wishes to look at those cases where a guardian's care for his duties was called into question—"

"The King's Grace decided them!" said Lord Tavish.

"The regent," said Queen Katherine, her voice thin but firm, "may judge as she sees fit. Not only in a case, but whether to judge it."

"You act as if the king's judgment was *long* unsound, *before* he fell prey to the wicked magic of the Misty Hills!"

Queen Katherine smiled and leaned back.

"If," said Lord Ewan, as belligerently as a popinjay whose lady's ribbons had been insulted, "the king's judgment was so sound, what harm could stem from looking again?"

Lord Tavish whirled on him, his robes swirling. "If the Queen's judgment is sound. If she receives *wise* counsel—"

Did he think to win the queen's confidence like this? thought John.

"Guardians have complained—" said Lord Roderick.

"That I have singled them out?" said Queen Katherine. "That I have not treated all alike?"

Lord Roderick's mouth twitched. John thought, studying his face, that Lord Tavish might have come to seek favors for nobles, but Lord Roderick had not.

Lord Tavish returned to questioning her judgment. John studied their faces. Madeleine's story, of how the king must have touched with the tarns of madness, had spread far. He resented, a little, such an acquittal.

Lord Tavish turned again, abruptly, and stalked off. A moment later, Lord Roderick followed. John bowed to the queen and walked after. They did not want to the queen's favor, to leave so rudely—he caught up to them. Lord Thomas would not want them wandering in the woods.

"Do you wish to see the king?" said John.

Neither man turned. "No more than the heir," said Lord Tavish. "We shall return at once."

In the great hall, Jasper and Madeleine sat at the board. Madeleine leaned over the pieces, considering her moves. At times, despite the nobles who came and went, Candlewood was as peaceful as the days before her marriage.

"Jasper," said John, his voice low.

Madeleine looked up. She had been so intent that he had not heard him coming.

Briefly, John told of the nobles. "They know *I* learned the way in and out."

Jasper grimaced.

Madeleine said, "I wonder if the young men of the Misty Hills would guard the queen again."

In a chair by the fireplace, Lady Isobel slept. Queen Katherine lay awake, admiring her tiny son as he nursed. Madeleine yawned and looked about. Someone should have woken her—even in the lull before the day.

The queen looked at Madeleine. Outside, the hill doves cooed. Busy though they were, they were safe enough that the queen had decided that her son would bear a fitting name.

"You and Lord John, I fear, are too lowly in birth to be Prince Leod's godparents," said Queen Katherine.

Madeleine, surprised that she had even thought of them, said, "I do not think it wise to draw *more* attention to us."

"Lord Ewan declined." The queen scowled as if baffled.

Madeleine bit her lip. It would be difficult for Lord Ewan to marry his godson's mother. She did not think he could quite forget that something might befall King Walter.

"Lord Magnus has agreed that he and Lady Elspeth shall serve, but since Lady Elspeth can not arrive in time, you will stand proxy for her."

"You do me great honor, Madame," said Madeleine.

The queen looked reluctant. "I am no longer in King Leod's position. I must take new ladies-in-waiting—unmarried and higher in birth than you and Lady Isobel."

"May I suggest you ask Lord Fergus about his niece?"

Queen Katherine seemed taken aback.

"Lady Annette helped persuade him to ask for that audience, and for her own safety, Lord Fergus sent her to her parents—you may not keep her long. She wishes to marry." Madeleine lowered her voice. "I think she wants a baby of her own."

Queen Katherine stroked her baby's hair and smiled. "My old ladies-in-waiting—I know I lost Lady Osla and Lady Beatrix to matrimony. I suspect I lost more."

He was known as Lord Thomas's son—but fewer men knew his face than John's.

Jasper looked about Candlebrook. The nobles seemed more restive. He strode through the houses, toward the trees. From the corner of his eye, he saw something glinting. He looked. A handful stood together. Nothing glinted now, but nobles spoke with roughly clad man, men whom Jasper almost thought he recognized. And the glint—he remembered Madeleine's tale.

He walked to the mist-wreathed trees, but not farther than to find John. When they returned, they did not have to step from the mists; the company had come closer.

John's voice was low. "Those are the men who bore supplies to the tower."

"They must have the charm that they used against the dragon," said Jasper.

The men came closer, and they both fell silent. John eased his way closer to the path. Jasper followed.

"The mists don't change," said one man, sharply. John caught his sleeve, and mouthed, "Lord Roderick."

"The mists," said a commoner, "are mist." His voice held more contempt than most baseborn man would have dared, addressing a noble. "It got us safe to the tower. He'll be safe there, too."

"If you're frightened," said another lord, scornfully, "you can flee as soon as we free the king."

Jasper let his breath out. A mad chase after the lords, just as John had chased after the wolf-hunt, then. At least his father had men enough to hold these off—

John whispered, "The charm?"

Jasper felt cold. Once they got to the tower—"How on earth would we get it away?"

John looked unhappy. "At Candlewood, there are more men to overpower them."

"And if they strike too quickly? You only went to the tower under the charm. I once tried on my own—"

"What's that?" said Lord Roderick, his voice fierce and frightened.

After a moment, Jasper laughed, loudly. It did not sound right, but from the stares, perhaps that was a help.

"What good is that charm, you knave?" said Lord Roderick.

"None at all!" shouted Jasper.

The nobles all flinched. One reached for his sword. The man with the charm stepped forward. "I'll drive it off!" He lunged into the forest.

Jasper let his breath out. Moments later, he and Jasper seized the charm.

They looked less grand now than they had, even when they had come to Candlewood to speak with her.

Then, thought Queen Katherine, in satisfaction, not only did they lack their robes of office, they were surrounded by nobles as great as they were; they could barely cram into the chamber, but it cowed the royal ministers.

Better yet, what they had tried was common knowledge.

"The king," said Lord Roderick, "is mad."

An unwise admission for you to make, thought Katherine.

"But he is kept prisoner here, without care! You have not summoned any doctor—"

"How many doctors know the magics of the Misty Hills?" said Queen Katherine.

"Wizards," said Lord Tavish, heavily, as if he expected scorn.

"I myself," said Queen Katherine, "saw what Morgan could do. He was the best that the King's Grace could find. We have every reason to be cautious when speaking of wizards."

"You are not the regent, to make such judgments," said another man. "Lord Osgar is the regent!"

"This is outrageous!" said Lord Osgar. He looked about the flower-filled pasture, at nobles gathered there. "*I am the regent.*"

Madeleine sat, tucked by the woods in case her testimony was needed. With little Prince Leod in his cradle beside her, Queen Katherine sat in a great chair, surrounded by flowers, and smiled. The king, his head tilted to one side, studied Osgar. Some nobles looked contemptuous, some amused, some embarrassed. Few met Lord Osgar's gaze.

"Is his authority the king's?" whispered John in her ear.

"He's a royal official, and nothing else," Madeleine whispered back. "No lands, and not from a great family."

John's mouth twisted. "No wonder—he has nothing else to grasp at."

"If, my lords, my ladies, you permit this woman to claim that she has done nothing to the king, you connive at treason!" His face flushed, Osgar drew a deep breath. "The king went to the Misty Hills before. He has seen these—tarns of madness before."

Madeleine laid her head on John's shoulder. "I told them that."

John smiled wryly. "So he was not quite to blame for Lord Magnus's arrest, having lost some of his reason?"

"The king lost his guide in the Misty Hills, and drank from the tarn without considering whether it was safe. His ill judgment was not all the water."

John nodded. A small smile appeared on his face.

Across the field, King Walter still watched Osgar with bright-eyed wonder.

"If they are harmless," said Queen Katherine, "then the king is well, is he not?"

The laughter turned Lord Osgar scarlet.

The new ministers looked uncomfortable in their robes. Perhaps it stemmed from their unfamiliarity with them.

Madeleine curtseyed to the queen. At the side of the room, three women whispered and pointed.

"My ladies have come to attend me," said Queen Katherine, "but your fidelity deserves reward." She gestured at a servant, who gave her a box. "Lord Patrick encouraged the king in his madness, endangering my life and Prince Leod's. For that, he will forfeit lands. Some border Summerfield. The kingdom shall see that virtue is rewarded, as crime is punished."

Madeleine curtseyed again.

"I will speak with your lord husband. But, for you, yourself—" She opened the box and drew out a necklace. Firelight made the stones glint rose red. After a moment, Madeleine thought, Rubies?

"When one has found a worthy wife, her price is far above rubies," said Queen Katherine, "and so, in truth, I give you a meager reward." She glanced at her ministers. "Do you think I have been prodigal at the jewelers'?"

One bowed. His voice was measured. "We know the treasures of the realm."

"The rubies, or the lady who receives them?"

Hill doves tolled from the branches. Edane looked at Madeleine with bright eyes as she nursed, and Madeleine cooed nonsense. The candles of Candlewood shone among the trees.

The mists were thinning again—slowly, but the peasants sneered about Morgan.

Madeleine's mouth twisted. Lord Magnus had dispossessed those nobles who had defied his summons—and had learned that Gilliane had left Summerfield with her dowry, for a convent. Madeleine wondered how long it would take before she was abbess there, but she had left Summerfield.

Sandy's laughter echoed under the trees. He careened about the corner, his father in close pursuit, until Sandy grabbed a tree and shouted, "Safe!" John threw his hands in the air, complaining of how Sandy outfoxed him, and Sandy hurled himself to his father's arms.

Madeleine stroked Edane's hair. John rose with Sandy in his arms and came toward her. Sandy looked exhausted.

"Any more news from the queen?" John said.

"Lord Patrick *will* forfeit some lands," said Madeleine. "And—the queen spoke with me privately. Some of those lands border Summerfield."

John's mouth pursed. After a moment, he said, "I hope that Lord Patrick did not neglect his duties while pursuing the throne."

"With the queen acting as regent now—she wished to reward us," said Madeleine. "For so great a service, she *must* reward us, so the kingdom will see that she rewards those who serve her. . . . She apologized, that she could keep neither me nor Lady Isobel as ladies in waiting. . . ."

"Neither Jasper nor I would approve!"

Madeleine smiled. "Just as well for Isobel. Her pregnancy is not *hard*, not like the queen's, but she tires easily."

After a minute, John savored each word. "We will return to Summerfield within a month."

Her smile deepened. "We will return in time to see your grandmother's roses."